CRUISE SHIP CRIME MYSTERIES

Murder in the Northwest Passage

PAUL DAVIS MD

Blewitt Pass Publishing

Seattle, WA

ISBN: 978-0-9885791-4-9 (Paperback)

ISBN: 978-0-9885791-5-6 (e-Book)

July 4, 2013

Blewitt Pass Publishing
Seattle, WA

This book is dedicated to my Mother who taught me an appreciation for writing at a very early age. Also to my sister and all the friends, co-workers & passengers I worked with on cruise ships over the years.

CHAPTER ONE

Not tonight Josephine!

THERE WAS SOMETHING EERIE – something fantastic – somehow indescribable – in the scenery before his eyes. Feathers and plumes of orange and blue, and white and gold seemed to hover or float above the Wenatchee Mountain Range such as immense birds or angels of serenity spreading their wings over the Blewitt Pass and the valley below. Yes, serenity and contentment were all words that lulled the day's adventure into a reminiscing picture of sheer beauty.

They had traveled through the central core of mountains that divide the wet coastal area from the dry central part of Washington State, starting at Seatac airport traveling to Cle Elum where they had stopped for groceries and the few items they would need during their stay at Eddy's Cabin. Eddy Leavensworth grew up in the region and could trace his family back to the gold miners that first came to the area and settled down. This was a very well built cabin on a private twenty acres, erected in the middle of several thousand acres of National Forest land. The Old Highway was maintained, somewhat, for fire access, logging, and cell towers on the mountain peaks. Eddy's cabin was located at 4250 feet and was definitely designed for all weather. It was built solidly in log cabin style. The logs were not from your typical 'prefab log cabin kits'. They were 3 to 6 feet in diameter and stained with products to preserve their long-term fitness. The cabin was fitted with all the latest electronics, solar panels and battery collectors, wind generators, and the like. The place was comfortable and well insulated so that one would never feel the cold or the heat of the outdoors. Eddy had been kind enough to offer the use of his cabin to Alan from time to time, and this was one of those times.

Alan turned to Tiffany sitting beside him on the swing on the deck of the cabin, and took a sip of wine before he asked, "Beautiful, isn't it?" still wondering how such a gorgeous woman would have remained "a friend" for the best part of three years now. Her blonde hair neatly tied in a bun at the back of her lovely head, Tiffany was not only stunning to look at, but to anyone who knew her, her intellect and her wit certainly matched her beauty.

"Is *beautiful* enough of a word to express the emotions they stir in my mind?" Her right arm rose and traveled in a waving motion to the mountains. "Peaceful perhaps would be a better way to describe these clouds. They change shapes every moment, the next more exquisite than the last."

Slipping his arm around her shoulders, Alan drew Tiffany closer to him. "I love you, Tiff," he whispered in her ear.

She turned her face to his and kissed him tenderly. Tiffany then peered into his eyes. "Did you kiss her too?" she asked.

Drawing his arm back, quite surprised by her question, he asked, "Who's that?"

"Yvette. Did you kiss her while you were in France?"

"I don't think I did."

Tiffany sat up and stared. "What do you mean 'you don't think'? Is that how you recall you kissing me?"

Alan laughed. "No, Hon, and that's because I cherish every one of your kisses like a jewel. So, if I did kiss Yvette, I don't recall – besides, I don't think I did."

"Yes, that's what you said," Tiffany replied in a huff that didn't seem serious enough to take it into account. "And you never told me what happened during all those months that you were working on the new vessel…"

"Not true," Alan countered, a teasing smile painted on his lips. "I gave you a 'blow by blow' every night – or when ever we were able to get on line or on the phone." He then returned his attention to the mountain ridge while slowly going down the memory lane of his trip to France and Yvette.

He had been hired by a renowned shipyard in France to oversee the construction and the equipment fitting of a medical center aboard *The Contessa,* the newest and most modern vessel of its class to date. The Global Cruise Line – a company created for the sole purpose of managing and maintaining the operation of this particular condo-ship – had appointed the shipyard two years ago to build the ship that was to sail the Northern Passage from Seattle to Boston with its first full passenger complement in June 2012.

The Contessa was a 200-passenger & 250-crew cruise liner. One could book a passage on this unique condo-ship or buy a condo and pay a maintenance fee equivalent to 10% of the cost of the property per year. The small condos were $1.5 million and went up to $32 million US for the luxury suites. You could book one or two cruises at a time – one-month minimum. The cruises were similar to those traveling the oceans every day, but with a very high price tag: Seattle to Boston from $35,000 for the smaller cabins. Global Cruises really only catered to the ultra wealthy: Saudi princes, Russian oil magnates, wealthy ranchers from the US, dot-com, cell phone, and other communications tycoons, etc. Most owners stayed on board for 3 to 5 months or flew in to meet the ship for a few weeks here and there, and then holidays.

Stationed for the better part of six months in Le Havre, on the coast of France, Alan had been in his element – he had been elated to be engaged in the design and building of the medical center on *The Contessa* –

it had been a dream of his for all the years he had been working as "a ship doctor" aboard the vessels of the Gold Cruise Lines. He always liked designing interiors of the places he lived and worked. Having worked in some totally ergonomically useless spaces that they called medical centers, it was great to be able to take the space provided by the company and really design an efficient center that would work-and even be able to use some artistic influence on its appearance. Since medical centers seldom are a source of great income for a cruise ship-'the necessary required evil', they are often crammed into the smallest space possible in the bowels of the ship. Here, they were providing a decent (not copious) amount of space to fit out a medical center even with several portholes for natural light.

Somehow coincidentally, Le Havre had featured prominently in one of Alan's previous cruises for being the location where the staff captain on *The Duchess* had been found guilty of slaughtering two love-birds and dismembering them to assuage his thirst for atonement to his sense of betrayal.

Arriving in Le Havre only months after the events, Alan saw no point in stirring horrific memories by knocking on the door of one of the young victims' mother, nor did he take particular pleasure in walking the streets that the couple had probably traveled several times a week, yet he had a job to do and needed a place to stay. He chose a little hotel not too far from the shipyard and located on a well-frequented thoroughfare where he could practically choose to eat at a different restaurant or bistro every night.

It was on one of those evenings when he had been walking down the sidewalks in quest of another little eatery that he found himself face to face with Yvette. Once upon a time – as the story goes – Yvette had been the pearl of his eye, the throb of his heart. She had this incomparable beauty and presence that takes a man into a whirlwind of emotions and physical discomfort, one should admit, at the mere notice of her. Her head, surrounded by black, luminous hair, bouncing down to her waist in lovely curls, featured the most attractive onyx eyes Alan had ever seen. They would pierce the heart of any man catching her gaze. And if that wasn't enough to render a poor fellow totally helpless under her spell, Yvette's body was all delicious curves and suppleness of movement.

He had never forgotten their torrid affair of one summer in France. They had gone to Paris on several occasions, delighting in all that French romance could bestow upon them, especially in the city of lights.

However, tonight Yvette went past him, without even turning her head. *Has she forgotten me?* Alan wondered as he retraced his steps and began following her until she entered a small grocery store – he waited for her to come out – and stood by the door. Alan had certainly aged with a lot less hair on his head, but so had she. Now her long curly hair had become a style consisting of small braids wrapped into a bun on the back of her head. The onyx eyes had not changed a bit.

She left the store, her delicate lips parted in a smile, which Alan could never obliterate from his mind even if he wanted to, she set her sight on him and closed the grocer's door behind her.

In her cutesy, but always proper French, she said simply, "I wondered if it was you?" handing Alan her grocery bag, which he took while returning the grin and falling in step beside her.

"You did recognize me then?"

"I wasn't sure, but when I recalled your face – we were so young then – I thought it couldn't have been anyone else."

"I am glad you did, Yvette," Alan said, lowering his gaze to the pavement.

"Why didn't you write or phone?" she asked, reproach audible in her voice.

"I don't really know. But I needed to break away from a life that would have spelled disaster for both of us."

"What do you mean?" She threw him a questioning glance.

"I mean you were intent in pursuing your career in interior design only in Paris and although I love Paris, as a foreigner, I was not allowed to practice medicine there. I wanted to do the medical volunteer work I had committed to in the Amazon basin and I had to complete the medical training I had started in Canada…"

"Oh, it's Doctor Alan Mayhew now, is it?" Yvette cut-in curiously.

"Yes, and I have been lucky I suppose"—he turned his face to her—"I have accomplished my goals in many ways. I mean, I have visited so many places in the world, set up a number of projects in developing nations that sorely needed health care, rolled up my sleeves innumerable times giving vaccinations and treating the sick and injured, but there are still places for me to discover."

"I am glad to hear that you've done what you wanted to do," Yvette concluded, a morose tone lacing her every word.

"What about you? What are you doing?" Alan asked, returning his gaze to the sidewalk stretching in front of them.

"I am not the designer I was hoping to become, and when my mother passed away, I stayed in Le Havre and took a job as a nursing assistant in a hospitals surgery department around here. Pretty routine, boring work really with no chance to be innovative or design anything…." She sounded disgruntled.

After a moment of silence between them, Alan asked, "Would you like to have dinner with me…? And you could tell me all that happened since we last saw each other?"

Yvette shook her head. "I can't, Alan. I am married now – or at least *was* married – but I have two children at home waiting for me…"

Alan stopped and waited for her to do the same. She turned to him.

"I'll be here for another four months, and I would love to sit down and have one of those delicious meals with you – any time." He looked at her pleadingly.

She smiled. "Okay…, I guess I could do that. Where are you staying?"

"Just down the road at the Oscar. It's not too lavish but it's a comfortable little place…."

"…Yes, you did, and I am grateful for that," Tiffany went on, jolting Alan out of his recollecting thoughts. "But you didn't say much about your meeting with Yvette, apart from meeting her on the street one night – so are you going to tell me…?"

Alan had to chuckle at the petulant way Tiffany demanded an

explanation. "Yes, I will tell you – but "not tonight, Josephine"!"

"Okay, but you know I'll pester you until you spill those beans of yours," Tiffany replied, tittering and cuddling against Alan's chest. "And no need to quote Napoleon to me – he died in exile, remember?"
Alan could only laugh while caressing Tiffany's back.

CHAPTER TWO

Fire! Fire!

AFTER TREKKING UP THE mountain trails for the better part of the day, Tiffany was all but spent of energy. She plopped herself down on one of the lounge chairs on the terrace and looked up at the sun going down beneath the horizon. She had just come out of a warm and soothing shower and was waiting for Alan to join her with a glass of one of those delightful Washington State wines. She slipped each of her hands in the opposite sleeve of her robe and watched the sky turn the colors on the palette of the painter busy stroking the firmament with his skilled brush.

"Ah, there you are," Alan said, still running a towel over his hair. "I thought you would be busy cooking dinner – not lazing about the terrace..."

The teasing words ignited a mocking titter out of Tiffany's mouth. "If you're hungry, Master, perhaps you should order the cook in you to get it ready and leave your fair maiden in peace?"

"How about the maiden and master going to the kitchen together and enjoy each other's company while preparing a feast deserving of the gods?"

Getting up from the lounge chair, Tiffany wrapped her arms around his neck. "By all means, my master, I wouldn't have it any other way." She giggled as Alan tried to grab her hands while she dislodged them from the nape of his neck.

The cabin – more a house than a vacation retreat – afforded an all encompassing view of the mountains and valley from the front living room while a huge and imposing fireplace, flanking the far wall and climbing to the vaulted ceiling, reminded the visitors that its nestled flames and embers would keep them warm, whatever storms blew outside.

Built of cedar logs, each room – including the kitchen – felt inviting and cozy. One could almost feel the stress or the discomfort of city-living leave one's being the minute one passed the threshold of this veritable mansion cuddling the soft pillow of the green forest surrounding it.

"All right," Alan said, pulling a salad bowl out of one of the kitchen drawers, "shall we have some salad, with spaghetti and some sautéed mushrooms, or would you prefer some stuffed mushrooms and water-cress salad?"

"Wow! Why do you always have to make it sound so delectable?" She threw him an appreciative glance across the kitchen island. "Spaghetti and salad would be just fine – thank you. Do you want me to cut the veggies while you busy yourself with the mushrooms and spaghetti?"

"Sounds like a plan," Alan replied, turning to the stove after taking bags and bags of vegetables out of the crisper.

"Let's not feed an army, shall we?" Tiffany commented, dragging a bag of carrots and a head of lettuce to her side of the counter.

"Oh, that's only water – the veggies I mean. They'll digest quickly enough and you'll still have plenty of space in your little tummy for the spaghetti, believe me."

"You know, sometimes I wish you weren't a doctor – you've got a way to describe one's digestion before having a meal that would destroy any one's appetite in an instant," Tiffany remarked, slicing carrots somewhat viciously and swiping the slivers into the salad bowl.

Ignoring her comments all together, Alan asked, "Would you like red or white tonight?" and turning to the half dozen or so bottles of Washington State wines they had brought with them (knowing full well that they would leave a few for Eddy).

"A scrumptious red, please," she replied, smiling up at him when he place the bottle of red on the island.

"It's a professional defect," he commented, taking two glasses out of the cupboard, "I'm sorry…"

"Talking about professional "defect" as you call it, do you think Susan will be alright?"

"Where does that come from?" Alan asked, surprised that Tiffany should refer to their long-time friend who had been a passenger on many of the cruises they had journeyed together.

"Well, it's because I've received an email from her this morning, saying that she was now out of surgery and looking forward to the trip. She said that she had never felt so near death and that she hoped the northern lights would somehow cure her for ever."

"That's sounds like she's hoping for a miracle…"

"Wouldn't you want a miracle if you knew that the big "C" could come knocking again anytime?"

Alan shook his head, resting his hip against the side of the counter beside the stove – watching the mushroom simmering slowly in the pan. "She's on her way to a full recovery, Tiff. In fact, I would suggest that she'll perk up to her old self once we're at sea. As for a miracle, she could only hope to live the best out of every day for the rest of her life. Cancer is a fickle disease, but it seems to shy away from people who take care of themselves with proper diet and exercise, maintain a positive outlook on life, and believe that a higher power is present in their lives to help them."

"What should I tell her then? Should I encourage her to turn away from the past and look to the future in a positive way?"

"Yes, but ignoring what she went through is not the answer either – she will grow from that experience…."

"Like the song says, *what doesn't kill you makes you strong…*" I guess."

"That's right while keeping in mind what may kill you in the end."

Turning her head to the windows, Tiffany exclaimed, "Oh my God, would you look at that moon? It's like a huge orange rising into the sky."

Taking his glass of wine with him, Alan went to stand in front of the terrace, looking at the scene before his eyes. "Extraordinary," he murmured as Tiffany joined him, slipping her arm around his waist.

"But, you know, that color is not a normal occurrence," Alan remarked, going to the sliding door and opening it wide.

The smell of wood burning and the bluish wisp of cloud on the mountainside were telltale of what was apparently happening several miles from the house. There was obviously a forest fire in the area. The sight and smell left both Alan and Tiffany unsettled for the rest of the night, especially when they still could see an orange glow on the horizon after the sun had set, in addition to the rising orange moon.

In the morning, Alan rose early from a restless sleep. The mere idea that a fire would chase them away from this piece of paradise on Earth and destroy Eddy's house, had been enough to keep him – and Tiffany in turn – awake for hours on end.

Before leaving, to make their way to the forest rangers down the valley, Alan took the hose from its hiding place in the well-stocked outbuilding, attached it to the water spout on the side of the house and sprayed all its sides liberally, hopeful the cabin would stay wet enough for a while. Once that was done, he and Tiffany climbed down the trail to the rangers' station. The air was still stifling hot and dry, a dryness that often spelled disaster for the forest-lined mountains of central and eastern Washington. Summers brought with them the menace of fires every year and every year literally millions of acres were destroyed by forest fires. This was not a matter to be taken lightly or ignored. A wind gust could shift the flames and in moments engulf everything in their paths. The speed with which such a fire could spread was unbelievable, reaching 50 to 80 miles per hour in some instances; the fire could easily chase a car down a mountain road and devour it, along with all its occupants, in seconds. Besides which the smoke enveloping entire regions surrounding the fire could affect their inhabitants and kill them in short order from smoke inhalation.

"Do you think we'll find some one at the station?" Tiffany asked as they were walking rapidly down the trail.

Alan nodded. "I should think they'd have someone on the computer to relay wind and weather info to the fire-fighters on location."

"What shall we do, if the fire gets too close?" The question demanded no answer. Both Tiffany and Alan knew that they would not dare return to the house or would be "evacuated" if there were the slightest threat of Eddy's cabin being in the fire's path.

"I don't think we would have time to go anywhere, Tiff," Alan said, grabbing her hand to cross the dry bed of a small creek. He looked both ways before reaching the other side and shook his head. "There's virtually no water left on this mountain," he groaned.

Gasping for air, when they arrived at the rangers' station, they took a couple of deep breaths before pushing the door open. The place was empty except for one man – as Alan had gathered – who had his back turned to them and didn't even notice them come in.

"Hello," Alan said, placing his elbows on the counter. "Can we interrupt you for a minute?"

The man raised a hand to indicate that he was intent on completing a report of some sort to who ever was on the line with him. He said a few words into the mouthpiece in front of his lips and then turned to the visitors.

"What can I do for you guys?" he asked, getting up from the computer chair and stepping up to the counter.

"Hi," said Alan courteously, my name is Dr. Mayhew and this is Ms. Sylvan"—nodding to her—"We're staying at Eddy Leavensworth's cabin up the north hill and we're wondering how close the fire is from us?"

"The name is Joe," the young ranger said, "nice meeting you. And to answer your question; let me show you." He pulled a map from under the counter and placed it in front of Alan and Tiffany. "Here is Eddy's cabin and here is the fire." He looked up from the map. "As you can appreciate the cabin is located across and over the ridge facing Blewitt Pass, so I wouldn't worry about it at this point. This being early June, the ground and trees are not as dry as they'd be in August and the guys told me they've got the fire practically under control as of an hour ago."

"What about the smoke and ashes, couldn't they carry igniting material over the ridge?" Tiffany asked, drawing a straight line over the map with her index finger.

"Yes, ashes are a risk, of course, but you're too far away to be in any danger. By the time any of the burning ashes come across the ridge, they would have disintegrated into dust."

"What about traveling back to Seattle, would that present any problem?" Alan asked, already wondering if the fire were to spread over the pass, how they would make the journey to the port of Seattle to meet *The Contessa* in time before it sailed.

Joe shook his head. "There shouldn't be any problem. We've kept the road cleared through the pass and so far there's no indication that the fire would spread that way."

Alan straightened up and looked at Tiffany who was still focused on the map. "Could we have a copy of the map?" she asked with a smile that warranted only a positive answer from Joe.

"Of course," he said, folding and handing it to her with a broad grin. "And I'll do one better"—he reached under the counter again—"here is a booklet describing all the trails in the area." He handed it to her. "I don't know how long you're staying around, but some of these trails are taking the route that Chief Joseph of the Nez Perce traveled between June and October 1877 when he finally surrendered saying, "I will fight war no more forever". Even if you don't have a chance to hike that way, it'll make for an interesting reading."

"Thanks for that," Tiffany said, taking the booklet from Joe's hand.

They were about to leave after saying their goodbyes when Joe added, "One thing I would ask you, though, is to make sure not to use the fireplace in Eddy's cabin."

Taken aback by this latest comment, Alan retraced his step toward the counter. "You mean there's a danger? I thought you said we were too far away...?"

"Yes, you are far from harm's way for this fire to touch you, but lighting a fire in that fireplace of yours wouldn't be a good idea since the land is getting drier by the minute around your place and one burning piece of wood – as small as a match actually – could burn Eddy's cabin and surrounding land into a firestorm."

Alan nodded when he realized what Joe was saying. "Okay, no problem, Joe," he said, shaking hands with him, "and thanks again for all the info."

CHAPTER THREE

Here we go again!

AFTER A WEEK OF STRENUOUS hiking while keeping constant vigil on the disappearing clouds of smoke for the last four days of their vacation, Alan and Tiffany were now packed and ready to take to the road back to Seattle, where *The Contessa* was waiting for their arrival to hail her departure in the next twenty-four hours.

"Alright, have we got everything?" Alan asked as he climbed behind the wheel of their SUV.

"Yes, I think so. But I think we would do well to check if we've forgotten to do anything to protect the cabin."

"Okay, what did we do?" Alan replied, already checking the inside of the house mentally while they were both looking at it. It was really a beautiful place, he thought, envious of Eddy's good taste in choosing this place in the mountains.

"You've hosed down the house, I closed all the doors, windows and locked everything down," Tiffany said.

"Did we take the laundered sheets and linen out of the dryer?"

Tiffany nodded. "Yeah – all folded in the linen closet. What about the fuse box, the generator, the inverter, the gas line, the solar generator; did you hit the main switches and all the other things that you told me to remind you about that Eddy wanted done before we left?"

"Sure did.... Okay then, I think we can go." Alan turned the key in the ignition. "I wonder what the road is like now," he added musingly. "I hope the fire trucks have not left too many gouging ruts in it."

An hour into the drive, they reached the paved road without incident and as if the gods had decided they were on safe and sturdy ground now, another hour towards the coast on the main highway, and the sky opened up in pelting rain.

"Wow," Tiffany exclaimed, that's as sudden as opening the shower tap. "Did you see that?"

"Yeah, that's the West Coast for you. This is rainforest region and although it can be dry as bones for weeks on end, when it rains it pours – literally."

The windshield wipers had a hard time keeping up with the job and they were now inching their way out of a deep valley at a snail's pace. A few minutes later, the rain not letting up, they heard a faint cry from somewhere ahead of them. Alan slowed the car down, not wanting to hit anything he couldn't see through the sheets of water draping the front of the car. When they heard the whining again, Alan pulled the SUV to the side of the road, and shut off the engine.

"Please help, please," they then both heard more clearly.

Not caring one bit about getting his uniform wet – or soaked – he opened the car door and jumped out, under Tiffany's mild protest. "Don't, Alan, maybe…"

He didn't respond and slammed the door shut, before hurrying across the road in the direction of the car that he could now see – it had veered off the pavement and had plunged into a ditch.

The driver had managed to open his window, but was trapped between the steering wheel, a deflated airbag and the back of his seat.

Again Alan didn't hesitate; he took his cell phone out of his jacket pocket and dialed 9.1.1. He spoke briefly to the person at the other end of the call, giving the woman their location – although his phone was fitted with a GPS and didn't need to do so – and asking for an ambulance to be dispatched to the scene of the accident as soon as possible.

Snapping the phone shut, he bent down to the passenger and said, "I am Dr. Mayhew – if you could tell me where you're hurt, and I'll try to help before the paramedics arrive. Could you do that?"

"It's my legs," the man said, cringing. "They're pinned under the steering column and I don't seem to be able to move them."

"Can you feel them?" Alan asked.

"Sure – they hurt like hell," the man uttered between gasps for air.

"Okay, let's take some deep, relaxing breaths, shall we? And tell me if you have any other medical problems, like heart problems."

"The name is Fred," the fellow said after he had taken a couple of breaths. "No heart problems, Doc, other than a broken one. It's because of my tires; I should have changed them, but … they're so expensive… and my ex-girlfriend took all the extra dollars…"

"Alright," Alan said, "time enough for hindsight later. Could you stretch one of your hands so I could check your pulse?"

Nodding, Fred put his left arm out of the window and winced. "Even when I move my arms, my legs hurt. Do you think they're broken?"

"Couldn't say before they've got you on a stretcher, but even a sprain could affect your entire body," Alan replied, trying to concentrate on the man's heartbeat. What he feared at this point was Fred going into shock – and his pulse was increasing rapidly and getting very weak. He let go of the arm saying, "Try not to move and I'll be right back, I am going to my car for my medical kit." And with these words, he rushed back to the SUV.

"Is he hurt?" Tiffany asked in a rush as Alan, dripping wet, sat in the front seat and passed his hand over his tousled hair.

"Yeah. I think he's injured his legs, but he's pinned down and I couldn't open the door." He turned to look over his shoulder. "Did you see the blankets in the back when we loaded the car?"

"I think so… let me check." To his surprise he then saw Tiffany getting out of the seat, literally climbing over it and slithering her way to the back of the car. "Here you go," she yelped, dragging a red blanket behind her on her way back to the front of the vehicle.

"Thanks, I'll be right back," Alan said, getting out again carrying the blanket and his basic medical kit. Alan always traveled with some kind of a medical kit – "part of being a Doc," he would always say. The extent of the kit depended on where he was going and the amount of space and weight he was going to be allowed to carry on the plane.

By this time the rain had eased to a showery mist, for which Alan was grateful, although his clothes and the rest of him were drenched by now.

When he reached Fred, the poor fellow was shivering and unable to control the tremors – his body was fighting against the injuries and was about to shut down. That's the last thing Alan wanted to see. "Here we are," he said, wrapping Fred's upper body in the blanket as best he could. He wrapped the blood pressure cuff around his arm. His BP was low for sure. His heart sounded audible and okay but fading fast. "Where were you going when you hit the ditch?" He wanted Fred to stay awake and attentive to his question rather than letting go.

"I... I was on my way to Cle Elum"—he stopped and then tried speaking again—"to... to get some groceries ... when the rain ... started..." He looked up at Alan and seemed to notice for the first time that he wore a uniform. "Are you a... a marine?"

Alan smiled and shook his head. "No, Fred, I'm just a ship's doctor – you know the guy that tries to keep his head above the watery ills of the cruise passengers."

"Nice," Fred said, cracking a timid smile while trying to keep the clattering of his teeth to a minimum.

"What about you? Are you firefighting in the park?"

Fred shook his head, but before he had time to respond, they both heard the blaring sirens of the ambulance, police and fire truck shattering the silence surrounding them. "Here we go, Fred, now you're going to get all the help you need. And please, don't worry about the legs – they'll be just fine," Alan added reassuringly.

Another hour had to pass before Alan and Tiffany were finally driving down the highway. In the meantime that Alan had been busy with the injured Fred, Tiffany had opened his suitcase, had taken a fresh set of clothes out of it and when he had climbed back into their vehicle, she had helped him get out of his wet uniform and into his spare set.

The gymnastic he had to perform to undress and put on his dry clothes could only be described as amazingly humorous to anyone who would have been watching them through the windshield. Yet, no one had paid any attention to them – the paramedics and firemen had been far too busy extracting Fred out of his car all the while this had been happening in the SUV.

"Are we going to make it?" Tiffany asked, looking at her watch. "I hope whomever our staff cap is, he's not a time-keeper."

Alan chuckled at the remark and shook his head. "No, I don't think he would mind if we're even two hours' late. I traveled with him before and he's a nice guy."

"Oh good – and what's his name?"

"Stephan Ivanov," Alan replied, shooting an amused glance in Tiffany's direction.

"Good God, not another Russian! I hope he's not the pawing or vodka gosling kind." Tiffany had instantly recalled their voyage aboard *The*

Duchess a few months back when they had dealt with a Russian spy – a German intelligence agent to be precise – who had been the picture-perfect of a Russian male specimen.

"None of the above – I can assure you. He's actually a tea drinker. I think he's got the best collection of teas I've ever seen. It's kind of a ritual with him. Every time he takes a break, he goes back to his cabin and has a cup of tea, brewed in an English teapot, complete with tea-cozy, sugar bowl and milk jug on a silver tray."

Tiffany was staring at her companion by this time. "You're joking, right? Are you saying he's Mr. England wrapped with a Russian bow?"

"Just about," Alan said, chuckling all the more after he noticed Tiffany's face. "But he's as smart as they come. Don't be fooled by his manners, he'll be on to you the minute you try to pull one on him. I've seen him in action on our way from Panama to Seattle. He kept everyone on their toes and nothing escaped his notice. I tell you the guy is sharp."

"Okay then, that's good to know, I wouldn't want to get on his bad side," Tiffany said, returning her gaze to the road.

"And he loves the well-mannered ladies, too," Alan blurted, knowing full well that Tiffany would give Stephan a run for his money, if he tried anything.

"All right," she said, "enough of that. I'll have to see for myself what the guy is like. And I bet he's going to be scrupulous as ever about our choice of entertainment – like what sopranos and pianists I've already cast for the trip."

Alan nodded. "He's an opera lover and he knows his classics – so if you need help in that regard, he'll be the person to ask."

A few hours later, after a frustrating trip in typical rush hour traffic through downtown Seattle, they finally returned the SUV to the rental agency just a few blocks from the famous Seattle Space Needle, the reminder that Seattle was the host to the world's fair in 1959, and now has a nice green space called Seattle Center with a so-so restaurant atop the imposing jutting tower. With bags in hand, they made their way in a rental agency courtesy car to the pier where *The Contessa* stood proudly at dockside.

"She is absolutely magnificent," Tiffany exclaimed, once they had alighted from the car and thanked the driver for his diligence.

Alan smiled as he lifted his gaze to the ship that was to be their home for the next few months. Glistening white on all flanks, her bow rose fiercely toward the sky as if saying, "No ice, no storm, no rain or swell will ever defeat me in my progress through the oceans of the north. I am indomitable."

As if he had heard the ship's unspoken words, Alan remarked, "She won't be easily beaten into submission, I'm sure."

CHAPTER FOUR

The Erebus and The Terror

And indeed nothing is easier for a man who has, as the phrase goes, "followed the sea" with reverence and affection, than to evoke the great spirit of the past upon the lower reaches of the Thames. The tidal current runs to and fro in its unceasing service crowded with memories of men and ships it had borne to the rest of home or to the battles of the sea. It had known and served all the men of whom the nation is proud, from Sir Francis Drake to Sir John Franklin, knights all, titled and untitled--the great knights-errant of the sea. It had borne all the ships whose names are like jewels flashing in the night of time, from the "Golden Hind" returning with her round flanks full of treasure . . . to the "Erebus" and "Terror," bound on other conquests--and that never returned.[1]

HIS ELBOWS RESTING ON the railing of the promenade deck of *The Contessa*, Alan was watching the beautiful shores of Puget Sound that stretched before him, thrilled at the thought of starting a voyage he had longed to make. He had always admired the beauty of the Arctic, the awesome natural events that had evolved before his eyes not so long ago; during a trip he had taken in Alaskan waters with a somewhat unsavory character that had turned out to be nothing more than a thief and a liar. He chased away the unwanted reminiscence in favor of the prospect of returning to the polar waters with some degree of relish. He had also ferreted some information regarding the forthcoming reconnaissance survey of the Northwest Passage designed to locate Sir John Franklin's lost vessels – the *Erebus* and the *Terror*. Both ships had sunk after being trapped in the ice in the summer of 1848 and were now thought to be located somewhere along the Adelaide Peninsula and perhaps near O'Reilley Island. His cursory research into the history of the *Erebus* and *Terror* had revealed that in 1850 the *HMS Investigator*, captained by Robert McClure, had endeavored to follow Franklin's route before being trapped in the ice for three consecutive winters. McClure returned to

---

[1] Joseph Conrad, "Heart of Darkness," Part One, *Blackwood's Magazine* No. 1,000 (Feb., 1899): 194

England in 1853 only to die a year later.

Alan shook his head, thinking of the onshore and submersible tours that would lead several passengers to a visit of the wreckage and the ship's salvaged vestiges on Banks Island.

Alan was silently hoping that *The Contessa* would be in the nearby waters if and when the Erebus would be located. However there was perhaps only a chance in a million or more of that happening.

"What are you thinking about?" Tiffany asked when she reached him and came to stand at his side.

Alan smiled as he turned to her. "I was just considering all of the facets associated with our excursions of the *HMS Investigator*."

"Ah yes, that famous boat which spent three whole winters trapped in the ice," Tiffany rejoined pensively. "I surely hope we won't be doing the same; I mean get stuck in the middle of the Arctic..."

Alan's chuckle interrupted her. "I can think of worse things than being trapped aboard a luxury cruise ship for three years with a beautiful woman in my bed, can't you?"

"Oh you're impossible!" Tiffany blurted, joining him in his renewed laughter. Gazing up at him, she asked, "Any plans for Vancouver?"

"None at the moment. I'll probably have to stay aboard with Evelyn and Angie to verify the inventory before setting sail northward and to participate in the safety drill that will undoubtedly be called for the day."

"Do you mean you won't even accompany me to take a leap at the suspension bridge?"

"What suspension bridge?" Alan asked with a frown across his brow. He was already thinking of the sprained ankles or broken legs that he may have to treat upon the return of the more adventurous passengers that would have crossed the gorge.

"The Capilano Suspension Bridge and overhanging walk, that's what I mean. Apparently that new walk around the cliff is amazing. The paving is made of glass or Plexiglas and it feels like you're actually walking "on air" above the gorge."

Alan shook his head and turned to face her. "I would prefer if you would accompany me to a little restaurant I've heard about on English Bay at the end of the day and before *The Contessa* sailed later tomorrow night – what do you say?"

Batting an eyelid with caprice, Tiffany wrapped her arms around his waist. "I'd love that," she whispered before giving him a peck on the cheek and quickly retrieving her arms to stand a discreet distance from him. Although Captain Middleton had made it clear to the both of them that he didn't mind the relationship, he had stated that he would have preferred for them to remain as discreet as possible in front of crew and passengers.

As they were about to part – Tiffany to arrange for tonight's piano recital at the onboard theater and Alan to sickbay for a meeting with both of his nurses – Babette trotted toward them waving. "You-hoo, you two"— she took in a breath—"finally I caught you!" She stopped at the railing and looked up at the two smiling faces looking at her. "I was afraid you would have decided to give this trip a miss when I didn't see either of you in the foyer when the horde got on board. Where have you been? Or should I ask?"

The famous New York playwright shot a reproachful glance at her friends and waited for an answer.

Alan had a hard time holding back a chuckle. The woman's effervescent nature always managed to put a smile on his lips. She was such a character. "My dear Miss Babette, I wouldn't have missed this cruise for the world…"

"Me neither," Tiffany piped in, "And I had every intention to come and find you before tonight's performance – I've got some questions about the introduction of our virtuoso…"

"No worries, dear child," Babette replied, "I'll be in my cabin when ever you need me. But for now, I wanted to talk to you, Alan, about this excursion to view the sunken ship; do you think I would be allowed or would I be fit enough to take "the dive"?"

"The dive?" Alan repeated, surprised. "Who told you that you – or anyone else for that matter – would have "to dive" to see the *HMS Investigator*?"

"No, no, Alan, not a dive per se – I mean the brochure said that a few passengers would be allowed, "to dive" down with a submersible to see the wreckage. Do you think I'll be one of those few?"

"If I have any say in the matter, you would be one of the first aboard the sub, my dear Babette," Alan replied helpfully.

"I guess then it's a question of being fit enough to go down, isn't it?"

Alan nodded. "Yes, but there is also a question of scientific priority…"

"What do you mean?" Tiffany queried. "Are there some old boring scientists on board that are going down…?"

"Yes, there are a handful of these "old fogies" who have already approached our captain and bought their passage on the sole conditions to be able to go down on the sub to view the sunken ship."

"But that's favoritism!" Babette exclaimed. "This is not a scientific expedition, or is it?"

"No, it isn't, but since Health Canada is helping us with the visit of Banks Island and have spent a great deal of time at our company headquarters devising the best way to handle these excursions, the least the powers-that-be could do was to allow a couple of their scientists from Parks Canada to visit the wreck with the sub. Politics, you know."

"Oh well, I suppose I'll have to wait my turn then, like all the other sheep on the ship," Babette said, visibly disappointed.

"It's not that bad, Babette," Tiffany said, putting an arm around her shoulders, "you're one of our most esteemed passengers and I am sure between Captain Middleton and our good doctor they'll manage to save you a seat." She looked up at Alan, seeking his approval.

"Absolutely. But, as you surmised correctly, we'll need to have you go through a rigorous physical medical examination whether you want to go down with the sub or visit the salvaged vestiges on the island. It also will include a testing by one of the personal trainers in the gym, so do your daily workout, please."

"Why would that be?" Tiffany asked. "What's the problem with going to the island?"

"Nothing definite yet, and I'd prefer waiting until we get to Juneau where we are to receive more information before I say anymore on the subject," Alan concluded.

"Alright," Babette rejoined, "since you want to keep this – whatever this is – a secret, I better keep this whole conversation to myself, hadn't I?"

"That would be my recommendation," Alan agreed, his gaze deadly serious.

CHAPTER 5

A hole behind you

IT SEEMED TO ALAN that the most seasoned staff had been assigned to crew the ship, a choice for which he was grateful. Captain Middleton, for instance, was one of the most respected and agreeable seafarers he knew. Endowed with fairness and understanding while keeping a tight rein on his officers, he was certainly one with a sense of humor that never seemed to abandon him, even in the worst of circumstances. Middleton had been the captain on *The Duchess* when '*murder and mayhem*' enveloped some of the crew and passengers with the horrific prospect of being the next target on the killer's list. But he had gone through the ordeal with a masterful mind, all the while maintaining his ship "steady as she goes" for the duration of the cruise.

As the ship was slowly sailing northward to Vancouver that night, the captain had convened his officers and principal staff around his table for a sumptuous dinner. He apparently didn't want to hold a formal meeting with his staff tonight – "I've had enough of these meetings on the way to Seattle to last me a lifetime," he had said to Alan when the latter had queried whether that typical meeting would be on the agenda on the first night – as it was customary.

Also invited to dine with the captain were the two scientists from Parks Canada and the two technicians that would oversee the submarine dive at the *HMS Investigator* wreckage site.

"Dr. Sullivan," Captain Middleton said genially, raising his glass to the man, "Welcome aboard *The Contessa* and by all means, and welcome to my table tonight."

"Thank you, Captain," Dr. Sullivan replied, nodding. "Dr. Lespierre and I are very fortunate to have been chosen for the voyage, and we are extremely grateful for the comfort and accommodation you have put at our disposal, indeed."

"Yes," Dr. Lespierre rejoined, "we are very pleased to be here. It is a great opportunity for us." The man's French accent had betrayed his background on the first syllable he had pronounced. He was perhaps a little younger than Sullivan but both men seemed to have worked together a long time for their manners and demeanors were identical in many regards. Their faces, bordered of sturdy-growing beards, were tanned as old leather – there was no mistaking it – these men must have lived outdoors for the best part of their careers and perhaps their lives.

"Has either of you visited the Arctic before?" Stephan Ivanov then asked, shooting a glance in the captain's direction. He didn't want to be the first to ask but his curiosity apparently got the better of him.

Dr. Sullivan smiled benignly. "Yes, Dr. Lespierre and I were actually on Ellesmere Island when we received word two years ago that the *HMS Investigator* had been located."

"Have you seen her already then?" Middleton asked, himself quite interested in the subject.

"Oh no. We were on another assignment and by the time we would have been able to reach Banks Island the crew would have gone back to Ottawa to report the find in person."

"But we did go to Banks Island last year when they first assembled the collected relics from the ship," Dr. Lespierre added. "We have seen the vestiges already and as a collector myself of sunken treasures, I could certainly tell you that they are magnificent specimens of the era."

Alan's ears perked up when he heard Middleton's next question. "Did you have an opportunity to visit the community on Banks Island while you were there?"

"Not really," Dr. Sullivan replied. "We were only there for the day and had to rejoin another party in Inuvik, so we didn't really have time to visit or go about the place."

"Is Inuvik where they get their supplies?" Alan asked.

"I believe so, since it's the closest airport town to many of the Arctic islands. But I'm not quite sure of their logistics, given that most of our assignments took us to the Northern Territories where we were dropped off and picked up by the Parks' aircrafts."

"That's most interesting," Captain Middleton commented before saying, "Why don't we have some dinner now, before everyone gets hungry – I wouldn't tolerate any such thing to occur at my table!" He then waved for the servers to bring the first course of their dinner.

When their appetizers and salads had been served, Tiffany looked at Stephan Ivanov – the man intrigued her. Built like a mountain, muscle-bound, his gentle face didn't match the rest of him. It was the face of a boy, unblemished by age. Although he appeared young, and with features that could be qualified as very symmetrical, it betrayed only gentleness and care for his fellow human beings. She shook her head unnoticeably and returned to eating her stuffed mushrooms.

As for the two technicians – the "divers" as Babette would have called them – they hadn't said a word ever since they sat down. Tiffany knew their names were Edward Barrington and Sam Ashton and they looked as English as they come. Both lanky and seemingly supple in their movements they bore the marks of men who watch their diets and go to the gym routinely. Again, Tiffany gathered they were in their thirties and perhaps had conducted such exercises quite often off the coast of England.

"No tea for Stephan I see," she remarked quietly to Alan sitting to her right.

"I guess not tonight, Josephine," he replied, throwing her a smirk before biting on a piece of bread.

That answer had Tiffany blush to her ears. "That reminds me," she said, shooting Alan a darted look, "you haven't told me all there was to tell about Yvette, have you?" Her voice had become a mere murmur – not wanting to attract the attention of the other guests at the table.

"Later, I promise," Alan said to her, almost in a whisper.

Having observed the little bantering between the two from across the table, Captain Middleton asked, "And what have you got for our passengers' entertainment tonight, Ms. Sylvan? I heard something about a Japanese virtuoso, is he as good as his reviews are claiming?"

Tiffany looked up, apparently unabashed by the captain's sudden interest in her agenda. "Yes, sir. I am not a music expert or even an authority, but Mr. Ashimoto has won many concert competitions since the tender age of five, I am told, and is now one of the concert pianists attached to the London Philharmonic."

"I love classical piano, especially piano concertos," Edward Barrington piped up, finally opening his mouth. "And I believe I have heard Mr. Ashimoto play in London the last time I was on leave."

"Oh you live in England then, Mr. Barrington?" Stephan asked, after wiping his mouth and taking the last sip of his wine.

"Absolutely. Sam and I work with the sub on the North Sea oil platforms and when we're on leave we go back to London – every three weeks."

"And, Mr. Ashton, are you also a classical music lover?" Captain Middleton asked.

"Yes, but I have an equal penchant for Jazz, though."

Edward turned to him and smiled. "Yes, Captain – when I go to a concert he goes to a Jazz haunt. But sometimes we go together...."

When the desserts were served, the first officer, Mr. Alderman, turned to Alan. "Doctor Mayhew, do you think we will encounter any difficulties during the passengers' visit of Banks Island?"

Alan knew the question would have to be raised at some point, but he didn't relish discussing the matter at this juncture and certainly not during dinner. "I couldn't foresee much difficulty at this stage, Mr. Alderman, but I'll have to differ making an assessment on the Banks Island's health hazard or conditions until we get to Juneau and receive the latest sealed written report from Health Canada."

"Does that mean there could be some health risks to the visitors then?" Captain Middleton asked, although he had been fully apprized of the health risks existing among many of the Inuit communities during their meetings with Health Canada in Ottawa while the ship was still under construction in France.

"Yes, Captain, is the short answer to that question at the moment. However, I have made all the necessary arrangements with the authorities concerned regarding our visit on Banks Island to address whatever the risk, our passengers or crew going ashore might face and they will be fully prepared for the visit beforehand."

Captain Middleton nodded his approval and then returned his gaze to his first officer. "I think this evening has been most informative, but now you'll have to excuse me; I must retire and catch some zees before we reach Vancouver. I dearly want to visit that city – she has a special place in my heart." He eyed Alderman. "I trust *The Contessa* in your capable hands then, Mr. Alderman. Try not to ram her against one of those islands while I'm gone, will you?"

"I'll do my best, Captain," Alderman replied, while the exchange had ignited a round of laughter among the guests.

"Good night," said the captain, rising from his chair and making his way to the door of the dining room.

The sun popped its head over the mountains lining the West Coast of British Columbia quite early the next morning. No sooner was the sun up – at 05:00 to be precise – a young alluring woman made her way to the holographic golf course installed on the fore deck of the vessel. This exceptional and unique optical illusion device allowed the golfer to visualize a golf course in front of him as he progressed through the links. The lawn at the young woman's feet extended before her until it met at the foot of the invisible screen. She placed a tee on the ground and swung her first ball into the air, not paying any attention to the man behind her. Apparently several people wanted to get their golf practice in before they went ashore to play 'the real thing' later in the day.

Taking turns, they progressively went through the course and while 'playing' on the front nine of the rather complicated course the man became confused as to where he was. He turned to the young woman playing ahead of him. He stepped up to her, explained his confusion and asked her if she knew what hole he was playing.

"I'm on the 7th hole," she replied, "and you are a hole behind me. So you must be on the 6th hole."

He thanked her and stood aside to let her take her next shot.

On the back nine, the same thing happened and he approached her again with the same request.

"I'm on number 14, and you're still a hole behind, so you must be on the 13th hole."

Once again he thanked her and returned to his play.

He finished his round and went to get a coffee where he saw the same lady sitting at another table.

He asked the server if he knew the lady.

The man said that she was a sales lady who had come aboard just for a part of the cruise, until they reached Alaska, and that he didn't really know her but that she had come to get coffee last night inquiring about the golf course.

The man got up and went to the lady's table. "Let me buy you breakfast in appreciation for your help," he said. "I understand that you're in the sales profession. I'm in sales also. What do you sell?"

"I'll tell you, but you're going to laugh," she replied, smiling.

"No, I won't, I promise," he said.

"Well, if you must know, I work for Tampax."

With that, he laughed so hard that tears ran down his cheeks.

"See," she said, "I knew you'd laugh!"

"That's not what I'm laughing at," he replied, "I'm a salesman for Preparation H, so I'm still a hole behind you."

CHAPTER SIX

A collector of sunken treasures

"DID YOU HEAR WHAT Lespierre said last night?" Alan asked Tiffany while they were having breakfast at the café before *The Contessa* was to reach her berth in Vancouver.

"Hum, yes," she replied, biting on a fresh croissant. "If you're referring to his visit of Banks Island last year, yes I did."

"Yes, that and the fact that he's a collector of sunken treasures." Tiffany nodded. "I wonder what his interest is really about in the *Investigator*," Alan wondered aloud. "Is he interested in securing some of the relics for himself perhaps?"

"You're impossible, Alan," Tiffany blurted between two bites. "You've become quite suspicious lately, haven't you? It's totally normal for a collector to have a particular interest in these sorts of things. Besides, I believe he's here to do just that – catalogue the relics first hand for Parks Canada, isn't he?"

Alan nodded, scooping the last of his cereal and munching on it concertedly. "Yes, but I would have thought these relics have been catalogued already and his interest may lie elsewhere…"

"Oh am I so glad to find you, Alan," a familiar voice behind them cut their conversation short. "I went to the medical center – what a magnificent mini-hospital it is. Just wonderful – and Evelyn told me where I could find you…. Anyway, how are you both?"

Susan Ashland hadn't left any breathing space in her speech so that neither Alan nor Tiffany could respond. She had pulled up a chair to sit at their table.

"Good morning, Susan; how are you?" Tiffany said before Alan could greet her. "Did you get my email?"

"Oh yes, and it gave me the boost I needed at the time, thank you." She turned to Alan. "I'm sorry, Alan, but I wanted to ask you if I could come for a visit later today – after I come back from Vancouver."

"Of course, but I would like to leave the ship at about six, would it be okay for you to come by the center earlier than that?"

"Yes, I should be back by three, at the latest. I wouldn't be well enough yet, I don't think, to traipse around the city for any more than a couple of hours this morning."

Susan Ashland was a beautiful woman, by any man's description. Her elegant stature, only made suppler by the years she spent on the stage as a ballerina, attracted the eye of anyone passing her by. Her face merely betrayed some of the signs of fatigue that had resulted from her recent surgery. She had lost quite a bit of weight but her skin seemed to have regained the luminosity of health and she was now looking at Alan and Tiffany in turn, a timid smile adorning her lovely lips.

"Have you brought your medicines with you, or do you need a new prescription?" Alan asked, knowing that, depending on the treating physician, patients needed to procure their meds from some of the port-of-calls at which the cruise was scheduled to lower anchor. And if they wanted to find any unusual medications, they had best procure the meds sooner than later – the further north they went, the harder it was going to be to get the meds.

"Oh no, Doctor Vaughn gave me a three months supply before I left Boston and an additional prescription if I needed anymore – so I'm all set for the journey." She paused and looked at Tiffany. "I told you, didn't I?"

"If you're talking about breast implants, yes you did," Tiffany replied, taking a sip of her coffee.

"And what do you think I should do?"

"Goodness, Susan, that wouldn't be for me to say. I have no idea what such a procedure entails…"

"Let me interject here, ladies," Alan said, gazing at Susan fixedly. "Let's talk about the pros and cons this afternoon, shall we?"

Susan nodded. "Yes, that's what I wanted to talk to you about, but I want some woman's advice beforehand as well," she said by way of a reply to Tiffany's mild rebuke.

"I know, Susan, but you need to hear the physical impact such an operation would have on your health at this point, and there is plenty of time – which is necessary – before you make a decision."

"Alright, you two, I hear you, and I'll see you when I get back from Vancouver," she concluded, getting to her feet. "Have you seen Babette this morning?"

Tiffany shook her head. "Oh I don't think she'll be up early this morning. She stayed up talking to Mr. Ashimoto after his performance…"

"How was he? Any good?" Susan asked, still standing by the table, yet seemingly anxious to be on her way.

"He was fantastic!" Tiffany replied all smiles. "He got three 'encores' and a standing ovation. For a first evening, we couldn't have wished for a better musician."

"I'm sorry I missed him then, but with these meds and Dr. Vaughn's new regimen, I have to get to bed like a mere child – so infuriating sometimes." And with these words, Susan gathered the colorful afghan she wore about her and left the dining café.

"Has anyone called for me?" Alan asked airily as he entered the medical center.

Evelyn turned from counting the drugs in the cabinet in the examining room to say, "No, Doc – no calls so far. No one is awake yet, I guess."

"And I gathered from the manifest that most of our passengers are the sort that will not come in for a nose bleed," Alan remarked, coming to stand beside her and taking a look at what his nurse was doing. "You know you can catalogue these with your electronic notepad…"

"I know, Doc, but I'm no wizard with these gadgets and since I found a printed list in the file, I thought I would do a manual check." She looked up at Alan pleadingly as if saying, "don't make me use that awful tablet, please."

Evelyn Develon had been Alan's nurse for quite a few years on various ship contracts. She was a gorgeous brunette that always reminded the doctor of one of those Egyptian deities; her features were so symmetrical that it couldn't escape anyone's notice.

Alan smiled. He understood her dilemma. "Let me show you." He went to the cabinet beside the drug storing shelves and took out a tablet and a small scanner. "Here is what you do; first you turn it on, touch your finger on the icon labeled 'inventory', and as you see, the list appears." He handed the tablet to her, which she took gingerly. "Okay, now with the scanner, you go over each canister and as it lights up"—he joined action to words—"the list on the tablet is automatically updated. See?"

"Amazing," said Evelyn, looking at the list running down before her eyes and each drug count being updated as if by magic. "Does it do anything else?" she asked, her fear of computerized equipment being quickly replaced by curiosity.

"This tablet only counts full bottles as part of the supplies for the center. But as you do know, most of our equipment is now also fitted with remote controls that enables you or I to raise beds, move heavy instruments such as the x-ray apparatus and the mini MRI without lifting a finger."

"That will save a lot of backbreaking efforts with broken legs and other bed-ridden patients – let's hope we don't have any of those before I get used to everything."

"Yes," Alan agreed, "and Angie and you can now attend to your nursing tasks without having to worry about filling out forms or updating paperwork."

"Did you give Angie the same instructions when she came over with you on your trip from Panama?"

"Oh yes. We went through every single piece of machinery together and although she was a bit reticent when it came to using the MRI, she fared pretty well."

"Will you go through everything with me as well?" Evelyn asked, visibly anxious not to be left out.

"Of course we will. Actually, you'll have the first crack at using our MRI this afternoon. Susan Ashland is due to come in at three for a talk about her recent mastectomy – and I'd like to get an MRI done on her before we go any farther on this cruise. If there is any reason for me to think that she should return to Boston, I'll make sure I have a clear visual understanding of her case before I make a diagnosis."

No sooner than Alan was explaining the reason for Susan's visit that afternoon, she entered the medical center. Evelyn's thoughts briefly drifted to her own sister – she had had a mastectomy over 5 years back and was now fully recovered and had moved on with her life; a thought that always pleased Evelyn to no end. After being asked to sit in on the discussion with Susan, she wished Susan would recover in the same way. The MRI went well with Evelyn learning the steps of the highly automated device very quickly, as usual, and fortunately for Susan, Alan's read of the scan looked good.

Five-thirty came around so fast, that Alan couldn't believe he still had reports to type for the main office, and... but he shrugged the tedium away and shut down the computer system with a hit of a digit on the keyboard. Since he didn't want to show up at the restaurant in his uniform, he decided to head for his cabin, have a quick shower and change into a casual suit. En route to his cabin, he was accompanied by the strong voiced tenor who had apparently performed in Vancouver three days previously and was to perform again tomorrow night. Alan and he exchanged some pleasantries. They had just passed one of the large-figured female passengers when all of a sudden she let go a very large expulsion of gas. Without missing a beat, she blurted out, "I was trying to match your beautifully strong voice and look forward to hearing you again." It was all Alan and the tenor could do to keep a straight face, and could not match that scenario with words!

Alan had no idea what Tiffany would be wearing this evening but he was sure it was going to be another one of the stunning dresses that seemed to fill her suitcase. Shortly after six he was waiting for her in the grand foyer near reception and the gangway to the pier where *The Contessa* had found her berth for the day and night she was to spend in Vancouver. The vessel had already been the subject of numerous curiosity seekers and tourists alike, taking pictures from the balustrade above the dock; as close as non-passenger were allowed to come to the ship. Everyone had to admit, she was a splendid ship. Her elegant lines and discreet features hid her immense power to cut through the swell of the temperamental Arctic Ocean or fray herself a safe passage through the worst of tropical storms.

After scanning their crew cards, and saying hello to the security officer on duty a few minutes later, Alan and Tiffany emerged onto the walkway along the pier facing downtown Vancouver that seemed to tower above them. Seeing Alan's beckoning wave, a cabby from the taxi rank close by, pulled up and asked, "where to, sir?" once the both of them had climbed into the backseat.

"The Boat House on English Bay," Alan replied.

Nodding, the cabby pulled away from the curb and pressed a digit on his on-board computer.

"So you've been to this place before?" Tiffany asked quietly, slipping her hand in his.

He squeezed it and turned to her. "Yes, but it's changed a lot apparently since the Olympics..."

"Are you sure the restaurant is still there?" Tiffany cut-in, turning an anxious gaze to him.

"Oh yes, the Boat House has been there for over sixty years I believe, and it's not moving anywhere, I can assure you."

"Is it close to the beach?"

Alan couldn't help but chuckle at her inquisitiveness. "Yes, across the street from it and overlooking the mountains beyond Stanley Park."

"Wow, that's sounds as inviting as if you had recited the advertisement off a brochure."

"But, it happens to be the truth. And it's a comfortable place. Actually you can choose to dine on the terrace, in the bistro or the formal restaurant upstairs."

"And what have you chosen?" Tiffany asked.

Alan shook his head. "I'll leave the choice up to you once you've seen the place."

Since they had escaped most of the rush-hour traffic, it took only a mere ten minutes, to reach English Bay and the restaurant from the pier.

Stepping out of the cab, Tiffany – dressed in a summer outfit, which fit her to a T – looked around her and stopped when she saw mountains looming high above the park and beach. "This is a gorgeous setting, Alan," she exclaimed, sliding her arm in his as soon as the taxi had departed. "But I don't see the terrace you talked about…"

"Let me show you," he replied, leading her down the sidewalk alongside the restaurant until he stopped and added, "Look above you."

When Tiffany lifted her gaze, her mouth dropped and closed quickly. "That's where I want to eat," she said, hopping beside Alan like a little girl who had just discovered the ice cream parlor.

"Well, that's where we'll go then," Alan said, taking her by the hand toward the stairs that would see them sitting at a table facing the ocean and mountains beyond a few minutes later.

"You know, Alan, we always see these cities from the ship's deck and they are all a wonder to look at from that vantage point, but, it's true, you need to see them from their hearts, from the point of view of the people living every day with these mountains surrounding them. Quite amazing the difference, really."

"And Vancouver is one of the cleanest cities in the world, which to me adds to her charm…"

"Would you care for a drink before dinner?" the server asked when he came to stand beside their table as unobtrusively as he could.

"I think we'll have wine with dinner, so no cocktails for me," Alan replied, looking at Tiffany to see if she would want an aperitif.

"Nothing for me either," she replied, smiling up at the waiter.

After the young man had enumerated the "specials" and "catches" of the day, Alan ordered some salads and other vegetarian delicacies from the menu. He also asked for a bottle of "Louis Latour" – his favorite wine –, which he knew the restaurant would carry.

"Very well, sir," the server said, "I'll be right back with the wine."

When a young woman came to the table to lay the cutlery on each of their placemats, Alan suddenly burst out laughing.

Both Tiffany and the waitress turned to stare at him – uncomprehending. "Did I do something wrong, sir?" the young lady asked.

"Oh no, my dear, nothing like that. I was just recalling a friend's story that had to do with cutlery – that's all." He looked up at her, his grin dwindling down to a measly smile when he noticed her dismayed face.

When the waitress was out of earshot, a befuddled Tiffany said, "And that's one I surely want to hear."

Alan shook his head, took his soupspoon and looked at it before he replied, "Maybe we should wait until we're finished eating before I tell you the story."

"Oh no, you don't – there are too many of these so-called stories that you have left out of our conversations already, so spit it out, Dr. Mayhew."

Her teasing scold didn't escape Alan's notice. "Okay then – here goes nothing." He paused as if gathering his thoughts, then began, "Some of the advertising consultants for the head office of the shipping line in Miami took some friends of mine and colleagues out for dinner after some strenuous meetings regarding the promotion of our *Contessa* cruises. One of them noticed that the waiter who took their order carried a spoon in his shirt pocket. It seemed a little strange.

"When the busboy brought their water and cutlery, my friend noticed he also had a spoon in his shirt pocket. Then he looked around and saw that all the staff had spoons in their pockets.

"When the waiter came back to serve the soup, he asked, "Why the spoon?"

""Well," he explained, "the restaurant's owners hired Mckinsey & Co., to revamp all our processes. After several months of analysis, they concluded that the spoon was the most frequently dropped utensil. It represents a drop frequency of approximately three spoons per table per hour. If our personnel are better prepared, we can reduce the number of trips back to the kitchen and save 115.27 man-hours per shift"."

"As luck would have it, during the dinner, my friend dropped his spoon and the waiter was able to replace it with his spare. "I'll get another spoon next time I go to the kitchen instead of making an extra trip to get it right now", he said.

"My friend was impressed. But he also noticed that there was a string hanging out of the waiter's fly. Looking around, he noticed that all the waiters had the same string hanging from their flies. So before he walked off, he asked the waiter, "Excuse me, but can you tell me why you have that string right there?"

"Oh, certainly!" Then he lowered his voice. "Not everyone is so observant. That consulting firm I mentioned also found out that we could save time in the bathroom. By tying this string to the tip of you know what, we can pull it out without touching it and eliminate the need to wash our hands, shortening the time spent in the bathroom by 76.39 percent".

Ever vigilant of US Public Health rules and regulations that govern any ship landing at a US port, Alan asked, "After you get it out, how do you put it back?"

"Well," he whispered, "I don't know about the others, but I use the spoon"!"

"Good Grief," Tiffany blurted, amid somewhat loud but muffled laughter, "Now I know why you thought it would be better to wait until we finished our meal...."

With a deadpan face, Alan added, "So we should be careful, when we visit a restaurant and watch if any of the waiters has a spoon in his apron pocket."

"And it's lucky we've got a female server to attend this table," Tiffany said, after her giggles had died down a little.

Following a tasteful meal and a delightful evening watching the sun set in the waters of English Bay, Alan and Tiffany returned to *The Contessa*, still a bit inebriated from the wine, each other's loving company and feeling on top of the world. When Alan reached his cabin after spending a couple of hours with the woman he dearly loved in his arms and making love to her in her cabin with the passion of a man that was now enjoying life, he opened the door and breathed a deep sigh of contentment. His sense of contentment however, was soon cut short when he saw a note pinned to his pillow on which he read a 'message' – if such could describe the words inscribed in bold letters:

> TEN
>
> AND
>
> THEN
>
> THERE
>
> WERE
>
> NINE!

Immediately recalling Agatha Christies' novel, where the ten characters described in her story managed to die one by one – each time the death followed by these exact words – "and then there were..." – and that until "there were none" left. He sat on his bed and wondered what it meant. Were they going to discover a body aboard *The Contessa* by morning and nine more during their journey? "Impossible!" he shouted to himself, throwing the note on his desk, annoyance written in the lines of his face.

He would have to do something about someone having intruded into his privacy, but for now, he didn't want to alert anyone of the breach of security or create an all-out search for the culprit in the middle of the night, and decided to take a calming shower and sleep the troublesome message off.

CHAPTER SEVEN

Nine what? – was the question

AFTER AN EARLY MORNING run on one of the promenade decks, and a refreshing shower, Alan decided to remain quiet about finding the note pinned on his pillow. Calling an all out search or starting an investigation this early in their journey wouldn't serve any purpose but to disturb the passengers, for what was probably a prank, albeit a puzzling one. Instead, he considered approaching Babette with the enigma. Perhaps, being well versed in meaningful literature, she would be able to shed some light on the perplexing note.

He found her in the chapel, apparently absorbed in some of her reading.

"I'm very sorry to bother you, Babette," he began, when she turned her head to see who was coming down the aisle, "But I would like your help…"

"Goodness gracious, my dear Alan," Babette replied quietly, while Alan took a seat beside her, "be sure to know that you're never bothering me when it comes to assist you, except of course, if it came to your health…"

Alan held up a hand to stop her going any further with her drawn out assumptions, and smiled. "Nothing like that, Babette." He took the note out of his breast pocket. "Have a look at this and tell me what it is about – if you can."

Babette didn't need her glasses to read the heavy print. She read the note and lifted her gaze to him. "Where did you find it?" she asked, a quizzical look on her face.

"Pinned on my pillow when I came back to my cabin last night – why?"

Babette returned to focusing on the piece of paper as if mesmerized. "You know, I'm sure, where the quote comes from"—she looked up at him again—"but it's the implication behind the words that are very somber in their meaning, Alan, almost menacing I would say."

"What makes you say that, or what is this somber meaning you mentioned?"

Giving the note back to him, Babette replied, "Well, the original work by Agatha Christie was entitled "Ten Little Niggers", which was later changed to "Ten Little Indians" for political correctness. Agatha elaborated the riddle on the basis of finding the person who was actually supposed to die, and until Hercule Poirot found who the person was, everyone around him would be killed."

"That's what I understood, the moment I saw the note," Alan agreed, "but as you mentioned the story began with ten people, and here we have only nine – unless I've missed something…"

But "Ten Little Indians" should be your first clue. Ask yourself which nine people or things would have been complete with the tenth member?

Is there anyone missing amongst the crew or staff? Or are there only nine items when there should be ten of them?

Babette shook her head. "I'm sure you haven't missed anything, Alan."

"You mean a "little Indian" or an "Indian object" is missing?"

"Make that an Inuit or an Inuit artifact, and you might get closer to the answer."

Alan frowned. "But we don't have any Inuit person or artifact on board – not that I am aware anyway."

With a gentle smile and closing her Bible into her lap, Babette added, "Maybe you should be looking at what is ahead of us, Alan. There is a shipwreck at the bottom of the ocean – which we may have an opportunity to visit – and in that ship there were treasures, artifacts or relics. Is there per chance one of these pieces missing or a piece that hasn't been discovered yet?"

"Good God," Alan exclaimed, "that's going a little far..." He stopped dead in his speech and peered into her eyes. "And we are looking at the *Investigator*, aren't we?"

"Exactly, Alan. The "Investigator" in the case of Agatha's story was Hercule Poirot, and his brain resealed the secret of the "Ten Little Indians", which in your case, would be the hull of our "Investigator"."

It was Alan's turn to shake his head. "I would never have thought of that in a million years, Babette. And that's probably why you're the playwright and I'm not." He got up and threw her a grateful glance as he made his way out of the chapel saying, "Thanks. I owe you one."

It was high time he had a chat with Dr. Lespierre; Alan thought when he returned to the medical center. He wouldn't have time to talk to the man this morning, but he was determined to corner him before the day was over. In the meantime, he wanted to have a second look at Susan's MRI.

Angie was on duty this morning. She was arranging some of the linen when he went to her. "Good morning, Doctor," she said with a broad smile on her lips. "I'd love to take some of these sheets home with me – really, they are the best..."

"I hope I don't notice any of them disappearing from the linen closet when we're back in Boston," Alan remarked, "Otherwise I'll know where to sleep next."

"I knew this cruise would spell trouble for me the minute I stepped aboard," Angie said, winking. "You're such a tease sometimes."

Chuckling, he asked, "Have you transferred Ms. Ashland MRI results onto my computer yet?"

Angie returned a blank stare to Alan. "No is the answer, Doc, because I didn't even know anyone had gone through an MRI so far – sorry."

"No, no need to apologize. My fault; I should have shown Evelyn how to do it before she left yesterday."

"Actually she told me about using the MRI yesterday, but I had no idea that she had omitted to upload the file. But I can do that for you now, if you like?"

"No-no, that's fine – I'll do it. Just take good care of the sheets for now..." And leaving Angie with a trailing laugh, he went to the MRI room to send the file to his system.

When he sat at his desk and scanned through the images of Susan's chest, he couldn't see any reason for her to worry or for him to send her back to Boston. *She should be fine,* he thought. *But if she wants breast implants, that's going to be tricky. She didn't have large breasts to begin with and now after the surgeries and radiation, her skin was taut to her chest not giving the customary laxity needed for the pouch needed in the typical silicone breast implant.... Anyway, we'll see,* he concluded, closing her file.

As he was rummaging through one of the desk drawers, he came across a little framed note that he had found in some store in England when he had taken Yvette to London for a weekend visit. He had bought it for Angie, knowing that she was always dealing with children and decided it was high time to give it to her.

He was about to get up when she appeared at the door of his office saying, "Would you want to have lunch here or will you go to the restaurant? I'm asking because I'm on my way to the café and I can bring you back something if you want..."

"Thanks, but I think I'll be eating at one of the restaurants today – I'm hoping to find Dr. Lespierre and..."

"Another doctor?" Angie interrupted, frowning. Another doctor on board would certainly disturb her well-established routine. And Angie was not a person who liked changes by any means. A nurse for many years, Angie was the portrait of neatness and practical demeanor. Never a hair out of place, always wearing a uniform that seemed to have come out of the box that very morning, she inspired confidence and often loving care for her patients.

"Oh no, he's not a doctor of medicine," Alan replied, "quite the opposite in fact – he is an archeologist attached to Parks Canada and won't be coming anywhere near the medical center, unless he's sick or hurt, of course."

That explanation seemed to allay Angie's fears for the moment when she said, "That's good – I'm not too sure I can take another flirt about the place."

"Well, if I am a flirt then maybe you'll accept a gift from this admirer?"

Angie opened her eyes wide, never knowing what to expect from her boss at any time.

"Here"—he extended a hand with the framed note to her—"maybe you'd like to hang it somewhere...?"

"Oh my, that's nice of you, Doc," Angie replied, taking the frame from him and reading the words quickly.

MAHATMA GHANDI

Mahatma Ghandi, as you know, walked barefoot most of
the time, which produced an impressive set of calluses on
his feet. He also ate very little, which made him rather
frail and with his odd died, he suffered from bad breath.
This made him a super calloused fragile mystic hexed by
halitosis.

Exploding in roaring laughter, Angie then said, "That's going in the waiting room! I'll hang it up as soon as I get back from lunch. Thank you, Doc. But where did you find it?"

"When I spent a few days in London during the ship's construction, I found a little store that had all sorts of these jokes and adages framed. I thought you might like it, since you're often treating kids during the cruises."

"Well, thanks again, Doc. I'll hang it this afternoon," Angie said, going back to the locker room, presumably to put the picture-note in a safe place.

When she was about to leave – her hand on the doorknob – she looked at Alan.

"What's on your mind, Angie," Alan asked, noting her hesitancy.

"Nothing much, Doc, but I thought about the number of crew physicals for this cruise. Will we have to put everyone through the examinations on this particular cruise? I know corporate will send us lists of which crew will be nearing the expiry date of their physical, but…"

Alan shook his head and got up from his seat. "Not everyone, no." He walked out of his office, locked the door behind him and added, "Let me walk with you to the elevator."

"Do we have a list already of the crew we need to put through their physical then?"

"Yes. Actually, but we will have more than crew members going through check-ups; you see, when we'll reach Banks Island, any passengers wishing to disembark to visit either the village or the place where they've collected the salvaged relics, or even those people who will go down in the sub to view the ship wreck will have to have gone through a detailed physical exam."

"Wow, that's going to mean a lot of lab work as well, won't it?" Angie remarked, as they reached the elevator.

"Yes, it will, but don't worry, we'll have help. Health Canada is assigning two lab technicians to join us in Juneau, to carry out the lab work."

"Whew, that's a relief! Because, I can't really see Evelyn and I handling the work-up for so many people by ourselves in addition to our usual work."

"But there won't be that many people going ashore, I don't think. Yet, we had better be prepared for all eventualities. You, Evelyn and I will work on involving the Health Canada techs into our routine and let the tax payer dollars be put to good use."

After exchanging a few more words in the elevator, Alan left Angie to go to the café while he made his way to the luncheon buffet, where he thought he would find either scientist – Dr. Sullivan or Lespierre – or both. Since it was still early and the luncheon crowd hadn't arrived yet, he decided to sit at the bar and wait to see if the archeologists would come in before sitting at a table.

"Hello, Doc," the bartender, Jimmy, said with a broad smile on his face. "What will it be?"

"Hi, Jimmy. Just get me a tall orange juice – no ice, will you?"

"Sure thing, Doc," he answered, placing a large glass on the bar and bending down to fetch the jug out of the fridge. "How have you been?" he asked while he poured the orange juice in Alan's glass.

"Just fine," Alan replied, taking a first sip. "What about you, anything happening around here?"

"Nothing much, except I've noticed the difference between these passengers and those I served on previous cruises."

"How's that?"

"Well, on most cruises, I get all sorts, like disgruntled husbands, rowdy jet-setters, or the occasional flirty ladies, but on this cruise, so far, I got people talking about business, their last golf tournament and wives chatting about their last purchases in Paris, New York or Athens." He shook his head, smiling, while wiping some glasses he picked up from under the counter. "They're really too quiet for my taste, Doc"—he lowered his voice to a mere whisper—"boring actually."

"I'm sure things will heat up once we're a bit further along," Alan said, drinking some more of the juice. "But, tell me, did the two archeologists come by already – I mean have they eaten or come to this bar since we left Seattle?"

"You mean the two professor-type pair that carry books and satchels everywhere they go?"

"Yes, that sounds like them. You've seen them coming in here then?"

"Oh yes, they were here last night actually. They sat at a table near the window and seemed to have an argument about something, kind of a lovers spat. They didn't look very happy anyway."

"Did you hear what they said?"

"Oh no, Doc. I was watching the Jay Leno show on TV and it was some show, I tell you, I didn't pay much attention to much else, other than my work, of course."

"That's alright, and what was Jay on about this show?"

"He found probably the funniest date story ever, first date or not. Jay went into the audience to find the most embarrassing first date that a woman ever had. The winner described her worst first date experience. There was absolutely no question as to why her tale took the prize!

"She said it was midwinter... Snowing and quite cold ... and the guy had taken her skiing in the mountains outside Salt Lake City, Utah. It was a day trip (no overnight). They were strangers, after all, and had never even met before. The outing was fun but relatively uneventful until they were headed home late that afternoon.

"They were driving back down the mountain, when she gradually began to realize that she should not have had that extra latte. They were about an hour away from anywhere with a rest room and in the middle of nowhere. Her companion suggested she try to hold it, which she did for a while. Unfortunately, because of the heavy snow and slow going, there came a point when she told him that he had better stop and let her go beside the road, or it would be the front seat of his car. They stopped and she quickly crawled out beside the car, yanked her pants down and started.

"In the deep snow she didn't have good footing, so she let her butt rest against the rear fender to steady herself. Her companion stood on the side of the car watching for traffic and indeed was a real gentleman and refrained from peeking. All she could think about was the relief she felt despite the rather embarrassing nature of the situation. Upon finishing however, she soon became aware of another sensation.

"As she bent to pull up her pants, the young lady discovered her buttocks were firmly glued against the car's fender. Thoughts of tongues frozen to poles immediately came to mind as she attempted to disengage her flesh from the icy metal. It was quickly apparent that she had a brand new problem due to the extreme cold. Horrified by her plight and yet aware of the humor of the moment, she answered her date's concerns about "what is taking so long" with a reply that indeed she was "freezing her butt off" and in need of some assistance.

"He came around the car as she tried to cover herself with her sweater and then, as she looked imploringly into his eyes, he burst out laughing. She too, got the giggles and when they finally managed to compose themselves, they assessed her dilemma. Obviously, as hysterical as the situation was, they also were faced with a real problem. Both agreed it would take something hot to free her chilly cheeks from the grip of the icy metal.

"Thinking about what had gotten her into the predicament in the first place, both quickly realized that there was only one way to get her free. So, as she looked the other way, her first-time date proceeded to unzip his pants and pee her butt off the fender. As the audience screamed in laughter, she took the Tonight Show prize hands down. Or perhaps that should be "pants down." And you thought your first date was embarrassing, Doc."

"And what were Jay's comments after that?" Alan asked, refraining from breaking in an all-out roaring laughter.

"He said, and I quote: "This gives a whole new meaning to being pissed off"."

At these words, Alan couldn't contain himself, and let out a hearty chuckle. "Oh and how did the first date turn out? Did they say?"

Jimmy nodded. "He became her husband and was sitting next to her in the audience."

Upon emptying his glass, after he had stopped laughing a little, Alan said, "Well, it looks like our two archeologists are not going to show up today," looking around him.

Jimmy bent down over the counter and replied, "Just wait for another ten minutes or so, and they should be here – like clock work they are."

Jimmy had been right on the money for Dr. Sullivan pushed the door open to let his partner Dr. Lespierre precede him into the bar, exactly ten minutes later.

CHAPTER EIGHT

Too many things to consider

WHEN ALAN APPROACHED their table, Dr. Sullivan seemed to shrink back in his seat – he obviously didn't want any company. As for Dr. Lespierre, a broad smile met Alan's gaze when the latter pulled up a chair from another table and sat down between the two of them.

"I'm sorry to interrupt your lunch, gentlemen," Alan began, "but ever since I heard of your interest, Dr. Lespierre, in ancient artifacts the other night at the captain's table, I was really intrigued to know how many pieces they have salvaged from *The Investigator*, and how many have not been recovered yet."

The geologists exchanged a surreptitious glance before Lespierre decided to respond. "Those are difficult questions to answer, Dr. Mayhew. And this is part of the reason for our participating in this journey." Alan nodded. "As far as the manifest states, the *Investigator* was, as you know, primarily a rescue vessel. It was assigned to locate the *Erebus* and *Terror* – Franklin's ships – but was also trying to find a Northern Passage from the Pacific to the Atlantic Oceans. However, the unrecorded – or I should say unofficial – story was that Captain McClure had other ideas as to the ship's ultimate destination."

By then, Alan was hanging on to Lespierre's every word. Not a fanatic of history per se, he was, nonetheless extremely interested in the lives and deeds (or misdeeds) of the explorers of the Great North. "Do we know what McClure's ultimate goal was?" he asked.

It was Sullivan's turn to reply. "According to some of his logs, we could only surmise that his final destination before returning to England was the nearest accessible port in the Hudson's Bay."

"What would he intend to do there?" Alan queried, all the more interested now.

"Well, that's difficult to say at this point, since his private log is not clear on the matter. But we – that is Dr. Lespierre and I – agree that it would have to do with the fur trade and the Hudson's Bay Company."

"But he was not a hunter was he? Or did he want to exchange seal or polar bear furs upon his arrival at port?"

"No, Dr. Mayhew, we do not think so," Lespierre replied, "quite to the contrary."

"How do you mean?"

Lespierre threw a glance at Sullivan before he answered. "Well, we're not sure of anything at this juncture, you understand, but we think that he intended to buy a large quantity of furs from either independent traders on shore or from the Hudson's Bay Company itself and bring the pelts back to England in order to sell them in London. He would have made a sizeable profit, if he had succeeded," the scientist concluded, visibly satisfied with his explanation.

Following a short silence, Alan asked, "But wasn't the Hudson's Bay Company a subsidiary of Harrods at that time?"

"Assuredly, Doctor; but, you see, carting furs from Canada back to England cost a great deal and since the *Investigator* was a ship already assigned on a reconnaissance and rescue voyage, paid by the British government, in essence, Queen Victoria herself would have paid the freight cost."

Alan slid back in his chair. "So, all McClure had to do was to buy the furs and haul them back to England free of shipping charges, is that it?"

"Exactly," Lespierre said, nodding vigorously. "And Harrods could sell the furs without having to fork out the shipping costs and pocket the profits made from the unknowing furriers."

"If such a scheme had been successful, Captain McClure would have not only completed the original Queen's mission but opened the door – or the waters as it were – to frequent trips for freighters of all sorts."

"Yet, to buy any number of furs from anyone would have cost a bundle even at that time," Alan commented.

"Oh yes, and that's why we are carefully analyzing the salvaged contents of the *Investigator*, Doctor. You see, if anyone, including Harrods, had assigned McClure with such a task, the person would have lined his pockets with gold coins."

"And the gold coins or coffer containing the money would not have been listed on the manifest, I gather?"

Both archeologists nodded in unison, like twins. "We have currently nine items of importance recorded on the manifest but if our conjectures are correct the tenth item should have been the captain's chest," Lespierre said, effectively giving Alan the answer he had been looking for since the previous night.

"May I ask what these nine objects are?" He looked at both scientists in turn.

"Well, compared to the captain's chest, they would appear to be of lesser importance, you understand," Dr. Sullivan said, "but if I remember correctly without consulting the ledger, there was a gold carafe and goblets, a jewelry chest – the dimensions of which are not precise – a series of instruments and a metal tube, which, we believe, contained maps of the Arctic and polar regions that the Canadian government had loaned to McClure before his departure from northern British Columbia."

"But didn't you say that you have seen some of these objects on display in the museum on Banks Island?" Alan asked, shifting his gaze from one to the other.

"Oh yes, but you see, the items that were on display were mostly typical maritime instruments – part of the list, yes – but essentially not what we were hoping to find."

"You mean the salvage operation of the *Investigator* has not been completed then?"

"Unfortunately not, Doctor. All the funds have now being diverted to finding *The Erebus* and *The Terror* – in which the exploratory mission itself will cost the current Canadian government more then they budgeted – so no more money will be spent on the *Investigator*, I'm afraid, especially in these politically charged economic times. When people are yelling about the government not spending enough on public education, you can imagine how they would scream if they knew that the politicians were designating money to finding gold bullion for a national museum."

"But you're here, aren't you?" Alan questioned encouragingly.

"Oh yes, we're here as you said, but only thanks to Parks Canada and the generous designated funding of an anonymous party."

"Anonymous party?" Alan's ears perked up.

Both Lespierre and Sullivan nodded. "Yes, being anonymous, we obviously don't know his or her name, of course," Lespierre replied, "but we suspect the person is a passenger aboard this ship – watching that everything goes according to plan, I suppose."

"And what would be the plan then?"

"Apart from cataloguing what is left aboard the *Investigator*, we couldn't say. And in order for us to do the cataloguing, we've been told that the two divers assigned to go down with the sub are also assigned to dive and examine the inside of the wreck."

"I see," Alan said musingly. There were many things to consider, he thought. Not only was there potentially a treasure chest aboard the *Investigator*, but there was also a patron who had probably forked out a fortune to recover the coins by paying for the salaries and passages of the two divers entrusted to find the coffer – if it ever even existed, in addition to the 'designated funding' to Parks Canada.

After sharing a light lunch with the two scientists, whom he quickly realized were more of a pair than just scientific colleagues, and talking mostly about the route *The Contessa* was to take through the Northern Passage, Alan needed to return to the medical center where work was sure to be waiting for him. However, he made a mental note to have a chat with the divers before long and to try finding who this "patron" was. Yet another item came to the forefront of his preoccupations – who had left the note on his pillow and what was the purpose behind leaving it there?

When he returned to his office, he found the medical center empty – Angie wasn't back yet. *Never mind*, Alan thought, *all the time she can take off now will make up for the extra hours she and Evelyn will have to put in later in the trip with all the physicals they were going to have to do.* Since no one was around, he decided to fetch one of the boxes he had brought on board before leaving France to see if any of the contents could be of use either in his cabin or in the office. He plopped it on his desk, opened it and rummaged through it for a few minutes before coming across a few items of interest. Firstly, there were several magnets collected in various ports to add to the wall in the medical center where an artistic collection of magnets was forming, as was customary on most ships on which Alan had served. Then he found his favorite mini-mouse with USB connection to connect to the office computer and his letter opener from North Africa – that looked more like a dagger, but very effectively opened letters. Alan mused that if he ever needed to, he could use it in self-defense, as it was very sharp. There was a nice silver framed picture of some Hindu goddess with very colorful surroundings and bangles he thought would look nice on the otherwise bland wall with the statutory list of regulations. Next, he came across a sheet of paper – the existence of which he had completely forgotten. He sat down and read it:

Church Ladies with Typewriters

These sentences actually appeared in church bulletins or were announced in church services:

1. Bertha Belch, a missionary from Africa, will be speaking tonight at Calvary Methodist. Come hear Bertha Belch all the way from Africa.
2. Announcement in a church bulletin for a national PRAYER & FASTING conference: "The cost for attending the Fasting & Prayer Conference includes meals."
3. The sermon this morning: "Jesus Walks on the Water." The sermon tonight: "Searching for Jesus."
4. Our youth basketball team is back in action Wednesday at 8 PM in the recreation hall. Come out and watch us kill Christ the King.
5. "Ladies, don't forget the rummage sale. It's a chance to get rid of those things not worth keeping around the house. Don't forget your husbands.
6. The peacemaking meeting scheduled for today has been canceled due to a conflict.
7. Remember in prayer the many who are sick of our community. Smile at someone who is hard to love. Say "Hell" to someone who doesn't care much about you.
8. Don't let worry kill you off - let the Church help.
9. Miss Charlene Mason sang "I will not pass this way again", giving obvious pleasure to the congregation.
10. For those of you who have children and don't know it, we have a nursery downstairs.
11. Next Thursday there will be tryouts for the choir. They need all the help they can get.
12. Barbara remains in the hospital and needs blood donors for more transfusions. She is also having trouble sleeping and requests tapes of Pastor Jack's sermons.
13. The Rector will preach his farewell message after which the choir will sing: "Break Forth Into Joy."
14. Irving Benson and Jessie Carter were married on October 24th in the church. So ends a friendship that began in their school days.
15. A bean supper will be held on Tuesday evening in the church hall. Music will follow.
16. At the evening service tonight, the sermon topic will be "What Is Hell?" Come early and listen to our choir practice.

17. Eight new choir robes are currently needed due to the addition of several new members and to the deterioration of some older ones.

18. Scouts are saving aluminum cans, bottles and other items to be recycled. Proceeds will be used to cripple children.

19. Please place your donation in the envelope along with the deceased person you want remembered.

20. Attend and you will hear an excellent speaker and heave a healthy lunch.

21. The church will host an evening of fine dining, superb entertainment and gracious hostility.

22. Potluck supper Sunday at 5:00 PM - prayer and medication to follow.

23. The ladies of the Church have cast off clothing of every kind. They may be seen in the basement on Friday afternoon.

24. This evening at 7 PM there will be a hymn sing in the park across from the Church. Bring a blanket and come prepared to sin.

25. Ladies Bible Study will be held Thursday morning at10AM. All ladies are invited to lunch in the Fellowship Hall after the B.S. is done.

26. The pastor would appreciate it if the ladies of the congregation would lend him their electric girdles for the pancake breakfast next Sunday.

27. Low Self Esteem Support Group will meet Thursday at 7PM. Please use the back door.

28. The eighth-graders will be presenting Shakespeare's Hamlet in the Church basement Friday at 7 PM. The congregation is invited to attend this tragedy.

29. Weight Watchers will meet at 7 PM at the First Presbyterian Church. Please use the large double doors at the side entrance.

30. The Associate Minister unveiled the church's new tithing campaign slogan last Sunday: "I Upped My Pledge - Up Yours!

When Angie returned to the medical center, ready to apologize for her lateness, she found her boss tearing in laughter.

"Have a read," he said, handing her the sheet of paper.

"What's that?" she asked, taking a seat across from Alan.

"Just read it..."

When she finished – even before reaching the last line – Angie was laughing so hard that she snorted, which provoked some more laughter out of both of them...until the door of the center opened and a man with a large laceration on his forehead stumbled in and fell to the floor before Alan even had time to get to him.

CHAPTER NINE

It escaped his mind

LITERALLY BOUNCING OFF their chairs, Angie and Alan rushed to the aid of the poor man – poor being a relative term since he was dressed in an expensive Italian suit now colored with a large red sash of blood, and looked as if he came out of a jewelry store with a diamond signet ring on his pinky, the latest Bulgari watch, a heavy gold tennis bracelet and neck chain, and a tie-pin that would have certainly emptied most people's bank account in a jiffy.

"Let's see what our friend is up to," were Alan's first words when he knelt down beside the fellow, and checked his pulse. "He's alive with a strong pulse and probably just fainted, but let's check his vitals," he added, looking up at Angie. She had brought him his stethoscope and blood pressure cuff without uttering a word.

Curious about the fact that she didn't seem overly concerned, Alan asked, "Do you know him?"

"I shouldn't say that I know him, but he's the reason I was late coming back from lunch," she replied, looking down at the injured man with visible annoyance.

"Why, what happened?"

"Nothing much except that the man has absolutely no manners what so ever. He was rude and obnoxious when I bumped into him coming out of the elevator."

"Is that it?" Alan queried, while deflating the cuff from the man's arm and noting that his BP was perfectly normal. "Anyway, let's wake him up before we address that wound of his, shall we?"

A second later the man opened his eyes and stared at Alan. "Who are you?" he blurted. "Where am I?"

"Very good questions, sir," Alan replied. "But answer me another; do you know what day this is?"

"How should I know," the middle-aged, bald fellow retorted abruptly and rudely, sitting up and then getting to his feet. "And I noted that you haven't answered my question – where am I?"

Without a word, Angie handed him a mirror while he brushed his trousers and adjusted his tie. "Good God! What happened? What did you do to me?" He looked terrified at his own reflection.

Alan decided it was high time to attend to his wound and asked the few questions that would confirm his early diagnosis. "Why don't you sit in that room"—he pointed to the first open door to his left—"and let me examine that laceration on your forehead?"

"Is this a hospital?" he asked, walking past Angie and going to sit on the chair beside the examining table.

Alan nodded to Angie – she knew he meant for her to gather what he would need to disinfect, suture and apply a dressing to the wound – and addressed the fellow, "Yes, this is the ship's medical center, sir. I am Doctor Mayhew. May I have your name?" Alan peered into the man's face.

A blank stare met his gaze. "To be honest with you, I can't recall, Doctor... I really don't know."

"That's okay; it will come back to you in a while." He paused while taking the providone iodine from Angie's hand and beginning to clean the wound. "Do you remember how you got that nasty cut on your head?"

Another blank stare. "I... I must have knocked against something... again I can't recall."

"Do you know if someone was chasing you when you came rushing in here?"

"I... I don't think so. I really couldn't tell you."

"Okay, this will sting a bit for just a moment," Alan said, instilling the lidocaine for local anesthesia, adeptly suturing the fairly deep wound and applying a dressing to the man's forehead. "Let's go to my office now and clear up what happened, shall we?"

With these words Alan showed the fellow back to his office and invited him to sit down across from him. "Angie, would you mind telling me how you met this man this afternoon?"

Reluctantly, Angie walked into the office and threw a critical glance at the new patient before she answered, "Well, I bumped into this gentleman coming out of the elevator on deck 6 about a half-an-hour ago..."

"Did you say anything that could help him remember...?"

Angie shook her head. "I'm sorry, Doc, but.... May I speak to you in private?"

Agreeing that it was probably best, Alan excused himself and followed his nurse to the storeroom where he closed the door behind the both of them.

"Well, what happened, Angie?" Alan asked, curious to know what the subject of the obvious altercation had been.

"I'm sorry, Doc, but this guy was so insulting that I let him have it verbally, of course. He said I was probably a f...king whore - and that I should watch where I was going or he would advise the captain of my rude behavior."

"I see," Alan said, crossing his arms over his chest and looking down at the floor beneath his feet. "Do you recall anything that would help identify him?"

"I'm not sure, but I'd say he probably came out of the restaurant on the fore-deck."

"Okay, that's at least a clue – and don't worry about what ever he said; the man is probably used to have people in uniform do his bidding at every turn." He smiled at her. "As soon as he comes out of his temporary amnesia, I'll have a word with him."

"Does he have a concussion?"

"Maybe, we'll do some testing to be sure. But he obviously bumped his head pretty hard against something quite sharp..." He turned and opened the door. "Let's call the maître d' of that restaurant and ask him to come in…, he might recognize him and be able to tell us who he is."

As soon as they glanced toward Alan's office they couldn't help noticing that the man had vanished.

Nonplussed and mostly annoyed, knowing full well that multiple forms and records yet had to be filled out for medical legal reasons, Alan rushed out the door of the center and looked around, hoping to find his lost patient – with the lost memory.

"Where do you suppose he went?" Angie asked, coming back into the center after she had had a look farther down the corridor for the ill-mannered fellow.

"I don't know, Angie," Alan replied, dialing the number of the restaurant.

Following a short but informative conversation with the maitre d', Alan shook his head.

"Well? What did he say?" Angie questioned, obviously curious to know if the maitre d' had been able to shed some light as to the identity of their elusive patient.

"He recognized the fellow almost instantly when I described 'the guy with the jewelry' and said that he had reserved a table for three people but that he had been left to dine alone and was quite angry that his guests had not shown up."

"Did he give you a name?"

"Yes. It's a Mr. Isaac Bornstein, and he has one of the larger condos on the upper deck."

"No wonder," Angie remarked. "Did you see that tie-pin? Must be worth a fortune."

"I'll have to have another chat with him…"

"And you think playing the loss of memory bit was just an act?"

"I would say so, Angie. The laceration was quite deep but just scalp – no bony involvement. What's more, I think he fainted not because he had a concussion, but because he simply was upset at seeing the blood. His blood pressure was perfectly fine."

"But then why did he rush in here the way he did?"

Alan snickered. "You know, Angie, these sorts of magnates, or despots I should say, abhor fainting in public. And he probably felt faint in the hallway and went in the first door he found. I bet he didn't mean to come in here specifically – we just happened to be the first door in his path."

"The devil he is, I tell you." Angie snapped, still exasperated. "If he ever crosses my path again, Mr. Bloody Bornstein, I'll have a couple of words with him, the nincompoop that he is."

Once Angie had returned to her duties and Alan had regained the solitude of his office, he decided to ask their chief of security if he – or his team – would please locate the fellow.

"Hello, Gerald, how are you on this beautiful day?" Alan asked airily.

"Well if it isn't my favorite doctor," Gerald replied amicably. "What can I do for you? Have you lost a patient by any chance?"

"Well as a matter of fact, yes, I did," Alan said – his laughter audible to the other end of the center.

Silence.

"I'm sorry, Doc, but I don't think that should be a laughing matter – even for you." Gerald's tone of voice was quite stern and admonishing.

"Well, you asked and I answered, didn't I?"

"Come on, Doc, what's this about? And don't tell me we've got a corpse on board this early in the cruise, otherwise I'll be likely to put in my resignation."

"No, nothing of the sort, Gerald, and please don't resign or retire until I do – I wouldn't know what to do with my corpses if you did."

"Okay, okay, stop it, will you, and tell me who you're looking for?"

"Mr. Isaac Bornstein."

"Oh yes? And what did our social network tycoon do this time?"

"You have heard of him then?"

"Who hasn't? He's one of the richest fellows on board this ship, Doc. He's treating everyone like his lackeys and has absolutely no consideration for his fellow man."

"I see." Alan paused. "Well, I'll tell you what happened and then maybe you could tell me where I could find him – I'll need to have a chat with him and fill in some paperwork following our treatment of his laceration."

"Okay, I'm all ears," Gerald replied.

Ten minutes later Gerald had been brought up to date as far as Mr. Bornstein's movements were concerned – the surveillance cameras aboard *The Contessa* had done their job – and located him in his suite; number 1007.

With a bunch of children sitting beside and around her, Babette closed her Bible, and said, "How about we have some lifesavers as a recompense for being so attentive during the Bible class?"

The shouts of joy overwhelmed her while she pulled out a roll of candy from her pocket. "I'll give each one of you one lifesaver and you tell me what they taste like, okay?"

"Oh, that's easy, Miss Babette," a small boy kneeling in the pew in front of her replied.

"I'm sure it is, but let's see…" She pulled the first candy out of the roll and handed it to a little girl beside her. "So, what does it taste like?"

"It's cherry-like," Annie replied, sucking on the lifesaver.

"And it's red, isn't it?"

Annie stuck her tongue out to everyone and said, "Sure is!"

"Okay, now let's try this one…" Babette offered the next candy to a little boy sitting on the other side of her.

He took it eagerly and planted it in his mouth. "It tastes like lemon," he said. "And it was a yellow one."

"Okay then – how about this one? It's green; would you tell me what it tastes like?" Babette asked another boy, handing him the lifesaver roll for him to pick out the candy. The little guy grimaced a bit and then declared, "It tastes like my mother's salad dressing! Yuk!"

Babette and the kids couldn't help laughing, watching the boy's face.

When they each had tasted and sucked on most of the colored candies, Babette offered the last one to another girl – a quiet little kid with beautiful auburn hair. She smiled when she pulled the *honey* lifesaver out of the roll. She then sucked on it for a while and shook her head. "I don't know, Miss Babette – I mean I know it's kind of brown, but I can't tell you what it tastes like."

"Well let me give you a clue; it's what your mother may sometimes call your father."

The little girl looked up in horror, spit her lifesaver out and yelled, "Oh my God, is that what an asshole tastes like?"

Amid the laughter, giggles and tittering, Babette tried to regain what ever was left of her composure. "Alright, children," she said, a little louder than she wanted to, "Just remember where we are, okay?"

When the hilarity died down, Babette accompanied the kids out of the chapel and took Elizabeth aside. "It must be awful for you to hear your mom speaking that way to your dad; does she do that often?"

"Just sometimes, I guess," Elizabeth replied shyly. "Usually not when I'm around, though."

"Anyway, I don't think your mom really meant those words... do you?"

Elizabeth shook her head. "It's usually only when Mom has had too many cocktails that she gets mad at Dad."

"Alright, and I'm sorry about that, but you know if one day you don't want to hear any of those things, you can just come in to my cabin"— Elizabeth smiled gratefully— "it's number 1006."

Nodding, the little girl left Babette at the door of the chapel and ran to join her friends in front of the elevator.

CHAPTER TEN

Haida Gwaii

THE CONTESSA WAS DUE to arrive in the archipelago of the Queen Charlotte Islands on the North Coast of British Columbia the following afternoon. Lowering anchor near the shores of Haida Gwaii – the Haida name for the two islands, Graham & Moresby – the passengers who would want to visit the north coast would be taking a small island ferry specifically designated to meet the cruise ships on their way to Alaska and beyond. Often referred to as the 'Galapagos of the North', Haida Gwaii is endowed with rare flora and fauna, in particular, the largest black bear known to exist, only on Graham Island, and to a sub species of black tailed deer.

Looking forward to taking the ferry and spending a few hours on the shore of the mysterious and mythical islands, Alan and Tiffany tried to plan their visit during dinner in the officers' mess. Although slightly better appointed than the crew mess (several framed pictures on the metal walls), and enjoying basically some of the same cuisine as the passengers dining in the restaurants of the upper decks, it was not luxurious and the presentation was not elegant. Food was unceremoniously plopped onto plain plates by the servers. Painted steel floors, plain portholes, stainless steel serving stations, plain Formica topped tables, utilitarian metal chairs with a modicum of padding on the seats, and plain tableware did distinguish it from the even plainer more basic crew mess. Alan was always trying to get the crew mess to upgrade its menu items to include salads, fresh fruits and vegetables, and to decrease the copious quantities of fried food. Of course the nationality in charge of the crew mess did have influence over the crew menu, and Alan and Tiffany did partake in some very good Indian curries when they were aboard a ship dominated by South Asian chefs. All of this of course, kept crew and officers separate from the passengers during mealtimes.

They were in the middle of eating a delightful dessert, when Alan's phone called him to instant reality. One of his friends, a passenger on the cruise was on the line.

"Yes, Herbert, what can I do for you? Is Karen alright?"

Karen and Herbert von Weglan were two Australians who were inveterate sailors whom Alan knew from his sailing days. Herbert and Alan even had an impromptu Rotary meeting at the equator one day off the coast of Ecuador when they were sailing together one year. Both Karen and Herbert were retired, he was an engineer and she had been a journalist for a big newspaper in Sydney, Australia. Karen was recovering from serious medical issues and Alan had made sure they had been able to rent a very pleasant cabin for this trip.

"She's fine, Alan. Thanks for asking. But I was just calling regarding the visit of Haida Gwaii tomorrow; do you think it will be too strenuous for Karen?"

"I shouldn't think so…"

"But you know her, Alan, she's adamant about going ashore…"

"Well then, I think you've got your answer; if she feels good and she is determined to go, and I see no medical reason not to, then you should be taking the trip and enjoy the walk through the forest."

"Will you be going too?" was Herbert's next question, his voice full of apprehension.

"At this point, Tiffany and I have no other plans"—Alan looked at Tiff's querying face—"so I don't see any problem in joining you both in the afternoon if you like?"

"Good show, mate! I'll feel better if you're able to come along… you understand?"

"Of course, no worries. And if something should come up between now and tomorrow afternoon, I'll be sure to let you know."

After a few parting words, Alan closed his phone and returned Tiffany's glance. "As you gather that was Herbert on the phone. Do you think we could accompany them on the visit of the island?" Alan knew that they had planned to be alone on the hike through the park, and he was afraid this change of plan would upset her a little. But she smiled.

"No, it'll be interesting to meet them again. They're such a nice couple. And I imagine Karen will not want to go too far inland…"

Alan nodded. "I have an idea that she's tired of being cooped up in their cabin with an over-protective Herbert looking after her."

They were about to leave the officers' mess when Gerald walked in and strode decisively toward Alan. The doc had always acknowledged Gerald's stature and presence. Initially trained as a "Seal", the man was forceful, and yet gentle. He had served in Iraq and later in Afghanistan, and upon his return to the States; the big man had chosen to enlist his services with the Company. He was not young, Alan knew, but his physique and impeccable behavior allowed him to pass for a much younger man in the eyes of anyone looking at him. His full head of blonde hair and the smooth skin of his face had probably a lot to do with his appearance of youth, too.

"Okay," he said, ignoring Tiffany for a moment, "I've got something on you know who, and I think you might be interested…" He looked to her, realizing his faux pas. "Sorry, Miss Sylvan; didn't mean to be rude…" He smiled as he took a seat beside Alan. "How are you?"

"Just fine, Gerald, and who were you referring to as "you know who" just now?"

"Sorry, Tiff," Alan said, "I didn't think of mentioning it, but I had a patient yesterday that left the center without giving me his name…"

"And you know who he is now? Should I be worried?" Tiffany asked, all tease and smiles.

"Nothing to worry about, Miss Sylvan," Gerald answered. "Mr. Bornstein is just money-loaded and bouncing his weight around everyone."

"And you said you've found something else about him?" Alan asked.

"Sure did, Doc. Apparently he's the one paying the bills for our two scientists and divers. Parks Canada paid their passage and any invoices with his money." He riveted his gaze on Alan. "Do you know anything about this?"

"Yes. When I talked to the two archeologists, they told me that someone had paid their bill anonymously."

"Well there you go. I'm going to run a background check on these two guys – there's something that's not quite right about them and their assignment."

"And what would that be, do you know?"

Gerald took a sheaf of paper out of his breast pocket and scanned through it. When he apparently found what he was looking for, he handed the sheet to Alan, pointing to the paragraph describing the divers' assignment. "See here"—he put a finger on the sentence in question—"it says that they're supposed to dive with the sub and a few chosen passengers and/or crew down to the wreck." Alan nodded while reading. "But then it does not say anything about them diving to the wreck without the sub – although the monies they're going to be paid include several solo dives as well."

Alan handed the paper back to Gerald saying, "When I spoke to Drs. Sullivan and Lespierre, they apparently were both aware of the divers' second assignment. But I don't think it's common knowledge."

"Okay then, I was right. They'll be doing something else than guiding the sub down to the wreck."

"Yes. But the person who would know a lot more about this is our Mr. Bornstein, since he's the one paying the bill."

"That's what I thought. Mind you, these guys can do whatever they want where ever they want – no skin off my back – but in this case, the insurance will not cover them if that second trip turns sour and they're killed in the process. Our company could be up for a hell of a lawsuit if anything happens to these guys."

"Okay," Alan said, "While you have a talk with Mr. Bornstein, I think I'll have a chat with the divers. Would that be okay with you?"

"Yeah, that would be fine with me. But if you feel uncomfortable talking to these two, I could send one of my guys to…"

Alan waved a hand in front of his face. "No need, Gerald, I don't think they would want to make themselves conspicuous at this stage by laying a hand on me. Besides, I'll need to have a chat with them about coming in for a complete physical before we reach Banks Island."

"Okay then, we'll do that," Gerald agreed. "You know, it might just be an omission in the description of their assignment…"

"Somehow, I don't think so," Alan countered.

"And what makes you say that?" Gerald asked, eyebrows raised questioningly.

"I think the error doesn't lie in the description of their assignment but in the payment for the second assignment together with the first."

"Now, you've lost me. Could you tell me what's going on?"

"Okay, here goes nothing," Alan replied. He then recounted his meeting with Sullivan and Lespierre and the reason he felt they were going for the solo dive.

"Well, I'll be the turkey at Christmas!" which remark sparked a quiet titter out of Tiffany's mouth. She had been listening to the exchange between the two men in silence; quite intrigued by the treasure hunt that seemed to be evolving before her eyes and ears.

"Okay then, now that I know we've got two guys going on an undisclosed and unauthorized dive, my approach to the meeting with Bornstein will be quite different, I can assure you."

"Hold on, Gerald," Alan said, grabbing the man by the arm, as he was about to get up from his seat. "I don't think it would be a good idea to tell the guy what we suspect. To my way of thinking, he would be liable to cancel the sub-dive altogether, which would hurt not only the Company but also Parks Canada. They've been instrumental in allowing us to take a look at the wreck, as you know, and foiling the show at this early stage would prevent our two scientists from completing the cataloguing of the ship's relics."

"Alright, I hear you, Alan. But I've got the insurance guys, HR, lawyers, etc. to think about. You know now with people coming on board looking for something to sue the company for, even before they get their first meal, we have to be careful. We passed the USPH very well, but there are so many other rules and regulations that we have to adhere to; our jobs have become more like administrators than security officers. Just the other day when we had that crew member who was stealing the real silver cutlery, I was not allowed to just throw him in the brig and then dump him off at the next port like I would have been able to just 10 years ago. No, I had to have that meeting with the HR manager, the staff captain, captain, general manager, you, and chief engineer along with the crew member's witness to 'discuss the situation' before we were 'allowed' to fire him and get rid of the thief. Times have changed, I tell you, Alan, times have changed. So how do we cover our backs should anything happen with these divers?"

"I'll tell you what; when I fill out the paperwork after the required divers' physical, I'll make sure to include some notation to the effect that they're fit to dive without the sub – should any passenger rescue be necessary, but that they need private insurance to cover any such activity. Would that cover us insurance wise?"

"Well, you know better about these things than I do, but I should say it would circumvent the problem, yes."

Hungry for her soft touch and caresses, as soon as they reached Alan's cabin, he took Tiffany in his arms and kissed her feverishly. They never seemed to tire of each other's presence. For more than three years now, their love and care had grown and flourished – much to Alan's amazement. He had never been a man to flounder in search of a woman; beautiful, intelligent women always found him. Not to say that Alan would look the other way at a nice figure crossing his path, though, it was more a matter of "look and don't touch" until Tiffany came along and she literally changed his life.

The night was still young when the two of them decided to take a stroll on deck before retiring – each to their own cabin. They were about to say goodnight when they heard Babette's unmistakable voice calling Alan in the distance.

As soon as she came within earshot, panting, she said, "I need... I mean... I need to tell you ... something, Alan..."

"All right, Babette," Alan said, taking their friend by the arm and leading her toward the nearest lounge. "Why don't you take a big breath"—they walked toward the couch—"sit down and tell me what's on your mind."

Babette nodded, sat down and looked at Tiffany. "I'm sorry, dear, but could you get me a glass of something fizzy, I'm not really in shape for jogging?"

Tiffany smiled knowingly and nodded. "No problem, I'll just be a minute," she replied, trotting away toward the nearest restaurant. Tiffany was trained to hear the plea behind the question. Babette wanted to be alone with Alan. *He'll tell me if she's okay*, she thought while walking briskly away from them.

Babette looked after her and smiled as she turned her head toward Alan's face. "What a jewel you've got there, Alan. Don't you dare lose her – under any circumstances – you hear me?"

Alan chuckled lightly. "I'm quite sure I'll keep her safe and away from any boogey man," he replied. "But I'm sure you haven't done that Olympic run just to tell me to keep myself in Tiffany's good books, have you?"

"No, indeed, Alan. It's much more serious than that. I mean... oh, I'm sorry I didn't mean... anyway, it's about Elizabeth Bornstein..." Alan's ears perked up. "She's in my 'bible-class for little ones' and this afternoon she made me aware, inadvertently mind you, of her mother's drinking habit and the subsequent foul language she uses to describe her husband – Elizabeth's father."

"It might be a problem for the child, I agree, Babette, but, as you know, we can't intervene."

"No-no," Babette cut in, patting Alan on the arm, "that's not the current problem. When I went back to my suite tonight, I heard a violent argument between two men and a woman emanating from my neighbors' suite. I'm not a snoop, Alan, as you know, but this was much too loud for me to ignore." Alan nodded. "So, I was about to phone reception and ask them to call on who ever lives in the next door cabin. Then I remembered when Elizabeth registered for bible-class she gave me her suite number... well, to make a long story short, Elizabeth is the daughter of that loud-mouth next door."

After a moment of pondering the problem, Alan bent down and placed his elbows on his knees. He turned his face to Babette. "I tell you what; if the man has anymore disturbing outbursts tonight – or any other night – you phone reception or directly to the Chief of Security, Gerald Tolberg. His name is on the officers' list in the packet you received when you boarded *The Contessa*. He'll straighten the guy out ASAP."

"That's good to know. Thanks, Alan," Babette said and before she could add anything else, she and Alan saw Tiffany coming back with that "fizzy" drink the playwright had asked for.

CHAPTER ELEVEN

Plants and medicine

LISTENING TO THE HAIDA shaman describe the medicinal virtues of the plants on the islands was nothing short of fascinating to Alan and to two of his friends in particular. Karen von Weglan and Susan Ashland were hanging on the man's every word.

"...Plants and the knowledge of them are a vital part of our culture, our language and our way of life. This knowledge is part of the plants themselves, and of the lands and waters in which they grow. The knowledge, the people, the culture, the language, the plants, animals, the land, bogs and lakes, and the ocean are all pieces of the whole of Haida Gwaii. All are intertwined and woven together.

"If the strands of this weaving are removed, the whole fabric is weakened. Plants, from the giant cedar and spruce of the rain forest, to some of the tiny flowering plants used in Haida medicines are integral parts of our existence on these islands. This is why we continue to be the watchers and guardians of Haida Gwaii. We are connected to the land and sea, and all of the living things here.

"Over 60 different plants are used as ingredients in medicines for the treatment of diseases, for maintaining good health and for acquiring spiritual power. The knowledge of how to use medicinal plants was given to one of our ancestors by a woman, Skil Jaadee, the Medicine Spirit, who lives on a high mountain on the west coast of the islands.

"Although some medicine recipes are known to many Haida people, most are the properties of particular families that have been passed down through the generations. Part of the reason for safeguarding the knowledge of medicines is the danger of poisoning that may occur if the plants are not used according to the exact prescription.

"Some examples of Haida medicine plants include the Licorice fern, Polypodium glycyrrhiza. The sweet-tasting rhizomes are valued as a medicine for colds and sore throats. Another commonly known plant is Fireweed, tl'ellaal (Epilobium angustifolium), used as a spring tonic and blood purifier. The young shoots are peeled and chewed."[2]

"Do you think that Fireweed medicine would be good for me?" Karen whispered in Alan's ear as they resumed walking through the forest and down a trail that would soon lead them back to the beach and pier.

---

[2] http://www.museevirtuel-
virtualmuseum.ca/edu/ViewLoitLo.do?method=preview&lang=EN&id=9794

"I don't think it would hurt, but as the shaman said, one needs to prepare these sorts of medicine with utmost care, otherwise they could be dangerous rather than curative."

Karen nodded, leaning on her cane to continue walking.

Susan, who had heard Alan's answer to Karen's question, came closer to him and asked, "Do you think they have some sort of lotion to soften the skin?"

Alan stopped and turned to both ladies. "I think you need to understand something about the people you are going to meet on this trip. As they will inform you, they will relate a great number of stories about their ancestry and their culture, yet whether it is a lotion or a tonic, the principle will be the same; they have been attuned to nature's gifts and power for hundreds of years and unless one understands and communes with their natural surroundings and accepts the gifts without ultimate expectation or skepticism, nothing could ever help redress a medical condition."

"Are you saying it's a state of mind as much as anything else?" Susan asked.

"Pretty much, yes. Your recovery and cure depend on lots of factors, but I would suggest the most important being your outlook on life and on your future."

Little Elizabeth Bornstein's mother was also along on the Haida Gwaii trip and encountered a frog. Susan was not sure how much she had had to drink, but she listened to her tell about it being a colorful frog and that it gave her three wishes. The frog told her that whatever she wished for she would get and Mr. Bornstein would get ten times more. So her first wish was: I want to be the most beautiful person. It was granted and she was told that Isaac will be ten times more beautiful. Her second wish was to be the wealthiest person on board *The Contessa*, which was also granted, and again, she was informed that her husband would be ten times wealthier than he already was. She hesitated a bit before telling what her third wish was. Then she came out with: "I want to have a very mild heart attack..."

As they continued walking down the path, Tiffany noticed how twisted the roots of certain plants or trees were. "Why do they look so tormented?" she asked the shaman.

He turned his head to her. He was a slender fellow but his carved muscles and bearing attested of a life spent in the outdoors. "*Tormented* is a good word, Miss Sylvan. As you probably know, Haida Gwaii is located at the edge of a tectonic plate which shifts from time to time and provokes earthquakes that could rate among the more serious ones on Earth."

"I didn't know that," Tiffany said, looking up at the man. "Do they happen often?"

"Yes, unfortunately. The latest one was in August 1949 and it was felt hundreds of miles from here. My mother told me the stories of my grandparents' house shaking and bursting at the seams. I am glad I didn't see it – I wasn't born yet – but these tormented roots are the results of their growth being interrupted during the quakes."

Little did the shaman know that, four months later, an earthquake measuring 7.5 on the Richter scale would hit Haida Gwaii again.

"As cold as ice, as sweet as sugar and everything nice," Tiffany was singing quietly on their way back to the ship.

"You sound very happy," Alan remarked as they climbed up the gangway.

"Yes, I am. That island and the walk through the forest with the shaman were so…"—she stopped briefly, turning her lovely face to him— "I don't know…. refreshing is not the word for it, but it was like taking a shower on a hot day. I don't know how to describe it, only to say it made me feel good all over."

Alan smiled. "Mother Nature must have touched you in ways that you didn't experience before, I guess."

"Yeah, it felt as if I was swaddled, lulled into a beautiful and peaceful state of mind."

Arriving at the guests' entrance of the ship, Susan walked up to them. "Would you two be able to join me for dinner tonight?"

"It's a yes for me," Tiffany replied, "but we've got Babette's play Grand Opening this evening, so if we could make it early, that would be better."

"Oh *mon Dieu*, really? I must have missed it on the entertainment schedule. And she didn't mention it when we had lunch." She looked at Tiffany. "And if that's the case, you're right, we should have dinner early – I wouldn't want to miss it." She waited for the doc to answer.

"Same here," he said, nodding. "I have quite a bit of work to catch up with before tonight, so if we could have an early dinner that would be great."

Susan's eyes went from Tiffany's face to Alan's in turn before she said, "Sorry, I keep on forgetting that you're both on duty. Anyway, yes, let's make it at about six o'clock at the fore-deck restaurant, if that's okay with you."

"Sure," Tiffany said, looking up at Alan to see if she got his approval. He nodded.

"See you then," Susan piped-up happily before turning around and leaving her two friends to look after her.

"Do you think we're going to be assailed again with breast-implant questions?" Tiffany asked.

"I'd say so," Alan replied as they walked to the elevator. "When I talked to her yesterday about her MRI results, she would have been ready to hop off the ship and register at the nearest hospital for aesthetic surgery at the earliest possible time."

"But that's crazy!" Tiffany exclaimed as the elevator doors opened and two young men came out.

"I'll see you later," Alan said, to Tiffany's surprise. "Go ahead; I'll take the next one," he added, while Tiffany was holding the doors open. Alan turned away to catch up with the two divers.

"Mr. Ashton, Mr. Barrington," Alan called after them. They stopped and turned to him. "Would you mind; I would like to have a word with you both."

"No problem, Doc," Sam Ashton replied, "We're on our way to the bar and if you'd like to join us, we could talk there." Edward Barrington nodded.

"Yes, that would be fine. I could use an orange juice," Alan said, falling in step with the two men.

When they reached the bar, Jimmy acknowledged Alan immediately. "Hello, Doc, how can I serve you this afternoon?" he asked as the two men sat on the stools facing him. "What about you, gentlemen; what will it be?"

"An orange juice for me," Alan said to Jimmy's nod.

"And make that two scotches on the rocks for us," Edward said.

"Were you able to go to the island?" Sam asked Alan.

The latter nodded. "What about you two?"

"Yeah," Edward said. "We didn't go inland to the forest though, we stayed mostly around the village. They've got a very interesting museum – did you visit it?"

Alan shook his head. "No, I opted for a walk through the forest with two patients of mine."

"Still on duty, even on shore, eh?" Sam asked, sliding the glass of scotch that Jimmy had just placed on the counter, toward him.

"Oh yeah. Most of us – the officers I mean – are on a 24-hour call and, especially on this cruise; I'm basically at my patients' disposal anytime."

"I guess since we're no patient of yours – not yet anyway – we are privileged then?" Edward remarked, sniggering.

"Not really," Alan said, taking a sip of his juice. "I wanted to talk to you two about your taking a complete physical before reaching Banks Island…"

"Ah," Sam cut-in, "I knew that would come up sooner or later. But I didn't expect it to be so soon."

"Yes," Edward nodded, "besides we went through a physical before leaving England already – insurance purposes, they told us."

Alan looked at both men in turn. "Yeah; I've got your files, but since I'll be overseeing your dives on both occasions…"

"Both occasions'?" Edward asked, apparently startled.

"Well yes, you see, our Chief of Security, Gerald Tolberg, has advised me that you're intending to dive with the sub to observe the outer shell of the *Investigator,* but that you also intend on taking a solo dive *into* the wreck – isn't that correct? Or was I misinformed?"

Sam and Edward exchanged a surreptitious glance. "Well yes, Doc, that's correct," Sam replied. "But I don't think either of us has informed Global Cruise of our intention… unless"—he focused his gaze on Edward's face—"you or our client mentioned something to them…?"

"Are you saying you have another client – I mean other than Parks Canada?" Alan asked feigning surprise.

"No, Doc, not really. Frankly, I don't know what's going on here, but all we know is that our client has funded our excursion to the wreck offshore Banks Island through Parks Canada, as you are aware, but he's also asked us to do a solo dive into the sub to help Drs. Sullivan and Lespierre with their cataloguing of the relics left on the ship."

"Okay then," Alan said, after emptying his glass, "but there is an omission in the description of your assignment in our paperwork. You see,

Parks Canada has received monies for this project and has asked Global Cruise to remit the amounts due to you both upon completion of the sub-dive. However, since Global Cruise wasn't aware of your intention of diving solo to the ship – without the sub – they don't know if you'll be covered by our insurance company."

Sam shook his head. "It's the same thing with our work in the North Sea." He swallowed a long swig of his scotch. "You see, we've got too many bosses – that's the long and short of it. The platforms or drilling rigs belong to one company, then you've got the oil & gas outfit operating the rig, and then we're working for a diving company that see us assigned all over the globe to dive for either or both of these companies." He looked at Edward, who nodded in agreement. "It's only one headache after another, especially when it comes to our insurance. And the premiums are sky-high in any case – whether we dive once, twice or as many times as required by the client."

After a moment of silence between the three men, Alan said, "But you now understand why I need to have you pass that darn physical before we get to Banks Island?" He threw a glance at each of the divers. "Besides, it won't be that bad, I've got two lovely nurses to put you both through the paces..."

Sam cracked up laughing, while Edward chuckled. "That's very nice, I'm sure they are nice, Doc, but you wouldn't happen to have a male nurse hanging about by any chance?"

Alan caught on instantly. "You mean you guys prefer men?" he asked, smiling.

"Yeah, you bet, Sam and I have been partners in many ways for years now. So, we'd prefer if you did the examination"—he shot an amused gaze at Sam—"and I promise we won't make any advances."

"Good," Alan said, laughing too, "because I don't think my girlfriend would appreciate it."

CHAPTER TWELVE

Act I

THE THEATER WAS GOING to be packed, judging by the number of people milling about the foyer before the bell would urge the guests to take their seats twenty minutes prior to the curtain rising on the first act. Babette's fame accompanied her everywhere. But tonight was to be a particular treat for the passengers of *The Contessa*. The play entitled, *Make Mine a Rumba*, was a sophisticated comedy, which Babette had partially written before she left Boston. For this play in particular, she wanted to work on the script in the comfortable confines of her home and only surrounded by familiar things, which was something her suite – even as well appointed and as convenient as it was – didn't offer.

"Don't you look smashing," Babette said as she approached Tiffany. "That dress is absolutely ravishing."

"Thank you, and so do you." That was true enough; the playwright was wearing an exquisite black dress, adorned with grey and black pearls around the neckline. It suited her and accentuated her figure in all the right places. "But you know," Tiffany went on, "we're supposed to be in uniform and I had to ask our staff captain if I could make an exception on this occasion – otherwise, it would have been my whites as usual."

"And where is the dear man?" Babette asked, her eyes traveling about the place, searching for Stephan Ivanov. "I should thank him personally for this "Grand Opening" – I really didn't expect any of this," she added in a whisper in Tiffany's ear.

"But you deserve it, Babette," Alan said, coming to join them. He looked around at the people attending this evening's play and was pleasantly surprised to see that it was a white-tie affair and all the ladies were dressed to the hilt. Although his eyes always came back to Tiffany – her red lamé gown suited her clear complexion and enhanced her coloring. "May I add that you two look absolutely wonderful?"

"*Tout flatteur vit au dépend de celui qui l'écoute,*" Babette said in French to Alan's ear.

"Meaning?" he asked.

"Meaning that flatteries will get you everywhere," Babette answered all smiles.

It wasn't long until the strident bell rang and all passengers filed into the theater. Always the observer, Alan noticed that the divers and archeologists were in attendance in pairs. He went to sit beside Stephan and smiled at him as he did so.

"She looks beautiful, doesn't she?" Stephan remarked, as soon as Alan was comfortably ensconced in his seat.

"Who's that?" Alan asked innocently.

Stephan laughed quietly before he replied, "Our entertainment director." He nodded in the direction of the stage where Tiffany was standing and preparing to announce the first act.

"And even lovelier tonight in her red lamé gown, thanks to you," Alan said pointedly. He knew about Stephan allowing Tiffany to wear the dress.

Stephan chuckled. "You know, you're the luckiest guy on this ship."

With a nod from the captain sitting in the front row, Tiffany began her introduction, and in a few minutes the curtain rose to the first act of . .

MAKE MINE A RUMBA

Written by

BABETTE

ACT I
SCENE I

As the curtain rises there is an empty stage. All is quiet and serene. Radio is playing softly. Dog is sleeping on rug. Suddenly there is a loud noise
Enters LEE

LEE: Alright! Now, who has it? Damn it, where is that kid?

ELIZABETH: (Enters from kitchen). What are you looking for?

LEE: I'm not looking for anything. Tell that "darling" son of yours to give me back my flashlight.

ELIZABETH: There you go accusing him again. How do you know he took it?

LEE: She says, "There you go accusing him again." That's right, defend your precious son. But you tell that kleptomaniac from me to give me back my flashlight.

ELIZABETH: Bill, you stop calling him names. You fool (in a whisper and looking off D. Left) I beg you not to call him those names.

LEE: Why shouldn't I call him a thief (to door left)? That's what he is. He is a thief. I paid $3.50 for that flashlight and I want it back.

ELIZABETH: (Not very angry) Then why don't you ask him for it like one human being to another.

LEE: Alright. I'll show you... (Shouting at door left) Give me back my flashlight, you brat.

ELIZABETH: Stop it. You idiot (whispering) can't you realize what you are doing to him?

LEE: Now. See I asked him nicely and there's no flashlight. Do you see a flashlight – is there a flashlight – here or here? (Now he pounds on the door). I'll give you five minutes to bring that light out, or I'm coming in there and get it. (Pounds the door – then hops around, shaking his hand in pain.)

ELIZABETH: (Furious now) You will not! (She puts herself in front of him at the door.) I won't let you. You . . . you sadist.

LEE: Now, see what your little darling did – that damn kid – oh my hand. (Dog barks.)

ELIZABETH: How could he have done anything to you? He wasn't even in the room. (Dog barks again.)

LEE: You didn't see that door open and close. (Starts for stairs to bedroom.) That's the trouble with you, you're blind. (Off to bedroom.)

ELIZABETH   Liar, Liar, Liar, Liar – Better stick your hand in some cold water. Wait a minute . . . I'll get you some ice. (Goes to door right.)

LEE: Leave me alone. Just wait until I get my hands on that brat.

ELIZABETH: (Back into room.) Is this what you are looking for?

LEE: (Entering) See, what did I tell you? Your little angel is growing up to be a regular kleptomaniac.

ELIZABETH: Now you listen to me, Lee Clarkson – no one took your flashlight – you just didn't put it away. If you put things where they belong, you wouldn't have to go around accusing people.

LEE: You just won't see it will you? (Music is lower) He sneaked around back there and put it in – where ever you found it.

(Mrs. Flater) (A woman walks around the patio, neighbors.)

ELIZABETH: For your information, he would have had to walk through the living room to put it in the kitchen. Remember – you wanted a house arranged like that, so there wouldn't be any raids on the fridge. You cheap skate you would rather hurt your own son for a lousy $3.50 flashlight.

LEE: It's not the money it's the principle.

ELIZABETH: You're the last person who should talk of principle.

LEE: Why do you have to get so nasty all the time? Oh boy... (Music up – dog barks – doorbell rings and again rings)

LEE: Probably the police for your son – madam (bowing low over to door).

ELIZABETH: That does it! You can sleep by yourself tonight (exits bedroom, right).

ENTERS Mrs. Flater (a woman in her 50's, bleached hair, the highest heels, young, expensive clothes (Loud, common with a vulgar laugh.)

MRS. FLATER: I . . . (presents card) I'm Mrs. Flater – of the Flater Real Estate.

LEE: (Reads) See you at 9 – Put a...

MRS. FLATER: (Takes back card and laughs). Wrong card – (gives him another card) Be my guest (nudges him, walks by him – Lee clears his throat) Nice place you have, Mr....?

LEE: Are you soliciting?

MRS. FLATER: Not right at this moment, but I'll be back.

ELIZABETH: If she is soliciting, tell her we don't want any.

LEE: I already did – I mean – no, that isn't what I meant. (To Mrs. Flater) Won't you come in? Will you come here a minute. (Elizabeth re-enters.)

MRS. FLATER: You must be Mrs . . . uh . . . what's your name? My card (starts to give it takes it back) No, on second thought, I'd better not. I'm Mrs. Flater of the Flater Real Estate (over to Lee) "The first with the finish".

ELIZABETH: I'm sorry, Mrs . . . ? What's your name? But this house is not for sale.

MRS. FLATER: Maybe not now, but could be very soon you never can tell; but that isn't what I came about. As you know the Gibbon house next door is for sale now. We have the exclusive and as the seller is very anxious to dispose of his property, I am only too happy to oblige and I wondered if you would do me a favor? Just a little one – you want nice neighbors and I want a sale. Nothing personal, mind you. You keep it quiet on your side – kids, dogs, fights and all that.

ELIZABETH: Thank you for your interest, Mrs. uh-uh, we hope you make your sale. Now, if you will excuse us. (Stands.)

MRS. FLATER: Well, if that's your attitude I can tell you a few things . . .

ELIZABETH: I bet you can, good day, madam.

MRS. FLATER: Look here, I was just trying to be polite but if you want to fight with your husband that's your funeral. (Moves towards door) One more thing – do you own that dirty truck out front?

ELIZABETH: Certainly not, we don't own a truck.

MRS. FLATER: Sorry, it looked like it belonged to you (exits).

ELIZABETH: Now see what you did, humiliated me before the whole neighborhood.

LEE: I didn't say a word.

ELIZABETH: Not much you didn't. I don't suppose you opened your big mouth or said a single solitary word. She heard everything and now the whole town will know we had a fight.

LEE: You're the one who always shouts and you practically called her a madam and kicked her out of the door. Why do you always blame me? (Phone rings.)

ELIZABETH: You answer it, it's probably you know who ('you know who' in disgust).

LEE: Hello, Mother (pause) (Elizabeth nods as if to say "I thought so") Oh we were just thinking about you. No, really she didn't say anything about you, no; I'm not lying to you. Everything is all right. No, don't come over now . . . I, um I mean we might have to take the children somewhere. Sure I want to see you, when can you make it? Wait, I'll let you talk to her.

ELIZABETH: (shakes her head and whispers) No, no, no.

LEE: Hello, Mother, she can't come to the phone right now, she wants to talk to you but she's taking a shower. No, Mother, she didn't just get up. I didn't make breakfast. No one is abusing me (pause). Now . . . I'm sure six o'clock will be fine. We'd love to see you – all of us, of course. Goodbye, Mother. I wonder why she called just now, woman's instinct I guess.

ELIZABETH: Woman's instinct, my eye, the Flater mouse had her little antenna buzzing and your mother got her hooks in.

LEE: She was just concerned.

ELIZABETH: Did she just get up, what a funny hour for a shower. No one's abusing me now – why does she always tell you that you're abused?

LEE: Well, aren't I?

ELIZABETH: Aren't you what? And, by the way, what was that six o'clock bit all about?

LEE: She is dropping over to see the children. I said you wouldn't mind.

(The McTeeges and the Real Estate women enter the other yard – and a rock hits the fence)

LEE: I told those damn fool kids of yours not to throw rocks.

(Lee and Elizabeth rush outdoors to the patio but stay out of sight from Mrs. Flater and the McTeeges.)

MRS. FLATER: That's Mr. Clarkson – a real television fan. They love westerns. Mrs. Clarkson is very emotional.

ELIZABETH: Emotional, am I?

LEE: Shhh . . .

MRS. MCTEEGE: Sounded more like a fight to me (over toward fence).

MR. MCTEEGE: (Mumbles) You ought to know...!

MRS. MCTEEGE: What was that?

MR. MCTEEGE: Yes, I said you ought to know more about the schools and such.

MRS. MCTEEGE: That's right, the kind of neighborhood we live in means a great deal. What about them (pointing to the Clarksons)?

MRS. FLATER: You'll like him; tall with wavy black hair (laughs) the kind you'd like to get your hands onto. He's a cellist with the symphony.

MRS. MCTEEGE: I don't like classical music.

MRS. FLATER: Now, Mrs. Clarkson, they say she comes from a good family (under her breath near the fence) You'd never know it though.

MRS. MCTEEGE: I take it their not the country club set.

MRS. FLATER: Now, on that side there is a couple you'd really like – Mr. and Mrs. MacHay. He's in wholesale plumbing and he can get you real bargains. I know she dresses very well. They have M O N E Y.

MRS. MCTEEGE: I'd like to meet her.

MRS. FLATER: And over there are the Hank Bergers. You've heard of them of course – they have two Cadillac's and you should see the house, my dear, their interior decorator told me that the sky was the limit.

MRS. MCTEEGE: My husband will soon be a vice president. He's in charge of radio and appliance sales. The contacts one makes are very important.

MRS. FLATER: I can see you're a wife who has her husband's future at heart. You'll find this a charming neighborhood (leads them into the house).

ELIZABETH: Charming indeed. What she forgot to tell them about the MacHays is that he beats his wife and she's afraid of him. Oh they have money, but no background and the Burgers are loaded especially the Mrs. This is her fourth husband, but she still keeps her boyfriend on the side. I wonder why she didn't tell him about Dr. Heerum; how he sent his first wife to the insane asylum, and plays patty cake with his patients and third wife. She shouldn't forget her. This is her third try at matrimony, and each time it was a married man.

LEE: I thought you liked your neighbors.

ELIZABETH: I do, most of them. I get along with all of them but they're not all my friends. Still it burns me up that she tells them about the few irregulars we have and forgets to mention such regulars as the Jones or why didn't she tell them about Dr. Craig, or Dr. Geracci – they're the real people.

LEE: It takes all kinds . . .

(Enter Flater and McTeeges)

MRS. FLATER: (Talking to McTeege) I'm so glad you have decided to take this house I could have shown you others, but I always like a satisfied customer. Now about the financing – what would you like to put down?

MRS. MCTEEGE: As little as possible. The monthly can be high. We've got a good expense account, but not much cash. (Ad-lib and fading as Mr. T. and Flater talk).

ELIZABETH: We shouldn't be listening....

LEE: Yes, it's none of our business (starts to go in – Elizabeth is in first. Lee picks up the flash light by the fence.)

MRS. MCTEEGE: (Strolls over to fence, as others talk) Hello, I'm Lucrica McTeege – but you can call me Lucy, everybody else does.

LEE: I'm Lee, Lee Clarkson, won't you come in, there's a gate right over there. My wife and the former tenants were good friends. Let me help you. (Gate sticks.)

MRS. MCTEEGE: You have strong hands.

LEE: (a bit embarrassed). It's been some time. (Gate opens.)

MRS. MCTEEGE: (Looking at patio and on into house.) What a quaint place you have.

LEE: My wife likes antiques, family hand me downs and all that – like to see it. (Enter Elizabeth.)

ELIZABETH: Welcome to our block.

MR. MCTEEGE: Looks like I've lost a wife and found a neighbor. May I come in?

MRS. FLATER: Isn't this cozy? I see you know each other already. Well I know when I'm outnumbered. (Exits saying,) It'll just lock up; don't worry about me I can take care of myself. (Laughs.)

MRS. MCTEEGE: Tell me what do you do all day?

ELIZABETH: Chief cook and bottle washer, butler, nurse, P.T.A. Board Member, church worker.

MRS. MCTEEGE: Take it easy, kid. What do you do for kicks, watch television?

ELIZABETH: Yes, that too!

MRS. MCTEEGE: Bridge?

ELIZABETH: I haven't time and anyway I don't like it.

MRS. MCTEEGE: What do you like?

ELIZABETH: Being a wife and mother – no housework though. I'd like a maid, I really would, I'm crazy about the theater and traveling and being with friends – auditing courses at college and helping people. What do you like to do?

MRS. MCTEEGE: First, give me an old fashioned, handsome man, some music, the right kind, and I'll know what to do.

ELIZABETH: Do you have any children?

MRS. MCTEEGE: One son, John Jr. We call him Jack but he doesn't like it, he is a teenager you know – 15 his last birthday. We all have our problems. I hate leaving him alone all the time, but it's good for him I guess, he's got to grow up some time and with John being on the road so much, I just have to have recreation. You know what I mean.

ELIZABETH: Our oldest son is 15 too, we must get the boys together (phone rings). Excuse me (as she goes to phone) I'm expecting the children to call me.

(The men, who have made a tour of garden and patio return.)

MRS. MCTEEGE: How's your golf?

LEE: I don't play.

ELIZABETH: Phone for you...

LEE: Who is it?

ELIZABETH: I don't know, he or she. Didn't give its name.
(Doorbell rings) (Elizabeth keeps on talking as she goes to door) Oh there you are. I thought you were going to call me. Okay. Be back at six. Grandmother Clarkson is coming. Liza, you be sure and dry your hair.

J. MCTEEGE: (While she's talking, J. McTeege to wife) What do you think?

MRS. MCTEEGE: Of her, (shrugs her shoulders) they won't do us much good; of course Jack could get his meals here and not dirty up our rugs. What about him? Any symphony connections?

J. MCTEEGE: You heard him; the man doesn't even play golf.

(Lee returns from phone) (Elizabeth goes to kitchen brings out tea table with ice tea, plates of sandwiches and cookies – napkins, silver dishes, lace tablecloth on tea cart – everything is proper).

LEE: (who has returned from phone, talks as he walks, goes over to record player to turn it up a bit) Do you like Brahms, Beethoven...?

J. MCTEEGE: Sorry, I don't know them, what's their line?

LEE: What music do you like?

J. MCTEEGE: I haven't given it much thought, but I have a wonderful collection of records and books; a whole library, science, music, art, literature; you name it, I have it.

MRS. MCTEEGE: And he's never read any. Isn't that wonderful? (Laughs and so does Mr. T. Lee smiles.)

(Elizabeth re-enters)

ELIZABETH: Well, who was it? A man or a woman? (Gives tea to Mrs. T.)

LEE: Neither – a musician.

ELIZABETH: Tea? (This to Mr. T.)

J. MCTEEGE: (Looks at his wife and says, "Queer". The McTeeges both laugh
and so does Lee. Elizabeth passes sweets, napkins, etc.)

MRS. MCTEEGE: Tell them that one about the two pansy fiddle players.

J. MCTEEGE: (Clears his throat.)

LEE: Go ahead, we're broadminded.

ELIZABETH: Anyway, Lee isn't a fiddle player.

MRS. MCTEEGE: Speaking of queers, I heard that the majority of American
males wish they were women.

J. MCTEEGE: Did you pick up that bit of information at a bar?

MRS. MCTEEGE: It doesn't matter where I picked it up. It's a statistic. It goes
on to say when men with overbearing mothers complaining or ill-tempered
wives, plus the stress of business, kids, homes, ulcers and all that – the idea of
being a homosexual or even having an operation appeals to some men.

J. MCTEEGE: What is sex anyway; just one endocrine calling to another.

ELIZABETH: Why would a man want to be a woman, or a woman a man?

LEE: Oh, I don't know, it might have its moments.

MRS. MCTEEGE: There's a perfectly wonderful doctor right here in this very
town and I understand from very reliable sources that he is giving some sort
of male hormones to women and female hormones to men. (Pause) What do
you say to that? (This directed to Elizabeth).

ELIZABETH: Endocrinologists and even gynecologists have been prescribing
that for years (passing cookies to Mr. McTeege). How about another cookie?

MR. MCTEEGE: No thanks, I'll pass this one up; I've had my vitamin E for the day. (Laughs.)

MRS. MCTEEGE: To get back to this doctor, he's doing marvelous things, simply marvelous, did you read that article in the Tribune where a man of 80 fathered a child?

MR. MCTEEGE: Don't you believe it, there's another rooster (door bell rings) in that woodpile.

(Enters BOBBY SALVA)

LEE: I thought I told you not to come to my house, I'm busy – I'll call you later.

BOBBY: (disregards what he says and breezes in.) Sorry, darling, I just had to tell you.... Oh, you have company (over to Elizabeth). You must be Mrs. Clarkson – I've heard about you.

LEE: Mrs. McTeege, may I present Bobby Salva.

BOBBY: Hi, you're the Mister, of course, (Mr. Mc T. stands up.) My, aren't you big. I like big men.

MR. MCTEEGE: We only meant to stay a minute. Thanks for the tea, you're a good cook – wish my wife could bake like that.

MRS. MCTEEGE: (Hands Elizabeth a card)

ELIZABETH: What's that for?

MRS. MCTEEGE: That's the doctor I was telling you about (looking at Lee) You need it more than I.

CURTAIN

Amid the laughter, the giggles and titters, and after arousing applause from the audience, Alan, Stephan and Tiffany followed the throng of passengers out of the theater for the intermission. The tables, brought into the foyer especially for the occasion, were covered with *amuse-gueules*, cheese, small fruits and, of course, the traditional champagne, wines and liqueurs of all sorts.

"Ms. Sylvan," Captain Middleton said, walking up to her, "you have outdone yourself, really a very entertaining play. The best of choices, I'm sure."

"Thank you, Captain," Tiffany replied demurely, "but all the praise should go to our wonderful playwright…"

"Too true, Ms. Sylvan, yet the choices of entertainment are yours, and you have my most sincere admiration for a job well done."

"Here, here," Stephan rejoined, lifting his glass of champagne in a toasting gesture, "three cheers for our Entertainment Director."

"And you, Doctor," the captain went on, "I heard you've caught on to a little scheme aboard our *Contessa*, haven't you?"

Pointed comments they were, and Alan wondered if Gerald had talked to the captain already. "Just a matter of insurance," Alan replied, making light of the treasure hunt that seemed to emerge out of the irregularities Gerald and he had found on the insurance papers.

"Yes, of course," the captain said somewhat dismissively. "But let's have a chat about this matter with our Mr. Bornstein, shall we?"

"Yes, by all means, Captain – whenever your schedule allows."

In a few minutes, the bell sounded again, interrupting the chatter and seeing the passengers re-entering the theater to return to their respective seats. This time, Tiffany came to sit beside the captain, as it was customary, smiling gently at him as she sat down.

"You know, I'm like a child waiting for the next episode of my favorite show," he remarked in Tiffany's ear. "Ms. Babette is excellent, indeed."

"Yes, she is, sir," Tiffany replied quietly as the lights dimmed and the curtain rose on: MAKE MINE A RUMBA, Act I, Scene II.

CHAPTER THIRTEEN

Make Mine a Rumba

ACT I
SCENE II

Symphony music is playing softly in the background. Elizabeth is reading a story off stage to the children.

LEE: (Enters from kitchen across the stage, he has one of Elizabeth's aprons on, flour is all over him and he has a mixing spoon in his hand.) Where's the baking powder?

ELIZABETH: (off stage) In the third cabinet on the second shelf.

LEE: (Turns up the symphony and repeats,) In the third cabinet on the second shelf (exit kitchen, right back on stage. Shouting from kitchen door) It isn't there – you better ask those brats what they did with it.

ELIZABETH: Shh! Liza's asleep and the boys are too. Darling, would you mind turning down the volume.

LEE: Damn it! (Center stage) I did turn it down. (Shouting) Don't you want me to hear it?

ELIZABETH: You can't hear it if you're shouting. Wait a minute... I'll get it for you.

(Elizabeth enters kitchen.)

LEE I'm not shouting – see it wasn't there. You'd better ask those kids, they're not asleep.

ELIZABETH: (Opening cupboard) Here it is in...

LEE: Where did you find it? Never mind – it will end up being my fault. You women have a way of twisting things. (He's opening the can of baking powder – the content spills all over the floor)

ELIZABETH: Look out, you're spilling it.

LEE: I suppose it's my fault someone didn't put the cover on properly.

ELIZABETH: I'll clean it up.

LEE: Never mind; I'm capable of doing it myself.

ELIZABETH: There are cookies in the jar and nut bread in the fridge. Why must you bake a cake?

LEE: Because, I want to. Is there any real crime in my baking a cake? I can't listen to the symphony because it might disturb your little darlings and now I can't even bake a cake in my own house (slams the door – exits – reenters immediately.)

ELIZABETH: (Picks up card) (Opens her mouth to say something.)

LEE: No, I'm not a homosexual, and I needn't visit your doctor. Oh, Oh (doubles up in pain).

ELIZABETH: What's the matter, darling?

LEE: Just leave me alone . . .

ELIZABETH: Lie down on the couch and I'll call the doctor.

LEE: I don't need a doctor – (groans).

ELIZABETH: (Throws a knit comforter over him) Where does it hurt?

LEE: (Points to stomach.)

ELIZABETH: (Starts to open his belt.)

LEE: Leave my pants alone.

ELIZABETH: (Looks at him funny) I'll call the doctor. (She brings the phone by extension to the couch.)

LEE: (groans and mutters) I don't need a doctor.

ELIZABETH: Hello, this is Mrs. Clarkson. May I speak to the doctor? Hang on darling, they're calling him, Oh no. Isn't there anyone else?

LEE: Tell him to hurry; this is bad (he curled up into a ball).

ELIZABETH: Tell him to hurry, (Pause) Mrs. Clarkson, 17 Pine Drive. (Hangs up.) The answering service said she'd have the doctor here right away; he's making a call in the neighborhood. (Door Bell rings) He is a fast one (goes to door) (Enters Bobby Salva, pushing his way in, hears the groans, runs to couch – followed by Elizabeth.)

BOBBY: Oh, you poor darling, you look awful. What have we here? (Sees belt is open, takes his belt off) Now isn't that better, (takes pillow from head puts it at his knees,) now isn't that comfy, (starts to rub his temples).

ELIZABETH: It's in his stomach (Door bell rings). Thank you for coming so soon, Doctor.

DR. ASSPAN: I was at a party up the street. Don't you worry we'll get to the bottom of this, where's the patient?

ELIZABETH: Right in here, Doctor, he's having terrible pains in his stomach.

LEE: (Eyes closed, head in Bobby's lap) Thanks for coming, Boyd.

ELIZABETH: It isn't Boyd, darling, he's out of town, but Dr. Asspan was available.

LEE: (Opens his eyes) You – (he stares at Elizabeth then at Dr. Asspan – pauses).

BOBBY: It's terrific, positively terrific, darlings. This is my doctor too – (gets up) and I just love him (bends over and hugs him – the doctor moves away, obviously not interested in Bobby's gesture of affection).

DR. ASSPAN: (feels his stomach and brushes his beard with hand.)

BOBBY: Isn't he wonderful, he always warms it first (Elizabeth turns towards Lee) it tickles you know.

DR. ASSPAN: (Disregards this, leans his head down, thinks better of it and uses the stethoscope. Opens his medical bag, takes out a bottle, prepares and gives him a shot. Writes out a prescription.) There, that will take effect in a little while, you'll be alright.

ELIZABETH: What seems to be the trouble with him?

DR. ASSPAN: Either an ulcer or the flu, we'll have to run some tests first, but I'll get in touch with Boyd and tell him (starts towards the door). Now don't worry, Mrs. Clarkson.

BOBBY: Darling, I'll look in on you tomorrow. I want to see if I can get a ride with Dr. Asspan (Runs). Wait for me, calling out . . .

ELIZABETH: I'm sorry, darling, I wish I could have it instead of you. Hurt very much?

LEE: Do you think it could be an ulcer? The first violinist had an operation . .

ELIZABETH: Remember you're not a fiddle player.

LEE: I think I'll snooze for awhile.

ELIZABETH: Okay, I'll sit here.

LEE: First, turn on the symphony.

ELIZABETH: (Turns on the symphony – light fades to denote time – voice overbearing, complaining, mother's ill temper, stress, and kids.) An ulcer, ill tempered wives; am I ill tempered? I don't mean to be – and now ulcers - oh God, not a homosexual. (Cries softly.)

LEE: (Opens his eyes) Honey, it's not as bad as that. I'm going to live – come on over here (pats sofa).

ELIZABETH: Do you feel better?

LEE: Much – (pets her hair) what soft hair you have; just like silk – (starts to play with her.)

(Lee and Elizabeth in a tight embrace, kissing, caressing each other until they hear one of the children calling)

CHILD: (off stage) Mommie?

ELIZABETH: I'm coming.

LEE: Oh, damn it. (Gets up and goes to turn up symphony.)

ELIZABETH: (Reenters) It's okay now, Lee, would you turn off the music?

LEE: Sure, if you'll rumba with me – (points to bedroom) in there (goes to turn off music).

ELIZABETH: (Smiles)

(Lee goes over to her – walks with arms around her – like position of a dance towards bedroom – music up, lights fade – blackout for a second.)

ELIZABETH: (Runs on stage – she is wearing a nightie, her hair is tousled. Picks up a card and says) "Homosexual indeed" (lets the dog in – goes back to bedroom.)

CURTAIN STARTS DOWN

LEE: (Enters in pajamas and goes toward phone.)

ELIZABETH: Lee, where are you, Darling?

LEE: I'll be there in a minute. (On phone) Hello, Bobby . . .

FAST CURTAIN

END OF FIRST ACT

Amid thunderous applause and a standing ovation, Babette took a gracious bow on stage. "Dear friends, thank you so much for your appreciation. Playwrights couldn't ask for a more appreciative audience, and you are the best. Thank you," she added, throwing a kiss to the still standing spectators.

Grabbing the cordless microphone from Babette's hand and smiling gently, Tiffany concluded by saying, "The second act of this wonderful play will be performed in a few days – while we'll be on our way to Banks Island and the frozen waters of the Arctic. Thank you once again for your warm welcome to our talented playwright, Ms. Babette...." Saying this, Tiffany put her arm around Babette's shoulders and both ladies bowed to the passengers and officers.

Striding toward the aft elevators, Alan shook his head and wondered why Mr. and Mrs. Bornstein had been absent – from what Alan had been told, it wasn't something that the tycoon would miss. Pondering the question, when he came out of the elevator, he bumped into Gerald.

"Oh, hi, Doc. I knew you would be at the theater so I didn't want to disturb you, but do you have a minute now?"

"Sure. Why don't we go to the medical center – we can talk there. Evelyn should be on duty tonight..."

"Does she know about this?" Gerald asked suspiciously.

"No, I don't think anyone knows about our treasure hunting patron"—he paused for a second—"except that our captain seems to have been briefed. Did you talk to him?"

"Yes. I had to let him know what was going on – my responsibility, you know."

"Well, he's anxious to have a conversation with me in the near future. Did you talk to Bornstein yet?"

"No, not yet. I wanted to leave it until the morning when we were at sea again."

Alan nodded.

As soon as they reached the center, both men nodded courteously to Evelyn who was dealing with an octogenarian passenger who wanted her to give him a double dose of Viagra. She had informed him that firstly, only the doctor could give that medication and secondly that it was not safe to use a double dose and if needed the doctor could give a daily dose of Cialis that was very effective. He explained that his reason for needing the double dose was that his 27-year-old girlfriend on board was 'very demanding' and that at the next overnight port, his wife was going to meet him to bring one of his suitcases he had forgotten. Evelyn asked if his wife was joining him to which he said, "Oh no, she gets seasick and never cruises with me." She assured him that, "The Doctor will see you after he is finished with the security officer, please have a seat here in the waiting room."

Alan led the Chief to his office past the passenger with a friendly nod and closed the door.

"Okay, what's up?" he asked, taking a seat at his desk.

"Well, it seems that our Mr. Bornstein is doing more than throwing his weight about the place; I received a call from our playwright last night..."

"Ah yes, she mentioned something about Bornstein having a loud argument with someone..."

"Exactly. It seems the guy is a bully and he's got a drunken wife and a poor little kid hearing rude remarks from her mother."

"But we can't do anything about that state of affair, or can we?"

"No, Doc, in principle we can't, but if this guy's behavior begins to disturb the passengers or turns abusive, I've got to put a stop to it – otherwise, we might have an exodus on our hands, if you know what I mean. Most of the passengers own their condo cabin suites; the value of their suite goes down if there is a loudmouth next door."

CHAPTER FOURTEEN

"Bombs away"

"THERE WERE STRANGE NOISES coming from suite 402," Samuel said to his supervisor.

"What sort of noises?" the latter asked, clipboard in hand and paying very little attention to Samuel's remark.

"Well, it was like loud snoring, then I heard the water running and then it was like two people were having a loud conversation..."

"Did you say 'two people' in 402?"

Nodding vigorously, the room steward went on, "then when I went in to clean the bathroom, there was toilet paper all over the place . . . you know, Jack, I've seen this before, but I tell you this was strange."

"Humph . . . well all I could tell you is to keep an eye on that cabin, because it says here"—he flipped a couple of sheets over the clipboard—"there should only be one person in there."

"But there's never anyone in the cabin when I go to clean in the morning – it's like the woman is never there."

Jack shrugged the mention of strange noises and Samuel's disquiet away and they both returned to their maintenance duties. However, later that day, the fire alarm from cabin 402 alerted the chief of security and elicited an emergency action on his part. Although engrossed in whatever task had retained his attention on that afternoon, a fire alarm aboard ship wasn't something he could ignore. Huffing and puffing – more in anger than anything else – Gerald arrived at the cabin and felt the door for added heat. Feeling none, he pounded on it so hard that Jack and Samuel, who had come rushing to his side, thought he would break it down.

"Here, I'll open it for you, Chief," Jack blurted, brandishing the master key card, which they knew Gerald had also. Yet, by banging on the door, he was probably just trying to make a statement.

Flinging the door open, Gerald was instantly assailed by an African Gray parrot, ready to claw at his face and bite his ear off.

"*What the hell...?*" Gerald hollered, grabbing the bird by both legs and immobilizing its powerful beak by clamping his hand around it. "Get me a box to put this thing in, so he won't hurt anyone," he yelled into Jack's stunned face.

When Samuel returned with a nice large box and some tape to secure it, the three men soon had their way with the very talkative parrot. After carving some holes in the temporary cage, Gerald carried the boxed bird to the captain directly.

He only knocked once on the open door, marched in and deposited the container on the captain's desk.

Middleton looked up, visibly annoyed by the intrusion. Yet, knowing the chief of security wouldn't burst in his office without good reason, he asked, "What have you got there?"

"A parrot, Captain," Gerald said as quietly as his irritated demeanor would allow.

"A parrot?" Middleton exclaimed, bursting in loud laughter.

Stunned by the captain's reaction, Gerald snapped, "I don't think it's funny, sir! It made sounds of a fire alarm, almost bit my ear off and clawed at my face when I entered the cabin..."

"Calm down, Gerald," the captain said, waving for him to sit down. "Is it an African Gray, by any chance?"

"Yes, it is. And the woman in 402 also seems to have a constant guest with her – so the steward says."

The captain shook his head. "Somehow I don't think that's the case, Gerald..."

"But Jack said that Samuel heard two people talking every morning when he walked by the cabin before beginning his cleaning rounds."

"That may be so – but you have to realize that these African Grays can talk your head off if properly trained, and..."

"You mean to tell me this creature could carry a conversation and no one would know the difference?"

Middleton nodded. "Let me tell you about a friend of mine. She had an African Gray parrot, Ricky Ticky, who picked up a great deal of sound imitations. He would cough, sneeze, make the sounds of a smoke alarm, bark like her dog, make the exact sound of her cell phone and then proceed to answer it with her voice, too. Unaware that it was Ricky Ticky talking, she would run into the room and pick up her cell-phone only to find it quite silent." Middleton smiled at the recollection. "Yes, and then he would make the sounds of the shower water, the water boiling on the stove, my friend going to the bathroom and even the sounds of when she was making a bowel movement. One time, when he was quite young, she made the mistake of saying "bombs away" when the bird flew over her at the moment he let it go. He liked this term and whenever he would do #2, he would proclaim, "bombs away"."

By this time, Gerald had relaxed and even emitted some laughter.

Undaunted, Captain Middleton continued, "She also relayed a time when she and some friends where having Bible study with one of the more long-winded members of their group. In the back of the minds of those in the group, other than the speaker, everyone was hoping that this long-winded member would stop speaking. Ricky Ticky apparently picked up on the vibe and started his imitation of snoring very loudly. The Bible study group broke out in absolute hysterics. The long-winded group leader then said, "I guess I should stop now," to which the rest of the group broke out in laughter again.

Wiping the tears of laughter that were menacing to course down the big man's cheek, Gerald said, "I guess we'll have to put down the fire alarm to a "parrot accident" then?"

"Yes, but as you know, we can't allow the passenger to keep an animal of any kind aboard this vessel, even though pirate captains of old used to keep parrots on their shoulders..."

"I know, Captain, but we're two days away from our next port-of-call; what shall we do with the beast in the meantime?"

"I think we should have the lady in 402 give us the parrot's cage or demand that she leaves it locked in until we reach the next port. At which point we'll have to ask her to leave the ship or make arrangements to have her pet flown back to where ever someone could pick it up and take care of it."

"Okay then, leave it with me, and I'll make the necessary arrangements," Gerald concluded, rising from his seat.

"Yes, but before you do that, make sure the lady is not a condo owner, otherwise, we'll have to address the matter with kid gloves, if you understand my meaning," to which the parrot answered, "Kid gloves, kid gloves."

"Sure, Captain, no problem." And with these words, the chief grabbed the box and walked to the door of the office.

He was about to close the door when the captain called him back. "Say, Gerald, how are we doing with Mr. and Mrs. Bornstein? Did you manage to talk to him yet?"

As he turned around, Gerald replied, "Not yet, sir, I'm still gathering intel on the divers – I want to have the facts straight before I approach the guy."

"Good show, yes, again, kid gloves… remember what the parrot said?"

"Oh yes, especially with him."

Nodding, the captain returned to his paperwork and Gerald marched out of the office.

An hour later and still unable to locate Mrs. Shaw – the resident of cabin 402 – Gerald decided to ask for Alan's help. He found the latter totally absorbed in paperwork and looking at his computer screen from time to time.

"Sorry to interrupt, Doc, but I need your help," Gerald blurted, poking his head at Alan's office door."

"Sure, what's the matter?" He shot a quick glance at the box. "What have you got there?" Alan asked.

"An African Grey parrot!"

To Gerald's utmost frustration, Alan, too, exploded in laughter, attracting Angie's attention right away.

"Not you too!" Gerald exclaimed. "Don't tell me; you've had an encounter with an African Gray before?"

"As a matter of fact I did," Alan said, leading the chief by the arm to the storeroom. "And I gather it's an African Gray that you have stowed away in that box?"

"Oh, poor thing!" Angie cried out, following the two men into the back room.

"This thing is dangerous. He practically gouged my eyes out and bit my ear off when he flew at me," Gerald said.

"Where was this?" Alan asked, taking the box from Gerald's hands.

"Mrs. Shaw's cabin – 402 – the bird made the sound of the fire alarm so loud we responded, and when we entered the cabin, he just attacked me!"

"And where's Mrs. Shaw now?"

"I have no idea. The steward says that she's never in her cabin when he goes in to clean it in the morning. The parrot must be hiding when he does."

"Okay, let's first attend to the boxed patient and then we'll see what we can do to find its owner," Alan said, opening the box, and grabbing the bird out of it.

"You look like you've handled a parrot before," Angie said, staying far enough so the bird wouldn't be able to reach her quickly.

"Yes – although I never owned one – I had a patient who had an African Gray just like this one. And she showed me a few tricks that kept the bird calm and attentive."

"Well that's good, because until we find a cage for him, I don't think I would want to come any closer to him than when he's in that box."

By this time, Alan had the bird firmly held by the claws and standing atop his hand. The parrot was quietly looking at the people around him, shifting his head from side to side. When Alan felt his heartbeat returning to normal by caressing his chest, he gently placed him on the exam table.

The parrot immediately proceeded to preen his plumage as if disgusted by the fact that someone had dared disturb his coat of gray and red feathers. Alan smiled and went to grab a stepladder and led the bird, who was atop his fist, onto the top rung of the ladder. Apparently unperturbed, the parrot resumed his preening. A moment later, though, he looked at the three humans and cocking his head to the side, distinctly uttered, "You son of a bitch!"

Alan, Angie and Gerald couldn't help but burst into renewed laughter, which encouraged the bird to do the same, with a good rendition of Angie's laugh.

Once the giggles and chuckles had died down, Alan said, "You know, that reminds me of another patient of mine and her husband who kept trying desperately to teach their parrot how to speak. Unfortunately, the bird would not even learn one simple word. One thanksgiving, when my patient, her husband's in-laws, two neighbors, one grandparent, and their children were all gathered around the table ready to say grace, from the corner of the room came the following statement in the exact intonation and accent of my patient, "God damn son of a bitch." Obviously the whole room turned around to see the parrot focus on my patient, since she had been the one who had unknowingly allowed the parrot to learn this phrase."

"I... I'm sorry, Doc," Angie blurted amid left-over giggles, "but are you intending to keep him in the stock room... I mean what if he flies at Evelyn or me when we open the door...? And, what about feeding him?"

Still smiling, Alan answered, "No need to worry about him flying out of control. These birds need peace and quiet; they hate violent movements or noises"—he looked at Gerald—"and that's probably why he flew at you when you opened the door after hearing you banging on it."

Turning to the parrot and bowing, Gerald sneered, "I'm so sorry, *your highness*, but you're the one who screeched the fire alarm sound."

CHAPTER FIFTEEN

I don't think so!

AFTER GERALD HAD PHONED to say that he had located Mrs. Shaw and that James III, the parrot, had been returned safely to its cage, Alan exhaled a deep sigh of disgruntled annoyance – the paperwork and the tasks still in hand seemed to be overwhelming. With some of the new human resource initiatives from '*the man in charge*', Internet had allowed all crew to make complaints to head office. The purpose was, of course, to keep managers in line and not overwork their charges. Unfortunately, it, along with a number of other initiatives, created a great number of pro-forma's and reports that all department heads had to complete on a regular basis. Alan, of course, was the titular head of the medical department and its budget even though the Managing Director was actually responsible for all the departments on board. Yet, it wasn't the amount of work that dismayed him, but the manner in which the head office had organized the tasks and duties of the medical officer. They were not organized in a logical or reasonable way. It reminded him of something…. He rummaged through the box he had brought out of the store room a couple of days ago for a minute until he found another piece of paper – the very thing he wanted to find. He plopped himself into his chair and read the note.

The Dead Horse Theory

The tribal wisdom of the Northern Native people, passed on from generation to generation says that, "When you discover you are riding a dead horse, the best strategy is to dismount."

However, in government more advanced strategies are often employed, such as:

1. Buying a stronger whip.
2. Appointing a committee to study the horse.
3. Changing Riders
4. Arranging to visit other countries to see how other cultures ride dead horses.
5. Lowering the standards so that dead horses can be included.
6. Reclassifying the dead horse as "living-impaired."
7. Hiring outside contractors to ride the dead horse.
8. Harnessing several dead horses together to increase speed.
9. Providing additional funding and/or training to increase the dead horse's performance.
10. Doing a productivity study to see if lighter riders would improve the dead horse's performance.
11. Declaring that as the dead horse does not have to be fed, it is less

costly, carries lower overhead and therefore contributes substantially more to the bottom line of the economy than do some other horses.
12. Rewriting the expected performance requirements for all horses. And, of course . . .
13. Promoting the dead horse to a supervisory position.

Maybe I should send this to the 'man-in-charge', he thought. Then remembered that it was the *'man in charge'* who had to deal with not only the politics of medical issues on board ships but things like the unions and politicians at the Port of Miami and with some of the new union rules, he did not want to give the poor guy a heart attack with the stress he knew was involved in that port. Fortunately, *The Contessa* was not scheduled to stop there in the near future.

As the medical officer for ships, it is the docs' responsibility to monitor all gastro-intestinal outbreaks and to test for Norovirus, one of the most contagious. When the log shows that 2% of the ship is infected with any gastro-intestinal disease, various sanitary measures are automatically put in place. Total wash down and sanitation of the ship has to be documented to the USPH and other authorities. Various announcements have to be done, etc., etc. In addition to these fairly common procedures, the unions in Miami insist that other measures are undertaken to ensure that the employees at the port get lots of work.

For example, when arriving at the Port of Miami, the ships crew is not allowed to touch the luggage, even in the ship's holds. Normally, the crew is very efficient at getting luggage that they have collected the night before from the ship's holds and to transfer it to specified places on shore for passenger collection. In Miami, one has to wait for the slow union longshoremen to collect the luggage and take it to the port building. If anyone dare tells them that they are going too slow or that they dropped a suitcase off a cart, they generally stop work completely until the union boss 'negotiates for a fee' and a resolution of the situation.

Of course when a ship does a turn around, there are new crew coming aboard and crew finishing their contracts, and anxious to make flights and go home. This all ends up with major delays in Miami because no crew or passenger movement can occur until all the luggage is off the ship. As soon as the luggage is off, the immigration officers can come aboard to do their thing and clear the passengers going ashore. Once all the passengers have been cleared, then the disembarkation of the crew can occur and is usually much more arduous for the crew than for the passengers. This is especially true as most crew is not from the US and has to have special visas just to transit to the airport in Miami for flights to their home countries. So with all this not having to occur in Alaska, Alan shook his head with a smile lingering on his lips, and returned to his duties.

However, it wasn't long before the medical center's door opened and a woman passed out as she was crossing the threshold.

Alan jumped out of his chair and together with Angie ran to the woman's aid. Her face was ashen, which was not a good sign. Alan checked her pulse and breathing – everything seemed to be stable until she began seizing. Alan's first thought was epilepsy. When her body ceased jerking and convulsing uncontrollably, and when she opened her eyes, Alan and Angie helped her up and led her into the room equipped for emergencies. Without being asked, the woman lay on the bed and seemed relieved for the momentary care and attention.

"What is your name?" Alan and Evelyn asked quietly, looking at the patient kindly.

"I'm Mrs. Shaw," the woman replied, returning the gaze.

"Oh, you are James's owner then?"

Mrs. Shaw nodded and smiled weakly. "Yes, and I'm so sorry for the trouble he's caused." A woman in her forties, Mrs. Shaw was endowed with a busty figure, a gentle face, bright brown eyes and a head of graying hair that obviously had seen too many salon treatments. Yet, she was exuding that certain kindness and care that personifies pet lovers.

"Did you know you're not supposed to have pets on board?" Alan queried.

"Yes, but you see, as I explained to Mr. Tolberg, I am on my way to Juneau with James to bring him to my clients. You see I run an aviary and these people bought the parrot when he was just a fledgling little guy."

"But couldn't you have sent him on a flight to Juneau?" Angie asked from the other side of the bed – her curiosity getting the better of her.

Mrs. Shaw turned her head to her. "Well, yes, normally I would, but you see these people didn't want the bird to suffer through a flight – which they often do – so they asked me to personally accompany James to his destination, and unfortunately, I left the cage open this morning when I went for a run." She took Alan's hand. "I'm sorry, Doctor, for all this, really I am."

Alan patted her hand with his other one and smiled. "That's okay; I wish we could have more passengers as entertaining as James." He looked up at Angie. "Would you mind getting the x-ray room ready for Mrs. Shaw?"

"No problem, Doc, right away," Angie replied, trotting away toward the room in question.

"What do you think is the matter with me, Doctor? I've never felt this way before – certainly never fainted before, that's for sure – I have had an irritating rash on my arms"—she pulled the sleeves of her blouse above the elbows—"and it's driving me nuts."

Alan examined the rash and lifted his gaze to the patient. I'm glad you showed me this, because it appears that you are suffering from a fungal infection…"

"You mean like a mold…?"

"Much like it, but this one, if I'm right, would be the result of you breathing tiny molecular fungi particles when you clean the birds' aviary and cages."

"Is that dangerous?"

"Well, it could be, but I think we'll be able to treat it right here on the ship, and you'll feel as good as new very soon."

"That's a relief." Mrs. Shaw said, lowering the shirtsleeves and relaxing her head against the pillow. "I couldn't see myself caring for my birds and scaring them with my fainting in the aviary – they'd be flying all over the place…"

"Yes, I can understand that, but once you return home and after the medicine, I recommend that you wear protective clothing and a respirator when you enter the aviary or treat your birds, otherwise you'll have a relapse."

A while later, Mrs. Shaw was resting comfortably in one of the wards of the center, after having gone through the tests Alan had required to confirm his diagnosis. And yes, the good woman indeed suffered from a fungal infection which had lodged itself in her left lung in the shape of a very small tumor, and portions of which, had spread to her brain, causing the seizure.

"More paperwork," he groaned to himself, as he strode out of his office. But the patient was on her way to be cured, which was what he always wanted.

It was almost five o'clock when he strode down the hallway that would lead him to Mr. Bornstein's suite. He was to meet Gerald there and interview the treasure-hunting patron in view of clarifying his intention behind the exploring of the *Investigator*.

Gerald, always punctual, joined him in front of the suite.

"Let's do this," Gerald said, knocking softly on the door.

"Who is it?" Mr. Bornstein's booming voice asked by way of a reply from inside the suite.

"Doctor Mayhew and Gerald Tolberg," Alan answered.

"Clarisse, why don't you get the door – I'll be right there."

Glass of wine in hand, Mrs. Bornstein – Clarisse – opened the door wide, a broad smile adorning her very red lips. "And two of them," she said, batting an eyelid. "Come on in, gentlemen, come on in, my husband will be right with you," she added, extending an arm in the direction of the lounge room. "I'm Clarisse Bornstein, and you handsome men are?"

"This is Doctor Mayhew," Gerald replied hurriedly, "And I am Gerald Tolberg."

"Are you a doctor too?" Clarisse asked, taking a seat on the sofa. "Do sit down, please; standing people make me dizzy."

Alan's eyes traveled around the heavily furnished room, reflecting upon the stuffiness he felt. The brocade upholstery, the golden frames surrounding all of the pictures hanging on the walls attested only of the money spent on the décor while good taste had been left to abandon.

Complying with the lady's request, both men sat across from the middle-aged woman who visibly had already had too much to drink. Her otherwise blue eyes were glassy, and her skin, although heavily made up, betrayed all the signs of her addiction. Her platinum blonde hair was carefully coiffed atop her head, emphasizing the wrinkles and bags adorning her long neck. Wearing some sort of multicolored afghan, she didn't seem to have bothered with any other undergarment – the nipples of her silicone breasts poking through the fabric attesting to the fact.

"Ah, gentlemen!" Isaac Bornstein erupted, coming out of the bedroom, "very good of the both of you to come for a visit." He threw a glance at his wife. "Did you offer these good people a drink, darling? They might be thirsty as you know?"

"No thank you, sir," Gerald replied, "nothing for me." He turned his head to Alan.

"Nothing for the moment," the doc said quickly.

"Okay then," Bornstein said, turning toward the liquor cabinet. "I'll have one with Clarisse – she doesn't like to drink alone generally." He opened the bar, pulled out a bottle of rum and poured himself a generous glass. "I love rum," he declared, joining his wife on the sofa. "What's your favorite killer, Doctor?"

"I prefer a good wine with dinner," Alan answered pointedly. "Hard liquors don't agree with me somehow."

"By the way," Bornstein went on, "thanks for fixing that cut on my head. It's healing very nicely, see"—he patted his forehead—"just an oversized Band Aid is enough now to protect it."

The man is a jackass, Gerald thought.

"And I see you've recovered your memory since the incident," Alan remarked. "Do you recall what happened, now?"

Bornstein shook his head. "Not really. I know I had a discussion with Sam Ashton, you know, one of our divers, and when I turned to open the door leading to the hallway, it was flung open in my face, after that I remember sitting in your office, and that's it." He paused to drink some of his rum. "It was the weirdest thing – never happened to me before."

"Oh I have some hors-d'oeuvres in the fridge," said Clarisse all of a sudden, rising from her seat. "Why don't I bring them over?"

Bornstein looked up at his wife. "Yes, darling, why don't you do that while the three of us have a chat?"

"Okay, okay, if you wanted me to leave the room, why didn't you say so?" Clarisse snapped, before marching out in the direction of the condo's kitchen.

"I'm sorry, gents, but as you can appreciate, my wife has a slight problem with her drinking and she flares up from time to time…"

"And where is your daughter, Elizabeth, if I might ask," Alan cut-in, still clearly worried about the little girl's well being.

"Oh, not to worry about our daughter, Doctor, I make sure that when we travel, her time is well occupied with what ever entertainment is available."

Having followed the conversation thus far in silence, Gerald now showed signs of impatience. The big man wanted to tackle the issue at hand. "I'm sorry, sir, but I would like to get back on track here with the purpose for our visit." He paused, opening the folder in his lap. "You see, we've come across a discrepancy in our insurance paperwork that may require your attention…"

"And what discrepancy is that, Mr. Tolberg? I thought I had arranged – or my secretary did, for all that bureaucracy to be taken care of before we boarded the ship. Is there something she's omitted to do?"

That's typical, Alan thought, *blame the secretary*.

"Well, we don't know if your secretary did or not, or if the error comes from farther down the line, but the insurance papers we've received do not describe the second dive that Mr. Ashton and Mr. Barrington are supposed to perform after the sub-dive tour. Although we've received complete payment for the both assignments, the insurance papers have not been filled out properly, as you can see"—he handed Bornstein the sheet Alan had read earlier—"…and we need to cover all basis, as you can understand, I am sure."

"Let me have a look at this," Bornstein said, depositing his glass on the coffee table and focusing on the insurance documents. "I see what you mean, and you are perfectly correct, Mr. Tolberg." He raised his gaze to the chief of security. "I'm glad you've caught that – thank you."

"And what would be the purpose for that solo dive, sir?" Gerald asked. "We've heard from the archeologists that you were intending to help them in cataloguing the remaining relics aboard the *Investigator,* is that correct?"

Taking his glass back and drinking it empty, Bornstein fixed his gaze on the chief before he said, "Yes, that's correct, Mr. Tolberg. Whatever has been left aboard *The Investigator* should be itemized and eventually brought to the surface."

"Yet, we've been told that Parks Canada has no more funds allocated for the salvage of the wreck or its contents – would you be intending to pay for the recovery of the remaining relics then?"

Bornstein guffawed. "Well played, Mr. Tolberg. Well played indeed. If you were trying to ask me if I would be interested in procuring McClure's treasure chest, and its recovery, the answer is yes, absolutely."

"But you know that whatever would be found aboard the *Investigator* will be the property of the commonwealth, don't you?"

"Yes, Mr. Tolberg, I'm perfectly aware of the law of the land, and I have no intention of infringing it in any way."

"That's all fine, sir, but have you informed anyone else – apart from Parks Canada, I presume – of your intention?"

"Absolutely not, and that's perhaps why the insurance papers haven't been properly filled out. I generally don't speak of my private ventures with anyone, because, as you are well aware, there are thieves and treasure seekers everywhere – and not all with the best intentions."

Alan drew himself to the edge of his seat. "Does your wife or child know anything about this?" he asked.

"Not that I am aware of, no, Doctor. You see, I don't trust Clarisse to keep anything to herself, and as for Elizabeth, I'm sure she has no idea other than that we're going to visit a museum on an Arctic Island."

Yet, Clarisse had listened to the entire conversation from the darkened part of the corridor leading to her room, with great interest.

So the bastard does not trust me, does he? And he's going to grab the treasure worth millions and have me wait on him for the rest of my life…? I don't think so!

CHAPTEEN SIXTEEN

Plastic surgery . . . or not?

"THIS IS ABSOLUTELY priceless. Have a read," Babette said, handing the ship's log newspaper to Susan. Both women were sitting down at the café, enjoying a morning latte.

"What is it?" Susan asked, taking the folded newspaper from Babette's hand. She began reading:

JACK (age 3) was watching his Mom breast-feeding his new baby sister.

After a while he asked: "Mom, why have you got two milk dispensers? Is one for hot and one for cold?"

MELANIE (age 5) asked her Granny how old she was. Granny replied she was so old she didn't remember any more. Melanie said, "If you don't remember you must look in the back of your panties. Mine say five to six."

STEVEN (age 3) hugged and kissed his Mom goodnight. "I love you so much, that when you die I'm going to bury you outside my bedroom window."

BRITTANY (age 4) had an earache and wanted a chewable aspirin. She tried in vain to take the lid off the bottle. Seeing her frustration, her Mom explained it was a childproof cap and she'd have to open it for her. Eyes wide with wonder, the little girl asked: "How does it know it's me?"

SUSAN (age 4) was drinking juice when she got the hiccups. "Please don't give me this juice again," she said, "It makes my teeth cough."

DANNY (age 4) stepped onto the bathroom scale and asked: "How much do I cost?"

MARC (age 4) was engrossed in a young couple that was hugging and kissing in a restaurant. Without taking his eyes off them, he asked his dad: "Why is he whispering in her mouth?"

CLINTON (age 5) was in his bedroom looking worried. When his Mom asked what was troubling him, he replied, "I don't know what'll happen with this bed when I get married. How will my wife fit in?"

JAMES (age 4) was listening to a Bible story. His dad read: "The man named Lot was warned to take his wife and flee out of the city but his wife looked back and was turned to salt. Concerned, James asked: "What happened to the flea?"

TAMMY (age 4) was with her mother when they met an elderly, rather wrinkled woman her Mom knew. Tammy looked at her for a while and then asked, "Why doesn't your skin fit your face?"

CONNIE (age 5) This particular Sunday the demonstrative pastor started his sermon with, "Dear Lord, Dear Lord, "Dear Lord." Slowly he extended his arms toward heaven and had an overly rapturous look on his upturned slightly obese face. "Without you... (long pause) ... we are but dust." He would have continued, but at that moment this very obedient 5-year-old daughter, who was listening for a change, leaned over to her Mother and asked quite audibly, in a very shrill, little girl voice, "Mom, what is butt dust?"

The most wasted day is one in which we have not laughed and not appreciated something around us in nature. Have a wonderful day on board . . .

As suddenly as she had burst into laughter, Susan stopped and looked at Babette fixedly. "Mon Dieu, mon Dieu, what am I going to do with myself?" I will never be that mother with wonderful children – do you realize that?"

Quite familiar with human behavior in general, and in particular with that of her friend, Babette shook her head and replied, "You have a whole life ahead of you, a whole new career in the Beaux Arts in Paris, what would you want with children at your age?"

"Yes, I know, but being de-feminized"—Babette opened her eyes wide, she had never heard that term before—"how could I possibly leave a legacy to anyone; I have no-one..." Tears pearled at the rim of Susan's eyes once again. The ballet dancer and patron of the arts had been crushed when she had heard that she had breast cancer, and now, although accepting her condition at some level, she was thoroughly resentful of the fact that her appearance had been damaged, perhaps beyond repair.

"De-feminized is probably the wrong word to describe what happened to you, Susan. You have lost nothing of your feminine allure or demeanor; you are still alive – and thank the Good Lord for that – and as for leaving a legacy, you could always teach children, young women, to go on with their lives..."

"Something like a finishing school, you mean?" Susan was catching on to Babette's idea.

"Yes, perhaps you could open a private school in Paris, your favorite city..."

"But that's a wonderful idea," Susan erupted – her vibrant and explosive attitude returning at a gallop. "But what about my breasts...?"

"Who needs them?" Babette replied, shrugging. "They're nothing but a burdensome pair..."

"Hold it right there," Susan cut-in, "what happens if I meet the man of my dreams? What would be there to look at, but that awful scar tissue – tell me, what do I do then? Most men will not understand, even though they will say it is okay."

"Listen to me, Susan. You're a beautiful woman regardless of your breasts and when your scars have had time to heal properly, perhaps you can consider plastic surgery. But in the meantime, get yourself ready to tackle the life that's been waiting for you in Paris.

Looking down at her chest, Susan's face returned to the portrait of sadness that she had displayed since boarding the ship. No one was giving her a straight answer. There were always those words, "perhaps, probably, possibly," and all those ambivalent expressions that people use when no one wants to steer you in any particular direction. Susan's dilemma was that she couldn't imagine her future without the specter of the big "C" returning to destroy her life once again. This is a plight that affects most cancer patients; a relentless and insidious fear that one day the doctor will give them the bad news. Some people, such as Susan in this instance, can't re-focus or believe that another day is at hand until someone else shows them the way to the rest of their lives. For Susan, life, as she once knew it, was dead and buried. She thought she would never be able to walk in a room without people staring at her chest, without hearing snide comments about her "flat chest", or without someone asking the inevitable question, "How are you coping, dear?" Susan wasn't coping very well, in fact. She focused on the past, rather than enjoying the moment or looking forward to her future.

"How long would it take, do you think, until I could have the operation? I can not wear these 'falsies' forever," she asked Babette.

The latter lifted her gaze from the paper, visibly flustered. "I thought we had this conversation a moment ago, dear. Besides, I am not a doctor or a seer to being able to predict your future. I believe, though, that you should heal your body and your mind first, before you go under the knife again."

"What on Earth do you mean by 'healing my mind'?" Susan retorted hotly. "Do you think I'm insane?"

Babette raised her eyes to the sky. "You haven't been listening, have you? Healing your mind is part and parcel of the process, Susan. You can't heal your body without healing your mind. You can't hope to recover from this atrocious disease without helping your whole attitude to change. Look around you"—she waved at the vast expanse facing them—"The Good Lord has seen to it that you are fortunate enough to travel the waters of His oceans and rivers and to cross His lands. He has put, at your disposal, an infinite natural grandeur for you to return to see the beauty of this wonderful world. But no, you shrug all of it off, and ignore your surroundings in favor of brooding over what cannot and will not change until such a time that you take a good look at what is right in front of you. Absorb the beauty and precious gifts that surround you day after day, Susan, and soon you will feel those thoughts of the past leaving you for ever."

Tears still brimming at the rim of her eyes, Susan nodded. "I guess I've been full of myself, haven't I?"

Babette smiled at the rejoinder and patted her friend's arm reassuringly. "Yes, my dear, you have. But now it is time for you to step on the stage of life and learn how to dance once again with a slightly different costume."

* * * *

Clarisse Bornstein, for her part, wasn't admiring the calmness of the ocean before her or the waves lapping the hull of *The Contessa* when she called Sam Ashton to meet her on the promenade deck. She was brewing, plotting and seething with an uncontainable anger. She had been the wife of a brute for far too long, she thought. She wanted out of the marriage but not before lining her nest with everything she felt he owed her. However, divorcing Isaac was out of the question. She had signed a pre-nuptial agreement that would see her destitute in case of a separation. *Elizabeth would get the lot,* she knew. The only way out of this situation was for her to force her husband to pay up, off the record, for a yet, undefined reason, she surmised.

When Sam came onto the deck, the evening was chilly and he would have felt the cold if it wasn't for the down-filled jacket he was wearing. He spotted Mrs. Bornstein immediately. No one would miss the elegant figure wrapped in a gorgeous fur-coat standing by the railing, waiting for him. Clarisse had found him handsome and powerful the minute she had laid eyes on him all those months ago when she and Isaac had engaged him and Edward Barrington during one of their trips to London. His haled face and rugged features were attracting her like a bee to the honey-pot.

"How are you, Mrs. Bornstein?" Sam asked when he came to stand beside her and put his elbows on the railing.

"Just peachy, Sam, just peachy," she replied, a devious smile already parting her lips. "It's just that I want to add a little caveat to your contract." She peered into his face when he turned to her.

"What sort of caveat?" he asked, not showing his surprise. "I thought we were done with the contract negotiation. Besides which, you are not a signatory party to the contract, so what would you think your husband would want to add at this stage?"

"Not my husband, my dear man; this is a matter between you and me – my husband has nothing to do with what I am planning…"

"Hold on a little minute, Mrs. Bornstein. Are you saying your husband is not aware of our meeting this evening?"

"Yes, I want to engage your services myself, and Isaac should not be made aware of any of this."

Sam remained silent for a moment. He was not about to work for this woman. Neither he nor Edward would want to be involved in any way with this woman. In the past few months they had noticed her behavior – and had no intention of being induced to work for her. They didn't need the money (together they had amassed a sizeable nest egg), and they knew how Isaac Bornstein could react if they were 'involved' in any way with that wife of his – they could kiss goodbye to any future assignments from him and their reputation.

"And what makes you think that Edward and I would accept to work for you, Mrs. Bornstein, and not your husband?"

She sniggered quietly. "Well, let me put it this way; my husband has this strange aversion to homosexuals – in fact, he hates them with a passion. So, if I were to tell him about you and Edward, I think you would be replaced at a moment's notice."

Little did Clarisse know that Sam and Edward had put their cards on the table soon after they had met Isaac Bornstein for the first time. They never flaunted their relationship with the people they worked with, but they didn't want rumors or unwelcome comments to burden their lives, so they always made a point of discussing the matter before accepting any assignment.

At this juncture, however, Sam thought he would play along with her and see what she had in mind – one never knows with people who suffer from any sort of addiction – sometimes they come up with the most marvelous ideas. "Okay then," he said, "I'm all ears. What do you have in mind?"

Nonplussed to say the least, when Sam returned to their cabin, Edward was waiting for him with the inevitable question. "So what did she want? Making advances to my handsome partner, was she?" Edward's tease didn't escape Sam.

"When I tell you, you probably won't believe me."

Edward frowned. He was sitting at the desk, emailing their friends with the latest diarized version of their journey. "I probably won't, but let's have it anyway – what did she say?"

"In a nutshell she wants to get *her* hands on McClure's chest."

Edward's mouth fell agape for a moment. "You're joking, right? And how did she hope to accomplish that feat? But more to the point how did she want to involve either or both of us in that scheme?"

"That's something we need to discuss you and I and then advice Gerald Tolberg before this thing goes too far."

"I gather her plan is not quite on the legal side of things, is it?"

Sam sat on the bed and took his shoes off before lying down. "No, it isn't," he answered, putting his folded hands under his head. "But if I were a thief, I would probably try it."

CHAPTEEN SEVENTEEN

Magnificent is one word for it

ENGULFED IN THE WATERS of the Gastineau Channel, on the Alexander Archipelago of Alaska, *The Contessa* slowed down to allow her passengers to admire the grandeur before them. Mount Juneau looming high above the horizon afforded the onlooker a view of its ice cap. Known as the Juneau Ice Cap, the large ice mass is the birthplace of more than thirty glacial floes. One of which, the Mendenhall Glacier, has been retreating steadily up-land for some two hundred years while leaving in its wake barren strips of earth where the Tongass National Forest is quietly reclaiming the ground inch by inch.

If not all of the passengers, most of them were on deck that morning. One could not miss being literally attracted by the powerful sights. All seemed to envelop one with awe and wonder. The shimmering blue of the water against the vibrant green of the forests plunging into the swell with abandon could not be ignored. And, as if on cue, a pod of whales came alongside the ship – a sight to behold indeed. As if in deference for their appearance, the silence aboard *The Contessa* was nothing short of reverent. The phone cameras didn't stop clicking everywhere. No one wanted to forget the images their eyes had witnessed in the early hours of that day. Mothers leading their young alongside them in a rhythmic dance in and out of the waters, while the males seemed to guard the flanks of the pods, like escorting soldiers returning to their ancestral homes. All this attested to the magnificence of Alaska.

Due to its smaller size, the Juneau Port Authority had asked Captain Middleton to moor *The Contessa* at one of the commercial piers – not in the downtown area where the mega cruise liners routinely stay during their stop. Alan often thought this was more of a directive from the business community. Having 3000 plus passengers descend on souvenir shops is much more profitable than having 200 plus people, even though *The Contessa's* passengers were more likely to purchase the high end items. Arrangements for a shuttle bus were made that would fetch the passengers desirous of visiting the town. Once those arrangements had been made, the captain asked Alan to come to his office for a short meeting. There were plans to be delineated regarding the health concerns that might hinder their voyage from that point onward. Juneau was the last major port-of-call before heading up the Northwest Passage. The captain wanted to re-assure himself that all measures would be taken in the days ahead to have all crew and officers go through their physical exams, and that all passengers who had signed up to visit Banks Island in particular, were prepared to pass an equally strenuous examination before disembarking.

"Have a seat, Doctor," Captain Middleton invited when Alan came in the office. Stephan Ivanov was already comfortably ensconced in one of the chairs. He threw a friendly welcoming smile at Alan when he sat beside him.

"Thanks, Captain," Alan replied.

"Alright, gentlemen, you know why I called this meeting and what needs to be done. However, I have one item that came to my attention since we last spoke." Stephan and Alan exchanged a quizzical glance. "Yes, the matter concerns Mr. Isaac Bornstein and in particular his wife, Clarisse Bornstein." Middleton landed his gaze on Alan. "Before Mr. Tolberg joins us, I wanted to know if Mrs. Bornstein – or her husband for that matter – had approached you with concerns about her addiction."

"No, not directly, no. When Gerald and I paid them a visit regarding the insurance paperwork, Mr. Bornstein acknowledged quite frankly that his wife is an alcoholic. But he didn't request any assistance for her, no."

"Well then, let me bring you up-to-date. I have it on good authority that Mrs. Clarisse Bornstein is trying to enroll anyone willing to snatch the McClure treasure chest off her husband's hands..."

Both men facing the captain burst into a chuckle. "That's out of a James Bond movie, no doubt," Stephan exclaimed. "How could she hope to do that under the nose of the security details we will have onshore at the time – and that is if the divers were able to locate the chest in the first place or raise it to the surface?"

"Exactly," the captain said, himself cracking a smile. "Yet, she seems determined to follow through with her plan in inducing anybody to take the bait."

"Excuse me, sir," Alan cut-in, "but how would she intend to grab the chest – does anyone know?"

"That's probably something Mr. Tolberg could answer – whenever he gets here." Impatience began to rise in the captain's facial expression. "However, I would like to know from you, Doctor, if there would be any way to stop the woman from disembarking on Banks Island before things get ugly...?"

Alan crossed his arms over his chest. "Well, yes, Captain, there is. Short of putting her in shackles, if Mrs. Bornstein wants to get ashore, she would have to go through not only a physical examination, but also the preparation briefing. And if she agrees to undergo the physical, which I doubt very much, she might be declared unfit to face the risks accompanying such a visit."

"I see," the captain said concertedly. "So, she could be stopped from going on shore – that's what you're saying?"

Alan nodded at the same moment as the three men heard a knock on the office door.

"Come in," Middleton shouted, "Come in, Mr. Tolberg. Have a seat"—he pointed to the third chair—"and tell us what's going on with the Bornstein's, please."

"I'm sorry, sir, but I had a hard time getting up here – it seems that all two hundred pax are roaming the outside decks of the ship at once." He sat down and opened the folder that he had placed in his lap. "Well, there isn't much to add to what you already know, I'm afraid, but quite a few precautionary measures to be put in place before we get to Banks Island." He looked up at the captain. "You see, Mrs. Bornstein is not a professional thief nor is she capable of carrying out her plan – what ever it may be – by herself. She will need help. And that assistance she would need to find aboard *The Contessa* or she would need to hire someone on the island, which would be harder yet."

"But couldn't she engage the service of some treasure hunters from somewhere else?" Stephan suggested.

"Absolutely, Mr. Ivanov – actually that is exactly what she will most likely do. She has approached our divers with a form of blackmail, which plan was subsequently foiled when they apparently told her to "go to hell", quote-unquote."

A guffaw erupted from the captain's mouth, which was accompanied by Alan and Stephan's quiet laughter.

"Yes, gentlemen," Gerald went on, "yet, we need to do something to stop her. And at this juncture, I can only see one way to prevent her or, at least, being aware of the contact she might have on the outside…"

"And what would that be, Mr. Tolberg?"

"Well…." Gerald hesitated. "I want to tap her phones and oversee her Internet communications for one thing…"

"Sorry to interrupt," Middleton cut-in, "but isn't that illegal?"

"Not unless the purpose of the investigative measure is to avert a crime from being perpetrated on board, sir. And I think such is the case in this instance."

"And you will need my permission to do that, I suppose?"

"Yes, Captain, I do."

"Okay. You have it. What else?"

Alan shifted in his chair. "What about here in Juneau? Wouldn't she be able to establish contact with a potential hired hand while she's in town?"

Gerald nodded vigorously. "Yes. And that's what I will need to address with the local authority when we get onshore."

"I think I can give you a hand with that one," Stephan piped-up.

"How's that, Mr. Ivanov?"

"Well, Captain, I have a friend who is based right here in Juneau – he's actually a U.S. Marshall – and I'm sure he'll be happy to help."

"Would that do, Mr. Tolberg?" Middleton asked him.

Gerald turned to Stephan. "Yes, sir, that contact would be very helpful for sure. Thank you."

"Anything else we should consider?" the captain asked, glancing at each man in turn.

"Well, yes," Gerald replied. "If Mrs. Bornstein is desperate enough, and since she already resorted to blackmail, I think my team will need to keep an eye on her."

"Yes, by all means," Middleton agreed. "And as for you, Mr. Ivanov, I would like you to ensure that every officer on this ship keeps eyes and ears open. We can't let this situation develop into something that would hinder this cruise in any way. Understood?"

"Yes, sir," Stephan answered. Alan thought he was going to get up and salute, so firm his reply had been.

"Okay, gentlemen, I think that about covers it. Let's get to Juneau and back to our duties, shall we?"

Getting to their feet, the three men then filed out of the captain's office quietly.

Alan's gut feeling was screaming at his mind. Mrs. Bornstein was in trouble – no doubt of it. When it came to alcoholism, an addict cannot control his or her urges and sees the world in a different light. The people surrounding them become enemies, whether they are or not. Alan's thoughts turned instantly to Elizabeth's safety. The little girl would soon become an encumbrance, an appendage that Clarisse would hurt if she crossed her path. One wrong word from the child and the woman could really do damage. He needed to address that problem, and fast.

When he opened the door of the medical center he came face to face with Babette.

"Oh my, Alan, am I glad you're here!" she burst out, putting a hand to her chest. "Evelyn told me"—she turned to the nurse—"that you were in a meeting with Captain Middleton and if you hadn't showed up just now, I would have gone up there to talk to either of you right away anyway."

Knowing a troubled or fearful face when he saw one, Alan said, "Okay, Ms. Babette, calm down and let's go in my office, shall we?" grabbing the playwright by the arm. He switched his gaze to Evelyn. "Would you mind getting a tea for Ms. Babette, please?"

"Right away, Doc. No problem," Evelyn replied, already heading for their lunchroom.

Once they were sitting down – Alan behind his desk and Babette facing him – he asked, "Okay, tell me, what was so urgent or so bothersome that you wanted to fetch me out of the meeting?"

"It's Elizabeth, Alan. She hasn't shown up for Bible class this morning..."

"Have you checked with her parents?" Alan interrupted.

Babette shook her head. "I couldn't – they're not in their cabin and I haven't seen Clarisse anywhere."

"Maybe she is with her parents on the upper decks taking in the view," Alan suggested quietly, trying to calm the fear that seemed to rise to his mind like yeast-filled dough.

"Here we are, Ms. Babette," Evelyn said, depositing a cup of green tea in front of her.

"Thank you, my dear," Babette replied, a dismissive tone to her voice, "and I think it will be just right to fix my worried head."

"Okay then," Evelyn said, seeing that Babette was going to remain attentive to her troubles. "I'll be in the other office," she said to Alan, "if you need me."

"Okay, Evelyn, thank you." The doc paused for a fraction of a second before adding, "Would you mind calling Mr. Tolberg and ask him to join us?"

"I'll do that, no problem," Evelyn answered, walking out of the office.

When the door closed on the nurse, Babette resumed, "You see, Alan,

Elizabeth is only six years old and very quiet for her age. I never hear a peep out of her during Bible class and I never see her with her parents at any of the restaurants. I tell you, that child is frightened, Alan. And since I heard this awful argument – probably between Clarisse and her husband – the other night, I have kept my eye on the little one. I'd feel a lot better if I knew where she was." She took a sip of tea. "Hum, this is very good – a lot better than what you get in some of the cafés on board even."

"Okay, you heard me asking for Gerald to join us. We'll see what he says about this situation, but he mentioned that almost every passenger was on deck this morning, so maybe the Bornstein's are somewhere admiring the scenery... and you should be out there enjoying the splendors of Alaska too."

"Yes, yes, and so you said, but missing Bible class is not like Elizabeth; I tell you something is wrong, Alan, I can feel it."

CHAPTER EIGHTEEN

Eight what?

PLANNING AND EXECUTING a search of the ship for a missing child was not something Gerald wanted to contemplate at this juncture. "I can understand your misgivings, Ms. Babette," he said while sipping gratefully on a cup of delicious mocha that Evelyn had brought in as soon as he sat down. "But you need to understand that we cannot initiate a search of the vessel unless one of Elizabeth's parents comes to me and inquires about her."

"Do you mean to tell us, we have to wait until either of those two ignoramuses advises you that their child is missing?"

"Yes, I'm afraid that's the law. Even if we had good reason to think that the child was missing or even in danger, we would need to find the parents first before we could act in any way."

"But that's paramount to ignoring what's in front of your nose..."

"Sorry to interrupt you, Ms. Babette," Alan said, focusing on his friend. "I don't think we should jump to any conclusion here. It's a simple question of asking the cabin stewards if they have seen the parents or the child this morning – and then, if we cannot locate any of them, take appropriate action at that point, since we already know the addictive medical issues of the mother."

"Yes, I think that's what I would recommend doing," Gerald agreed, drinking some more of his coffee.

"All right then, you boys get on your horses and get me some answers," Babette declared, rising from her seat – visibly unsatisfied with the "boys'" suggestions. "I'll be in my cabin if you need me," she added, marching out of the office.

Looking after her, Alan said, "I don't think you can or should ignore her fear for the child's safety, Gerald. She is very astute and quite attuned to children's behavior for one thing, and right now, I would bet that she's on her way to search the ship."

"But that's ludicrous, Alan. If the child is in some sort of trouble, Ms. Babette will put herself in harm's way..."

"Exactly, and by that time, you'll have to get off your duff and help her, won't you?"

Gerald's eyebrows shot up. "Good heavens, I think I should have stayed with the Seals; life was much simpler than on these luxury cruise ships."

Chuckling at the big man's visible annoyance, Alan said, "You don't know the half of it, my friend. If our playwright is on a scent, she'll be like a dog with a bone buried two feet down..."

"Well then, I'll let her have the bone and chew on it," Gerald quipped.

"No, but seriously, do you think Elizabeth is in danger?"

"Personally, I have a hunch that her mother is the menace right now. She's the one you propose to follow and monitor carefully, that's good, but let's not ignore the fact that if Elizabeth was in her way – and not by design, but by chance – Clarisse would regard her as an enemy."

"What about mother's instinct and all that, wouldn't she stop?"

"No, Gerald, an alcoholic mother is no mother at all in most cases."

"Alright, I hear you," Gerald concluded, getting to his feet, "I'll go to the Bornstein's cabin right now and if they're not there, it will give me an opportunity to plant some bugs about the place and wire any computer they have on site."

"Will you question the cabin attendants too?"

"Yes, I'll have to now, since I've got one of our most celebrated passengers watching over my shoulder, don't I?"

Stephan and Gerald made their way to the rather bland looking building of the U.S. Marshall's office in an otherwise quaint looking downtown Juneau to talk to a man by the name of Larson McDonald. They stopped for a coffee at one of the local coffee shops. When they went through the doors, an awkward and uncomfortable silence fell over the local patrons. All eyes turned to the two uniformed men until they took a seat at the far end of the premises.

"With the hundreds of cruise ships that stop in this place, you'd think they would have seen officers before," Stephan whispered to Gerald. "I don't know if it means they like us or they hate us."

"Probably a bit of both," Gerald answered, lowering his head across the table not to be heard.

A pot of steaming coffee in hand, the matronly waitress strode to their table decisively and asked, "Coffee?" handing them a menu.

"Sure," Gerald replied, smiling up at the middle-aged woman. Dressed in a pink uniform too tight for her ample bosom, she showed all the signs of a woman who had seen too many husbands in her bed, perhaps too many rowdy kids about the place, no exercise, and a diet that was far from ideal.

"I'll have an apple pie a la mode," Stephan said, handing the cardboard back to Tracy – or so said her nametag.

"I'll have the same," Gerald rejoined, while Tracy poured the coffee in the two mugs that were already on the table.

"Okay, be right back," she retorted in an unfriendly tone as she turned away.

"You know, Officers," an old man sitting at a neighboring table said, "we've seen so many of you people coming in and out of here that we don't like it anymore," turning to face them.

"And why's that?" Gerald asked

"Because, see, people come here, go up to Mount Roberts, and traipse all over the place – leaving their garbage everywhere – a real shame I tell you."

"So you see a lot of cruise ship passengers coming in this place then?"

"Oh sure – by the thousands I tell you – and all as dirty as the next."

"That must keep everyone busy and employed," Stephan rejoined.

"Oh yeah," the old man said with a shrug of the shoulders. "I tell you if it weren't for their garbage we would pay no mind to them, but it's by the boat-load, I tell you, that we've got to clean up."

"But apart from their dirty habits you must have met some interesting and nice people, haven't you?" Gerald remarked.

"Oh sure, and then some. There was a guy who came last week – he was on a cruise and he told me about their organist...." He smiled at the recollection.

"Are you going to tell us?" Gerald queried, seeing that the man was apparently lost in thought for a moment.

"Oh sure... sure," he said, getting up and rounding his table to come and sit beside Gerald. "It'd be better if the others don't hear me," he added. "They're none too interested, I'd say."

"Okay, Fred," Tracy said, approaching the table with the two servings of apple pie, "are you gonna bother these good officers with your silly stories again?"

"You know me, Trace, I have to keep our visitors company so they don't feel lonely," Fred replied, with a broad smile deepening the lines of his friendly face.

"If he's becoming a bother, you just let me know," Tracy said to Gerald, "and I'll make it a quick business to shove him outta here, okay?"

"No bother at all, ma'am," Gerald answered, laughing quietly.

Once Tracy was out of earshot, Fred put his forearms and elbows on the table and began re-telling his story. "See, this guy told me that they had an organ at the ship's chapel and that for several weeks, they had a very big-busted organist playing it. Her breasts were so huge that they bounced and jiggled while she played the organ." Fred stopped, chuckled and shook his head. Stephan and Gerald snickered. "Unfortunately, she distracted the passengers that congregated considerably. A few of the regulars to the Sunday service were down right annoyed, if you get my meaning. The guy told me the busybodies said something had to be done about this or they would have to get another organist even though they had none other on board. So, one of the ladies approached her very discreetly and told her to mash up some green persimmons that she knew the chef had in the galley, and rub them on the nipples of her breasts and maybe they would shrink in size. They warned her, though, not to eat any of the green persimmons because "They are so sour they will make your mouth pucker up tighter than a fish's rectum and you won't be able to talk properly for a while." She agreed to try that method. The following Sunday morning at the ship's service, the new pastor who had only been on board for two weeks got up to the lectern and said: "Dew to thircumsthanthis bewond my contwol, we will not hath a thermon tewday!"

If the three men had wanted to keep this conversation as discreet as possible, they were out of luck. Their loud laughter and chuckles were enough to attract the attention of everybody still sitting in the coffee shop – and even got a smile on Tracy's lips.

"You're a fantastic story-teller," Stephan blurted between leftover chortles. "I should get the cruise director to hire you as a comedian for a show onboard."

"Oh no, Officer, not me – Juneau is enough of an audience for me. See, couldn't stand in front of a public – I'd be down right jittery if I'd tried."

An hour later, Stephan and Gerald were finally sitting across from Marshall McDonald. And after the introductions and friendly chitchat was over, Gerald steered the conversation to Mrs. Clarisse Bornstein's troubling plan.

"You see, Larson, we've got all the safety, surveillance and security measures taken aboard *The Contessa*, but when it comes to keeping an eye on her in this town, or up the coast of Alaska, we need your help."

With a head of copper hair as hirsute as a bramble bush, Larson was a big fellow – huge as it were – but his demeanor could easily be compared to one with a heart of gold. He was gentle and soft-spoken, surprisingly enough. "After what you fellows explained, I can understand you'd want my help. But my problem is that I don't have the manpower to tail the woman around when we've got to look after all the cruise passengers while they're in town or up country. This isn't Boston"—he looked at Stephan pointedly—"so, I just don't know what else I could do to help."

Gerald nodded. "Yes, I see what you're up against, but maybe you could circulate the photo I gave you among your men and let me know if anyone has seen her..."

"I can do that – no problem – but you said something about her daughter; will that little girl come with her, do you think?"

"That I don't know, Larson. All I know at the moment is that the woman in question may meet someone here to try and strike a deal in order to go after the treasure before our vessel reaches Banks Island."

"Ah-ah," Larson exclaimed, stretching to the back of his chair, "that's something I can help you with," and shaking an index finger at Gerald.

Stephan and Gerald exchange a smiling glance.

"Yeah, see, since we don't have any roads leading in or out of here, we can stop anyone taking one of the regular flights we've got landing here every day."

"But that's a lot of people to screen," Stephan suggested helpfully.

"Not as many as you'd think, Steph, and we carry out a check anyways – after nine-eleven we have to." Larson turned his gaze to Gerald. "So if you'd come up with a name or better a photo of the hired-hand, we'd be only too pleased to stop him (or her) before the person makes contact with our lady."

"Well, that's even better than anything I could have expected," Gerald said. "And as soon as I have some intel to forward, I'll transmit the data to you."

* * * *

The Contessa was abuzz with activities that evening. Everyone was aware that the famous soprano, Kerry Konawa, had flown into Juneau that morning and was due to sing tonight for the exclusive passenger audience aboard the vessel.

When Tiffany entered Alan's cabin for a brief respite before the show was due to begin, he didn't say a word and just handed her a note.

Tiffany's eyes grew wide when she read it.

> TEN
>
> AND THEN
>
> THERE
>
> WERE
>
> EIGHT

"Good Lord, where did you find it?"

"Just as I did the previous one – pinned on my pillow when I came in to change a half-an-hour ago."

"But what do they mean?" she asked, sitting beside him on the bed.

"Honestly, I don't know anymore," Alan replied, obviously at a loss to find an answer to the riddle. "You see, when I first talked to the two archeologists, they told me that there were ten items 'of importance' – as they put it – aboard the *Investigator*, so I immediately assumed that the number mentioned on the note pertained to the number of relics recovered or to be recovered from the wreck. But I guess I was wrong," he added ruefully.

"Listen, I think you should put it down to a prank of some kind. We've got enough on our plate as it is to worry about some idiot who writes riddles and pins them on our doctor's pillow."

"I know what you're saying, Tiff, but this is not something I can or should ignore entirely. I'll mention it to Gerald and perhaps he could place a camera in this cabin and catch the perpetrator red-handed – if he or she comes in again with another note."

"Good idea." Tiffany cracked a smile. "As long as we know where it is and we turn it off, you know, when..."

Although in no mood for laughter, Alan chuckled. "Yeah... I think one of our, shall we say amorous embraces, would be a bit too much for our Chief of security to watch."

Tiffany's smiling eyes soon drew a concerned frown across her brow. "And I suppose you know Babette is none too pleased with Gerald at the moment?" Alan nodded and looked down to his lap, taking one of Tiffany's hands in his. "When I talked to her backstage, she was really worried about Elizabeth Bornstein..."

"Yes, I know she is, Tiff, but I'm more worried about that mother of hers..."

"How's that?"

"Well, you know I've told you that she is an alcoholic and that she's now determined to put her hands on the McClure's treasure..."

"So you said, yes. But isn't Gerald taking care of that situation?"

"Yes, apparently he was going to plant some surveillance devices in the

Bornstein's cabin this afternoon and Stephan and he were going to the U.S. Marshall in Juneau to have her followed, if need be. But all that is not going to protect Elizabeth from harm if she gets in the way of her mother's delusional activities which is way too easy to happen with a chronic alcoholic."

CHAPTER NINETEEN

No worse for wear

IF ANYONE IN THE MEDIA had had the privilege to hear the arias with which Kerri Konawa endowed her audience that night, there would have been nothing but raving reviews in the papers and over the airwaves the next morning.

"She was absolutely splendid," Isaac Bornstein commented when he and Clarisse exited the theater. "I'm more of a jazz man myself, as you know, darling, but this woman stole my heart. She really did indeed."

"If you say so, dear," Clarisse rejoined, hanging on the arm of her husband to prevent her legs from wobbling under her. "But now, I sure could use a drink," she declared, looking around her to see if the bar was still open. Unfortunately, the cocktail tables that had been installed before the intermission had now disappeared as if by magic. "Where did they go?" Clarisse asked, apparently bewildered at their vanishing act.

"Who's that, darling?" Isaac asked.

"The bar... where did it go? And where are all the people going?"

"To their cabins, I suppose," Isaac suggested helpfully, guiding his wife toward the elevators. "And there's plenty to drink in our suite – I'm sure you'll find the bottle you want in the liquor cabinet."

Clarisse looked up at him. "And will you have a night-cap with me...?"

Isaac shook his head. "I don't think I would want to be late for my next meeting, darling..."

"You mean you've got another meeting...? But this is the middle of the night," she blurted as they entered the elevator. "Is she pretty? Just tell me," she demanded, turning her gaze up to the man she now loathed.

"She is not a 'she' – it's a 'he' and no, he's not pretty."

The half-a-dozen people riding the elevator with the couple tittered and giggled quietly at Isaac's remark.

"Don't you start laughing at me," Clarisse exclaimed suddenly, raising her voice, her eyes traveling around the enclosed space. "Don't you see...? He's cheating on me? He's... he's having an affair aboard this damned ship and I can't divorce the beast..."

Gratefully the doors opened on the upper deck at the same moment, enabling the shame-filled passengers to exit without another glance at the woman.

Incapable to subdue Clarisse's ranting, Isaac grabbed his wife by the arm and literally dragged her hopping down the corridor in her high heels toward their suite. "You are nothing but a drunken bitch, you know that?" he said, his voice laced with all the rage he felt, pushing his wife indoors. As soon as the door closed on them, he grabbed her and started shaking her. "And now you're going to tell me where Elizabeth is!" He peered into her eyes. "Come on, what have you done with her?"

"Nothing…" Clarisse blurted between sobs, trying to shake herself off his gripping hands. "Let me go!" she screamed. "I've done nothing to or with your bloody brat."

"Oh no? And what's this I heard that she hadn't been to Bible class today, hey -- tell me that? And our steward hasn't seen her"—still firmly clamped in his grasp, Isaac led his wife toward the child's bedroom—"and tell me now, before I open this door that she's in bed, go on, tell me?"

Clarisse twisted and shook – to no avail. "Let go of me… you're hurting me."

"No, darling, I wouldn't dare hurt you or you'll probably grab something else to bash my head in, like you did the last time." Still panting with untold rage, and only letting go of Clarisse's one arm, he opened Elizabeth's bedroom door. The bed hadn't been touched and the room was eerily quiet. "As you can see, she's not here, and it is well past her bedtime," he said more quietly, as if his last hope of finding his daughter resting in her bed had been dashed.

Surprisingly, Clarisse burst out in loud laughter, which engendered an immediate reaction from her husband. He slapped her so hard that she stumbled backward and fell on her backside, hiccupping.

Striding decisively over her, Isaac made his way to the door and with a hand on the doorknob, he turned to his wife, saying, "I've got a meeting with the chief of security – and I hope for your sake they've found her!"

And with these words, Isaac marched out of the suite, slamming the door behind him.

Rubbing her bruised face, Clarisse got up and waddled down to the liquor cabinet. She opened it, brought out a bottle of gin and drank a long gulp of the clear liquid before stepping to the sofa and plopping her aching body onto it – bottle still in hand, now a glass in the other.

A few minutes later, Isaac was sitting across from Gerald in his office. The business tycoon's masterfully studied demeanor had all but abandoned him.

"Where was she?" was Isaac's first question.

"In a linen closet," Gerald replied. "She had been bound and gagged and it's only by chance that we found her when I questioned one of the stewards on your deck. The man had noticed something moving behind one of the shelves but paid no mind to it at the time, since he was already late for his rounds."

"And how long do you think she had been in there?" Isaac asked.

"She told me that her mother had locked her in there in the early morning sometime – but she didn't know the exact time."

"I see," said Isaac, lowering his gaze to his lap. "And you said that she's now in Ms. Babette's cabin…?"

"Yes, Ms. Babette was worried about her since she hadn't shown up at Bible class, as I told you on the phone this evening, and since we didn't think appropriate to leave her alone anywhere after her ordeal, after the Doctor checked her over, Ms. Babette offered to take her in."

"That's very nice of the lady, I must say," Isaac said, obviously grateful not only to Babette for her compassion and care, but to Gerald for finding his daughter unharmed. "Do you think I would disturb her if I went to fetch Elizabeth at this hour?"

"I think it would be best if she remained with Ms. Babette until we can sort this out."

Isaac frowned. "What else is there to sort out, Chief? Is there something else I should know?"

Gerald nodded. "I'm afraid so, sir." He looked down at an opened folder on his desk. "We discovered a couple of days ago that your wife had tried to persuade your divers to directly bring the McClure's treasure to her, once it would be raised to the surface..."

"Is this a joke?" Isaac expostulated, getting visibly angry.

"I'm afraid not. Now, calm down, sir." Gerald waved a hand in front of his face. "Your wife's attempt at blackmailing them failed. Thanks to the divers' integrity, as soon as they realized that something was amiss with Mrs. Bornstein, they came to me with the story. After that, I got the okay from Captain Middleton to place some surveillance devices in your living room and den – and more importantly, I tapped your wife's computer in view of intercepting any message she could have sent to some treasure hunter off the ship..."

"Hold it right there, Chief," Isaac blurted. "What about my business; some of the communications I have with my company are totally confidential..."

"I can assure you that none of your business dealings are of any interest to anyone in this office. We only want to apprehend a criminal and prevent the theft of one of Canada's treasures."

Seemingly reassured that Gerald had not prodded into his affairs unduly, Isaac asked, "And have you obtained any communication of value – something that could inculpate that wife of mine or her contact yet?"

"Nothing so far, sir, but it's only been a few hours since we've started monitoring her communications."

Isaac got up. "Alright, Chief, as long as we keep Elizabeth away from this affair, I'll be okay with what ever you decide to do."

"What would you intend to do with Mrs. Bornstein, if I might ask," Gerald queried, lifting his gaze to the man facing him.

"I intend to send her back to Boston in the morning, Chief. And once she gets there, I'll have my lawyers serve her with divorce papers." He paused, took a handkerchief out of his trousers' pocket and wiped his brow. "And since she's seen fit to molest our daughter, I'll make sure she has no further contact with her."

Seeing that Isaac's face was turning ashen by the moment, and that his hands were trembling, Gerald said, "Why don't you sit down for a few more minutes, sir. It's been a long..." He couldn't finish his sentence when he saw Isaac Bornstein collapse in the chair and grab his chest, in the throes of a probable heart attack.

Throwing some ice water on him from the open bottle on his desk, and grabbing the phone, Gerald dialed Alan's emergency number.

Having attended the second part of this evening's delightful entertainment, Alan and Tiffany had retired to his cabin for what promised to be an even more pleasant interlude before his beautiful lady would return to her own cabin. Alan was in the middle of taking a shower when he heard his phone blare him out of his daydream. "Oh shit," he cursed, "what now?" However annoyed he might have been, the ring-tone told him that he needed to hurry – this was no ordinary call, but a real emergency.

Tiffany had heard the insistent and strident ringing too, and was already re-dressed and waiting for Alan as soon as he came out of the bathroom.

"What is it?" she asked.

"It's Gerald. He's got an emergency in his office." He stepped to her and kissed her.

"...Phone me when you're back," Tiffany suggested, disentangling herself from his embrace. "Okay?"

"I don't want to wake you up, but I'll text you if I'm late coming back."

When they left Alan's cabin, Tiffany made a beeline for the aft elevators while Alan hurried in the opposite direction toward the front of the ship.

As soon as he reached Gerald's office, he pushed the door open – without knocking – and noticed Isaac Bornstein slumped helplessly in the chair, his breathing irregular and labored, and the pallid color of his face.

"When did this happen?" Alan queried, already taking the big man down from the chair and laying him on the floor with Gerald's help.

"Just before I phoned your number," he replied. "Will he be okay, do you think?"

The question engendered a frown on Alan's face. "Would you mind calling Angie – she's on duty tonight – and have her bring the emergency cardiac kit?"

Gerald didn't reply and was already relaying the message to Alan's nurse by the time he had finished examining his patient. He put a nitro-glycerin tablet under his tongue when he saw that Mr. Bornstein was becoming more alert.

"It's my chest, Doctor," Isaac groaned, "It's like somebody's sitting on it."

"Just try to relax, Mr. Bornstein, I'll get you some oxygen and other medicine as soon as Angie gets here." Alan kept checking his heart sounds and rate, while he asked, "Have you experienced chest pains before?"

"No, not really, I have had twinges. That's all – but nothing like this."

"How's the pain now?"

"Bearable," Isaac answered.

"Okay, we'll get you down to the medical center where I'll keep you under observation tonight. After that, we'll decide on the next step."

"I'll... I have to get ... back ... to the cabin, Doc.... Clarisse, I... I don't know..."

"Not now, Mr. Bornstein," Alan urged, "we'll talk when you're stabilized, okay?"

An hour later Isaac Bornstein was still lying in one of the emergency beds of the center, apparatuses to monitor his heart rate, blood pressure, oxygen saturation, etc., were hooked to various parts of his body. He seemed more relaxed and certainly breathing more easily.

Alan came to sit down at his bedside, his stethoscope still wrapped around his neck. "Okay, now tell me what happened tonight to land you in this bed?"

Once Isaac had recounted the incident preceding his heart attack, Alan realized that, as he had predicted, Clarisse was showing all signs of delirium and was becoming extremely dangerous. He was glad for Babette's assistance in taking Elizabeth under her care for now, but that was not a duty she should have to assume as a passenger for any length of time.

"Thanks for speaking to me frankly, Mr. Bornstein. In the morning, Security and I will have to take measures to send your wife to a specialized hospital in Boston. I can make arrangements for you to be admitted to a hospital in Juneau for your recovery, or if the testing you will have done at the hospital is okay, we can address your care here on the ship. Your choice. As for Elizabeth, if you do stay aboard when you're back on your feet – which I don't think will take any more than a few days – she could rejoin you in your cabin and remain under your care for the rest of the trip. That is, of course, if you wish to continue the cruise with us."

"Yes, Doc, I would like that very much. And I don't think my returning to Boston would bring me any more peace of mind." He smiled. "Besides, I want to see that treasure brought back to the surface… if it even exists."

"Okay then," Alan said, getting to his feet. "I'll leave you in Angie's care tonight and I'll be back in the morning with the orders for the hospital tests."

Isaac Bornstein cracked another smile, visibly relieved that he was in good hands.

CHAPTER TWENTY

A thief

WORRIED THAT MRS. BORNSTEIN would try to attempt suicide or commit some other crime that could tarnish the cruise line's reputation or disturb other passengers unduly; Gerald decided to pay Clarisse a visit. Using the steward's master key-card, he and another member of his team entered the Bornstein's suite to find the woman snoring on the sofa – the empty bottle of gin lying on the floor beside her.

"Okay, Neil, let's get her out of here, shall we?" Gerald suggested, looking at his companion.

Neil was a hunk of a young fellow with muscles bulging all over the place, but that intelligent face of his told anyone looking at him that he had a good head on his shoulders. "Where to?" he asked, having already lifted the woman in his arms.

"Let's put her in one of the lower deck cabins, so we don't lose her before her transfer flight back to Boston."

"She'll fight tooth and nails when she wakes up, though, and ruin the cabin. How about putting her in the brig?" Neil said quietly, "No one likes to be sent packing or find themselves somewhere new after a bender..."

"I know, but this woman has kidnapped her own kid, locked her in a closet and drank herself into oblivion; so I think she's going to get what she deserves. After that... if it were me, I'd send her to a detox center. But, with her husband, I think she'll be in for a rapid divorce experience."

Once Clarisse was resting comfortably on the bunk of one of the inside cabins near the security center, and locked in, Gerald decided to get a few hours' rest before he would accompany Mrs. Bornstein to the airport in Juneau. However, it wasn't long before Neil phoned him to say that Clarisse's computer had just received an email from a guy going by the name of Cecil Legato – a renowned thief and treasure hunter. This Cecil hadn't given his name but Neil had traced the IP address back to him.

"And what did Cecil have to say?" Gerald asked, annoyed at the interruption. He was just about to fall asleep.

Neil replied, "He says that he'll be landing in Juneau at 1500 hours tomorrow and expects to see her in the arrivals' lounge."

"Okay, just send him a reply saying that you'll be there to meet him and to describe himself and what he will be wearing," Gerald said. "And once you've done that, send a message to Larson, the U.S. Marshall, with intel on this Cecil Legato and tell him we'll be there also to meet the guy as he deplanes."

"Okay, will do, Chief," Neil replied, hanging up shortly afterward.

Getting in at 3:00 pm will give us time to set the stage for him, Gerald thought as he nodded off to sleep again.

When Alan reached the medical center in the morning, he found a middle-aged man waiting for him in the anteroom, and Evelyn working at her desk. She didn't lift her head when the doc approached the man.

"My name is Doctor Mayhew, can I help you, sir," he asked as the man stood up, throwing a curious gaze in Evelyn's direction.

"I hope so, Doctor," he replied, looking up at Alan and extending his right hand to shake. "I'm Sir Reginald Faulkner, and I am really sorry to trouble you, but, on the other hand, I think it is quite imperative for me to get an answer to my dilemma."

Alan shook the man's hand and said, "We can talk in my office if you like," seeing that Sir Reginald looked positively embarrassed by whatever was ailing him. He extended an arm in that direction and shot a quick glance to his nurse – she still hadn't lifted her head from her paperwork.

"Yes, yes, that would be much better indeed," Sir Reginald replied, preceding Alan into his office.

When both men were sitting down, Alan asked, "So, tell me what's troubling you, Sir Reginald? You seem in perfect health, judging from all outward appearances."

"Yes, yes, and so I thought, until last night that is," Sir Reginald said quietly. He was a man probably in his fifties with a splendid head of white hair and a complexion that only accentuated the deep blue of his peering eyes.

"What happened last night then?"

"Well..." He hesitated. "I don't know how to explain this, but, you see... Helen and I have been married for twenty-five years, and I can't recall such a thing ever happening to me...."

"Did you have some difficulty...?"

"No-no, Doctor, nothing of the kind, it's just that when... I mean, when..."

"Alright," Alan cut-in since he noticed that Sir Reginald was becoming more embarrassed by the minute. "Do you want me to carry out a private examination?"

"I don't think that would be necessary, I'll just have to say it, won't I?"

"Is it your wife? Does she have a problem?"

"Again, no, I mean yes – oh, I don't know, it's only that she told me that my... my penis tasted funny...!"

Alan pinched his lips, trying to prevent a loud chuckle from escaping his mouth. "Alright, Sir Reginald," he said after he had regained some of his composure, "you may have an infection of sorts, and I would need to take a swab before I could confirm what we're dealing with here."

Once Sir Reginald had left the medical center, Alan went to Evelyn's desk and she looked up at him. He noticed that she had been crying.

"What's the matter, Evie? What happened?"

"*Of all the nerve,*" she exploded, literally jumping off her seat to face Alan, "I still don't know who he is or what he's told you, but the guy is offensive!"

"And why would that be?" Alan took a couple of steps back.

"He came in here, barely talked to me, unzipped his trousers and wanted me to look at his... I mean... you know what I mean!"

Alan smiled.

"Don't you dare think this is funny! He's probably some kind of pervert – I don't want to have anything to do with he or his 'medical problem'." She took a tissue out of the box on her desk and wiped the tear that was menacing to course down her cheek again. "What did he want, anyway? I saw that you took him to one of the closed rooms... does he have a real problem?"

"Yes, he does, and I think he simply didn't know how to approach a woman with it but to come *right out with it*, but please process his chlamydia culture."

"OH, you're as bad as he is," Evelyn concluded, sitting down again and blowing her nose.

This was promising to be a very busy day. Alan had to meet with the Canadian Health Authority's rep later that morning, and get some of the lab technicians set up in the medical center's lab, and then, he wanted Angie and Evelyn to start with the preliminary physical examination process of the passengers that had put their names down for a visit of Banks Island. However, before all that, he wanted to pay Babette a visit. He wanted to thank her personally for taking care of Elizabeth and to tell her that the child would be able to return to her father's suite the next day. Isaac Bornstein had an angiogram in town that showed no major blockage and only minimal damage from the heart attack. The cardiologist on call said he was doing well and put him on meds that would regulate his cardio-vascular functions pretty well as long as he did some mild exercise, ate appropriately, decreased his alcohol intake to nil, and tried to relax – and no major stressful situations.

"How did this whole thing start?" Babette asked, once Alan had related what he knew of the events that had taken place the night before.

"I'd suspect that Clarisse heard Gerald and I mention the treasure when we were interviewing Isaac. After that, it snowballed into her thinking that she could grab the McClure's chest before we reached Banks Island and run away with it..."

"But that's preposterous, Alan. How could she even contemplate succeeding with that plan?"

"She's not a well woman, Babette, and her drinking has led her to delusional thinking, that she could do anything she wanted."

"The only good thing out of this ordeal is that Elizabeth won't have to be afraid of her anymore – the poor child was horrified at the mere mention of having to face her mother again."

"How is she doing, by the way?"

"She's fine now. I read some stories to her last night and she fell asleep quietly. And this morning early – too early for me, mind you – we went to the café on the upper deck and had some fresh croissants and chocolate milk." She paused with a thoughtful smile on her face. "I'm telling you, that little girl is very smart for her age."

"Where did you two go after that?" Alan was curious since he hadn't seen any sign of the child in the suite when he came in.

"Oh, it happened all at once. We met the von Weglans and Elizabeth took to Karen right away. So, the three of them went for a visit of Juneau..."

"But was Karen alright to do that? With her arthritis and her latest operation, you're sure she was okay?"

"Oh, you're such a worry wart, Alan," Babette said, giggling. "Karen will be just fine. She needed an outing like that. She's a strong woman and having a child beside her gives her renewed hope. You'll see I'm right when they come back."

"Well, all I could say is that you deserve a medal for all that you've done so far on this trip, Babette."

"Tut-tut, Alan, I will have none of that. Caring for a child, even for one night, is a blessing. So don't you come and thank me – just thank the Good Lord for his generosity."

Alan smiled and bowed his head. Babette was right; he needed to be grateful for his own blessings, for he had so many to be thankful for. He lifted his gaze to her. "Anyway, when they get back, will you let Elizabeth know that her dad would like to see her?"

"Sure, I'll do that; and now, you go on your way and leave me – I've got to get back to my writing...."

Without another word but with a broad grin on his face, Alan left Babette's suite.

* * * *

"Babette was right, wasn't she?" Tiffany remarked when she and Alan were finally alone and having a quiet lunch at the officers' mess.

"Yes she was, and I'm glad Gerald heeded her words, otherwise Elizabeth could have spent a whole night in that linen closet."

"And what's going to happen now? Are they going to catch that guy – I mean the treasure hunter that's supposed to come in this afternoon?"

"I hope so, otherwise, the U.S. Marshall can look forward to a manhunt before we leave Juneau."

"What happens if they don't catch him?" Tiffany asked, swirling her spaghettis around her fork with visible delight.

"Well, I don't know, but the good thing is that he could only escape by air or taking the ferry back to British Columbia. There are no roads out of here; they end after forty-five miles into the Alaskan mountains. And somehow I don't think anyone would relish climbing these mountains at anytime of the year."

"Are you going to be there when they arrest him?"

Alan ate some of his salad and after munching on a piece of bread, he replied, "I sure hope not. I've got enough to worry about as it is. I'm going to meet the rep from the health authority and take the three lab technicians on a tour of the ship before they settle themselves in the center." He finished his plate and looked up at his apparently hungry lady. "What about you? What are you doing?"

"Oh, I've got rehearsals with some of the cast for the next act of Babette's play and then I've got some Inuit Sunset Dance to organize for the last night in Juneau." She wiped her plate with the last piece of her bread roll. "So, yes, I've got enough to keep me busy, in case you were wondering."

Alan smiled. Once again he reflected on the fact that he was so 'blessed' to have Tiffany as his friend and companion. *She is even beautiful with tomato sauce dripping down her chin.*

CHAPTER TWENTY-ONE

The Red Dog Saloon

NEIL HAD BEEN RIGHT when he had said that Clarisse would fight tooth and nail when it came time to take her out of the cabin and escort her to the airport. Disheveled, obviously enraged and blabbering, she threw herself at Neil, fists pounding his chest, as soon as they opened the cabin door. "What's the big idea? You let me out of here"—she tried squeezing between Neil and Gerald through the doorway—"you've got no right to hold me in this hole." She took a breath and suddenly looked as if she was about to cry, but hollered instead, "My husband will have you in jail for abduction..." She resumed her pounding of Neil's chest while he held her by the upper arms and pushed her backward toward the bed.

Once inside the cabin and as soon as he had time to get a word edgewise, Gerald said, "Okay, Mrs. Bornstein, we're here to take you to the airport..."

"I'm not going anywhere, you bastard," Clarisse snapped. "You can't do anything like that to me..."

"Oh yes, we can and we will," Neil retorted, making sure the woman remained seated on the bed.

"What about my clothes?" she asked as if all of a sudden realizing that the two men meant every word. "I can't travel in this dress, now can I?" She tried getting up. Neil pushed her back down.

"No worries," Gerald said, the steward got your suitcase all packed and you'll get your coat when we get down to the pier."

"What about Isaac? Does he know what you're doing?"

"Oh yes, and I'm glad you ask, because we've received instructions from him – he sends his regards from the medical center, by the way."

That statement seemed to have knocked some sense into Clarisse. "What happened to him? Did you hurt him too? ...Because if you did, he deserved every bit of it." She touched her bruised cheek. "See what he did to me...? And that's not the first time either."

"Yes, we know all about the slap across your face, Mrs. Bornstein, but, if you recall, that was only because you locked your little girl in a closet..."

"I never did such a thing – where is she...? Have you kidnapped her too?"

"No, Mrs. Bornstein, we leave that sort of thing to you," Neil remarked, lifting the woman by the armpits. "And now, if you're ready to go without any fuss, I won't have to handcuff you and we'll get down to the pier."

"I can't go anywhere looking like this." She turned to look at herself in the mirror above the dresser. "I look like a drowned rat."

In fact, Mrs. Bornstein looked every bit as if she just gotten out of a sewer, but Gerald had no desire to let her go anywhere – not even to the bathroom – until the woman was at the airport and in the hands of the U.S. Marshall's female officer. In short, he didn't trust her.

Outside, the wind had picked up and some clouds were gathering overhead. Everything looked as if painted gray. *She'll look like a drowned rat all right, if the rain comes down soon*, Neil thought, and smiled. He had no compassion or understanding for a woman who treated a child the way Clarisse had treated Elizabeth. Drunk or not, to him, a woman shouldn't mistreat a child. The hand that held her by the arm tightened until he got the handcuffs on.

"You're hurting me." Clarisse yelled, throwing him an angry glance. "And if you think you've heard the last of this, you're in for a surprise. As soon as I get home, I'll file a complaint against this bloody cruise line – it's a disgrace to be treated like a criminal..."

"But, isn't it what you are, Mrs. Bornstein?" Gerald asked, turning his face to her while the three of them were walking down the back stairs.

"What on Earth are you talking about? I've done nothing wrong."

"Oh no? Then why did you tie and gag Elizabeth in that closet?" Neil queried. "And what about your emails to Cecil?"

"What about them?" Clarisse groaned and then suddenly stopped in the middle of the last flight of stairs. "How did you know about my messages? Did you bug my computer too, you miserable bastard?"

Neil didn't answer and pulled her down the rest of the way until they reached the gangway. Gerald preceded them onto the small platform and then moved her ahead of him into the arms of one of Larson's men.

"Everybody is in place at the airport," the young officer said, grabbing Clarisse by the arm in the same way as Neil had done.

"Okay, let's go then."

* * * *

Holding Elizabeth's hand tightly, Karen progressed slowly down the street looking up at some of the colorful buildings. "Aren't those nice," she asked Elizabeth.

"Yeah, they all look like doll houses. Can we go inside and visit?"

"Oh no, dear, these are private homes, but we could stop at the coffee shop if you like?"

"That'd be great," Elizabeth answered, looking up at Herbert.

He smiled and said, "It's getting a bit cold this afternoon. And maybe a hot cocoa is just what we need."

"Okay then, let's go," Karen rejoined, hurrying as much as she could on her fragile legs. Her bones had seemed as if made out of straw when she first started walking again after all the chemotherapy, radiation and hospitalization, but now, after months of physical therapy, she was on the mend. Although, she could look forward to another surgery in the not too distant future, she now knew what to expect and how to cope with the post-surgical time.

Inside the coffee shop, there were mostly locals having coffee, cakes, and other Alaskan sweets. There were also some of the passengers from *The Contessa* that had come for a visit of the town and surrounding areas.

"Can I have some cake too?" Elizabeth asked, looking at the display above the counter top with the eyes of a child looking at candy canes at Christmas.

"Sure," Karen said, throwing a glance at her husband who hadn't taken a seat yet. "Why don't you have some with me, Hon?"

"Alright then, and cocoa for everyone, right?"

"Yes, please," Elizabeth piped up gleefully.

There was no doubt the little girl was happy to keep the von Weglans company – and vice-versa.

* * * *

When the plane taxied toward the airport terminal, Larson, Gerald, Neil and two other fellows – were waiting to see if Cecil Legato would come down the gangway as expected.

The five men had taken a good look at the mug shot that Neil had passed around that day and were obviously searching for the face of a man resembling Cecil's. They also looked for anyone dressed the way Cecil had described in his email to Clarisse.

Once the thirty or so passengers had disembarked, Gerald and Larson exchanged a quizzical glance.

"Either he's been delayed somewhere, or we've missed something, because I could bet my bottom dollar the guy wasn't on this plane."

* * * *

Unaware of the events that had taken place that afternoon and too busy to divert his thoughts away from the tasks at hand, such as getting the three technicians settled, showing them around the lab with Angie and Evelyn's able assistance, Alan had decided to take a break from everything and to ask Tiffany if she would accompany him to Juneau for a bite to eat at the famous Red Dog Saloon. She had readily agreed – her day had been a long and stressful one as well – and they were now standing in front of the swinging doors of the saloon.

"You sure it's okay to go in there," she asked, looking up at the façade curiously.

"Yeah, I've been in there before and believe me it's rather fun to listen to the locals telling their stories."

"What if they don't allow me in?"

"Come on, Tiff, this is the twenty-first century and this saloon welcomes tourists of all kinds – white, red, black and even polka-dotted ones, I'm told."

Bursting into happy giggles, Tiffany took Alan's arm and they both walked in. The place was very colorful. It was as if the whole saloon had been plucked out of the nineteen century and planted on the corner of the street. From the sawdust covering the floor to the flag-draped ceiling, from the gun once owned by Wyatt Earp in its display case, to the walrus tusk and various other 'trophies' punctuating the walls, the place was similar to a haunt frequented by the cowboys of old.

As soon as they sat down at a table below a moose's head, a waitress came to their table and asked what they wanted. She was dressed in a costume of the era – her red hair pinned atop her head with a blue feather, and earrings dangling down her neck – she looked the part, no doubt of it.

"We'll have a bottle of your best red," Alan answered, a broad smile crossing his lips.

"Sure thing, Mister," the lady replied, "and what about some grub?"

Tiffany opened her eyes wide. *Grub? Is she for real?*

"How about some stewed beans and some bread," Alan said.

"Any meat with that?" the woman questioned.

"No, just the beans and the wine will be fine, thank you."

"Okay then, I'll be right back."

Tiffany and Alan smiled at each other while looking at the woman and ignoring for a moment the two men talking at a nearby table.

Their laughter soon attracted their attention and unwittingly they eavesdropped on their conversation.

"You know these Canadian and lower 49'r tourists are priceless," one of the fellows was saying, "I knew an American once who decided to write a book about famous churches around the world."

"Oh yeah, and did he find all of them?"

"That I don't know, but listen – this is quite a story." He paused, drank a swig of his beer and then began. "At the beginning, he bought a plane ticket and took a trip to Miami, thinking that he would start by working his way across North America from South to North. On his first day he was inside a church taking photographs when he noticed a golden telephone mounted on the wall with a sign that read "$10,000 per call (per llamada)". The American, he was intrigued, and he asked a priest, who was strolling by, what the telephone was used for.

"The priest said that it was a direct line to heaven and that for $10,000 you could talk to God. The American thanked the priest and went along his way. Next stop was in Atlanta. There, at a very large cathedral, he saw the same golden telephone with the same sign under it. He wondered if this was the same kind of telephone he saw in Miami. He asked a nun what its purpose was. She told him that it was a direct line to heaven and that for $10,000 he could talk to God.

"O.K., thank you," said the American. He then went to Indianapolis, Washington DC, Philadelphia, Boston, and New York. In every church he saw the same golden telephone with the same "$10,000 per call" sign under it.

"The American, upon leaving Vermont decided to travel up to Canada to see if Canadians had the same phone before returning to the US to cross west.

"He arrived in Canada, and again, in the first church he went into, there was the same golden telephone, but this time the sign under it read, "40 cents per call."

"The American was surprised so he asked the priest about the sign.

"Father, I've traveled up the eastern seaboard of America and I've seen this same golden telephone in many churches. I'm told that it is a direct line to Heaven, but in the US the price was $10,000 per call. Why is it so cheap here?"

"The priest smiled and said, "You're in Canada now, son – it's a local call"!"

Alan and Tiffany's loud laughter echoed those of the two fellows and soon many of the other patrons who had listened in were chuckling, too.

"That was a very good story," Alan ventured, addressing the man who had recounted the exploits of the author. "You should be on stage – really."

"Well, my good sir, I'll have you know I was in my young days," he said, grinning at the recollection. "The name is Tom, what's yours?" he asked extending a crippled hand to Alan.

"Doctor Mayhew"—he turned to Tiffany—"and this is Ms. Sylvan," he replied, shaking Tom's hand.

"Ah, you're the doc on one of them cruise ships then, are you?" Tom asked.

"Yeah, that's me." Alan paused. "When were you on the stage then?"

"Oh that'd be many years ago, Doc. But now, I'm enjoying life in this blessed place." He looked around him. "It's got everything the Good Lord has ever given to this world; sunshine in the long days of summer and the white-outs with the long nights of winter. What else could a good man want?"

"And good health, I see," Alan rejoined, averting his gaze from the man's tortured hands.

"That'd be the one thing He's taken from me, but I pay no mind to my aches these days, because I've got all the help I need from our local people, and I don't suffer anymore. And that'd be for ten years now. See?" He extended both hands toward Alan. "No more pain and no more ugly, swelling joints either, just the left over of what the doctors in Virginia couldn't fix."

Alan was interested now. This was extraordinary. Usually rheumatoid arthritis would progress without fail until the patient would lose total use of his limbs. Yet, in this case, he had indicated that the disease had been stopped in its tracks. He turned the man's hands over and then lifted his gaze to him. "Would it be possible for me to talk to the doctor who treated you?"

"He ain't no doctor, Doc. He's just an Inuit that lives in the mountains and has got medicines that he brews himself. And he ain't selling anything – it's just for us who live in these parts." He looked at his companion sitting across the table from him. "Sorry, this is Den"—he returned his attention to Alan—"he's also been to see the Inuit, haven't you, Den?"

"Nice to meet you, Doc," Den replied, looking up at Alan. "And yeah, I've gone to see him, but with me it was because I couldn't sleep. He cured that, but not with potions or anything like that. He's just taught me a few tricks and now I sleep like a baby."

"That's great," Alan said, "But you're sure, I couldn't talk to the man? I would love to learn from him and use some of his "tricks" on my patients too."

"Always glad to be of service, for sure, Doc, but I don't know where he lives, and I don't know that he'd come to town before you guys are ready to leave," Tom said, shaking his head.

"But we could ask Gloria to send a message to him, couldn't we?" Den suggested.

"That'd be an idea," said Tom, "And we could let you know if he'd come down to see you, if that'd be okay with you?"

"Absolutely! I'll come back anytime he's available – before tomorrow night though. That's when we're due to leave."

CHAPTER TWENTY-TWO

Just call me Long Life

AND THERE IT WAS – another note pinned on Alan's pillow. The riddler had struck again. This time the note advised Alan that "there were seven left" – "seven what?" he asked himself for the umpteen time.

Although it was already late into the night, Alan decided to call the security office to see if Gerald was still on duty. He was.

"What are you doing up so late?" was Alan's first question when Gerald picked up the phone.

"What about you? Aren't you supposed to be in bed too?" the Chief retorted, a lilt of amusement in his voice.

"Well, I was about to get there, when I saw another note pinned on my pillow – just like the first two…"

"Hold on, did you say the first *two*? Was there another one besides the one we discussed?"

"Yeah. I received the second one a couple of days ago and with my being busy with all sorts of things, I forgot to mention it."

"So, I assume this one mentioned only "seven left", if my abacus is correct," Gerald said jocularly.

"Exactly. But I still don't know what the seven things are and I wanted you to put some cameras in my cabin to catch this joker red-handed – unless you have some other ideas."

"No, I think getting a couple of cameras in your room sounds like the right thing to do, but we will only be able to enter your cabin tomorrow…"

"That's fine," Alan interrupted. "I don't think the guy will come back tonight anyway."

"But have you thought about privacy?" Gerald asked, smiling to himself since he was well aware of Alan's frequent little tosses under the covers with Tiffany.

"Well… if you show me where the cameras are and how to switch them off, I think that will do the trick."

"Okay, Doc, I'll get that organized in the morning for you, but for now, I'll have to bid you good night – I've got a seemingly endless ream of paperwork to go through before I'd be able to get out of here."

"But before you go, Gerald, one more question, how did it go with Mrs. Bornstein; is she on her way to Boston? I just wanted to know if I can get her husband back in his suite…."

"It went fine, she should be home by now, and yes, Isaac Bornstein can get back to his cabin. And before you ask, Elizabeth can join him in the morning too."

"Good. That's all I wanted to know…"

"Hold on a minute, I almost forgot to ask, have you seen our diving duo anywhere – or talked to them today?"

"No, why?" Alan replied. *That question doesn't sound good,* he thought. "It's just that we can't seem to locate them. I had a couple of questions for them regarding their dives and they've not answered their phones nor has anyone seen them all day."

"Maybe they're staying over in Juneau tying one on with some friends..."

"Somehow I don't think so. My gut tells me something's wrong."

"What exactly got you so uptight all of a sudden?"

"Well, to make a long story short, the guy that Mrs. Bornstein had supposedly hired to retrieve the treasure before we got to Banks Island didn't show up today at the airport..."

"You mean the guy was supposed to meet her in Juneau?"

"That's what his email implied, yes..."

"But that doesn't make sense, Gerald," Alan erupted over the line. "If the man was supposed to get down for a visit of the *Investigator* before we arrived, what would he be doing here, in Juneau?"

"Exactly my thoughts, Doc. But the fact still remains that I've got two passengers missing and no answers, and I don't know where our treasure hunter is at this minute, and that bugs me."

"Okay, let me talk to our archeologists in the morning and maybe they'll have some answers."

"If you don't mind doing that, it would help. I don't want to approach these two without good reasons – and I don't have any at this point."

* * * *

As expected, the next morning was populated with a slew of activities in the medical center – mostly passengers and crew who had been scheduled to have a physical. However, all this didn't stop Alan from going to his cabin with Gerald to see where his team had installed the two cameras and to learn how to switch them on and off. Both men were on their way back to their respective offices, when someone called to them from the other end of the deck.

"Chief, Chief!" the man yelled.

"Neil... what's going on?" Gerald asked when his man stopped in front of them, catching his breath.

"You better come to the lower deck, Chief."

"For what?"

"We've got a problem, sir..." Neil looked at Alan. "And I think you better come too, Doc."

"Hold on, boy, first you tell me what's going on and then we'll follow you..."

"Not here, Chief... please!"

"All right, but do you seriously think we should bother Dr. Mayhew with what ever you've discovered?"

Neil nodded emphatically. "I think so, yes."

More curious than worried, Alan said, "Okay, Neil, let's go then. But let me stop by the center to pick up my bag..."

"I don't think you'll need it," Neil said, almost whispering now. "The guy is beyond help."

That remark got the three men to the elevator without another word.

When they reached the cabin, which had been occupied by Mrs. Bornstein only 24 hours ago, they stopped in the doorway.

There, lying on the bed was the man Gerald and Neil knew as Cecil Legato.

"I'll be damned," Gerald exclaimed, "how the hell did he get here?"

"Who is he?" Alan asked, stepping inside the room cautiously. He was conscious of the fact that a forensic team would eventually need to examine this cabin and he didn't want to disturb or touch anything unduly.

"Let me introduce you to the late Cecil Legato," Gerald replied from the door, "former treasure hunter and precious pelts trader."

"Interesting," Alan remarked, bending over the dead man. "I am no expert in these matters but I think the man has been killed with an arrow through the neck."

"An arrow?" Gerald repeated, astonished. "You mean like in a bow and arrow type of thing?"

"Yes. Come and see for yourselves."

Both Neil and Gerald walked into the room as cautiously as Alan had done and bent over the corpse.

"All I can see is a blackened hole below his Adam's apple – how could you tell it's been made by an arrow?" Gerald queried, lifting his gaze to Alan.

"The shape of the hole is quite different than that made by any other weapon. You see"—he pointed to the wound—"there are two breached extensions on both sides of the entry hole, which is typical of an arrow penetrating skin tissues."

"Well, all I could say is that we've got a mess in our hands and more questions than we have answers at this point," Gerald concluded, shaking his head and stepping away from the side of the bed. "Could you give us a time of death, though?" he asked.

Alan touched the victim's wrist, lifted it and said, "I'd say he died in the last 12 hours – rigor mortis hasn't set in yet – I could be more precise once I'll have examined the body for temperature and other vital signs."

"Okay then," Gerald said decisively, "You do what ever you need doing here while Neil and I go back to the office and get an investigation started." He turned to Neil who had been silent throughout the other two men's conversation. "And how did you come about the man?"

"It's the steward who came in to clean the cabin this morning who phoned me while you were out with Dr. Mayhew. When I came down and saw what was happening, I got the steward to stay in another cabin before he talked to anyone and came to get you."

"Good man. And where is that cabin?" Gerald asked.

"Two doors down, sir. Do you want me to get him?"

"No, not right now, and not until we've got the body out of here. I want this room sealed up as soon as you finished with our victim, Doc..."

"That won't take long," Alan answered. "I'll get my bag and get a transport gurney to move Mr. Legato to our morgue tonight."

Gerald nodded. "Yes, Neil and Travis will help you with that – you just tell us when, and we'll come down."

An hour later, Gerald was sitting in Alan's office. The latter had closed the door and lowered the blinds over the glass panels surrounding the room. He had often thought he would regret having an office with glass walls, but given the many situations that could eventuate in a medical center, Alan had wanted to keep an eye on things while maintaining a modicum of privacy when working at his desk.

"Okay, I've got an approximate time of death for you, Chief. Your Cecil Legato died yesterday evening between eleven and twelve o'clock. More precise than that I can't say."

"Well then it's a good thing we found him when we did, otherwise he'd be stiff as a rod by now, wouldn't he?"

"Absolutely, and Neil and I have already placed him on the gurney and into a preserving bag, ready for the morgue or whatever."

"Good. But now, what about this arrow business? Are you still contending that he was shot with a bow and arrow?"

"Not exactly. He was killed by an arrow alright, but not shot with a bow."

"You mean somebody planted an arrow through the guy's neck? Could it have been while he was asleep?"

"Yes, that's what I think happened. Although, I'd say he would need to have been drugged or restrained somehow beforehand, because, as you saw, he was a big man, physically fit, and even if he was sound asleep, the mere approach of someone near his bed would have alerted him – he was a hunter of some sort, remember – and he would have put up some form of resistance before being killed."

"Could you determine if he did?" Gerald asked.

"Once rigor mortis has come and gone, I'll have a look for any sign of restraints, or if the man fought before he was finally killed."

"Could he have been poisoned, you think?"

Alan nodded, crossing one leg over one knee and lacing the fingers of both hands behind his head. "Yes, that's another possibility. I can get several drug samples including a tissue sample and see if there are signs of any poisons having been administered before death."

"Do you think we should look for that arrow?"

Alan shook his head, unfolding his legs and placing his forearms on the desk. "You could look for it, but I bet money that it's at the bottom of the ocean right now."

"You know, Doc, it seems that every thread I pull out of that skein, doesn't lead me anywhere, but to more tangled wool."

"I think you need to find our divers and ask them some of the hard questions. These two seemed very aloof and a bit too carefree for my liking. I don't know if it's the kind of business they run or because it's in their nature to shrug off everything as if it was inconsequential, but to me, that's a sign of irresponsible behavior." Gerald nodded. "On the other hand if they were into some sort of competition to get at the McClure's treasure, they have the lead at this juncture and would have no reason to kill the competition."

"Yes, but if we look at this thing from a different angle, then these two would have every reason of getting rid of the competition."

"Yes but, they have the backing of one of the most respectable business men around? Why would they? No, Gerald, somehow I think our divers are game players but not killers."

"I just hope you're right, Doc. And I wish I could find them before this thing gets too complicated."

Once the corpse had been stored in the medical center's morgue, Alan returned to the mounting paperwork on his desk and was engrossed in the task at hand until a phone call from Gerald disturbed him again.

"What's up, Chief?"

"Sorry, Doc, I know you're busy, but I've got our two divers down on the pier wanting to bring someone aboard. Apparently the old guy wants to talk to you..."

"Hold on, Gerald, are you saying the divers came back to the ship and they're bringing someone with them?"

"Yeah, that's what I said..."

"Okay, stay right where you are – I'll be down to meet you in a few minutes," Alan told him, ready to hang up – but not before Gerald shouted over the line.

"But, Doc... Doc?"

"What?"

"Do you know this old guy?"

"Just hang in there – I'll be right down."

"Okay, okay. I'll wait."

A few minutes later Alan was making his way down the gangway when he saw an old fellow, watching him with a broad smile across his face. Standing on either side of him were Sam and Edward, the two divers, and Gerald, looking thoroughly confused.

"Sorry, Doc," said Sam as soon as Alan was in earshot, "but we met this man"—he turned to the old guy—"on our way down from a hiking trip up the local mountain, and he told us you wanted to see him."

"Yes, I did, Sam," Alan answered, "I sure did." He smiled at the old man. "Please, sir, do you want to come up?"

"Oh no, Doctor, I do not want to be a bother. It's just that Tom told me that you wanted to hear about my potions..."

Gerald was impatient as ever. "Okay, Doc, let's have it; what's this all about?"

"This is a local medicine man, Gerald, a man who should be treated with the highest respect." Alan took the man's extended hand in both of his. "May I know your name, sir?"

"Just call me "Long Life", Doctor." He looked at Gerald. "I am very sorry for the disturbance, Officer, but I just came with these two young fellows – they showed me the way..."

"Alright, Mr. Long Life," Gerald cut-in, "if it's only the doc you wanted to see, we can bend the rules a bit and let you board without the customary 48 hours notice if you like. Please give the officer at the gangway any government issued ID to photocopy, and we'll leave you with the Doc. You will need to be off the ship by 10:00 PM, enjoy a nice meal-I hear we have fresh salmon tonight in the crew mess. " He nodded to Sam and Edward. "Let's go, guys, I've got a few questions for you two now that you've come home."

And with these words, the three men made their way up the gangway, Sam and Edward saying, "See you later, Doc."

"Would you like to come aboard or go somewhere else to talk," Alan asked Long Life.

"Yes, I think we will go to the forest, and I will show you a few of the plants that I believe may help you in your search for answers."

"Lead the way," Alan replied, falling in step with the old Inuit. This man was perhaps in his late fifties but his skin was as smooth as silk and his movements agile. He had the presence of one in communion with nature. His long, black hair partly covered the collar and shoulders of his leather jacket, while surrounding a gentle face with penetrating and intelligent eyes. Alan had always been attracted to people who befriended nature or who made an effort to learn from it, but Long Life seemed to have a more mysterious or more "ancient" knowledge solidly lodged in that mind of his.

Alan was keen as ever to learn from Long Life everything he could in the short time they would be together. In fact, at that moment, he wished he could stay in Juneau for days, weeks or months – how ever long it would take for Long Life to teach him what he wanted to know.

CHAPTER TWENTY-THREE

How did he get onboard?

IF THERE WAS ONE QUESTION that encumbered Gerald's mind and came at the forefront of all others right then, it was the one regarding Cecil Legato getting aboard *The Contessa* without anyone noticing him. For a non-passenger or registered crew, to board a cruise ship was not generally a simple matter of walking up the gangway and making your way to whatever was your destination; it required showing the officer on duty – day or night – that you were a passenger with an entry card, or a crew member returning to your assigned post with a scan coded crew card updated daily. Therefore, Cecil must have posed as a passenger or a crewmember and had somehow obtained a false ID pass with his picture on it to enable him to gain access to the ship. Gerald was still tossing the possibilities about his tired brain when Sam and Edward came back to the office for a debriefing and interview. Gerald had trusted these two since the day they alerted him of Mrs. Bornstein's deceitful plan, but now there was the little matter of a murder having occurred aboard *The Contessa*, which was clouding his thoughts and changing his manners towards the divers and everyone else on his list of suspects.

"Okay, Sam, Edward, I'll put it as delicately as I can," Gerald began, "and give it to you straight: this man"—he put Cecil Legato's picture in front of them—"was found dead in one of the lower cabins of this ship. Do you know him?"

Sam and Edward exchanged a querying glance before Edward answered, "I've never seen him before, Chief." He turned his face to his companion. "What about you, have you ever seen him?"

Sam shook his head. "No, I can't say that I do, no. Who is he?"

"Well, guys, that man was a treasure hunter and a fur trader, known to the British MI5 and Interpol as Cecil Legato."

"Was he a passenger?" Edward asked.

"Not by any description, no," Gerald answered. "Yet, he was found in a cabin and until we know a lot more about him, we can't determine if he was really a passenger in disguise, or maybe he was a stow-away…"

"But isn't that a practical impossibility given the level of security you've got on this ship?" Edward suggested.

"You would think so, yes. But there are a few ways you could pass as a passenger on this ship – the simplest being in buying a passage and climbing aboard at whatever your port of departure."

"Did he have aliases?" Sam asked.

"Probably did, and that's another question Interpol or MI5 will be able to answer – I'm hoping they will anyway," Gerald said, shaking his head. He took a deep breath. "But that's not really of your concern right now. In fact the reason I wanted to have a chat with you guys is to clear up a few details regarding your activities in and around Juneau yesterday and today."

Again Edward and Sam exchanged a glance.

"What do you want to know, Chief?" Sam asked.

"Well, first, I'd like you to tell me where you were, then I'd like to know why you didn't answer your phones – either of you – and last but not least, I want to know where you were between 11 and 12 o'clock last night."

"Okay, Chief," Sam began, "this may sound a little strange to you, but after we told you what happened with Mrs. Bornstein, Edward and I decided to stay away from the ship for as long as she was in Juneau aboard the ship."

"And why was that? Were you maybe afraid of what the woman might do to you when she'd learned that you ratted on her?"

"Yes, that about sums it up," Edward answered. "You see, Chief, that woman was an alcoholic at the best of times and delusional most of the time. We had pegged her as unstable the first time we met with her and her husband in London. And neither of us wanted to find ourselves with a bullet through the skull. This was especially after she tried to blackmail Sam into that thieving scheme of hers."

"Well, if you had stayed in touch, you would have learned that Mrs. Bornstein is now out of reach – back in Boston as it is – and that she won't be harming any one around here anyway."

"And how did that happen?" Edward inquired, wide-eyed.

"After tying and gagging her daughter and shoving her in a closet, it was the only thing her husband could do from his hospital bed…"

"Hospital bed…? What are you saying, Chief?"

"I'm saying that your benefactor had a mild heart attack when he learned what his wife had done to his daughter and then instructed us to send her packing."

"Good Lord," Edward blurted, putting a hand to his mouth, "Is he going to be alright?"

"Oh yes, thanks to Dr. Mayhew he'll be going back to his cabin today."

Both men looked down to their laps, visibly embarrassed now.

"Alright then," Gerald resumed, nodding, "let's get back to my last question; why didn't you answer my calls today?"

"Probably because we were out of range around Mount Roberts, Chief," Sam said.

"Yes, but that doesn't tell me why you didn't return my calls as soon as you got back in range from where ever you went – so why didn't you?"

"After you saw us with the old guy this afternoon was the first time we looked at our phones…"

"Okay, so you were gallivanting through the forest with that medicine man"—Edward and Sam smiled when they heard Gerald describe their outing as 'gallivanting through the forest'—"for two days, is that it?"

"Not the two whole days, no, Chief," Edward said, looking at Sam a little sheepishly.

"What we mean is that we were alone, I mean together in the beautiful peace and quiet of the forest, for the whole of yesterday and only met the man on our way down from Mount Roberts. He wanted to come with us to the ship to meet the Doc, as you know."

"Alright, that clears up a few things for me, but tell me something else now; has either of you ever used a bow and arrow?"

That got Gerald a chuckle out of both divers. "No, Chief, we're not into that sport at all, not our cup of tea. But, we've got a friend on one of the rigs who uses an arbalest in competition..." Sam stopped, seeing the question mark painted on Gerald's face. "Sorry, Chief, you probably call the weapon a crossbow, which in England is slightly different than the arbalest, but does the same thing; it can reach a target precisely at 300 yards."

"Okay. And would this friend of yours ever use an arrow as a weapon without his crossbow?"

"Not that I know of, Chief, because those things cost a fortune and he stores his arbalest under lock-and-key and I've never seen him using an arrow without the weapon – why do you ask?"

"Well, I've got a problem," Gerald said, relaxing now, "Dr. Mayhew has determined that our guy has been killed using an arrow and piercing the fellow's neck with it. So, when you tell me that these archers don't like to use their arrows without the weapon, I am beginning to wonder where that arrow came from."

"But, Chief, wouldn't it have been simpler to use a knife if the murderer didn't want to use a gun?" Edward queried.

"Exactly. What I think is this; who ever pierced Mr. Legato's neck wanted to make it a symbolic gesture. Since our victim was a fur trader, maybe his killer decided to inflict the same sort of wound as a hunter would on an animal."

The three men fell silent. Gerald's latest conjecture easily added another dimension to Cecil Legato's murder. Perhaps someone other than a very exclusive circle of treasure hunters had been after his head.

Food for thought, Gerald concluded to himself.

"Okay, guys, thanks for coming in," the chief said, getting to his feet, "but the next time you decide to take time off from this expedition, and given the latest events, I'd like you to let me know, if you don't mind."

Both men nodded and rose from their seats; Sam saying, "If you needed to talk to our friend about that arbalest, let me know, and I'll give you his email address."

"I don't think that will be necessary, but if I do, I'll let you know. Thanks."

While Gerald was carrying on with his various interviews, Alan had returned from his extended walk with Long Life through the forest bordering the town. Now, Alan was in the middle of a physical exam – this one for a middle-aged woman passenger who wanted desperately to visit Banks Island. When Alan questioned her about the reason behind her desire to visit the island, she said, "I have been traveling all over the world,

Doctor, and Banks Island will be my last stop in the hope to find *a penis.*"

Alan stopped examining the lady and frowned, not sure if he should check his hearing or stifle a smile. He was sure he had heard the two words correctly, but wanted to find out for sure, given that Lady Archer had a distinct South Asian accent.

"And you're hoping to find it on Banks Island?"

"Yes, yes, you see, I have gone to many countries and I found some fun, some enjoyable, sometimes just a little, some full of colors, but not much giving me any satisfaction, no."

More puzzled than ever, Alan couldn't do anything but smile. *If she wants to find the right penis for her, who am I to question her intention,* he thought.

"Will you return to India after you found "the penis" you're looking for?" Alan queried as innocently as he could without cracking up.

Lady Archer burst into timid and embarrassed laughter, partly covering her mouth with a trembling hand. "Oh no, Doctor, I am sorry, my accent in English is terrible – I mean to say I have not found *happiness* – although I have found much *penises* along the way, you know," she whispered amid giggles so that no one but Alan could hear her.

* * * *

Still chuckling under his breath thinking of Lady Archer's quest, that evening Alan joined Tiffany on one of the open but protected upper decks for a short presentation of the Inuit Dance that the passengers were deemed to enjoy under a starlit, and cool sky. Everyone was clad in warm clothes, jackets or overcoats – the temperature having dipped considerably in the afternoon.

Much as many other cultures worldwide, the Inuit of the Arctic have used drums in some of their traditional music for centuries if not millennia. The Inuit drum dancing generally forms an integral part of family celebrations or the greeting of visitors to their communities, as such was the case tonight. The tambourine like drum made of caribou hide is stretched across a hoop, which is struck rhythmically with a sturdy stick on the one side and then, with a flip of the wrist, struck on the other.

Dressed in what could be described as black and brown cassocks and shod in leather boots adorned of fur tassels, the Inuit danced and "sang" to the delight and admiration of their audience. Although the meaning might have been lost on most of the passengers, the message the two men conveyed to the spectators was well received.

At the end of the presentation, and to Alan's surprise, he found Long Life talking to some of the drummers. He went to him with Tiffany.

"I am sorry to interrupt, Long Life," he said to the old man, when the latter turned to him, "but I'd like to introduce you to my lady friend, Ms. Tiffany Sylvan."

"Ah, my dear lady, what a pleasure it is to meet the lucky woman chosen by this man."

Tiffany didn't want to stare, but did. "Very pleased to meet you, Long Life. I haven't heard much about you yet, but I am sure I will after tonight."

"I hope you will, my dear, because your doctor has been a very good student when we traveled for a short time together and I am sure he will be able to impart some knowledge to you as well as I did."

"I am looking forward to it, sir, and I must thank you for coming with the dancers tonight – it was an unexpected pleasure to see you attend the celebration, I'm sure."

"Oh but I always come to greet our visitors – it is not often that I have the opportunity to do so, but when they are called upon I always come to make sure our spirits accompany them in their journey through the supreme spirit's land."

"I am sorry, but I must ask," Alan interposed, "where have you been schooled? Your English is impeccable."

Long Life burst in mild laughter. "I always try to hide the past, for I look onto the future with a happier heart, but since you have discovered my secret, I will tell you. I was educated at a Canadian university thanks to a very generous man who was in love with the North a long time ago."

"Well, I can see that his generosity hasn't been wasted, Long Life. And I hope you have benefited from your education in the same way as many people seemed to have benefited from yours since your days in school."

Throughout this complimentary exchange, Tiffany's eyes had not left Alan's face. She was discovering another part of the man she loved – she was sure – a trait of character that she would consider as an immeasurable treasure from now on. Alan was in love with life itself.

Drawn away from her daydream, Tiffany suddenly felt a hand on her shoulder. She spun on her heels to find herself face to face with Captain Middleton.

"Oh, I'm sorry, Ms. Sylvan, I didn't mean to startle you," the captain said, smiling at her, "but I wanted to congratulate you personally for this evening's interlude. It was very interesting and quite entertaining indeed."

"Thank you, Captain," Tiffany replied demurely, "but all the credit should go to the dancers and drummers – they were the perfect conclusion to our visit to Juneau, I thought."

"I couldn't agree more." He paused and looked in Alan's direction. The latter was still chatting with Long Life. "But tell me, who's this man Dr. Mayhew is talking to?"

Tiffany looked around and replied, "That's Long Life, sir. He's the medicine man around these parts and he took the doc on a short visit through the forest this afternoon to show him some of what the Inuit have been using as herbal medicine for centuries."

"How very interesting," the captain said, obviously genuinely interested. "I think I'll go and have a little chat with the man myself, perhaps he can tell me what I'm doing wrong when I can't fall asleep..."

"Why don't I introduce you, Captain," Tiffany cut-in politely, not interested in hearing anything more about the captain's sleep disorder."

"Hum, yes, why don't you do that, Ms. Sylvan – much appreciated."

A half-an-hour later when many of the passengers had returned to their suites or cabins, a group of young women attracted Tiffany and Alan's attention. They, too, were about to leave the deck when they stopped to eavesdrop on their conversation. The focus of their amused interest rested on a young woman dressed in designer jeans and a beautiful red leather jacket, giggling the night away it seemed. When she had turned her back to Alan and Tiffany, the two of them had noticed why her friends seemed to question the young woman about her gorgeous jacket. There was a sign pinned onto her back that said,

BEAUTIFUL, EXPENSIVE JACKET
I AM PROUD OF IT.
PLEASE ASK ME ABOUT IT.

"...I purchased it on line, and since it was the first time I bought something this expensive through one of the e-retailers, I didn't really know what to expect, but when I opened the package, I was so pleased with it.... Anyway, I am so happy that you guys noticed it..."

"We couldn't have missed it," another girl in the group remarked. "You just have to look at the back of it to know that it's expensive, and that you're very proud of it...!" She laughed along with her friends.

"Come on, take it off and let's see," one older woman suggested.

"Oh why not," the owner of the jacket said, taking it off. And as she was about to hand it to the woman, she burst out in laughter, realizing that someone had pinned a note on her back. "Who... who's the smart ass among you?" she asked still chuckling at the joke.

* * * *

A smile painted on both their faces, Alan and Tiffany then made their way quietly to the elevator. It had been a day they would not soon forget.

CHAPTER 24

The Northern Passage

"ALRIGHT GENTLEMEN," Captain Middleton began, "thanks for coming in this morning." He stood up and turned to the screen behind him and pointed to the map. "We're on our way to Kodiak Island now, which will be our last stop until we enter the Bering Strait and the Northern Passage. The weather promises to be cooperating for the next five days, so, I don't expect any surprises until we're actually treading the waters of the Arctic Ocean. Next stop will be Prudhoe Bay. Nothing much should happen after that stop because we'll be following the northern Alaskan and Canadian coasts until our next port of call – Tuktoyaktuk. This is where things will start to get interesting if not precarious. It's iceberg season after the early thawing and we will take our time while crossing to our next stop and the highlight of our voyage – Banks Island." He focused his gaze on Alan. "This is where Dr. Mayhew and his team will take the reins as far as the passengers' visit of the island village and museums are concerned."

The captain paused and was about to address the two archeologists when Sam Ashton asked, "Sorry, Captain, how many days will we stay on Banks Island?"

"I was coming to that, Mr. Ashton, but the answer is four days. I hope that will be sufficient time for you to dive with the submarine to the *Investigator* and complete your second dive to the wreck."

"Thank you, sir, that should do it," Sam replied, shooting a quick glance to Dr. Sullivan sitting to his right.

"What about you, Dr. Sullivan," the captain asked, "Will that be sufficient time to catalogue the artifacts left aboard the wreck?"

"Yes, that should be fine, Captain." He turned to Dr. Lespierre. "Do you see any problem in completing the work in four days?"

Lespierre shook his head. "No problem that I can see," he agreed, "but if we were to discover something complex aboard the wreck of any significance, I don't think we would have time – in four days – to raise it to the surface."

"Yes, of course," Middleton said, "that's the next point of consideration. But since this is a condo cruise ship and not a ship dedicated to raising relics out of the ocean, we will have to confer with Parks Canada's representatives once we arrive on Banks Island and perhaps then, you two gentlemen will have to stay behind with our divers to oversee the operation. We may have the ability to change the timing of our departure a bit, but that also depends on our corporate office."

The four men concerned with that venture nodded in unison,

knowing that further discussions on that topic could not be had at this time.

"Now then," the captain resumed, returning his gaze to the map, "Once we leave Banks Island, we will tackle the most difficult and perhaps the most dangerous part of our journey. The weather will be unpredictable all the way through to Cambridge Bay – our next stop. From there we'll start veering southward to Igloolit, our last port in the Arctic Ocean before we head to Cape Dorset and the Northern Atlantic Ocean." He turned away from the screen then, and returned to his seat. "And there you have it, gentlemen, that pretty well summarizes this voyage ahead of *The Contessa.*"

The men in the room fell silent for a moment until Stephan Ivanov stood up and turned to face the people that had been invited to attend. "Okay, all I have to say is that the whole crew – including the officers on board – will be entirely dedicated to their duties and to helping *The Contessa* tread these waters as carefully as possible, so that the passengers' journey will be one to remember for being one of the most daring and yet one of the most pleasant and interesting." He paused and looked at all the faces staring at him. "To that end, the officers will remain on watch 24 hours a day during the weeks that it will take to traverse the Arctic Ocean. When we reach the Bering Strait and enter the treacherous part of our voyage, most of the officers will be forgoing social functions, and will be available, of course, if there is an emergency. As you can understand our vigilance is of prime importance and the lack of it could cost the lives of more than four hundred people. So, if you have any questions regarding the operations on Banks Island – or any other of a technical nature – I would suggest asking them before we reach the Arctic waters."

"Sorry to interrupt," Edward piped up, "But what if we get stuck in the ice, what happens then?"

Stephan smiled and shook his head. "Well, Mr. Barrington, I shouldn't think that would happen, since we have an ice-breaker preceding us and we're constantly in touch with the various northern stations along the way in order for us to avoid most of the difficult passages."

"What about medivac evacuation? We do have a helipad for that sort of thing? Right?" Sam Ashton asked, "Just in case something goes wrong during the dive."

"Yes, we do, Mr. Ashton. And our medical center is very well equipped to handle first medical interventions should an accident occur." Stephan looked at Alan, who nodded. "If you like you could discuss the matter with Dr. Mayhew after this meeting – would that be okay, Doctor?"

"Sure, I can give you both a grand tour of the facility and discuss your concerns at length before we get to Banks Island."

"Okay, I think that concludes this part of the meeting, gentlemen," Stephan said. He turned his face to Middleton. "But I believe our Captain would like to have a further word with Dr. Mayhew and Chief Tolberg."

"Yes," the captain rejoined. "If you don't mind staying behind, gentlemen; this won't take long."

The two archeologists and the divers stood up, mumbling some words of thanks to the captain and left the office quietly.

Once the door was closed on the four men, Gerald and Alan returned their attention to the captain.

"Alright, Mr. Tolberg, I've read your report about this Mr. Cecil Legato, anything to add at this point?"

Gerald opened the folder on his lap and said, "Yes, Captain. This morning we were able to ascertain that Mr. Legato boarded the vessel as a passenger under the name of Denis Merchant upon arrival in Juneau."

"Good. So, the email to Mrs. Bornstein was some sort of diversion I suppose?"

"Yes, Captain, it looks that way. I now believe that the man probably wanted to meet Mrs. Bornstein at the airport. He was perhaps even there when he saw the US Marshall escorting her to her flight and hot footed it to the ship."

"Yes, yes, I would tend to agree with you," Middleton said. "But what about the actual murder; did the surveillance cameras reveal anything?"

"Only shadows, sir, although it was still daylight; the sunset had hardly gone down..."

"If I may interrupt here," Alan cut in, "I think I would like to revise my first assessment of the way the man died." Three pairs of eyes were riveted on the doc now. "You see when I first viewed the body I thought he had been killed in the bed where we found him. However, since we have now been able to ascertain that he had not been sedated prior to death, nor had he been restrained in any way, or fought against his aggressor, and since there was minimal traces of blood around the wound, I had to conclude that he had been killed somewhere else than in that cabin."

"Then why transport him in that room after his death?" the captain asked.

"I suppose the murderer wanted him to be found in Mrs. Bornstein's cabin for some reason," Alan replied.

"Maybe because he knew that the cabin would be opened the next morning and the body discovered then," Gerald suggested.

"Yes, but more to the point," Alan added, "The killer didn't want us to know where he had been murdered."

"Because the location was perhaps too close to where the murderer could be identified," Stephan put in.

"Exactly my thought," Alan agreed.

"So, what you're saying is that we should look at the surveillance tapes that are located near the people we suspect could be involved in this affair," Gerald concluded.

"Yes, I think that would be the next step, Mr. Tolberg," Middleton said. "And now, Dr. Mayhew, how are we doing with the physicals?"

"Well, while we were in Juneau, we concentrated on the officers and crew that remained aboard, and some of the passengers that have signed up to visit Banks. But the list is a long one..."

"A long one, did you say?" the captain interrupted, "but I thought only a few passengers had signed in, isn't that the case?"

"Yes, a few since Seattle but every day, another one or two have signed up."

"I see, and will we have enough protective suits for everyone?"

"Yes, because, I don't think we should allow everyone to disembark at once, Captain. And when it comes to passengers taking part in the submarine dive, I think there should be only four people allowed on board the sub apart from our archeologists and divers."

"And who are the four people that have requested to participate in the sub-dive?"

"Mr. Bornstein should be stable enough, I believe, to participate. Then I would recommend that Ms. Babette be allowed to take the trip along with Mr. and Mrs. von Weglan."

"Ms. Babette of course, I can only concur, but what about the von Weglans – why would you choose them?"

"It's a matter of providing the lady with an unforgettable journey after surviving a cancer and having not much else to look forward to except for another operation and chemo treatment once she's back in Boston. Anyway, I just thought it would give her a boost."

"Yes, of course, but will she be fit enough to make the trip?" the captain asked.

"I should think so, but if she isn't, I'll be the first one to take her off the list." Alan paused. "Besides which when it comes to the visit of the island, we will only authorize people who have passed the physical – which may yet reduce the number."

"Yes, of course, given the conditions on the island, I think it would be wise to have only a half a dozen people disembark at any one time." Middleton then stood up, indicating that the meeting was at an end. "Okay then, but let me know if there are any PR problems in that area – and I'll handle it myself."

"Thanks, Captain," Alan said, relieved to hear that Middleton would be talking to the people unable to visit Banks Island – he was in no way ready or looking forward to that sort of confrontation, especially with this group of passengers and or owners who were used to getting their own way with everything.

When Alan and Gerald left the captain's office, they were silent for a moment before Alan said, "You know, Gerald, that arrow pierced Legato's neck with such a force that it fractured both C4 and C5 vertebrae before coming out at the nape of his neck."

"So are you now saying he was shot with a bow and arrow?"

"Probably, but I would be in favor of a crossbow rather than the regular bow and arrow."

Looking up at the doctor, Gerald said, "You know that's very interesting, because when I interviewed our divers, Sam was quick to call my attention to the use of an arbalest as a weapon of choice in this instance."

"Yes, that's interesting, as you say," Alan rejoined, "Because with an arbalest you don't have to worry about wind interference as much as you do with a bow. The force of ejection is such that the arrow prevails against wind or motion – quite a weapon in fact, if you are trying to do someone in."

"Yes, that's what Sam Ashton said. He told me that his friend's arbalest cost a fortune and that he wouldn't likely spare an arrow for much of anything, which brings me to think that the weapon is still on board — these archers are apparently very attached to their crossbows."

"But this is a very cumbersome weapon," Alan remarked, "and not very easily disassembled I'm told. It's not like a gun that you can hide each piece separately in your luggage."

"I can imagine it'd be a problem, Doc, but most of these passengers have literally "moved in" when they bought their condos and an arbalest could have been hidden in one of their crates."

"Yes, maybe you're right. Anyway, when you have had a look at the tapes, let me know if anything pops up — I'll help you all I can."

"Okay, Doc, I'll probably take you up on that."

* * * *

When Alan got back to the medical center, an older fellow was waiting for him. The doc smiled and asked, "Are you here for your physical, sir?"

The well-dressed man stood up and returned the smile, extending a hand for Alan to shake. "Yes, Doctor, I am. The name is Rabbi Fienberg."

"Please to meet you, Rabbi," Alan replied shaking the man's hand. The latter had the allure of a jolly-good fellow. His sparkling eyes and ready smile inspired immediate confidence if not amity. "Please, come this way," Alan added, pointing to the examining room. "So, you're looking forward to visiting Banks Island, are you?"

Rabbi Fienberg began to undress as he replied, "Oh yes, but before that I am really looking forward to taking a gander at those bears on Kodiak Island. They told us that we'll be able to participate in a guided tour to view those beasts — very powerful and handsome they are, I've been told."

"I see," Alan replied, helping the Rabbi onto the examining table. "But you wouldn't want to face one of them alone, I suppose?"

"Ha-ha, ha-ha, ha-ha, no I wouldn't indeed, Doctor, not like that friend of mine who practically died at the paws of one of them."

"You mean your friend was attacked by a Kodiak bear?" Alan queried, curious to hear the story.

"Well, it was an ordeal he soon won't forget…"

"What happened?"

"Well, on that one day that those three were on Kodiak Island; there was a priest, a Pentecostal preacher, and my friend — also a Rabbi. They all served as chaplains to the students of the University of Montana who were on a field trip in Alaska at the time. They would get together two or three times a week for coffee and to talk shop.

"One day, someone made the comment that preaching to people isn't really all that hard. A real challenge would be to preach to a bear. One thing led to another and they decided to do an experiment. They would all go out into the woods, find a bear, preach to it, and attempt to convert it."

"Take a deep breath," Alan asked, still listening to the Rabbi's unbelievable story. "And another.…" When he flung his stethoscope around his neck, he then asked, "Did they go out and find themselves a

Kodiak then," humoring the man.

"Well yes they did. And seven days later they're all together to discuss the experience.

"Father Flannery, who had his arm in a sling, was on crutches, and had various bandages, went first. "Well," he said, "I went into the woods to find me a bear. And when I found him I began to read to him from the Catechism. "Well, that bear wanted nothing to do with me and began to slap me around. So I quickly grabbed my holy water, sprinkled him and, Holy God, he became as gentle as a lamb. He related that the bishop was coming out the following week to give him first communion and confirmation."

"Reverend Billy Bob spoke next. He was in a wheelchair, with an arm and both legs in casts, and an IV drip. In his best fire and brimstone oratory he claimed, "WELL brothers, you KNOW that we don't sprinkle! I went out and I FOUND me a bear. And then I began to read to my bear from God's HOLY WORD! But that bear wanted nothing to do with me. So I took HOLD of him and we began to wrestle. We wrestled down one hill, UP another and DOWN another until we came to a creek. So I quick DUNKED him and BAPTIZED his hairy soul. And just like you said, he became as gentle as a lamb. We spent the rest of the day praising The Lord."

"Then they both looked down at the rabbi, who was lying in a hospital bed. He was in a body cast and in traction with IV's and monitor wires running in and out of him. He was in a bad shape. The rabbi looked up and said, "Looking back on it, circumcision may not have been the best way to start."

"Well, Rabbi," Alan said between bursts of laughter, "all I could say is that if you have any desire of converting one of the Kodiaks, please DO NOT – even though we've got very comfortable beds around here where you could rest and recuperate from your encounter."

"Thanks, Doc, I'll keep that in mind – but I don't think I'll begin with a circumcision anyway."

CHAPTER TWENTY-FIVE

Very little to do with shipbuilding

TIRED AND RESTING HER HEAD on Alan's chest, Tiffany asked, "What about Yvette?"

"Where does that come from?" Alan said, lifting her face to him. They were both lying in bed after an evening filled with enjoying each other's bodies during a fervent interlude of lovemaking. "I thought we had gone over that story back in Washington…"

"Just the way you met her, but after that you never told me how you two spent time when you were on leave from your ship-building assignment."

Alan chuckled at the comparison – his overseeing the construction and assembly of the medical center aboard *The Contessa* had very little to do with actual shipbuilding. "Well," he began, shifting his position to look at his lovely lady, whose head now lay on the pillow next to his, "we didn't have much of a chance to get together – she was working and I was "on leave", as you call it, anytime I could, which wasn't regularly nor ever falling on a weekend. Yet, when we did, she was the one who showed me around the town, and once we drove to Paris where we stayed for a couple of days…"

"What do you mean 'stayed' in Paris?" Tiffany cut in, pushing herself up on her elbow, her eyes flaring with the fire of jealousy.

Alan smiled and shook his head. "She knew I was involved with you by that time, Tiff, and we 'stayed' in separate rooms – even on separate floors – and only played tourists for the best part of the day and a half that we were walking through the city." He tousled her hair and lowered his head to kiss her.

Returning the kiss, Tiffany plopped back onto her pillow. "Did you tell her about us then?"

"Yes, I thought it was important that she knew if we were to go anywhere together there wouldn't be any hanky panky between us."

"Why then – if this little adventure of yours was on the up and up – didn't you tell me anything about it when we were on Skype or on the phone?"

"Because, I didn't want to put ideas into your lovely head, and have you worry about me flirting with my old girlfriend – that's all."

"Ah-ah, you admit flirting with her then?" Tiffany snapped, turning her face to Alan, a teasing smile across her lips.

Laughing now, Alan swung his body over hers and covered her face with some more kisses, preventing her to utter another word.

An hour later Alan was back in his cabin lying on his bed wide awake, his thoughts drifting to the enigmatic riddler. Since the cameras had been installed, no one had entered his room and pinned another note on his pillow. *There must be a meaning to them,* he mused. *And what does he hope to accomplish by keeping me guessing?*

What were the ten items (or people) that had been or were to be eliminated one by one since their departure from Seattle? He couldn't think of any single item that had been eliminated from anywhere, and as for people, there were two that had now "been eliminated" from the ship – Clarisse was one and Cecil was the other. Yet, the dates at which these two "left" *The Contessa* were one day apart and had nothing to do with the dates at which each of the notes was left on his pillow.

Maybe the answer is in Agatha Christie's story, was Alan's last thought before he closed his eyes that night.

* * * *

The morning came far too early though, yet Alan woke up with renewed vigor and actually looking forward to some, if not all of his numerous tasks. As he was toweling himself dry after an invigorating shower in his tiny cabin stall, an idea popped into his head. *What about those items that had never been brought ashore on Banks – the relics that were left aboard the Investigator? There were ten of them, including McClure's chest, and now only seven left?*

He dressed quickly and decided to join Drs. Sullivan and Lespierre for breakfast on the upper deck. He knew these two were creatures of habit and had seen them having breakfast there on a couple of occasions.

When he reached the café, he was relieved to see that he had been right; the two men were involved in what seemed to be a heated lovers quarrel-discussion while partaking of a copious breakfast.

"Gentlemen," Alan said, as he approached their table, "would it be okay if I joined you? I've got a couple of questions for you."

Slightly startled, both men looked up and Sullivan nodded, wiping his mouth with his napkin. "By all means, have a seat, Doctor, we were just talking about our upcoming operation on Banks Island," he said, taking another bite of his toast, the jam oozing off the toast onto the tablecloth.

"Thank you," Alan said, taking a seat between the two men. "How are you, Dr. Lespierre – also looking forward to your return to Banks Island?"

"Hum, yes, Doctor," Lespierre answered after drinking a sip of his coffee. "In many ways we are, of course, but there are time constraints, you see, and I frankly don't think four days will be enough to accomplish everything we've set out to do."

"Are you concerned about bringing back some of the relics still on board the *Investigator?*"

"Yes, of course, but you see, one dive won't be sufficient I don't think to confirm what's left aboard the wreck."

"But before we go into those details," Sullivan interrupted, "perhaps we should let Doctor Mayhew tell us what brought him to our table this morning." He shot a reproachful glance at his colleague. "Go ahead, Doctor, what's on your mind?"

"Well, my concerns are not much different than yours, as it turns out. I was wondering if you perhaps have a tentative list of the items that have been left aboard the *Investigator*." Alan paused and looked at the two archeologists in turn. "You see, I am really questioning if you know precisely what sorts of relics were left on board that vessel before it sank."

"If it is descriptions you need, yes, we do have some that we've elaborated ourselves after studying the ships' manifest and the number of items that have been recovered so far," Sullivan replied, wiping his plate clean with the last bit of his toast. "But this is where we have a problem. As we've told you before, there are items of importance and others that could be considered as having very little historical value. And apart from the McClure treasure – if that chest does in fact exist – there are nine items that we would love to recover."

"And you have a list of those items?" Alan asked.

"Yes, we do," Lespierre interposed, "but may we ask why you would need the list or have any interest in it?"

"Curiosity primarily, I suppose. On the other hand, I think a copy of the list should go to Chief Tolberg before we reach the Arctic waters, so that he can arrange for sufficient security during and after the dives."

"Yes, of course," Sullivan said. "Actually, Chief Tolberg asked us to meet with he and Mr. Bornstein and our divers this morning after breakfast. And we could bring the list with us, yes."

"Okay then," Alan concluded, "that's all I wanted to talk about, and if you have other concerns – or details regarding timing – I think it'll be a good idea to put all your cards on the table now, rather than later." He got up from his chair, adding, "And if time permits, I might see you at the meeting."

"Good," said Lespierre, returning to eating his croissant, "Although all these considerations might not be relevant to you, we think your presence at the meeting would be most appreciated."

* * * *

A few minutes later Alan was sitting at Gerald's desk, looking at him. "So you can expect, and even demand to see that list," he said after he related his conversation with the two archeologists to Gerald.

"But why would you think that list would be so important to us? We've got nothing to do with the relics really – none that I know of anyway," Gerald said, reclining in his swivel chair.

"That's where I think you're wrong, Gerald. I think that list has everything to do with us or the murder, to be precise, and in turn with my little notes."

"How do you figure?" Gerald was all ears now.

"Let me go over the events if you don't mind, and then I think you'll see," Alan replied. "First, I receive a note stating that "there were nine left", then a few days later I get another one stating "there were eight left", and then nothing until the eve of Cecil's arrival aboard *The Contessa*. Next, I get the third note just before he gets himself killed in Juneau and before Mrs. Bornstein gets sent back to Boston. Then nothing… do you see the pattern?"

"No, not really," Gerald replied. "What is the pattern?"

"Okay, let me explain it another way. We know Banks Island is a dangerous place to be as far as your health is concerned. That particular strain of TB is no laughing matter – it kills. So, what if Cecil Legato had been aware of the treasure lying in the wreck long before Clarisse Bornstein even got involved with him? And how did she get in touch with him – it's not like Cecil would advertise his services on the net, now would he?"

"I see," Gerald put in, "What you're saying is that Cecil had been engaged by someone else long before Clarisse came into the picture, right?"

"Yes. And who ever hired Cecil initially wanted to have all ten items on that list raised to the surface *before* we arrived on site. They knew no one would be foolish enough to venture on the island without adequate protection and medical supervision."

"But why killing Cecil then? Obviously, and according to your deduction, there are seven items left plus the treasure chest, so why kill the golden goose?"

"I think that happened when Clarisse got involved, and Cecil left Banks Island to join her – some other party didn't want to share the treasure with anyone else, especially with someone the likes of Clarisse Bornstein."

"Okay, let's suppose you're right, what happens next?"

"I think it's happening right now – who ever was left on Banks Island is now recovering the relics as initially planned, and when we get there, there will be none left to find."

"And do you expect to find another note on your pillow anytime soon then?"

"I'd say so, because we're back at sea now, and from here we have very little recourse against who ever is on the island."

"But why alerting you of the treachery – what would it accomplish?"

"Precisely what it did accomplish; making us aware that some pirate is at work looting the treasures aboard the *Investigator*."

"Is he a vigilante or a riddler, do you think?" Gerald asked.

"Probably both – he wants to see justice done, but doesn't (or can't) come out with it without risking his own life."

"So, if I understand you; what you're suspecting is this," Gerald said, pen poised now and prepared to take notes, "You're telling me that Mrs. Bornstein found out about Cecil Legato already working on the island; then Bornstein himself gets her out of the way under the obvious pretext that she's overstepped her boundaries when she bound and gagged their daughter in that closet. Next, we have your riddler who apparently knows about the plan and operation on Banks Island; and then we have two archeologists who have a manifest of the ten items remaining on the wreck – one of which is the McClure's chest; and finally we have someone or a crew left on Banks attempting to retrieve what ever they could before we get there." Gerald raised his eyes from his note pad to Alan. "Does that sum it up?"

"Sure, but there is an inevitable conclusion to be drawn from that series of facts – we have a treasure thief and a murderer aboard."

"And who's your first pick?" Gerald asked.

"I'd say Bornstein is the thief, because I don't see how Clarisse would have known about Cecil any other way. Bornstein must have been corresponding with Cecil through his business connections for some time and Clarisse discovered the plot somehow."

"But he's no murderer – he was in your hospital when Cecil was killed, remember?"

Alan nodded emphatically. "And he wouldn't be capable of handling an arbalest by any stretch of the imagination, even if he hadn't been in the process of occluding off a few coronary arteries – sorry, his heart attack – when Cecil was killed."

"Okay then – someone else has shot that arrow to stop Cecil in his tracks – but who?"

"I don't know yet," Alan answered, "But the man should be a marksman of note. That shot wasn't a simple one to take. It required skill and precision."

"Plus, he would have been aware of Mrs. Bornstein being stashed away in that cabin-brig for a night..."

"He's observing each of the players' moves, Gerald. Nothing is left to chance. He is very calculating, that's all I can say," Alan concluded.

"What about the riddler? Do you have any idea who he might be?"

"Not yet, but I'd say he's not a sharp shooter or a daring fellow. I would think his best strategy is to stay hidden and hope that I understand what he's trying to tell me."

The two men sat in silence for a moment until Gerald tapped his pen on his notepad and said, "You know that old saying – the best form of a defense is an offense?" Alan nodded. "Well then what I was thinking is for us to leave our own note on your pillow, since you believe that your riddler is going to show up again soon."

"I think that may work, but we would need to be as astute as he is, otherwise he won't show his hand or even could quit the game once he knows that we've discovered what he's up to."

"Alright, let's discuss this a little later," Gerald said, "because now I've got a meeting with our prime suspect – Mr. Bornstein – as you know, and I don't want you anywhere near him or the archeologists when I start questioning them or the divers."

"Okay, no problem – I've got plenty on my plate anyway," Alan replied, getting to his feet. He looked at his watch and blurted, "Evelyn is going to hang me out to dry one of these days, sorry, Gerald, I've got to run!"

CHAPTER TWENTY-SIX

A flash drive . . . ?

DURING THE HOURS THAT followed Alan's meeting with Gerald, and during Isaac Bornstein's interview, the latter denied all knowledge of Cecil's existence or the man's involvement with raising the treasures still aboard the *Investigator*. And in order to confirm his denial, he invited Gerald and Neil, the computer wizard among the Chief's team, to go through his business files and correspondence on his laptop, which Neil did with a fine toothcomb.

Later, when they met again, Neil related, "There is nothing here remotely related to Mr. Bornstein's alleged involvement with Cecil Legato," when he closed the tycoon's laptop and prepared to return it to him. "And there isn't anything by way of correspondence related to the treasures or the *Investigator*'s operation other than emails and Skype records with the archeologists and the divers."

"Okay then," Gerald said, visibly disappointed. "It was a good lead, but it got us nowhere."

"And we still don't know how Mrs. Bornstein found Cecil Legato in the first place," Neil said, shaking his head.

"Yes, it's a puzzler alright. But she's still alive and well in Boston. Maybe we could ask the CIA or Interpol to have a chat with her, given the fact that we have valid proof that she had contact with our victim."

"Do you want me to contact Agent Silverton," Neil asked, raising his gaze to the Chief who was standing by the young man's desk.

"No, leave that one to me. I'll have a chat with him on Skype and see what he says."

"What about the riddler, Chief? Have you decided how you want to word that note yet?"

"No, not yet. But I'd like to have another little brainstorming session with the doc, before we put anything on paper."

"Okay then," Neil said, standing up, "I'll return the laptop to Mr. Bornstein and maybe go and have a chat with Dr. Mayhew..."

"Don't," Gerald said, shaking his head, "the man is in the middle of physicals right now, and disturbing him unduly before tonight will amount to a worthless effort since his mind is on medical issues, not composing notes. Let's leave it until I've had a chance to talk to Silverton in Washington."

When the afternoon drew to a close and Alan found himself alone in his office after a grueling series of physicals, he checked the calendar of events for that day in the hope that Tiffany would be free for the evening. Unfortunately, he soon realized that it was the night when the Second Act of Babette's play was going to be presented. He looked at his watch and rushed out of the medical center. He just had time to shower and change into his formal uniform before the curtain would rise in thirty-five minutes.

On his way to the elevator, he bumped into Gerald who came around the corner.

"Ah, just the man I want to see," Gerald said, stopping dead in front of the doctor.

"Sorry, Gerald, no time to chat – I've got to get ready for tonight's presentation of Babette's play…"

"Good God," Gerald exclaimed, looking at his watch, "I didn't realize it was that late. And you're right, I better get my guys organized – they'll have to get organized around the theater and the access to the power supplies for the theater on the double," he added, following Alan to the elevator.

"What did you want to see me about anyway?" Alan asked.

"I've interviewed Mr. Bornstein. I also had Neil go through the tycoons' laptop files this morning and there's nothing in there to indicate that he had any knowledge of Cecil being involved in the piracy operation, and I wondered if you had any ideas where to go from here…?"

As the elevator doors opened in front of the two men, Alan said, "Just ask him to give you any flash drives he has in his possession, or better yet, have his room searched, if you can, for any flash drives, including the one I noticed in his business card holder – it just looks like a thicker business card."

"That's a good idea, and that reminds me; I should ask the guys who packed Clarisse's bags if they found any flash drives in her effects – because if Isaac has no record of involvement with Cecil maybe his wife had some between the two."

"Exactly," Alan replied, before exiting the elevator near his cabin. "I'll see you later, Gerald, but now I've really got to get going."

"Okay," Gerald said before the doors closed on him.

CHAPTER TWENTY-SEVEN

ACT II

As soon as Alan arrived in the foyer, he made a beeline for Tiffany before she headed backstage.

"Looking very elegant as usual, Ms. Sylvan," he whispered as he reached her.

"Well, thank you, Dr. Mayhew, not so bad-looking yourself," she replied, a teasing smile crossing her lips.

"Do you have time to have an orange juice with your "not so-bad looking" man then?" Alan asked, leading her gently by the arm before the people already waiting in the foyer would notice her presence and capture her attention.

"Sure, but let's make it a quick one – I should be backstage already. You know from what I hear, Babette had a devil of a time with the cast yesterday during dress rehearsal apparently."

"Well, I'm sure she's straightened every one out by now, knowing her," Alan rejoined, turning toward the server behind the cocktail table. "Two orange juices, please, Andrew."

"By all means, Doc. Of course that would be without ice for you, right?" Andrew asked, looking up at Alan.

"Same for me," Tiffany said, "and make it a small glass – I've got to go...."

"Glad to see your proper use of the ice scoop, Andrew," Alan said aside, looking at Tiffany with sincere admiration. Once again she was beautifully dressed. The blue gown highlighted her coloring and, to him, she looked like an angel tonight.

"Here you go," said Andrew, handing them their glasses. "Break a leg," he added to Tiffany, smiling gently.

"Thanks, Andrew," Tiffany replied, turning toward the passengers who had begun to fill the foyer in great numbers.

A few minutes later the bell rang announcing the Second Act with Babette off to the side, stage right....

ACT II
SCENE I

Latin American music plays softly in the background - stage is bare.

MRS. MCTEEGE: (Enters carrying a box wrapped as a gift - looks to see if anyone is about - sees no one, so peers into drawers and things) Hello anyone home – Liz? (Opens door to bedroom) Liz, are you decent?

ELIZABETH: (Enters from kitchen) Hi there!

MRS. MCTEEGE: Are you still working? Come on girl - sit down here beside me. I brought you a present.

ELIZABETH: Oh, you shouldn't have.

MRS. MCTEEGE: Open it and see if you like it.

ELIZABETH: It's beautiful - I don't know when I've seen a lovelier towel or washcloth.

MRS. MCTEEGE: I wanted to get you something personal and what could be more personal than a towel. (Nudges her.)

ELIZABETH: What is the occasion?

MRS. MCTEEGE: It's a sort of a thank you present. Jack's eaten so many times over here and sleeps over here I just wanted to pay my way. I always say you never get anything for nothing.

ELIZABETH: Beautiful as it is, I couldn't accept it under those conditions.

MRS. MCTEEGE: Of course you can, you earned it. (Phone rings.)

ELIZABETH: Excuse me (Goes to phone) Hello, Lee is not here - who is this? Oh it's you Bobby (At this, Mrs. T. turns around). No, really I don't know where you could reach him. Yes, he was broadcasting this morning. Well, he could be at a rehearsal or a quartet practice. He might even be on his way home. Yes, yes, I promise I'll have him call you when he comes in. Goodbye.

MRS. MCTEEGE: What gives with this Bobby and your husband?
(There is a big pause) I didn't mean to pry, but you know me, by this time, little helpful Lucrica, that's me. (Stands) I guess growing up in the slum area makes a person kind of neighborly. But maybe you'd like to be alone.

ELIZABETH: No, don't go - please don't.

MRS. MCTEEGE: Get it off your chest - and you'll feel like you just stepped out of a tight girdle.

ELIZABETH: (Laughs) you're good for me. (Sits)

MRS. MCTEEGE: (Goes over and gets herself the cut crystal wine bottle and pours herself a large drink and says) I wish you'd go in for whisky or gin. John could get it for you wholesale. This will have to do for now (Goes back and gets the whole bottle). Now I'm quite ready – so take all the time you need.

ELIZABETH: Does John ever get calls from people like Bobby?

MRS. MCTEEGE: In his business he gets all kinds of calls. I'm sure glad he's in appliances and not women's lingerie. Have you spoken to Lee about it?

ELIZABETH: I've asked him, but he always passes it off and never really answers me. The only time he actually says anything to me is when he is mad.

MRS. MCTEEGE: And that's getting oftener and oftener.

ELIZABETH: How do you know?

MRS. MCTEEGE: Remember me, I live next door, what I know about my neighbors I could write a book. What he really gets hot about are the kids. Well you can't drown them so what are you suppose to do?

ELIZABETH: I don't know. And I don't understand it either. If he really loves me, as he used to say he did, then he'd love my children too. Men even marry women with other men's children and love these children like their own. What's the matter with me? I try very hard to be a good wife and mother and I try to be a good housekeeper and God knows I hate keeping house...

MRS. MCTEEGE: Why don't you buy yourself some luxurious clothes and see if his eyes don't bug out of his head.

ELIZABETH: We don't have that kind of money; the boys will be in college in a short time.

MRS. MCTEEGE: How about your credit rating? As far as I know you don't even have one. I even looked you up.

ELIZABETH: We never charge. What ever we have, we own.

MRS. MCTEEGE: I can see that (Elizabeth looks at her).

ELIZABETH: Anyway, Lee is generous enough about money matters. Whatever he has is mine too.

MRS. MCTEEGE: I wonder about that (This has a double meaning). What is he really giving Bobby?

ELIZABETH: What could he give Bobby?

MRS. MCTEEGE: Of course you'd know more about that than anyone else.

ELIZABETH: No, I think it's me. He just doesn't love me anymore, and I don't blame him. I'm not beautiful or brilliant and I have an awful temper - (Breaks down and cries) and I'm overly sexed.

MRS. MCTEEGE: You're what?

ELIZABETH: Overly sexed.

MRS. MCTEEGE: Where did you get a queer idea like that?

ELIZABETH: When I was a girl I was thought of as being rather proper and after I was married, Lee said, "I was awakened" and that I was oversexed.

MRS. MCTEEGE: Oh, how I can just hear his mother saying, "So, my boy, you look so tired, what is that overly sexed wife of yours doing to you?

ELIZABETH: You do listen in. Lee says that statistics show that married women are taking pills and shots to keep themselves quiet and not all sexed up. I like to think I can control my emotions and I do, but lately he's been so tired at night and he's actually getting worse with the children. (Phone rings) If that's Bobby I think I will call the police.

MRS. MCTEEGE: No, Liz, no, think of the scandal in the neighborhood, your husband's career and the children. Here, let me answer. I'll take care of him. Hello, you have the wrong number. (Hangs up) When you come right down to it, how do we know Bobby is a fairy?

ELIZABETH: We don't for sure, but the way he walks and talks, his actions; he's a typical flaming gay. My psychology professor didn't agree.

MRS. MCTEEGE: I should hope not, why, the psychologists say, you can't tell straight men from real gays by voice, looks, or even profession. They say many of the male athletes are that way, it doesn't always have to be the musicians, and the Army is full of gay fellows with their big guns. (Phone rings again) Let me handle this.

ELIZABETH: (Starts for phone) I should take it, it might be important.

MRS. MCTEEGE: "House of laughs" what's your problem? (Hangs up.) That's what my Jack always says - leave it to (Doorbell rings - Elizabeth goes to door - Mrs. McTeege hears voices of a man and of Elizabeth. Mrs. McTeege runs over to listen but doesn't quite make it out. Rushes back.)

ELIZABETH: Tell me I'm imagining things? That was a police officer, and he was looking for Lee.

MRS. MCTEEGE: For Gods sakes why?

ELIZABETH: He didn't say.

MRS. MCTEEGE: He must have said something. I heard his voice.

ELIZABETH: I'm not trying to keep anything from you. I'm just so confused.

MRS. MCTEEGE: (Brings her a drink, Elizabeth refuses it. Mrs. T. drinks it herself) It's your funeral.

ELIZABETH: Don't say that. They're looking for him.

MRS. MCTEEGE: Start at the beginning and tell me exactly what the policeman said.

ELIZABETH: First he asked if this was the Clarkson residence, and I said it was. Then he asked me who I was.

MRS. MCTEEGE: I know all that. Get to the point.

ELIZABETH: I identified myself to him and he said is Mr. Clarkson in. I said no, but I expect him any minute. Oh, officer is there anything wrong? He didn't tell me like they do on TV that it was just routine. He said those awful words.

MRS. MCTEEGE: (Gulps down another glass of wine) Yes, yes.

ELIZABETH: He said, he said we are looking for a child predator in this neighborhood but I wasn't to be alarmed. He said that he wouldn't hurt me. Could it be my poor Lee? Oh what can I do to help him and the children? We could move to Hollywood, nobody could tell the difference there. (Doorbell rings.)

MRS. MCTEEGE: (Goes to door.) You do have troubles kid. Don't worry we'll think of something. (Bobby enters.)

BOBBY: (At door) I must have the wrong house, I want Lee Clarkson.

MRS. MCTEEGE: So does somebody else. I don't live here. Come on in as long as you're here.

ELIZABETH: (Under her breath) How could you, how could you?

BOBBY: You know then. But he told me he didn't want you to know, about it I mean.

MRS. MCTEEGE: If I were a gossiping woman I'd tell my husband John about you. He's big enough to fix you.

BOBBY: He sure could fu... I mean, fix me, oh, would you tell him that would be very nice. But it will have to wait until another time. I must find Lee. Well, tell him I was here. Goodbye for now darlings (At door) would you mind if I used my key after this? I don't want to bother you all the time. (Exits humming and dancing a rumba.)

MRS. MCTEEGE: You better see a lawyer, Liz. If he has given him a key already, some nerve.

ELIZABETH: Thanks for helping.

MRS. MCTEEGE: Don't thank me this is more fun than.... (Doorbell rings) I thought he had a key – why doesn't he use it.

ELIZABETH: It could be the police again (At door) what shall I tell them?

MRS. MCTEEGE: The same thing you did the last time.

ELIZABETH: Yes, oh, Dr. Asspan, do come in, Dr. Asspan.

DR. ASSPAN: Are you very busy? I tried to reach you on the phone. Something must be wrong with your line, it crosses with a psychotic. You had better report it to the telephone company. I see you have company.

ELIZABETH: Mrs. MCTEEGE, may I present Dr. Asspan.

DR. ASSPAN: Did I hear you correctly? You did say Mrs. MCTEEGE - not John

MCTEEGE?

MRS. MCTEEGE: Yes, do you know John or his Aunt?

DR. ASSPAN: I must speak to you on a very personal matter. I wonder if you'd excuse us, Mrs. MCTEEGE.

MRS. MCTEEGE: Sure, sure, I think I need a drink anyway. (To Liz) call me later. I'll be waiting. So long, Doc, I'll tell John you were asking for him. (She exits.)

ELIZABETH: (Sits) Won't you sit down, Doctor?

DR. ASSPAN: Thank you; you wouldn't have a small one, would you? (Pantomiming a drink with his fingers).

ELIZABETH: (Goes to bottle – it is empty) How about a cup of coffee?

DR. ASSPAN: Don't bother.

ELIZABETH: No bother at all - it would only take a minute.

DR. ASSPAN: Some other time. What I have to say is not easy and frankly I'm at a loss to know where to begin.

ELIZABETH: Is it about my husband's ulcer?

DR. ASSPAN: I wish it were as easy as that. No, but it does. Go back to that evening when I received the emergency call and came over to see your husband... (Stands) you must understand, Mrs. Clarkson that we of the medical profession are over worked and very underpaid. It's true I own a small home free & clear, a swimming pool, a car, a little stock, but.... That isn't what I started out to say; I wanted you to know that I am dedicated to my profession. Sometimes a person makes a mistake, he doesn't mean to... well, take a musician he can play a sour note and nobody thinks anything about it, it's a different story with a doctor.

ELIZABETH: What are you trying to tell me, Doctor?

DR. ASSPAN: In my practice I do a great deal with endocrinology, that is, things that have to do with the glands...

ELIZABETH: Yes I know, you mean my husband's glands are not normal?

(Bobby enters and stands on steps)

DR. ASSPAN: Not exactly. If you recall the evening I attended your husband I gave him an injection. (Stands) I believe it was... (Sees Bobby)

BOBBY: Hi, don't mind me, darlings. Well, you needn't look at me in that way – I wasn't the one who gave him the shot. (Puts key away)... I know when I'm not wanted (Goes to bedroom)... I'm going in here and wait until Lee gets back. (Slams door.)

DR. ASSPAN: How long has this been going on. (Music up, a rumba, from bedroom) (Phone rings) (Doctor ad-libs – it's just a mumble.)

ELIZABETH: Hello - I'm sorry can't hear you; you'll have to speak a little louder.

DR. ASSPAN: I said, how long has this (Pointing toward the bedroom) been going on?

ELIZABETH: Fifteen years. (Into phone) no not you. There's so much noise I can't hear myself think. Please hold on a moment (Puts phone down) (Goes to bedroom door) Bobby I'm on the phone, will you please turn the music off.

BOBBY: (Sticks head out of the door) I will not. You might accuse me of listening. (Slams door – turns up volume)

DR. ASSPAN: (Dr. Asspan follows Elizabeth.) You say this attachment to... to Bobby has been going on for 15 years?

ELIZABETH: Oh no I thought you meant, how long we have been married. I don't think Lee has known him too long. What are you getting at, Doctor?

DR. ASSPAN: Shouldn't you answer the phone.

ELIZABETH: (Goes to phone.) Sorry to have kept you waiting. Would you mind repeating what you said before? (Puts finger in other ear, takes the phone as far from the music as possible) this is the Clarkson home, you want???? - Dr. Asspan - just, a minute, he's right here. It's for you.

DR. ASSPAN: (Elizabeth trying to get Bobby to turn down the music) Hello, Dr. Asspan speaking no, no, I don't expect to be long. If anything comes up in the mean time I'll be at the Vencello. Yes, he's in a bad way. After that you may reach me at home. Well my dear I'll look in on you again. That is I'll call back when your husband is in (Starts to go to the door).

ELIZABETH: (Runs ahead of him stands in front of door facing the audience) Oh no you don't! You didn't finish telling me what you started to say.

DR. ASSPAN: I thought I had. I told you I had given him an injection. Now there's (Walks down stage) nothing to get alarmed about (Takes off glasses and wipes them) I think I might have given him the wrong hormones.

(Dead silence - Doctor exits.)

CURTAIN

Once the applause had died down, it was time for the doctor, Stephan Ivanov and Captain Middleton to follow the passengers into the foyer for the intermission.

"So, Doctor," the captain asked quietly, "any progress?"

Alan turned his face to him. "Yes, sir. Thanks to our nurses and the three technicians, we're going through the physicals on schedule."

"Hum, yes," Middleton said, sounding unconvinced for some reason, "what I was really asking about is finding our murderer – any news on that front?"

The three men were passing through the doors of the theater when Alan said, "I believe our chief of security has made some progress in that regard, yes."

"Is he here tonight?" Stephan asked, looking around him for the man.

"He should be," Alan said, his eyes also traveling around the room. "I saw him just before coming down myself."

"Okay, let's have a drink, shall we?" Middleton said, going toward the cocktail table, Alan and Stephan in tow. "I'll have a chat with him in the morning. We need to find the guy before we reach Kodiak if possible," he declared adamantly. "I don't want this sort of person aboard *The Contessa*. He's a walking menace and the sooner we find him, the better."

Alan couldn't agree more, but somehow he knew it wouldn't be all that simple, besides, finding the murderer came second on his list to finding the riddler – unless he was lucky and the two were one and the same person.

Fifteen minutes later, the bell called the spectators once again to their seats – the curtain was about to rise on Act II – scene II of Babette's play.

ACT II
SCENE II

(Stage is empty - rumba is still blasting in bedroom - Bobby dances on the stage. He is dressed in one of Elizabeth's dresses, high heels, furs, hat, jewels - the dress is tight over his buttocks. He is doing a rumba. As he finishes the doorbell rings – Bobby pauses – bell rings again).

BOBBY: Isn't anyone going to answer the door? What a bunch of queers - (Goes to door, peers out – jumps up, starts to race across floor muttering). The cops, they mustn't catch me like this. (He runs to bedroom).

(Off stage) Mom, somebody's at the door.

BOBBY: (Bobby comes on stage dressed in an overcoat goes to the door - in high voice) Go to sleep, dear. Did you want something officer. (Voice off stage) I'll tell him - thank you, Officer. Who am I? I'm sort of a member of the family. (Closes door - goes to mirror, fixes hair, and takes off coat still dressed in Elizabeth's evening clothes, lights fade.)

(A cigarette - using a long cigarette holder, Bobby sits on couch) (Enters Lee - looks about stage - sees what he thinks is Elizabeth on the couch. Goes quietly over to her - puts his arm around 'her' and starts to pet 'her' – Bobby keeps his face turned away from Lee and is obviously enjoying this immensely.)

LEE: I'm beat but how about you? I'll bet you want to rumba.

BOBBY: (Bobby turns his face to Lee and kisses him; a teasing sort of kiss). (Elizabeth enters - stands muted) (Lee jumps up stares first at Elizabeth - then at Bobby) I can't wait until later, darling (he exits quietly).

ELIZABETH: (Starts toward the bedroom) This time, I mean it - I'm leaving you.

LEE: You can't do that.

ELIZABETH: (Stops) Why not?

LEE: Because, I don't want us to split up.

ELIZABETH: Ha - that's a laugh.

LEE: Ha-Ha it may be a laugh to you, but to me marriage is a serious business. That's what makes me so damn mad at those kids. They're the ones who are breaking us up.

ELIZABETH: You haven't contributed one single thing. You honestly think it's all the children's fault?

LEE: What else?

ELIZABETH: I'll tell you what else. You say marriage is serious business. I wish it were more than mere words to you.

LEE: It is. Believe me.

ELIZABETH: I don't believe you any more. I'm not the starry eyed little girl you married. I'm a grown woman. So I don't ask you for jewels, bobbles, and luxuries.... I do ask one thing, I ask you for respect, not only for me but also for our children. For kindness, faithfulness and understanding.

LEE: What do you want me to do? Hold down two jobs, so you can buy more things for those precious brats of yours.

ELIZABETH: Listen to me, Lee (She is crying now). Please, please, please listen to me.

LEE: What the hell do you think I have been doing for the last fifteen minutes, but listen?

ELIZABETH: Sure you listen, but you never really hear what I say. I've never asked you to make more money. I've always managed. Didn't I help you when you went to Italy to study? I worked. I don't dress like Jacqueline Kennedy, do I?

LEE: I keep telling you to get new clothes; I can't buy them for you, can I?

ELIZABETH: It isn't the clothes, it's kindness and understanding I want you to give the children. This is a big way of showing your love for me. Not just in there (Points to bedroom).

LEE: What's the matter with in there?

ELIZABETH: (She keeps talking does not wait for him.) You've promised me so many times and then...

LEE: All right - I won't promise you anymore. I'm not perfect. Sure I love them, so they get me mad and I blow. Why make so much over it? (Lights a cigarette) So I'm not the most demonstrative guy in the world - is that a crime?

ELIZABETH: It is when you make love to Bobby.

LEE: So that's what it is - you're jealous. Ha-ha, ha-ha...(laughs and laughs).

ELIZABETH: (Picks up the phone) Hello? How soon can you send a cab to? (Lee hangs up the phone. Elizabeth starts to dial again.)

LEE: (Hangs it up - yanks the phone out of her hands) you're crazy; you're really stark raving mad. Oh, brother, what you need is a psychiatrist. (He starts to double up) I'm sick - really sick.

ELIZABETH: You're not sick, you're a hypochondriac, every time there's a crisis in your life, you hold your stomach and say 'I'm sick - really sick'.

LEE: (Staggers to couch - lies down) That's all right, forget it. I'll make out - just call mother, she'll know what to do.

ELIZABETH: I sincerely hope she does (dials) Hello, mother Clarkson, this is Elizabeth - you know Elizabeth Clarkson who married your baby. Yes, well that's a matter of semantics. Oh well, at the moment he's laying on his cute little pink - you know what - and kicking his itzy-bitsy feet in the air - calling for mama. You'll come - I knew you would.

LEE: She's coming?

ELIZABETH: Right away - (Turns) oh yes, she wanted me to tell her sonny boy, 'mammas coming right away to protect her baby boy from that woman'. Why is it that mother and son can't remember a simple name like Elizabeth? (Dials) Dr. Asspan, this is Elizabeth Clarkson - I think you had better come. I know you're at Harlan's party but unless you want a lawsuit for mal-practice I would advise you to jump into your kitty kar and get right over here. Yes - I know your dedication. That's why I know you'll come. (She hangs up.)

LEE: (As soon as Elizabeth said "Asspan" Lee starts to ad-lib a protest first in pantomime, then in actual words.) I told you, I don't want that handholding...

ELIZABETH: Hello, Georgia. Lee - Elizabeth Clarkson. Is Boyd in? May I speak to him? No, I don't think it's too serious.

LEE: (Groans) Why didn't you call him in the first place? Not too serious she says. What do you want me to do, die? Not serious (Snorts) I bet you'd like that; I do have $100,000 in life insurance (Groans).

ELIZABETH: It's not enough - so you can't die. (Groans) stop groaning - I can't hear if Boyd's there. Hi Boyd — it's Lee again, looks like the same old trouble. I've called Dr. Asspan - (Lee groans louder) already. Yes, I made sure he'd know, I mean did he tell you?

LEE: What?

ELIZABETH: He thinks he gave Lee the wrong shot - something to do with hormones....

LEE: (jumps up, doubles up with pain.) What do you mean — hormones?

ELIZABETH: Wait a minute I'll look (Takes out tape measure puts down phone - goes over to Lee, sets him down - examines his chest feels it - feels his vocal box - goes back to phone - Now Lee is feeling his voice box and his breast). I guess I'm no expert - I can't tell! You'd better come over - (Lee tries to grab the phone - Elizabeth has hung up.)

LEE: (Goes to mirror) - (Looks at voice box, says) Hello? (Fingering his voice box - over and over again. Elizabeth shakes her head and goes off since the children answered; "hello — hello" off stage.)

BOBBY: HELLO (Enters Bobby) Hello?

LEE: (Does not see him, he jumps at the change - the change in his voice - he stares at himself, starts to say hello).

BOBBY: (Sings out) Hello - hello - now can we...?

ELIZABETH: (Off stage) Go to sleep now or you'll never be able to get up for school tomorrow.

LEE: (Tries to say something but he has lost his voice - pantomimes Bobby to go - but Elizabeth is getting closer...)

ELIZABETH: (Off stage) "Sleep well and dream sweet.".

LEE: (Pushes Bobby under couch).

BOBBY: I'd do anything for you, darling, but this...

ELIZABETH: You won't find what you've lost on the floor. Come on and lie down.

LEE: (Starts to say something – no voice comes out. Bobby is looking up and out from couch.)

ELIZABETH: Don't be afraid, dear. I won't leave you.

BOBBY: Thank you, darling.

ELIZABETH: (Taken aback by voice - adds) yet. (Goes to bedroom to get blanket). I'll get you a blanket - I won't be a minute.

MRS. MCTEEGE: (Wanders on stage) Hi, Lee.

LEE: (Tries to say something – nothing comes – he waves.

BOBBY: Hi, darling.

MRS. MCTEEGE: (To self) It's even worse than I thought (To Lee). Same old complaint (Lee nods - points to stomach - but Bobby is helping)

BOBBY: Wouldn't you know it, not even five minutes of rest between pains - mercy it's just awful.

MRS. MCTEEGE: Sounds like labor pains to me.

LEE: Much worse, darling (Lee is kicking Bobby to be still - he yells "ouch")

ELIZABETH: (Runs on stage with blanket and over to Lee and starts to fuss over him, as he moves away the couch is pushing into Bobby, who keeps yelling: "OUCH! Help!" - Lee must pantomime for Bobby - the dog comes in - starts pulling at Bobby and growling - Mrs. MCTEEGE is pouring herself a drink - music up - phone rings.

MRS. MCTEEGE: (Answers phone) wrong number.

(Doorbell rings – Elizabeth goes to the door – someone is pounding on the door as THE CURTAIN SLOWLY DESCENDS – pantomimes and goes between Lee and Bobby and threatens Bobby – Bobby is trying to get away – Dog and Lee hold back.

(Off stage): Where's my baby what have you done to my Sonny Boy?

CURTAIN

A large bouquet of roses in her arms, Tiffany joined Babette on stage and bowed to the applause after she handed her the splendid flower arrangement.

Microphone in hand now, Tiffany said, "Ladies and gentlemen, you've been a fantastic audience this evening and it is with great anticipation that we shall wait for the presentation of the third and final act of "Make Mine a Rumba" by our famous playwright – Miss Babette."

Tiffany bowed again under the thunderous applause, before handing the microphone to Babette.

"Thank you, thank you so much for coming tonight," Babette said as the applause abated, "I am really gratified to have such a pleasant audience, and it always gives me great pleasure to write a play during our cruises. But this play would only be scribbles on a few pages if it were not for our marvelous cast and for Ms. Sylvan, our entertainment director. Without her none of us would have had anything to look forward to tonight." She turned to Tiffany and handed the mike back to her.

"Thank you, Ms. Babette." Then Tiffany returned her attention to the audience. "The next act will be presented when we reach Prudhoe Bay, just before entering the Polar Circle. Thank you, everyone, and Good Night!"

CHAPTER TWENTY-EIGHT

An interview with Clarisse

IF ONE HAD TO DESCRIBE the décor of the Bornstein's apartment in downtown Boston, the words plush and exquisite would have come to mind. The furniture, the ornaments, the paintings and even the leather bound books that lined one of the massive bookshelves in the den spelled money.

A man in his early fifties, Agent Devon Silverton, was a lean and mean-looking fellow, although to everyone who knew him, he was a gentle-mannered investigator.

"Have a seat, Agent Silverton," Clarisse invited, plopping down in the sofa across from him and depositing her cocktail glass on the heavy wrought iron coffee table separating them. "You were not very clear on the phone as to what would bring you all the way to Boston, but I gathered it has something to do with that awful cruise line..."

Silverton waved a quick hand in front of his face. "Let me stop you right there, Mrs. Bornstein; I'm not here about the cruise line, no, I am here on a different matter..."

"And what could that be? I'm sure you know that my husband is intending to serve me with divorce papers..."

"No, Mrs. Bornstein, my visit here has nothing to do with your marital trouble either."

"Then what is it?" Clarisse asked, grabbing her glass from the table and taking another sip of what looked like a martini.

"It's about your alleged involvement with Cecil Legato..."

"Who? I don't know anybody by that name, so how could I have any involvement, as you call it, with a man I don't even know?"

"You know that's not quite true, don't you, Mrs. Bornstein? In fact you knew him well enough to have sent him several emails regarding the *HMS Investigator* and the treasure chest it is supposed to contain."

"No, Agent Silverton, I don't recall emailing anyone about that wreck; all I know is that my husband hired two divers to go after the treasure."

Clarisse's statement sounded truthful enough, but Silverton wasn't going to let it go at that. "Would the name Denis Merchant ring a bell then?"

"No more than your Mr. Legato does, no," Clarisse answered, seemingly relaxed.

"Well then, I will need to see your computer or laptop, if you don't mind?"

"Do you have a warrant?"

"No, Mrs. Bornstein, I don't need a warrant to search for any items that would be in plain view or would help me confirm my suspicion in a case of collusion with a well-known art thief."

"Before you go on searching my apartment, I'll call my lawyer," Clarisse declared, getting up from the sofa. "He'll soon see you out the door."

"Well, in that case, Mrs. Bornstein, I will have no choice but to apprehend you on suspicion of fraud and even murder," Silverton countered, standing up too.

"What are you talking about? What murder?"

"The murder of Cecil Legato, Mrs. Bornstein."

That rang a bell in Clarisse's mind all right – better than that even – she stopped and turned to the Interpol agent, aghast. "You mean he's dead?"

"That's what being murdered usually means," Silverton replied, cracking a malicious smile.

"But I left the ship before we met…"

"Ah, then you admit knowing the man?"

"No, I am not admitting to anything," Clarisse flared. "I was to meet someone, yes… but that's none of your damn business." Her eyes riveted on the agent, she was ready to claw his face by the looks of things.

"Oh but it is, Mrs. Bornstein, but if you want to clear your name from any accusation or complicit involvement with his murder, you just have to let me see your laptop and all of your flash drives, that's all." He put his hands in his jacket pocket and waited.

"What about the fraud? I've done nothing wrong. I've just talked to Denis, because Isaac wanted me to…"

At that moment everything clicked in Silverton's brain. He knew what and who the thieving scheme involved. All he needed now were the evidential items he knew she had to corroborate his findings.

* * * *

Two hours later Silverton was waiting for the attendants to call the passengers aboard the flight that would take him back to Washington DC that evening. When he had left Clarisse's residence he had contacted the authorities in Boston to keep her under surveillance until Interpol could connect all the dots in the case. With the flash drive in his pocket, *it shouldn't present too much of a problem*, he thought.

* * * *

"If I were to paraphrase Edgar Watson Howe," Gerald said, "I'd say that wise is a man who knows how to keep a secret, but wiser is a man who has no secret to keep". And you, Mr. Bornstein, are wise but not the wiser in this instance."

The two men were sitting face to face in Isaac's suite the morning after Gerald had received Silverton's report.

"And what secret would that be, Chief?" Bornstein asked, stretching to the back of the sofa. "I've given you every opportunity to check my laptop, and computer and you found nothing, have you?"

"True enough, Mr. Bornstein, but you were wise enough to involve your wife in your scheme, knowing that she would do whatever you ask for fear of being beaten if she didn't."

"How could anyone in their right mind involve an alcoholic into such a delicate business? I would have been a fool to do so, wouldn't I?"

"Oh but you have, sir. She was the one who contacted Cecil Legato once you found out that he would be the right man for the task. And when things began to happen, it was time to get rid of your wife..."

"I did no such thing," Bornstein flared.

"But you did; when she emailed him to come to Juneau, and she shut your daughter in a closet, you saw the perfect opportunity to get rid of your wife. You demanded that she be sent back to Boston where she would wait for your lawyer to file the divorce papers that she would have gladly signed. Then, once she was out of the way, you would have been able to recover the McClure treasure in due course, and claim it as your own, without having to share the loot with her."

"That's a fantastic story, chief, but without proof this is only a story. First, I think I should tell you that there is a pre-nuptial agreement in place and Clarisse wouldn't get a cent dead or alive. Moreover, I don't think the email my wife supposedly sent to that Cecil Legato could be connected to me in any way. She could have found the name anywhere – she is a very resourceful woman as you know."

"That she is, Mr. Bornstein, however, Interpol has spoken to Mrs. Bornstein in Boston, and she has spilled the proverbial beans, and has given us a flash drive that she had kept 'for insurance', she said."

Bornstein's face reddened. "Okay, Chief, I think it's time for me to ask you to leave my suite"—the big man got to his feet—"while I call my lawyer."

"Yes, sir, as you wish," Gerald said, rising from his chair, "but there is something I'd like you to consider at this point."

"What's that?"

"The fact that we have someone on board that has killed your thief and, by my way of thinking, wouldn't hesitate to eliminate you, since you were the one who hired Cecil in the first place."

"As I've told you before, I've got nothing to do with that thief, so why would the murderer be after me?"

"Come on, sir, you're no idiot," Gerald blurted, "you know we've connected the dots and if you were even close to a free pass out of this mess, I suggest you start talking and cooperating with us now!"

"What do you mean by a free pass?" Bornstein asked, visibly interested now.

"If you were willing to help us in our investigation and assist Parks Canada in the recovery of the treasure, as you originally planned, we could overlook your trespass and falsehoods, and put it down to your eagerness for fame in recovering the relics before anyone else in the world did."

Suddenly seeing a way out, Bornstein sat down again – and so did Gerald. "Okay, Chief, can you put that down on paper?"

"After I've received a full statement from you, yes."

"But I cannot tell you anything about the murder, for the simple fact that I don't know anything about it, you understand."

"Yes, I do, sir, but nonetheless, your statement will be most helpful in driving our investigation to finding our murderer."

Bornstein nodded and put his elbows on his knees. "But what about protecting me and my daughter from that killer? We can't very well stay locked up in here until we reach Banks Island, now can we?"

"Your daughter is of prime concern, Mr. Bornstein, and I think until we find our killer, it's best that she stays somewhere else."

"And where would that be?"

"We'll have to determine that with Captain Middleton's assistance..."

"And I guess you'll do that quickly, won't you?"

"Of course, sir." Gerald paused. "But as for you, I suggest we move you to another cabin as soon as possible where you could remain with a bodyguard..."

"I don't need any bodyguard..."

"You may think you don't, sir, but our killer will stop at nothing at this point, so two is better than one when facing someone who has nothing to lose."

"Okay, okay, I hear you," Bornstein agreed. "What about that statement then; can we do that now?"

"By all means, sir," Gerald replied, taking a small recorder out of his pocket and placing it on the table.

* * * *

To say that Alan was tired would have been an understatement. He was exhausted. Taking on such tasks as all the physicals for the passengers over and above the regular crew physicals, patient visits and check-ups, obligatory captain's meetings, public health checks, safety briefings, and the other duties that he had to attend to every single day, was starting to take its toll on his own health. Yet, not one to complain, he looked at everything positively. He had two dedicated nurses with a well-functioning, well-stocked medical center in which he could carry out a relatively high-level medical practice, considering the surroundings. But, perhaps the most helpful of all was to have Tiffany at his side, so to speak. She was his emotional anchor and her realistic attitude seemed to rub off on him.

The one person that afternoon who occupied Alan's mind was Karen von Weglan. She wasn't feeling ill or showing any symptoms of relapses but her outlook on her future didn't sound good to him the last time he had a chat with her. He had explained, at length, that the type of tumors that had originally encroached themselves upon her spine were not as dangerous as they sounded. The fact that before boarding, the last of them had obviously been removed and that with the tungsten rod that had been inserted to support her vertebrae, she could look forward to walking normally again and living a long life. However, all the talking did nothing to remove her fear of paralysis. Moreover, she felt alone in fighting this battle even though her husband was a great support, she would always say, "It is not his body."

When Gerald told him what had been concluded regarding the issue of his interview with Isaac Bornstein, an idea sprang to mind. Elizabeth would be the perfect temporary "grandchild" for Karen. Besides, the killer would have observed the von Weglans with Elizabeth in Juneau and perhaps thought that the little girl would not be a further obstacle to the proposed assassination of the last remaining pawn in that treasure 'chess' pursuit.

CHAPTER TWENTY-NINE

The face of a riddler

AND THERE IT WAS AGAIN – another note! "And then there were six left" it said. Without unpinning it from his pillow, Alan went to check the camera facing the bed. He had forgotten to turn it on the night before. Swearing aloud, he grabbed the note and rushed out of the room. This was beginning to unnerve him. Not only did he want to find the person – alive if possible – but he wanted to stop him before someone else was found with an arrow through their body. This whole thing was maddening.

When he burst in Gerald's office, the man was in the middle of transcribing Bornstein's statement onto his own report. "What's happening?" he asked, noticing immediately that Alan wasn't in the best of moods.

"This is what's happening," the doc replied, flinging the note in the middle of Gerald's desk.

"But that's good, isn't it?" Gerald stopped and stared up at the doc. "Oops, you didn't turn the camera back on before you left the room, did you?"

Alan shook his head. "No, I didn't. I forgot all about it, to tell you the truth."

"Okay, okay, don't worry about that now…"

"But I'm nothing else but worried, Gerald. We've got an assassin on board and a riddler that is in touch with the thieves on Banks Island, otherwise how would he know how many relics are still aboard the wreck?"

"True, but we have taken measures to protect Bornstein and he should be okay until we nab the murderer…"

"You don't get it, do you?" Alan blared. It was not like him to lose control, but right now, frustration and fatigue had gotten the better of him. "We need to catch the riddler before we can even think of putting our hands on the assassin. And who's to say that they're not one and the same guy? Or that this killer is not taking orders from the riddler? Just tell me that?"

"Okay, okay, Alan. Believe it or not I've thought about all those possibilities myself, but short of searching every god-damned cabin, I don't know how to find your riddler at this point."

"What about the surveillance cameras? I'm sure you've got one riveted on my door, haven't you?"

Gerald nodded. "Yes, but Neil hasn't seen anything out of the ordinary in any of the latest recordings…"

"Can I see the tape for this afternoon?" Alan asked.

"Sure, but I don't know what you're hoping to see."

"I know it's a long shot, but I just had an idea...."

"Okay," Gerald agreed, getting up from his desk and leading the way to the inner office, where Neil was sitting in front of a set of flat screens projecting most of the common areas of the ship, such as restaurants, pools, promenade decks, etc., and those covering the bridge, gangway area, main crew corridor...

"Oh, hi, Doc," Neil said, swiveling his chair to face the two men, "how are you?"

"Okay, thanks," Alan replied.

"Neil, would you mind pulling up the tape for this afternoon – from the camera we placed in front of the doc's cabin for us?"

"Sure, Chief, but I've had a look at it before writing my daily report..."

"No commentary please, Neil, just pull it up on the screen, will you?"

"Okay, no problem, Chief," Neil replied, turning his chair back to the keyboard and the bank of screens in front of him. "There you go... that's from twelve noon to six this evening." He turned his face to Alan. "What approximate time are you interested in, Doc?"

"Between 3:00 and 6:00 but more precisely I want to see that cabin steward going in and out of my cabin. There should be only two instances when the steward goes into the room – one, to change the towels, and second, to pick up laundry."

"Alright," Neil said, "I'll fast forward to each of the images showing the steward."

While Neil did so, Gerald asked, "You think there was one more steward than usual or the same steward entering the room more than twice, is that it?"

Alan had only time to nod before Neil stopped the tape at 4:45 when a steward could be seen entering Alan's cabin carrying clean towels and coming out a few minutes later with dirty ones that he placed in the hamper beside the door. "Okay, that's one," Alan said. "Can you print a still picture of that man?"

"Sure, Doc," Neil replied, hitting a few keys on the keyboard. "And here comes the next man."

The three men stared at the screen – the man was definitely smaller in stature and there was an unusual manner about his gait that Alan noticed.

"Okay, can we have a closer look at his face?" Alan asked.

"Sure, Doc, but the resolution is lousy..."

"Just do it," Gerald ordered, visibly annoyed now.

Neil was right; all they could see is a blurred picture of the man's profile as he opened the door to Alan's cabin.

"Okay, print this one too," Gerald said, "And if you don't mind, try enhancing the resolution on both of these guys, okay?"

"Okay, Chief, I'll do my best. It'll take me a few minutes though."

"Never mind, take the time you need to get us as good a picture of these two faces as you can."

A half-an-hour later, after Alan had left the security office, Neil came out of the inner office, brandishing the new printouts of the two enlargements. "Okay chief, here they are," he said, "not much better but there is something on the smaller man that the first picture didn't pick up. Look"—he put the photo in question in front of the Chief—"he's got a tattoo on the right side of his neck."

"Good work, Neil," the chief replied, taking the two photos and rising to his feet, "You watch the shop. I'm going to see the doc," and walked out.

* * * *

In the interim and after taking a quick shower, before he would go down to the officers' mess to meet Tiffany for dinner, Alan took out the list of relics supposedly left on board the *Investigator* and tried figuring out which of the nine relics had already been raised to the surface. He thought only the small items would have been picked up, because the larger ones would have required some sort of hoisting net or other device to lift the items out of the water. And that's when another idea came to his mind. *Are the people on Banks Island and those working at the museum aware of what's going on?*

He was about to pick up the phone to call Tiffany and ask her to bring up a 'doggy bag' for the both of them when he heard the knock at his door.

When he opened the door wide to Gerald, he said, "Just the man I wanted to see. Come on in; I've just thought of something…"

"Oh, and what's that?" Gerald asked, entering the room.

"Have a seat," Alan invited, pointing to one of the two chairs crowded into his small cabin. "If our assumption is right and someone is raising relics out of the wreck, they would've had to involve someone on the island – maybe even the people guarding the museum – because they couldn't very well do anything under the cover of night, since there's no nighttime to speak of at this time of year." He fixed his gaze on Gerald, and waited for the chief's reaction.

"Yeah, except that the wreck is not near shore; it's about three miles from the beach, and the only way to go down to the wreck would be to dive from another vessel…"

"That's even better, Gerald," Alan exclaimed. "If our thieves need a ship or a fishing boat of some kind to haul the relics up, they must be anchored just off shore Banks Island, wouldn't they?"

"I would think so, yes. So what are you saying?"

"Don't you see? If Interpol could get a satellite image of the vessel, they could send a chopper from another island or another boat to stop these treasure hunters before they finish their job and slip out to the Atlantic Coast."

Gerald nodded, but his face wasn't the portrait of total agreement. "I hear what you're suggesting, Doc, but we've got two problems that I can see. First, the hunters' vessel is probably fitted with a radar device that could detect any other vessel approaching their position miles from where they are…"

"And they could pull anchor before anyone was near, is that what you're saying?"

"Yes, and besides, even if they didn't move, these are Canadian waters and Interpol doesn't have enough evidence to launch any form of intercept against a vessel anchored near Banks Island."

"What about alerting Parks Canada of what's happening and have them intervene?" Alan asked.

"If we alert Parks Canada now, Bornstein will pull out his funding and we can all kiss the McClure treasure goodbye – if the darn thing even exists."

Sitting on the second chair and facing Gerald, Alan put his elbows on his knees. "Okay, but we can at least ask Interpol for that satellite photograph, can't we?"

"Sure, and before we do that, I wanted to ask you if you ever saw this man before…?" Gerald handed Alan the photo of the man with the tattoo.

Alan peered down at the picture of the smallish man for a moment before he said, "No, not that I recall. He is definitely not my regular steward. I can look through the medical files and see if I can match the photo with the one in his medical chart, as you can with the employees' files."

"It's the tattoo that's interesting and maybe the stewards on your deck would know the guy, given the fact that he must have a uniform from their supplies and a card key to enter your cabin."

"Yes, that's a good idea, because even on this picture"—Alan tapped the photo with his index finger—"you can see that it is a standard issue uniform."

* * * *

Leaving Alan to his tergiversations, Gerald went back to his office, looked at his watch and hoped it wouldn't be too late to call Silverton in Washington. *I'll get him at home, if he's left his office already,* he thought.

And he did. "Hi, Devon, sorry to get you at home," Gerald said as soon as the agent picked up the phone.

"Don't be, the wife is out with the girls, and the game is not on yet, so what's up?"

Gerald explained what they had discovered on the surveillance tapes and asked, "If I send you a copy of the original tape, would your guys have the equipment or software to enhance the frames of the two men…?"

"We can even do better than that, Chief, once I get the copy of the tapes, I can have one of my guys see if the small steward has a record anywhere."

"But wouldn't you have to get a more complete photo of his face to do that?"

"I know what you mean; and the answer is no, we can either see if we have a profile in file or do a facial reconstruction from the image you've got."

"If you could do that, it would be great. I'll get Neil to send you the tape via secure-download, if that's okay?"

"You do that…. Anything else?"

"Well yes, but I don't know if this will even be possible."

"Come on, Gerald, let's have it; what's on your mind?"

"It's just that we know the hunters' boat must be anchored about three miles off shore Banks Island, and Dr. Mayhew was wondering if there was any chance that you could confirm its presence with a satellite photo."

"We could do that, sure. But, that's not going to stop these hunters from going after what's left of the relics, is it?"

"That was my point to the doc, and from where we are here, I can't see any way to stop them. They're in Canadian waters – if they're anchored near Banks – and we haven't got anything to prove their intention or anything to show what they've been doing."

"Okay, I think I've got a solution for you, and by the way, isn't it about time for you to get up to date with the latest surveillance technology"—Silverton chuckled—"your surveillance cameras make you sound like an old tar using a sextant to find the nearest shore."

"Thanks," Gerald replied, chuckling too. "So, what's that solution of yours?"

CHAPTER THIRTY

The Northern Rover

APART FROM DOING THE passengers' physicals and the crew members' mandated check-ups, Alan had to see to crew and passenger patients who came in with one complaint or another.

On the morning before *The Contessa* was nearing Kodiak Island, one older fellow came in the medical center, sat down in one of the chairs facing Alan's office and looked definitely bothered about something. Since Evelyn was busy drawing blood from one of the crewmembers, Alan got up and went to see what the man wanted.

"Doctor," he said, raising his eyes to Alan, "Sorry to bug you about this, but this darn ear has been keeping me awake all night, and I wondered if you could have a look at it."

"Sure... Mr....?"

"Oh, sorry; it's Stromberg, Mike Stromberg," the man said, standing up.

"Okay, Mr. Stromberg, why don't you go to the examining room"—he stretched an arm toward the open door—"and let me have a look at that ear."

As soon as Stromberg had climbed onto the table, Alan grabbed the otoscope from the side table and looked into the fellow's ear. He readily saw the start of an inflammation of the membrane encircling the eardrum.

"Okay, I can see why it's been bothering you," he said. "You have the beginning of an infection and I'll give you some antibiotics that will kill the bacteria and prevent it from spreading any further than it has already."

"Ha-ha, ha-ha, ha-ha," Stromberg erupted in good humored laughter. "Are you saying that you're not up to date with the latest cures?"

With a surprised grin on his face, Alan asked, "What do you mean?"

"Well, let me tell you a little story, Doc..."

"Okay, go ahead, *I'm all ears!*" Alan chuckled. "Sorry for the pun, I couldn't resist."

Stromberg smiled and shook his head. "Alright here goes. In 2000 BC, the doctors of the time gave their patients a root for their earaches. In 1000 AD, the doctors told them that the root was heathen, and to say a prayer instead. And that went on until 1850 AD when the doctors said, "that prayer is all superstition, instead you should drink a special potion." Alan's grin didn't abandon his lips. "Then in 1945 AD," Stromberg went on, "the doctors told their patients that the potion was ineffective to combat infection, and that they should swallow a pill." He laughed and punched his knee with an opened palm. "But in 1984, the doctors decided that the pill was not working, so they prescribed stronger antibiotics, like you just did." Stromberg chuckled some more to Alan's stare. "And that went on till last year, when the doctors decided that the best remedy for an earache was to eat a certain root."

Alan shook his head. When he finally stopped chortling, he said, "You know, you could be right. When we were in Juneau, I met this Inuit medicine man – you probably saw him; he came with the drummers on our last night there – and he gave me not a root, but a potion he had prepared from ground roots, which he said would fight 'most infections'."

"See, what did I tell you? That man was way behind times and probably way ahead of our time, too." Stromberg's smile disappeared. "So, what is it gonna be, Doc, the potion or the antibiotics?"

"In all good conscience, Mr. Stromberg, I can't give you the potion – I haven't had a chance to test the ingredients – but if you want to eliminate that ear infection right now, I have to prescribe the antibiotics."

"Okay, I hear you, Doc. But do me a favor, I'm on this ship for the long haul; I own a condo on the upper deck, you see. So, when ever you get around to test that potion of yours, let me know if it would have cured my earache, won't you? My wife and I have always been interested in the natural way, if possible."

"I'll do that, Mr. Stromberg, because I, for one, have a preference for less harmful medicine and would like nothing better than being able to prescribe medicines from a natural source over our currently available chemical ones."

When Mr. Stromberg left the medical center, Alan returned to his office and fished out his notes from his walk through the forest with Long Life. He had not had time until now to research some of the suggestions Long Life had made, nor had he had a moment to think how this list of medicinal herbs and plants could help his patients.

He sat back and began reading.

Long Life's Herbal Lessons

The native people originally led a short but healthy life. They ate a great quantity of Omega 3, 6 & 9 fatty acids from the salmon, herring, sardines and nuts/flax seeds that they collected in the fall. Dietary supplementation with essential fatty acids (EFA) has been considered useful for rheumatoid arthritis (RA). It is interesting to note that the prevalence of RA in Inuit people, who consume large amounts of oily fish rich in n-3 EFA, is low. Long Life talked about the EFA's having unique roles as precursor molecules of chemical regulators, the so-called eicosanoids, including the prostaglandins (PG), leukotrienes (LT), and thromboxanes (TX). These compounds are synthesized and released by almost every tissue in the body, and participate in many biological functions, including the inflammatory and immune processes, which is why they are felt to be beneficial to people suffering from arthritis. These fatty acids also kept their minds young, as has now been discovered by modern science.

Alan put down the notes and gave some thought to Long Life. He got his undergraduate degree in biochemistry, he obviously kept up with the field in the journals he read and knew of these developments. He attributed his long life and good health to growing many greens and drying them for the winter. He would add these to his fish and nut based diet in the form of teas and ground concoctions. Some of these greens were, of course, the herbs.

Long Life reiterated many of the benefits of herbal medicines. Firstly, he explained that they are extracts from plants and flowers used to prevent and treat illnesses. Herbal remedies have been used for a wide range of conditions, from headaches to depression, to insomnia.

Alan knew that most modern health stores in Canada and the US carry hundreds of bottles or packages of tablets containing various herbal preparations; some helpful and some dangerous for certain patients to take. Although there is some scientific evidence showing that certain herbs have health benefits, much of the information is limited to individual reports or small scientific studies. Many have not yet undergone the same testing and approval procedure as prescription and over-the-counter medications. Many herbs can affect prescription and non-prescription medications and should not be taken by people with certain medical conditions. In Canada, a Natural Product Number, or NPN, is assigned to herbal products. A similar designation is given in the US and many other countries. This does not mean that the herbs, or the claims that they profess are tested or genuine.

Long Life stressed that it was most important for the patient to know if there was evidence to support the use of a particular herb, if the herb can interact with other medications or vitamins, what side effects are associated with the herb, what medical conditions for which the herb should not be used, and how to take and store the herb properly. Of course, many of the herbs that Long Life routinely used were teas or extracts grown or traded in the north of Canada and would never find their way to any health food store. The herbs that did not get routinely used because of toxicity or harmful interactions merely got eliminated from his armamentarium. Long Life knew well that although many of the hunters would use the herbs kava and ma huang (ephedra) to make their treks across the tundra more tolerable, these were not healthy for those taking it, and he would advise against it in excesses of alcohol. Alan also knew that this was a recognized recommendation given by western medical practitioners.

Returning to his reading, he noted that some of the more common herbal remedies Long Life mentioned included descriptions of the plant-based remedies, because for countless generations, the Inuit attributed natural curative powers to various plants that grew in their environment. These included:

Qisiqtutauyak:

The Ground Juniper plant (JUNIPERUSCOMMUNIS) is a shrub from the CUPRESSACEAE family. It is found growing in sandy areas along the coast and in dry, rocky soil, not in the forest. The coastal Indians for some of the forest products often traded it. It is traditionally boiled whole to produce a tea for the treatment of colds, lung problems, bleeding and bladder problems.

Arpiqutik:

Cloudberry (RUBUSCHAMAEMORUS) is a plant of the ROSACEAE family. In parts of Canada, it is known as bake-apple. It grows in damp areas near water. The fruit of the cloudberry resembles an orange-colored raspberry, and is popular for making jam. Only the leaves are used in the making of medicinal tea and are harvested only after the berry-picking season has ended. Cloudberry leaves were boiled to make a tasty beverage for the treatment of kidney problems and stomach disorders.

Paurngaqutik:

Crowberry (EMPETRUMNIGRUM) is a plant from the ERICACEAE family that grows in abundance throughout Nunavut. It can be found along the coast and in sandy rocky areas, often growing in isolation from other types of plants. The berries resemble blueberries, of which the Inuit used an infusion to soothe upset stomachs like the Chinese used ginger.

Of particular interest to Alan was the family of Inuit herbs that were used for arthritic pains (in addition to other ailments). These included:

Mamaittuqutik

Labrador tea plants (LEDUMGROENLANDICUM) are the best known of all the plants used for traditional Inuit tea. Like crowberry, it belongs to the ERICACEAE family. It can be found through almost all of Nunavut, usually growing in dry rocky areas or in peat bogs. He said that this shrub is easy to recognize by its white flower buds and distinctive leaves that are smooth on top and fuzzy beneath. Tea, including both leaves and flowers, which give it a sweet perfume, are used as a treatment for aches and pains, and other ailments.

Ukiurtatuq

This plant (LEDUMDECUMBENS) is a close cousin of the Labrador tea, and with its straight leaves and white flowers, it resembles Labrador Tea but in a smaller size, and can be found growing through most of Nunavut. The flowers, stems and leaves of the plant can be used for treating gastrointestinal (stomach and digestive) problems and sore joints.

Another treatment for arthritis was a slightly more difficult one for him to 'swallow', literally. To ease pain in joints and other sore parts of the body, Long Life described using a heated stone or sand (wrapped in cloth) and used like a "hot water bottle." Over an ointment made from Labrador tea and seal fat. He also said that the fried fat might be rubbed all over the body after the person swallows a spoonful of it.

One of the herbs also traded was the yellow colored herb Turmeric. Turmeric belongs to the ginger family. This spice is a good way to relieve the symptoms of arthritis and in particular, psoriatic arthritis. That's because it presumably reduces proteins that can cause inflammation. The effectiveness of turmeric differs from one person to another. For some people, the effects are extremely mild and barely noticeable. For others, Long Life said that they experience great relief when they include this spice in their daily diet.

* * * *

While Alan was concentrating on Long Life's notes and recommendations regarding the use of naturopathic medicine, Gerald, for his part, was engrossed in the information he had received from Washington.

"Extraordinary," he said to himself while looking at the set of photographs Devon had sent him via secured download over night. Several pictures showed a forty-foot vessel, going by the name of *Northern Rover*, anchored right above the known location of the *Investigator*'s wreckage. The other photos showed three men alternatively diving or minding the boat's position. But the more interesting photo was the one depicting several open crates on the aft deck. Gerald presumed those were probably used to store the relics the men would pull up from the wreck.

Yet, Devon's solution to the problem didn't stop there; Interpol had now intercepted radio and other forms of communications between that boat and *The Contessa*. The only thing they were now waiting for was the next telltale conversation the men would have with someone on board the cruise ship.

The only problem Gerald could see now was that if the men aboard the hunters' boat found the McClure treasure before they recovered the rest of the relics, they would raise anchor and resume their journey back to wherever they came from. And that last piece of the puzzle was also something Devon promised to find out for him. If Interpol could find out where the boat had usually been berthed, maybe – and if all else failed – they could nab the thieves as they returned to their port of origin.

In the meantime, Gerald needed to find the riddler and the assassin, which he firmly believed was not the same person. To him, the riddler was trying to help matters by alerting Alan of the progress of the relics' recovery, but he was not the one who killed Cecil Legato. That person was still hidden aboard *The Contessa* and maybe would remain so until their return to Boston or until he killed both the riddler and Bornstein. "But why would he want to do that? And why did he kill Cecil in the first place?" Gerald wondered aloud. It didn't make sense. Everything was going very well until Cecil decided to meet with Clarisse – and that was another question that demanded answers: *Why would he want to meet the woman?*

* * * *

Later on, and still pre-occupied with finding that 'second steward' and who the blighter was, Alan decided to have a chat with the cabin attendants on his deck and the one who normally was assigned to his cabin. *He wouldn't be hard to recognize,* he thought, *with that tattoo on the side of his neck. Yet, he might not be easily found now that he had delivered his latest note.* With similar queries pervading his mind, he walked to the cabin attendants' preparation room where, at this time of the afternoon, he knew he would find them getting ready to make their rounds after their afternoon breaks.

"Hi, Doc, what can we do you for?" one of the men asked jocularly as Alan walked in.

"Oh hi, Mark, how you doing?" Alan replied, walking to the fellow he knew was his regular steward.

"Fine, Doc... and if it's about that check-up, I'm due to come in tomorrow morning..."

"No, Mark, it's not about the check-up..."

"What is it then?" Mark asked, a frown appearing on his brow.

"Do you recognize this guy?" Alan asked, pulling a photo of the suspicious steward out of the folder he had brought with him.

Mark looked at the picture closely. "It's not very clear, but I think that's Sam, Sam Wilcox. He's got that same tattoo..."

"And is he a regular steward?" Alan interrupted.

Mark shook his head. "He only fills in for anybody who's sick or on leave. Why?"

"Well, it's because I think he's been in my cabin a couple of times and I wanted to meet him, besides which, I haven't got his name on the list for having his physical," Alan replied indifferently, not wanting to alert the whole crew of the real reason behind his query.

"Okay," Mark said, his voice almost down to a whisper, "it's like this; I let him change the sheets and towels in your cabin when I need a bit of time off..."

"Time off for what?"

"Well, Doc, there's only a few hours when I can talk to my girlfriend back in Boston, and by the time I finish up here, she's sleeping, so Sam relieves me when he can."

"Okay, and don't worry, I'm not going to report you for this, but can you tell me where I can find him right now?"

"That I can't tell you, Doc. I don't even know where he bunks. I only have his cell number and when any of us need a hand he usually appears on time."

Alan thought about that for a minute and then said, "Why don't you call him now and tell him that you've got some sort of emergency at home, and that you need him to relieve you for part of this afternoon?"

Mark looked up at the doc, frowning again. "What's this about, Doc?"

"I just want to find him, because, as I said, I haven't got him on my list, and I want him to have a full physical before we get to Kodiak, if possible."

"Okay then, let me call him." Joining actions to words, Mark took his cell phone out of his vest pocket and dialed.

The conversation lasted less than a minute with Mark getting Sam to agree to report to the stewards' preparation room on the double.

A few minutes later, Alan was waiting for the guy, he was sure was the riddler, with his back leaning against the wall beside the door. Sam Wilcox wouldn't see him as he entered the room.

* * * *

In the meantime, Devon had contacted Gerald saying that he was forwarding a full-face picture of the second steward – a man by the name of Hans Grover, who far from being a wanted felon was actually a CIA agent undercover, assigned to follow the 'exploits' of Cecil Legato. He further told the Chief that the guy was really good at what he did apparently and apprehending him would not only break his cover but endanger the CIA's investigation.

As soon as he received the copy of the photo, Gerald went to the man's cabin – he was traveling under the name of Sam Wilcox and his cabin was on the sixth deck. Finding no one at home, the chief then made his way to the medical center where he found Evelyn. She told him that the doc had left without a word a half-an-hour ago.

Before leaving the center and at a loss to know where Alan could have gone, suddenly, he fished his cell out of his trousers' pocket and dialed the doc's emergency number.

* * * *

Sam Wilcox burst into the stewards' preparation room and made a beeline for Mark without looking around him. By the time Mark was pointing back to the door, Alan had blocked the fellow's escape with his back now leaning against it.

"Okay, Sam," Alan said, "why don't you come with me to the medical center; we need to have a chat about your physical, don't we?"

Visibly stunned, Sam walked to the doctor without a word, except for, "Okay, Doc, I just hate needles…"

"Me too," Alan replied, grabbing the fellow by the arm, and turning to Mark, he added, "Thanks, I owe you one."

"Don't mention it, Doc," Mark said, laughing as the two men went through the door of the stewards' preparation room.

In the corridor leading to the medical center, Alan felt his phone vibrate in his pocket. He ignored it until the vibrating tone told him it was an emergency. He pulled it out and answered it.

"Where are you?" were the first urgent words Gerald pronounced as soon as the line was open.

"I'm on my way back to the center, why?" Alan answered.

"The riddler is a CIA agent, Doc, and I'm trying to find him now..."

"Don't bother," Alan said, "I'll meet you at the center," closing his phone down. He looked at Sam and added, "Okay, let's go and have that chat, shall we?"

"Sure, Dr. Mayhew, and don't worry, I won't give you the slip."

"I sure hope not, I'm really tired of receiving anonymous notes from you..."

"But they worked, didn't they?"

"That they did, but I still want to know why you didn't come right out and tell me what you had found out?"

"I'll tell you what you want to know, but you'll have to play ball with me..."

"And why would I want to do that?"

"Because if you want to catch a killer, that will be the only way to do it."

"Alright, and I suppose you know who he is, don't you?"

Alan only got a nod as an answer to his question.

CHAPTER THIRTY-ONE

He is a she – really?

WHEN ALAN AND SAM reached the medical center, Gerald was waiting outside, his back leaning against the doorframe.

"Chief Tolberg, this is Sam Wilcox," Alan said, before Gerald could open his mouth, "otherwise known to us as the 'riddler'."

"Well, I'll be damned," Gerald said, a sneering grin appearing on his face, "and where have you been hiding?"

"Not really hiding," Sam answered, entering the medical center with Alan and Gerald. "If you found me you probably know that I am a passenger…"

"Yeah and a CIA agent," Gerald groaned quietly as the three men stepped into Alan's office.

"That's right. My name is Hans Grover, but around here I'm Sam Wilcox."

"Okay, have a seat, Sam, and you too, Gerald," Alan invited, sitting himself down at his desk.

"Before we go any further, I've got one question for you, Sam," Gerald said, "Why this elaborate prank, pinning notes on the doc's pillow? Why not identify yourself right off the bat when you boarded the ship?"

"I thought you would ask that, Chief," Sam replied, smiling. "I was originally hoping not to involve anyone in Cecil Legato's deceitful scheme, until I had received intel regarding the *Northern Rover*. Once I was informed that the hunters' boat was anchored and the divers were actually starting their recovery dives, I thought it would be best for me to stay away from the action and away from you, Chief, until they actually retrieved some relics…"

"But why continuing to keep us in the dark for all this time – we could have foiled their plans if you had come to me…"

"No, Chief. You couldn't have done anything. You don't have the resources aboard this ship to go after a band of treasure hunters, believe me."

"Alright, I accept that, but we could have stopped the killer from murdering Cecil Legato…"

"Again, Chief, we couldn't have known things would have turned out the way they did. And when Legato went to meet his maker, I really wanted to stay out of it…"

"Why?" Alan blurted, getting annoyed. "Had we known there was some sort of plan to steal the relics, our security officers could have been more vigilant…"

Sam shook his head. "I'm sorry, Doctor, but, since the beginning, the CIA didn't want me to alert anyone of my presence on board. And that's why I devised the riddles, so that you, at least, would be aware of something happening."

"Alright," Gerald said, "I guess your handler has a short leash on you." Sam nodded. "Besides which, we can't undo the past now. But we can certainly try joining forces to prevent another murder"—he peered into the agent's eyes—"or are you going to tell me that your CIA wants to handle that one too?"

"No, I'm not going to say that. The CIA was only after these hunters and their investors. The murder was something we didn't expect. Actually, the Canadians aren't too happy about us meddling in their investigation either, since the *Northern Rover* is now anchored in Canadian waters. You see, my assignment was to keep an eye on Isaac Bornstein and keep the line between he and the hunters open so that we could nab the whole lot of them red-handed, as it were."

"But your plans have changed now, after we've placed Mr. Bornstein under protective custody, haven't they?"

"Yes, they have, Chief. I'm now working with CSIS – the Canadian Secret Intelligence Service – to stop the illicit raising of the relics from the *Investigator*."

"Okay, if that's the case, who's in charge of finding the killer?" Gerald asked again.

"Well, since Cecil Legato was an American citizen, I guess you're looking at him, even though the Royal Canadian Mounted Police (RCMP) will be involved."

"And don't tell me," Gerald said derisively, "You know who the killer is."

"I don't know for sure, Chief, but looking at the list of passengers there is only one possibility…"

"Oh yeah? And who might that be?"

"Listen, Chief, before I put my cards on the table, and as I've asked Dr. Mayhew before coming in here, can you assure me that I remain out of sight and out of your reports?"

"Well, that depends… if you give me enough evidence to work on, I might be able to do that, yes."

"And what sort of evidence would you need?"

"A background check, a rap sheet, or something to justify anyone's suspicion – but you know that as well as I do."

"Okay, I'll get my supervisor to send you what I've got and then you can take it from there, would that work for you?"

"And if this evidence leads to a dead-end, what then?" Gerald asked.

"I can help you ferret out more intel on other people you might suspect, but I think I am right when I say that the woman…"

"Did you say 'the woman'?" Alan erupted, advancing his chair closer to the desk.

"Yes, Doctor, that's the only person that would fit the profile…"

"And who's that?"

When Sam and Gerald left his office, Alan was nonplussed. But the woman was in all outward probabilities their killer. She was an actress by avocation, she was perfect to play the part, and no one would think twice if she appeared on the scene unexpectedly wearing one disguise or another. On top of which, she is athletic enough to handle an arbalest without trouble.

Alan shook his head when he picked up the phone and dialed Babette's number. *She needs to be told*, he thought, *before she gets ready to rehearse the third act of the play.*

"Good Gracious!" Babette exploded over the line when she learned that a member of her cast was probably a murderess. "And how am I supposed to play this one, Alan? I can't very well go up to her and tell her, "Oh, sorry, dear, but I've got to *replace* you under suspicion of murder," now can I?"

The twist in the statement had Alan smile. "No, Babette, but I suggest you get her an understudy until Chief Tolberg is ready to arrest her."

"And when is that likely to happen?"

"It won't be long now, since the CIA is providing the chief with all the information he needs to make an arrest."

"Okay, leave it with me, Alan, but I tell you right now, I don't like it."

"No one does, Babette, and I promise when you go down to the *Investigator* with the submarine, it will have been all worth it."

"You mean it? I'm going down," Babette shouted enthusiastically over the line. "Really? That would be absolutely wonderful…"

"So, will you please prep an understudy?"

"I'll even play the role myself, if it comes to that…!" She paused, but Alan could hear her giggles. "That would be too funny though. Anyway, I better return to whatever I was doing before you dropped that bombshell on me."

"Okay…"

"Oh, by the way, could you and Tiffany join me for dinner when we're anchored in Kodiak? And before you say anything, I won't take no for an answer. You know that I know the rules, and if you're breaking any, I'll talk to our captain myself."

"Alright, alright, Babette, I'll tell Tiffany to call you to arrange to have dinner with you in Kodiak. How's that?"

"Perfect!"

* * * *

That conversation reminded Alan of another matter that he needed to attend to before arriving in Kodiak. They were soon to be reaching the Arctic Circle and at that latitude he was now aware of another looming problem. He had received an advisory memorandum from Health Canada that very morning and when he had read it, he was not sure he wanted to believe its content. During the Arctic summer, where there is always a proliferation of biting insects, in some of the northern regions, some of these insects – namely Aedes aegypti mosquitoes – were carrying Dengue Fever. This is a viral disease, which infects 50 to 100 million people worldwide, leading to half-a-million hospitalizations, and approximately 12,500 to 25,000 deaths a year. Normally it is usually seen in tropical areas and not in northern Canada. Unfortunately, there had been reported cases of Native Canadians being infected with the disease, and, according to Health Canada, there was no doubt these cases were viral Dengue-related and a few cases of Dengue Hemorrhagic Fever, the more severe type of the disease, had also been reported.

As unbelievable as it is, medical science has no vaccine or other medicine for the disease. The only treatment is supportive (IV fluids) and Alan needed to teach the passengers and crew aboard *The Contessa* appropriate prevention. The first time one gets the disease, it usually manifests as a very bad flu. The second time one is infected by the mosquito bite, the victim can develop the more dangerous and fatal hemorrhagic variety of the disease (bleeding, low levels of platelets and blood plasma leakage). The only prevention is to spray the body with strong repellents and to cover *all* exposed skin. The memorandum recommended that people on any of the islands north of the 65th parallel, would do well to cover themselves with protective clothing, gloves, nets, and even goggles. The Aedes mosquito prefers breeding during daylight hours and favors clean waters to algae-ridden ponds. And there was plenty of both clean water and sunlight in the northern areas of the Arctic at this time of year, which was undoubtedly why it had evolved so far north. One more concern, in addition to the endemic community acquired tuberculosis, for the passengers and crew aboard *The Contessa*.

In preparation of the passengers and crew whom were to go on Banks Island, Alan decided that it would be imperative to have a memo distributed to all the passengers before they reached Prudhoe Bay – the next port of call after Kodiak.

* * * *

The following morning, which came almost unnoticed since, at that latitude, days merged into evenings and mornings floated out of the nights nearly within an hour of each other, Alan decided to have an early run on the upper deck while *The Contessa* was approaching the coastal town of Kodiak. From his vantage point, he stopped in awe. The small community spread over a few miles along the island's coast and on the other side of a bridge that linked two neighborhoods. The ferry, which was berthed alongside the port facility, sounded its horn in a resonant welcome as soon as *The Contessa* made its appearance.

The green hills behind the town, the colorful houses, and the freshness of the landscape gave Alan a sense of newness, a feeling of rejuvenation. He abandoned his jogging and stood – his forearms against the railing – to admire the beauty of it all.

A few minutes into his reveries, Tiffany came to join him and stood silent beside him for a moment before she nudged him. "Have you been here long?" she asked.

Alan shook his head. "Not long enough, Tiff." He turned to face her. "I was thinking of how lucky we are to spend a great deal of our time visiting places such as this one." He pointed to the port of Kodiak. "I know, most of our long hours are part ordeal, and part endless drudgery, but when I look at a place like this one, I can't help but feel grateful for who I am and for what I do."

"Wow, aren't we philosophical this morning," Tiffany said, slipping an arm into his. "But I have to agree with you – we're lucky. Most people when they're done with their jobs have to face endless hours in traffic, and problems at home, seeing to the kids, making dinner, washing dishes or seeing to the shopping for the week and sometimes shoveling snow from the front drive, before they can relax in front of their TV's – if they ever do."

"Exactly. And that's why I wouldn't want to do anything else," Alan agreed, wrapping his arm around his lady's shoulders. "Talking about dinner, have you been able to call Babette to see if she is available tonight for us to have a late supper with her?"

"Yeah, and she said that she needed to talk to you about something before dinner." Tiffany looked up at Alan inquiringly. "Do you know what it's about?"

"I think I do, yes." Alan hesitated. "I didn't want to tell you anything about it until the person's identity was confirmed, for one thing, and I am still not sure that we've got the real culprit."

"You mean you have uncovered who the riddler is?"

"Oh yes, and in his case, there's no doubt of it – he's the riddler alright."

"But you just said you're not sure…"

"I was not talking about the riddler, Tiff. I was referring to our killer."

"And how does he concern Babette?" She stared up at the doc. "Don't tell me she knows who the guy is…"

"Who the girl is," Alan was quick to correct.

"What are you saying, Alan?" She shook her head. "Never mind that; all I want to know is if Babette is in danger… and if she wants you to call her urgently, shouldn't you call her NOW?"

"I will talk to her, don't worry, and no, she's in no danger…" Alan stopped talking, pulled his phone out of his pocket and dialed Babette's suite.

She answered at first ring. "Oh, so glad you've called, Alan," Babette said in one unnerved breath, "I got up early – couldn't sleep since you called last night – and went down to see if I could find anything in the woman's dressing room…"

"And have you?" Alan cut in.

"No, nothing, and I mean that literally. It's as if the girl has vanished. There's nothing left in that room but the costumes for the play."

"Do you know which cabin she occupies?"

"Yes, yes, and when I went to see if she wanted to come down to Kodiak with me – just as a pretext to see if she was there – I found Chief Tolberg and another guy talking in front of her wide open cabin door."

"Are you saying she's disappeared?"

"I don't know, Alan, and frankly I don't want to know."

"Yeah, I think that's best for all concerned." He paused for a fraction of a second. "Okay, I'll go down and see what's happening, and you don't move from your suite, okay?"

"No problem. Don't worry; I have no desire to come face to face with that woman now. But you let me know when the 'coast is clear', won't you?"

"Yes, of course. And if you still want to go into Kodiak, maybe we should all leave the ship as soon as the gangway is down – I've got a few items to collect from their pharmacy supplier anyway."

"Good. I'll talk to you soon then."

When Alan hung up, Tiffany was still staring. "Okay, what's going on now?"

"I can't tell you right now, Tiff. It's enough that I've talked to Babette about it." He hugged her and whispered, "Let's go down together this afternoon, shall we?"

CHAPTER THIRTY-TWO

It's as simple as that!

YET BEFORE ALAN COULD go down into Kodiak with Babette and Tiffany, he had several crewmembers to put through their physical examinations. Most were routine check-ups but one of them came early with an unusual complaint.

The gorgeous Ukrainian, known to be a sexually loose woman, was a cabin steward whom Alan had already examined when they were in Juneau.

Surprised to see her, he asked, "Any specific problems you should tell me about?"

"Well, I have noticed lately that if I get even the tiniest cut, it seems to bleed for hours," she replied. "Do you think I might be a hemophiliac?"

That question took Alan aback. Helena certainly didn't display any of the symptoms generally attributed to hemophilia. "Well," he replied, "Hemophilia is a genetic disorder and it is more often found in men, but it is possible for a woman to be a hemophiliac. Tell me, how much do you lose when you have your period?"

After a moment, during which Helena seemed to be lost in thought, the curvaceous crew member said, "Oh, about seven or eight hundred dollars, I guess."

Bursting in loud laughter, under Helena's puzzled gaze, Alan then said, "I see what you mean, but that's not exactly what I wanted to know..."

"No? What then?"

"I meant how much *blood* are you losing during your period?"

Laughing in her turn, Helena said, "Just enough to prevent me from working with my 'regulars' for at least four days!"

When Helena left with some recommendations regarding solving her problem, he asked Evelyn to take over – he needed to get down to their suspect's cabin or find out what was going on with that cast member.

Having found no one near the woman's cabin, Alan made his way to the Chief's office. As soon as he entered, he saw the lady he knew only as Mrs. McTeege sitting across the chief's desk.

"Ah, Dr. Mayhew, glad you could come in – I was about to call you actually," Gerald said, pointing to a chair beside Mrs. McTeege's. "Let me make the introduction: this is Ms. Kristina Korsakov of the Russian Secret Service"—he turned his face to Alan—"and this is Dr. Mayhew."

"Pleased to meet you," Kristina said, smiling at Alan.

"Same here," the doc replied perfunctorily. He switched his gaze between the agent and Gerald. "And how does a Russian agent come to play a role in a theater performance aboard a condo-cruise ship?"

"Ha-ha," Kristina snickered. "I was just explaining to Chief Tolberg the reason for my being aboard *The Contessa*, when you came in, Doctor. But I think the better question would be; what is your interest, or your role, in this affair?"

Alan saw Gerald's face redden with every syllable the woman pronounced. He knew the chief didn't like anyone taking control of an interview.

Alan waited to reply.

Gerald was fuming when he blurted, "Ms. Korsakov, if you don't mind, let me ask the questions here. But for your information, Dr. Mayhew has been instrumental in locating the person who made us aware of the relics being stolen from the *Investigator*..."

"You mean Hans?"—Kristina shook her head—"that's no great revelation, I knew about him even before he boarded this ship."

"And if you were aware of the CIA's investigation and the ramifications this affair entailed even before Mr. Legato was murdered, why didn't you contact my office with that information?" Gerald demanded.

"Because, Chief Tolberg, Russia has no obligation to give your office or other American entities any information or conclusion we draw from our investigation. It's as simple as that!"

"No, Ms. Korsakov, it is *not* as simple as that! On this ship, I am responsible for the safety and security of all passengers and crew, and in that capacity, I should be able to get the information we need to solve any crimes that may have been perpetrated on board. In this particular case, you have been hindering my investigation by not divulging the names of the people you knew were involved..."

"But..." Korsakov interrupted.

"NO, Ms. Korsakov – I'm not finished. And, we're still in American waters at the moment; so, it will take me great pleasure to oust you from this ship as soon as the gangway is down and surrender you to the appropriate authority." Gerald shrugged. "What happens after that doesn't concern me."

"But don't you want to know who Legato's killer is?"

"At this point I don't know if I want to trust you with anything you might want to tell me, Ms. Korsakov. I don't want to spend precious time verifying everything you say or even try comparing notes with you. You could always tell me who you suspect is the murderer, and I'll take that intel under advisement – it's simple as that!"

After a long moment of silence, Alan turned his face to the Russian agent. "You know, Ms. Korsakov, you're right, I initially didn't want to be involved in any of this, but as it stands, I am – involved that is – and I would like you to answer me one question; why were you ready to leave this ship even before Chief Tolberg here apprehended you?"

"Who said I was ready to leave?" Korsakov asked, visibly obfuscated.

"The 'who' is not important, but the 'why' is, Ms. Korsakov?" Gerald interposed. "So, why were you prepared to 'abandon ship' today?"

"Simply because I have somewhere else to be, that's all."

"Alright, have it your way," Gerald groaned, getting up from his chair and then shouting, "Neil, get in here NOW!"

"Yes, Chief?" Neil said, appearing in the doorway within seconds of being summoned.

"Would you please accompany Ms. Korsakov to her cabin and lock her in there. Make sure there's no luggage or personal effects, like computers or cell phones, left in that room, before you come back here."

"Okay, Chief," Neil replied, stepping to Ms. Korsakov's chair and waiting for her to stand up. "Please come with me, ma'am..."

"You should do well to address me by my title, young man. I'm Agent Korsakov, you understand."

"Yes, yes," Neil said impatiently as the woman got up, "I'll do that, but now come with me."

What happened next would remained etched in Alan's memory as one of the most outlandish incidents of his career; Kristina maneuvered her left arm around Neil's neck, dragged him in front of her, stepping backward to the door and, with her right hand, pointed a small Beretta that had been concealed in her jacket's sleeve to the Chief and Alan in turn. "Okay, gentlemen," she said surprisingly calmly given the circumstances. "Since I was ready to leave the ship anyway, I will do so right now, with Neil here, and when I am satisfied that no one is on my tail, I'll disappear." Her gun didn't waver for a moment from the Chief's face.

That woman is a professional, Alan thought, *she won't hesitate to kill to achieve her goal.*

"And believe me, if I am bothered in any way while I'm in Kodiak, you are the one who will face the repercussions of an international incident. Is that clear?"

"Sure," Gerald said, nodding.

Korsakov then turned to Alan. "As for you, Doctor, I hope you don't involve yourself any more than you are in this affair, otherwise, I could see to it that you find yourself pushing paper in some medical institute or other, okay?"

Alan nodded in response.

* * * *

A quarter of an hour later, Neil was preceding the Russian agent down the gangway until they reached the pier. From the deck, where they were standing, Alan and Gerald watched the woman walk away unhindered toward the end of the pier and then climb into a 4x4 that sped off in the direction of the town.

"That's it then," Gerald said resignedly, shaking his head. "She knew who the killer is, didn't she?"

Alan nodded. "She probably did, but you know, Gerald, it's much better this way..."

"How do you mean?"

"Well, first off, you couldn't have stopped her without creating an incident aboard this ship that would have probably seen most passengers packing their bags, and then I don't think any of us would particularly like to be interrogated by any agents of any sort – especially Russian ones – during the rest of this trip."

Gerald smiled. "My sentiments exactly, Doc. In fact, I'm glad she's gone and I would bet my bottom dollar that she has been warned off from Banks Island by the RCMP's and that's the reason she wanted to leave so quickly."

"Talking about that; where's our CIA agent? Why wasn't he at this meeting?"

Gerald chuckled suddenly. "He was otherwise occupied." Alan looked at the chief wide-eyed. "He was sifting through the Russian woman's luggage actually."

"Good one, Chief." Alan laughed. "And has he found anything?"

"I don't know yet, but from what I looked at before he began his search, there wasn't any arbalest – or parts thereof – in her suitcase."

* * * *

Not wanting Babette to remain locked in her suite after Ms. Korsakov had left the ship; Alan went to her door and knocked on it lightly. A couple of seconds later Babette opened the door wide, asking, "So, where is she? Is she alright?"

Alan nodded. "Yes, Babette, she is. And she is off the ship – never to return."

"Wow, that's a relief," Babette said, exhaling a sigh. "But don't just stand there; come in, come in." Alan did. "But if she's off the ship, she wasn't the killer then – or have they arrested her?" She closed the door and went to sit opposite the doc in the small lounge room.

"No, she was not the killer…"

"Who then? And why was she ready to leave so quickly?"

Alan smiled. Babette's querying mind was working overtime. "We don't know who yet, and she was ready to leave because her assignment was completed apparently."

"Come on, Alan, what assignment? I hate playing twenty-question, you know." Babette's impatience was obviously reaching the boiling point very quickly.

"She is a Russian agent, Babette, and that's all I can tell you about her. She didn't say anything else."

"And Chief Tolberg didn't get any more information than that?"

"As incredible as it sounds – and I was there when it happened – she was not prepared to say anything about anything."

"Well, doesn't that beat all!" Babette exclaimed, getting up from the sofa. "I wish I had known who she was beforehand; I would have questioned her myself." She got up and stepped to the refreshment cabinet. "Would you like a juice or something before lunch?"

Alan waved a hand in front of his face. "No, thanks, Babette, I should go actually. I need to get to the pharmacy supplier in town this afternoon," he said, rising to his feet. "Tiffany and I will come and get you at eight o'clock to go to dinner – is that still okay then?"

"Sure, that will be just fine – I've got tons to do now that I have to find another Mrs. McTeege." Babette lifted her glass to Alan. "Here's to,

'two steps forward and one back', Alan."
"Well said, Babette!"

CHAPTER THIRTY-THREE

"It is good," Satan said.

SITTING QUIETLY, TRYING TO get his thoughts together after returning from his errands in town and dealing with the locals, Alan pondered a lot, and for some reason, he started thinking about the state of medical care in the US today. He remembered one of the comedians joking about God and Satan fighting about food. Alan grinned and wrote on his computer, a little item that reflected his thoughts, in light of the latest check-up he had given to one of the passengers.

In the beginning, God created the Heavens and the Earth and populated the Earth with broccoli, cauliflower and spinach, green and yellow and red vegetables of all kinds, so Man and Woman would live long and healthy lives.

Then using God's great gifts, Satan created Ben and Jerry's Ice Cream and Krispy Crème Donuts. And Satan said, "You want chocolate with that?"

And Man said, "Yes!" and Woman said, "And as long as you're at it, add some sprinkles." And they gained 10 pounds.

And Satan smiled.

And God created the healthful yogurt that Woman might keep the figure that Man found so fair.

And Satan brought forth white flour from the wheat and sugar from the cane and combined them. And Woman went from size 6 to size 14.

So God said, "Try my fresh green salad."

And Satan presented Creamy Ranch Dressing, buttery croutons and garlic toast on the side.

And Man and Woman unfastened their belts.

God then said, "I have sent you heart healthy vegetables and olive oil to sprinkle on them."

And Satan brought forth deep fried fish and chicken-fried steak so big it needed its own platter. And Man gained more weight and his cholesterol went through the roof.

God then created a light, fluffy white cake, named it, "Angel Food Cake," and said, "It is good."

Satan then created chocolate cake and named it, "Devil's Food."

God then brought forth running shoes so that His children might lose those extra pounds.

And Satan gave cable TV and remote controls so Man would not have to toil changing the channels. And Man and Woman laughed and cried before the flickering blue light and gained pounds.

Then God brought forth the potato, naturally low in fat and brimming with nutrition.

And Satan peeled off the healthful skin and sliced the starchy center into chips and deep-fried them so they might indulge while watching the cable TV. And Man gained pounds.

God then gave lean beef so that Man might presumably consume fewer calories and satisfy his appetite even though he knew beef was not healthy.

And Satan created McDonald's and its 99 cents' double cheeseburger, and then said, "You want fries with that?"

And Man replied, "Yes! And super size them!"

And Satan said, "It is good."

And Man went into cardiac arrest.

God sighed and created quadruple bypass surgery.

Then Satan created HMOs, the American answer to Canadian and British socialized medicine, none of which truly worked, from what Alan could see.

To prove his point, Alan added a final note:

There is more money being spent on breast implants, facelifts and Viagra today than on Alzheimer's research. This means that by 2040, there should be a large elderly population with tight faces, perky boobs and huge erections and absolutely no recollection of what to do with them.

Closing his computer with a smile on his face, Alan then went to meet Tiffany before the two of them would go with Babette for dinner in Kodiak.

"So, what's the latest on your quest for *The Contessa Killer*?" Tiffany asked with a smirk on her face when she opened the door to Alan.

He couldn't do anything but smile at the quip. "The latest is that we still have a murderer aboard *The Contessa* and we're no nearer to finding him (or her) than we were yesterday."

He took his beautiful lady in his arms and hugged her tenderly for a few moments. He needed her more than ever – he felt the tiredness of the long hours bearing down on his body. "Shall we go then?" he asked her, releasing her from his embrace.

"Sure, I'm ready," Tiffany replied, zipping up her winter jacket.

"I hope they have decent food where ever we're going," Alan remarked, escorting Tiffany out of her cabin and closing the door.

"Well, the tourist bureau has recommended a little place near the harbor that sounds very nice."

"Oh yeah, what's it called – maybe I know it," Alan said.

"It's called *Henry's Great Alaskan Restaurant*, near the port. Have you been there?"

Alan smiled. "Yeah, and if you want healthy food – fish, pasta or veggies – the selection is very limited, mostly, you've got burgers and fries. But if you wanted a better choice or more comfortable seating, for Babette especially, we could go to the Best Western, which is not far from Henry's place. Up to you."

"How about we let Babette choose? After all she invited us," Tiffany suggested on the way up the elevator.

"Good idea. Let's see if she's ready first...." Alan knew that sometimes Babette wasn't the most punctual person in the world, yet that thought was soon forgotten when the lady of the stage opened her door wide to her guests.

"What do you think?" she asked, spinning around to show all of the features of her apparel.

"That's beautiful, Babette," Tiffany exclaimed, while admiring the blue jacket with the trimmed hood and matching pants. "You look gorgeous. I'm sure you'll turn heads in that suit."

"I sure hope so," Babette replied, "I want to be noticed – it cost me enough for no one noticing it. I tell you, my producer better pay his next bill..." She laughed. "And where are we going then?" She looked up at Alan who had his arms crossed over his chest, grinning.

"With that outfit, I think you deserve to show it off at the best hotel in town, wouldn't you say?"

"I agree," Babette replied, slipping an arm into Alan's. "Let's go then," she added cheerfully.

Although it was past eight o'clock when they arrived at the hotel's restaurant, it was still broad daylight outside.

"You know, Alan, this interminable day time plays tricks on my sleeping habits," Babette said, taking a seat at a table across from the salad bar.

"It does on everyone, Babette," Tiffany agreed, unzipping her jacket and sitting down beside Alan.

"And the opposite is true in the winter – people can't seem to get enough sleep in these parts, unless they use their light visors or sit in front of their light boxes for 30 minutes a day to avoid what we call Seasonal Affective Disorder or SAD," Alan agreed. "Actually that reminds me of an experiment some physicians carried out years ago on speleologists who spent a great amount of time in caves without natural daylight."

"What did they do?" Babette asked, visibly interested.

"Did they sleep all the time?" Tiffany rejoined.

"No, actually. They were given no watch to tell time. They began to have longer and longer periods of sleep, and the curious thing was that they stayed awake much longer as well. In the end, the four men and women who participated in the experiment were sleeping twenty-four hours at a time and then staying awake for twenty-four hours."

"Wow!" Tiffany said a little louder than she wanted to, "and what happened when they got out?"

"It took them a couple of weeks before they got back to a regular rhythm."

"Thank goodness for clocks then," Babette said. "I don't think I could stand writing for twenty hours or so every day, my producer would have a fit…!"

During dinner, the inevitable topic of the McClure's treasure and the killer still being aboard *The Contessa* came up.

"Why do you think Kristina Korsakov wanted to leave the ship?" Babette asked.

Tiffany started giggling unexpectedly. "Is that really her name?" She looked at Alan.

"Yeah, that's the name on her passport apparently – why are you laughing?"

"It's just that I thought of Rimsky Korsakov – you know the Russian composer…?"

"Oh yes," Babette said, "very good, Tiffany." She turned her face to Alan. "Did you know that Rimsky Korsakov was a naval officer?"

Eyebrows raised in amazement, Alan replied, "No, I had no idea." He stopped abruptly and seemed to be suddenly engrossed in his thoughts. "I'm sorry, ladies, but I've got to call the chief…"

"You mean Chief Tolberg?" Babette asked.

"Yes, I've just made the connection between Ms. Korsakov and who ever she met at the port when she disembarked this afternoon." Alan got up from his chair, and added, "Just order dessert, I'll be right back."

As he was making his way to the men's room, Tiffany and Babette exchanged a quizzical glance.

"What do you think Alan meant by finding the connection…?"

"I have no idea, Tiffany, but obviously it has something to do with Ms. Korsakov, and the McClure treasure."

"Do you think he knows who the killer is?" Tiffany asked, almost whispering the words.

Babette nodded. "If he doesn't know the name, he's very close to finding out who he is, I should think."

"But what has it got to do with Rimsky Korsakov?"

"That I could not say. All I know is that Korsakov was a member of a group of composers called "The Five", and his most famous piece is Scheherazade, the story of a concubine who spent a thousand and one nights recounting fables to the sultan in order to avoid being beheaded."

"Wasn't that the sultan who believed that all women were false and faithless?"

"Exactly. And maybe, our Ms. Korsakov was telling tales such as Scheherazade did to save herself from being killed."

"That would be all too fantastic – but what else could you expect from a Russian agent," Tiffany remarked musingly.

CHAPTER THIRTY-FOUR

A piece of ass

A FEW DOORS FROM THE hotel where Babette, Alan and Tiffany were having dinner, and after having been served in the Kodiak cocktail lounge, a real southern gentleman beckoned the waitress back and said quietly, "Miss, y'all sure are a luvly, luvly lady; can ah persuade y'all to give me a piece of ass?"

"Lord, that's the most direct proposition I've ever had!" gasped the girl. Then she looked around the room, smiled and added, "Sure, why not? You're nice lookin' too and it's pretty slow here right now, so why don't we just slip away up to my room?"

When the pair returned half an hour later, the man sat down at the same table and the waitress asked, "Will there be anything else, sir?"

"Why yes," replied the southern gentleman. "Ah sure 'preciate what y'all just did for me; it was real sweet and right neighborly, but where ah come from in Albama, we lack our bourbon real cold, so ah still need to trouble y'all for a piece uh *ass* for mah drink..."

* * * *

Not wanting to take too much time away from the dinner table, Alan, meanwhile, tried to make his conversation with Gerald as short as possible.

"I gathered as much," Gerald said, in reply to Alan's suggestion. "Tell you what, if you don't mind, I'll come on shore and join you for dessert, would that be okay? Just tell me again which hotel you are having dinner at?"

Alan hesitated. "Sure, why not, but Ms. Babette is having dinner with us..."

"That's fine, Doc, she's been a real sport about it all, so getting her involved might give us another take on this whole situation."

"Okay then, we'll see you in a few minutes."

"Yeah, give me fifteen at the most."

* * * *

When Alan returned to his seat at the dinner table, two pairs of eyes were riveted on his face.

"Sorry, ladies, but I thought it couldn't wait..."

"What was that? I mean what couldn't wait – your bladder?" Tiffany smiled.

"Well, when you mentioned Rimsky Korsakov, Tiff, and you told me that he had been a naval officer, Babette, I thought there must have been a connection between our Russian agent and the killer aboard *The Contessa*."

"So, what's or who's the connection, you think?"

"The only naval officer I could think of at that moment ..."

"...is Stephan Ivanov," Tiffany blurted, taking in a breath.

"You mean, the staff captain?" Babette asked wide-eyed.

"I think so, yes. But that connection doesn't mean that he's the killer."

"And it's not because he's Russian that he's connected to Agent Korsakov, is it?" Tiffany argued.

"No, you're right, Tiff. But when you piece this puzzle together, Stephan is a very important corner in this whole picture." He paused, looking down at the dessert menu the waitress had left on his placemat. "Did you order already?" he asked, looking at Babette and Tiffany in turn.

The two women exchanged a glance and Babette said, "No, we were waiting for you; but what did Chief Tolberg have to say about your suggestion?"

"I think we should wait until he gets here – he'll tell all of us what he's concluded from this line of thought."

A broad smile drew up on Babette's face. "Finally, we'll get some answers!"

Alan looked up. "Haven't I given you most of the answers so far, Babette?"

Babette tapped on Alan's arm. "Of course you did, Alan, but hearing it from 'the horse's mouth' sort of thing will be much better. Besides, I think I'll have a few questions of my own to ask." She turned her face to Tiffany. "And one in particular; like Tiffany mentioned when you were on the phone, Alan, our Ms. Korsakov seems to be a real Scheherazade – telling you and the chief all sorts of lies probably – so why did he let her go so easily?

"Because she's a Russian agent, Babette. The chief didn't want to create some sort of international incident at this juncture..."

"Well, that's all fine and dandy, Alan, but I think you let her go a little too soon."

At that moment, Gerald bounced into the restaurant and made his way to the table, saying, "Thanks, Doc, for letting me out of my cage for a bit. I needed the break." He nodded to Tiffany with a smile on his lips. He then turned to Babette. "And don't you look nice this evening, Ms. Babette, that white turtle neck is very becoming."

"Ah, there is a man after my heart," Babette said, grinning. "And flatteries will usually get you most places with me, Chief – but tonight, don't count on it!"

Bursting in laughter, Alan pulled a chair for Gerald to sit. "Glad you could make it too, Chief."

Approaching the table discreetly, the waitress asked, "Will you have dinner, sir?"

"No thanks, just dessert with these folks, if I may," Gerald answered.

"Oh yes, and now that we're all here, why don't we order," Babette suggested. "I'll have Jasmine Green tea and some vanilla ice cream."

"Good choice," Alan remarked, "but chamomile tea would also be a good option, Babette, it would help you sleep and it's good for the digestion, too." He looked at the menu again.

"I'll have your chocolate mousse and an espresso," Gerald said, smiling up at the waitress. "Sleep is the last thing I need tonight." He chuckled.

"I'll have some fruit salad and some jasmine tea," Tiffany rejoined, giving the menu back to the patient waitress.

"Make that the same for me," Alan said last.

"Okay, coming right up," the lovely girl replied, trotting back to the kitchen.

"Alright, Chief Tolberg," Babette began, "do tell us what's going on with that Scheherazade of yours?"

"Who...?" Gerald looked at Alan, his face the portrait of puzzlement.

"It's the woman who told a thousand and one stories to the sultan to avoid being beheaded," Tiffany tried explaining.

"Has someone lost their head, besides me?" Gerald quipped, looking at Alan.

He and the two ladies burst out laughing.

"Okay, okay, guys, I know I'm not the smartest one around this block, but could you tell me what you're talking about?"

"Okay, Chief, forget about Scheherazade for a minute and go back to our connection between Stephan Ivanov and our Russian agent – what have you deduced from that conjecture, if anything."

Gerald grunted. "Hum, yes, well, as I said to you on the phone, Alan, Agent Korsakov seemed to be in a hurry to leave the ship because, as we both saw, someone was waiting for her at the end of the pier."

"Yes, and I thought it might have been someone who had known the ship's schedule and was ready to pick her up as soon as *The Contessa* docked."

"Precisely. Although all of the passengers and crew were well aware of our date and time of arrival, only a few would have had a reason to contact someone on land and have a car ready to pick the person up in a hurry. We have no passenger disembarking in Kodiak at this point – none that we're aware of anyway – but we have two persons of interest who needed to get away in a rush and rejoin their party on Banks Island before our arrival..."

"You mean the killer and one other," Babette interposed.

"Yes; and the other being our Agent Korsakov."

"Are you saying that the killer was the one driving the car that picked her up?" Tiffany asked.

"And the staff captain could be the one who arranged the whole escape?" Babette blurted. "Is that the connection then?"

"In a word, yes," Gerald replied.

"But why – why would a reputable officer do such a thing?" Tiffany was visibly not satisfied with that surmise.

"Probably because he needs money," Gerald answered.

"Money? Is he gambling his salary away or something?" Babette inquired.

"Not exactly, Ms. Babette, but I think it may have something to do with some sort of blackmail." Gerald paused. "Before coming down to join you, I sent a quick email to our Interpol agent in Washington, asking him to dig in Mr. Ivanov's past or to give me some indications as to why he'd be blackmailed."

"What about questioning him, Chief?" Alan asked, crossing his arms over his chest.

"Yes, well, if we want to find his body pierced with an arrow in the morning, we could do that, yes!"

"But, Chief, didn't you just say that the killer has probably left the ship with Scheherazade – I mean with the Korsakov woman?" Tiffany asked.

"Yes, I did, but if I am wrong and we question Mr. Ivanov, and then find him dead the next day, I'll find myself in the brig for the rest of the trip – not a pleasant prospect, I can assure you."

The waitress chose that moment to bring everyone's desserts and teas and coffee. "Would there be anything else?" she asked once everything was on the table.

"Just the bill," Alan said.

"Oh no you don't, Alan," Babette erupted. "This was my invitation, besides which, I haven't had this much fun since I don't know when, so it's my treat." She looked up at the young woman. "Let me give you my credit card right now, Lucy"— the name on her nametag—and just bring me the receipt, will you?"

"Yes, ma'am," Lucy said, smiling and taking the card from Babette's extended hand. "Be right back."

"Thank you, Ms. Babette," Gerald was first to say, when Lucy had left the table. "But I didn't think this situation should be taken lightly…"

"No-no, Chief, and don't misunderstand me; you see, it's the thrill of finding answers to convoluted problems that always excites me. To me the fun is in the chase, the drama resides in the discovery, and the sadness comes after the ordeal is over."

"Wow!" Gerald exclaimed, before bringing a spoonful of chocolate mousse to his lips, "I hadn't heard anyone explain what I do put quite like that before."

"So, why don't I have a chat with Stephan tomorrow, if you can't question him officially?" Alan suggested after munching on a piece of kiwi fruit.

"That's a good idea, Doc, but let's wait until I hear from our guy at Interpol; I'm sure he may have some intel that you could use during your interview."

CHAPTER THIRTY-FIVE

"That red thing bit me!"

WHILE STILL IN KODIAK, two of the passengers decided to take a hike along a trail leading outside the city. They didn't take a guided tour since they wanted to take a bit of a break from their wives' company. The trail didn't go far up the foothills but as soon as they left the town's outskirts, they noticed the increasing amount of insects swirling about them.

"Voracious aren't they," Ed remarked to his companion.

"Sure are," his friend, Tom replied, swatting a couple of beasties off his face. "And to tell you the truth I didn't expect to see any mosquitoes this far north either."

"Didn't you read the memo?" Ed asked.

"What memo?" Tom inquired, stopping and turning around to look at his friend.

"The memo from the med-center that said that we've got to watch for these insects – apparently some of these blasted mozzies carry some sort of viral fever..."

"You've got to be kidding me – really?"

"Yeah – but the memo also said that we don't have to worry about it till we get farther north."

"Well, don't that beat all!" Tom shook his head to get some of the nastier biters away from his baseball cap. "Wilma and I came on this cruise to get away from the tropics, and here you are telling me that we've got to look out for mosquitoes like we did in Africa!" He waved his hand in front of his face. "Well, in for an ounce, in for a pound, as they say." He shrugged and resumed walking ahead of Ed.

A little farther up the trail, Ed tapped on Tom's shoulder, saying, "Stop for a minute, okay? I've got to take a leak."

"Sure, there's nobody around here to take a look at your dick anyway," Tom said, turning away to leave his friend on his own.

Not ten seconds later, Ed hollered, "I've been bitten! That thing bit me! Tom...? Come over here!"

As Tom rounded the tree behind which Ed was standing, he saw his friend sitting on the ground looking at his genitals with a desperate look on his face. "Look," he said, "this thing bit me so bad, I'm bleeding...What do you think it is? Do you think it's one of those Dengue mosquitoes that got me?"

"What's that you said? Dinged mosquito – is that the fever one?"

Ed nodded. "It's called Dengue, the memo said."

Tom looked down at the small but bleeding wound and grunted. "I'll call the medical center on the cell. The Doc will know what to do with your injured...."

About 8 minutes later, Tom was on the line with Alan.

After Tom had explained what had happened – but not revealing exactly where Ed had been bitten, except to say that it was somewhere on 'his neck' – Alan said, "Okay, you're too far out of the city for me to get help over there right away, so you need to suck the wound as hard as you can and spit out every bit of blood you can suck out."

Not sure that he had heard the doc correctly, Tom lowered the phone from his ear and looked at it – his face the picture of incredulity. Replacing the cell close to his ear, he asked, "You sure that will do the trick, Doc?"

"Yes, I'm quite sure your friend will be okay, but it's better to be sure than sorry. And when you get back, tell your friend to come to the medical center as soon as he's boarded the ship, okay?"

"Okay then, Doc, I'll tell him. Thanks." And with these words Tom shut his eyes and the phone and then looked down at his friend.

"What did the doctor say?" a visibly anxious Ed asked.

"You and I are going to be a lot closer than hiking buddies; and you can NOT tell my wife about this – pull your pants down a bit further!"

* * * *

When Ed came through the door of the medical center, his face was white as if he had just received a kick in the stomach. He slumped in the chair beside the door, and with pleading eyes, he said to the approaching Evelyn, "Nurse, please help me, I've got Dengue fever...!"

"What makes you say that, sir? Have you been bitten recently?" Evelyn asked, looking up in the direction of Alan's office and waving to him to come out.

"Yeah...," Ed said in an almost inaudible murmur. "It was one of those red beasties; it came right at me and just landed and then it bit me..."

"You must be Ed Bunter," Alan said, coming out of his office. "Were you on a hiking trail with Tom Hastings...?"

"Yeah, Doc, that's us. The wife and I got your memo about the Dengue fever mozzies and I think I've been bitten by one of these critters."

"Where were you bitten, sir?" Evelyn cut in helpfully.

"Yes, and could you describe the mosquito for us?" Alan rejoined.

"Well..." Ed hesitated and raised his eyes to the doc. "I... I mean... I was just having a pee..." He looked up at Evelyn, silently pleading for her understanding. "...and then this huge red thing landed on... well... you know where, and took a chunk of my dick with him..." Evelyn stared at the patient for a second before she succumbed to irresistible giggles, turning on her heels and rushing out of the room.

Ed looked up at Alan, terribly embarrassed now. "I tell you I've never seen a mozzy like that one – they're big and red..."

"I think what bit you is not a mosquito, Mr. Bunter," Alan said, trying to keep a straight face.

"No? What was it then?"

"I think it was a flying red ant. They're ferocious alright, and they bite, but the only thing to fear from them is a burning sensation around the bite and a temporary rash that could be soothed quite easily with calamine lotion – nothing more."

"Are they like the red harvester ants that we get in the South?"

"Yes, they're of the same family, but this species breed in the prairies and the mountainous regions throughout Northern Canada and Alaska. They're more vicious than their southern cousins but they're not dangerous and they don't carry any diseases, so I think you're quite safe."

Ed frowned, the color on his cheeks returning. "Are you telling me that Tom had to suck on the bite on my dick for bloody nothing!?" He stood up. "The blighter better not tell anything about this to anyone, or I'll have his hide and yours for that matter! I don't want some fairy coming to ask me to do it too."

His arms crossed over his chest, Alan smiled. "I shouldn't blame Mr. Hastings for what I told him to do; in fact, what he did might reduce the chance of you experiencing any discomfort around the wound, so you and your wife can still enjoy each others company."

Not calming down any, Ed went on, "Sure, sure, why don't you tell him to brag about his exploits while you're at it, Doc. This is insane!"

"Alright, Mr. Bunter, why don't I have a look at the bite, disinfect it and see if there's any sign of inflammation?"

Relenting a little, Ed nodded. "Okay, but, please, Doc, not a word of this to anybody, okay?"

"Okay – not a problem."

* * * *

A little later, Alan was still thinking of that red ant that must have bitten Ed Bunter. He had some experience in the North, and remembered well his first hike over a bog in Newfoundland where there were more flying, biting insects than the blueberries he was trying to collect. He was glad he had passed that memo around to everyone for it seemed these 'beasties', as Ed called them, were really going to be a bother. Still pensive, the phone on his desk called him to attention.

"Doctor Mayhew," he said as soon as he picked up the receiver.

"Hi, Doc, this is Stephan"—Alan straightened up in his chair—"would you mind coming to my office – I think we need to talk."

"Yes, I think we should," Alan replied. "I'll be right up."

"Okay, I'll be waiting."

When Alan hung up, he looked at the phone for a minute before picking it up again. He dialed Gerald's office.

"Chief Tolberg; what can I do for you, Doc?" Gerald said as soon as he heard Alan's voice.

"I've just been called to the staff cap's office – do you know what it's about?"

"Not off the top of my head, no." He paused for a brief moment. "But didn't you say you were going to have a conversation with him?"

"Yes, but I didn't have time yet, so I was wondering if I should tell him what we suspect. What do you think?"

"Well, in such circumstances, I usually let the man speak and take it from there. If he comes up with some answers or explanation or even a confession, then I'm sure you'll know what to do."

"Okay, that's what I'll do then. Oh, by the way, did you get anything from your Interpol guy yet?"

"No, not yet, but I don't think there'll be much to tell. To my way of thinking, our staff cap is probably as clean as a whistle, unlike some this line has hired."

"Maybe you're right – we'll see. I've got an over-active imagination, I guess."

"Maybe not, Doc. It's always better to get ideas out there sometimes, than finding oneself in trouble later because we've kept things to ourselves."

* * * *

The door of the staff captain's office was open when Alan arrived. He knocked lightly on the door, drawing Stephan's attention to him.

"Come in, Doc, and have a seat," he said, closing the folder in front of him. Alan sat down. "The reason I think we need to have a talk is this..." Stephan got up and went to a tall cabinet standing along the far wall of his office. "Someone left this in my room," he added, pulling a sturdy-looking arbalest out of the cabinet.

Alan stared. "When was this? I mean when did you find it in your cabin?"

"This morning – after breakfast." He handed the weapon to Alan. "And the reason I wanted to talk to you about this is because I've had a visit from our CIA agent..."

"You mean Sam Wilcox?" Alan laid the arbalest against the edge of Stephan's desk.

"Yes – actually his official passport says Hans Grover. He apparently found this ugly thing in a storage closet on one of the lower decks and was going to give it to Chief Tolberg when it disappeared again and found its way to my cabin."

"But, Staff Captain, may I ask why you wanted to discuss this matter with me – and not Chief Tolberg?"

"I'm going to have a chat with him as well, don't worry, but since Sam Wilcox told me that he had been advising you of the current thieving going on near Banks Island and had discussed this matter with you a few days ago, I thought I would get all my facts straight before I returned this weapon to our chief of security."

"I don't think I could add anything more to what Agent Wilcox might have told you, Staff Captain, except for the fact that I found it strange that we had a Russian agent aboard *The Contessa* for awhile, who left abruptly upon our arrival in Kodiak."

"And you think she's had something to do with the killer?"

"More than that, Staff Captain..."

"Between us, you can call me Stephan," the staff cap cut-in, smiling at Alan.

"Thank you, Stephan, and as I was saying, I think Agent Korsakov knew the killer and has now left with him (or her) when she disembarked as we docked here in Kodiak."

"But if that's true, it appears that someone is playing games, wouldn't you agree, Alan?" Stephan said as he rounded his desk and went back to sit down. "Agent Wilcox had that weapon in his possession, and then someone swiped it from him to drop it off in my cabin – why?"

"It doesn't make much sense, I agree. But someone is surely trying to implicate you in this affair, Stephan. And I should think this is all a matter of diverting our attention from the real problem…"

"Which is…?" Stephan asked.

"Which is the fact that we have five people on board this ship that would have a lot to gain by having the upper hand on the raising of the relics aboard the *Investigator*."

"Five people? Who are they?" Stephan asked, his eyebrows furrowed.

"Well, we've got Mr. Isaac Bornstein for one – he's still the prime instigator of finding and raising of the relics. Then we've got our two archeologists, who would have a lot to gain if their assumption regarding the existence of the McClure treasure was correct. No one at Parks Canada believes the treasure exists, and if it happened to be removed from the wreck *before* we arrived on site, anyone of them could say that they were wrong and share in the bounty once the treasure was hauled off somewhere and sold to the highest bidder. And finally, we've got our two divers. Without them, proving or disproving the existence of the treasure would not happen. And in their case – again – having found no treasure when they dive with the sub, they could return to England safe from any queries when, in fact, a portion of the loot would be waiting for them when they return."

The two men sat in silence for several minutes, each considering their next move.

Then Stephan said, "How can we stop this whole thing from happening – any suggestions?"

"Only one, Stephan, and mind you, it's only a suggestion on my part; I would encourage Chief Tolberg to have the RCMP show their presence near the treasure hunters' ship and arrest the lot of them before they have a chance to finish the job and return to where ever they came from."

Stephan nodded. "Yes, I think that's what Gerald should do." He paused for a moment. "But what about the killer? Do you have any idea who he is?"

"I can't point the finger at anyone right now, Stephan, but at this point, I would really question the presence and credentials of the Russian agent – Ms. Korsakov. She is the one person who knew all of the players since the beginning of this affair, plus, being Russian, she could have been commissioned by some other party to eliminate Cecil Legato – who was perhaps in competition with some other pirates that have wanted to put their hands on the McClure treasure and relics."

"Are you thinking of mutiny or some such thing, Alan?"

The doc nodded. "I wouldn't call it that really, but with Bornstein engaging the services of one party – in locurence Cecil Legato – who's to say that some rival or other hasn't taken over the job."

"And we're coming back then to our four protagonists, aren't we?"

"In a round about way, yes. The two archeologists and the two divers have probably been taken over, so to speak, by someone with the means and resources to pull this off."

"Okay, Alan, let's leave it at that for now, but let's you and I talk to Gerald as soon as possible. We need to stop these thieves for one thing and we need to get that treasure – if it exists – in the proper hands. Besides which, I think I'd like to rip that Korsakov woman to bits myself…"

Alan chuckled. "Somehow I would think you would do a wonderful job of it!"

CHAPTER THIRTY-SIX

Annette

"I THINK I FOUND MY replacement for Mrs. McTeege," Babette was saying to Tiffany when the two women were having a light breakfast at the upper deck café.

"Oh yeah, and who's that?" Tiffany asked, spreading some jam on her croissant.

"I don't think you've met her, but she's about the same size as our Scheherazade and learning her lines for the third act in the next week or so shouldn't be that much of a problem for her."

"That's good, and I guess she's no Russian agent either," Tiffany said, giggling.

Babette sipped some of her tea and shook her head. "Believe me, this time I took the precaution of asking Chief Tolberg if she had a "dossier" of some sort anywhere – but no, she's just the daughter of one of the passengers who is interested in the performing arts."

"And how did you find that jewel so quickly?"

"Oh, that was sheer coincidence really."

"How's that?"

"Well, at the end of the second act, I spent a bit of time with some of the passengers after most of the people had gone back to their cabins, and there she was – Annette's her name – with her father. She wanted to talk about the theater in general and in particular the writing of plays. We talked for a while and Annette impressed me as a very articulate young woman with a lot of aplomb. So, I called her yesterday, and after we had a chat, she read a few lines for me – and I think she's going to be perfect."

"And you already got information on her from Chief Tolberg – that was fast," Tiffany remarked.

"Oh, I asked him last night and he phoned me back early this morning with the answer. I think he's got a good friend at Interpol that he can contact anytime."

"Isn't that the guy Gerald mentioned when we had dinner – or dessert I should say – with him?"

"Yes, I think that's him. But no matter who he is, I'm just glad to have found the person I need before Prudhoe Bay – otherwise, I would have had to take over the role myself."

Tiffany had to smile. Somehow she couldn't imagine Babette playing the role of the vulgar Mrs. McTeege.

"Yoo-hoo - yoo-hoo!" A voice from behind Tiffany suddenly interrupted her momentary reveries. "Oh, am I glad I found you both here," Susan said, hurrying to take a seat between the two ladies. "I've got the most wonderful news to tell you..." As usual the former ballet dancer managed to attract everyone's attention. Dressed in a white winter outfit, she looked nothing short of 'resplendent' in the morning sun.

"My goodness, Susan, where have you been all this time?" Babette queried, visibly taken aback by their friend's unexpected but welcomed appearance.

"Oh, everywhere, Babette..."

"Isn't that a bit difficult on a cruise ship?" Tiffany asked, tittering.

"No-no, actually, I think all my prayers have been answered." Susan paused, switching her gaze from Tiffany to Babette. "I've met the most wonderful, handsome man in the whole world – he's simply a dream, I tell you!"

"Well, that's good news indeed, my dear," Babette said, not as excited perhaps as Susan had expected her to be. "And who is the lucky fellow?"

"Oh that's the strange thing," Susan went on, her voice dwindling down to a mere whisper. "He's someone I had met years ago when I was in Paris. And now, would you believe it; he lives in Boston – not two blocks from my place! I couldn't believe it myself when he first told me."

"And he's a passenger on this ship?" Tiffany asked, a disbelieving frown appearing on her brow.

"Yes, yes. You see, we didn't recognize each other at first – it has been years since we've talked – but when he noticed me going to the golf links, just to watch, mind you, he approached me and finally got the courage to ask if I was Susan Ashley – and the rest is history, as they say."

"And you told him about your... I mean you told him what you've been through last year?"

Susan nodded emphatically. "Oh yes, mind you, it took me sometime before I could spill the beans, but as soon as I told him, he said that I was "an extraordinary woman", to quote him. And that made me feel absolutely wonderful – it was like someone had lifted a massive burden off my shoulders."

"And did he tell you as much about himself, like how he came to live in Boston?" Tiffany asked, curiosity lacing her every word.

"Sure, and he's been married, and has only one daughter who just happens to be very interested in the performing arts..."

"Her name wouldn't be Annette by any chance?" Babette ventured, thinking it would be all too fantastic if the girl was the same Annette she had just cast in the role of Mrs. McTeege.

"Why yes, that's it – but how on Earth did you know?"

"Well, my dear, call it serendipity or extraordinary coincidence, but when I had to find a replacement for a member of my cast, Annette's name popped into my head and I've just cast her in the role of Mrs. McTeege."

"Hold on a minute, Babette, can you backtrack a bit – how did you lose a member of your cast? What happened? Is the previous Mrs. McTeege sick or something?"

Babette fixed her gaze on Susan for a minute before answering. She wasn't sure she should divulge what she knew of the story to Susan. "No, she wasn't sick, but she had made arrangement to meet somebody in Kodiak when we arrived – or so she said – and she left me stranded."

"Of all the nerve!" Susan exclaimed. "Why on Earth didn't she say anything sooner?"

"I have no idea," Babette lied. "But, to tell you the truth, I think Annette will make a much better Mrs. McTeege. She's got the makings of a very good actress, I think."

Tiffany had remained silent through the exchange but a question was menacing to burn the edge of her lips – she couldn't hold back anymore. "But, Susan, do tell us about this gentleman; is he tall, dark and handsome – I mean you already said he was handsome – but what does he do for a living? And what brought him to Boston? Has he told you?"

Susan laughed under the puzzled gazes of her friends. *Not a laughing matter*, Tiffany thought. "Don't look at me like that, Tiffany, please." Susan giggled some more. "Of course, I asked him all of these questions and many more in fact. I'm no spring chicken anymore and I don't want to find myself with a broken heart and an empty purse at the end of a romance again, even as passionate and enticing as it might be. So, yes, I asked him what he does for a living and the answer is…" She paused for effect. "He is in boat salvage operations. He's got several salvage ships docked in Boston apparently. And it's because this cruise is headed to the site of one of the most daring and intriguing salvage operations in Arctic history that Auguste Sauvage – that's his name by the way – is making the journey to Banks Island. Isn't that wonderfully interesting?"

Babette and Tiffany couldn't help but stare at Susan.

"Wonderfully interesting" isn't quite what I would call this whole thing, Babette thought. *More like adding another dimension to the puzzle and another suspect on Chief Tolberg's list.*

* * * *

While Babette and Tiffany were learning about Mr. Auguste Sauvage's past and current endeavors, Gerald was reading the latest report Devon had sent that morning. The report included added intel on Annette's father. Mr. Sauvage didn't have a 'dossier' with Interpol, the CIA, CSIS in Canada or even the RCMP, but he certainly had a history of salvaging shipwrecks all over the world and possessed a fleet of salvage boats that were all generally docked in or near Boston Harbor. What intrigued him the most, though, was the fact that one of his ships by the name of the *Itinerant du Nord* was currently on a voyage that was supposedly taking it to Hudson's Bay. *What would he be doing in Hudson's Bay*, Gerald asked himself. And the ship's French name also caught his attention. Not a French-speaking person, Gerald asked Neil if they had a bilingual dictionary somewhere in the office.

"Well, no, Chief, but why don't we ask the doc, he speaks French, maybe he could help."

Gerald nodded and picked up the phone. Alan, Gerald and Stephan had had a long chat the previous day and Gerald had taken Alan and Stephan's advice to ask the RCMP to get some help in stopping the illegal salvage operation that was going on near Banks Island. But Gerald soon found out that CSIS was the only outfit willing to launch an operation of this magnitude, requiring the dispatching of a vessel to Banks Island on such short notice. CSIS had suggested sending a helicopter to the island and see if a fishing boat would be available to take the agents to the hunters' vessel.

"Hello, Gerald, what's up?" Alan said, when he saw the security office's number on the call display.

"Do you speak French?" was Gerald's first and surprising question.

"Well, yes, a little, why?"

"I guess you would since you spent all those months in Le Havre getting your med-center ready... anyway, could you translate "Itinerant du Nord" for me?"

"Sure... "du Nord" means "of the north" as you probably gathered, and "Itinerant" means "voyager" or "rover"..." Alan stopped, looking at the phrase he had just scribbled on his notepad.

"Could it be translated as the *Northern Rover?*" Gerald asked. He knew the answer already.

"Of course – yes. But what's this all about? Why are you asking?"

"I just can't say right now, Doc. I'll get some more intel on this little mystery and talk to you once we've left Kodiak, okay?"

"Well... yes. But just answer me one question; are the Canadians doing anything to stop the hunters from raising the relics at this time?"

"I don't know yet, Doc. That's something else – I'm still waiting on CSIS to give me an answer on their potential intervention. You know, I wish to God, we were somewhere else than the bloody frozen Arctic – no one seems interested in going anywhere fast around here."

The frustration in Gerald's voice was obvious and Alan decided to leave the man in peace for now – he would talk to him at dinner, he thought. However, Alan knew there was now something else to question – the *Northern Rover* and the *Itinerant du Nord* were probably one and the same vessel traveling under different names.

CHAPTER THIRTY-SEVEN

Mr. Sauvage

AFTER BREAKFAST, TIFFANY decided to find Alan – she wanted to tell him about Mr. Sauvage and his salvage boats. Something about Susan's story didn't sound right. She found him in the library of the ship, reading a paper with a grin on his face.

"What are you doing here?" Tiffany asked in a hushed voice, sitting down beside him.

"Have a read of this," Alan replied, passing the paper to her and pointing to the classified ads of a British newspaper – a few days old, judging by the date at the top right-hand corner of it.

Tiffany looked at Alan first, wondering what he was on about, and then read:

FREE YORKSHIRE TERRIER
8-years-old. Hateful little bastard. Bites!

FREE PUPPIES
1/2 Cocker Spaniel, 1/2 sneaky neighbor's dog.

FREE PUPPIES
Mother is a Kennel Club registered German Shepard.
Father is a Super Dog, able to leap tall fences in a single bound!

COWS FOR SALE. NEVER BRED
Also 1 gay bull for sale.

WEDDING DRESS FOR SALE
Worn once by mistake. Call Stephanie.

JOINING NUDIST COLONY!
Must sell washer and dryer. $100.

FOR SALE BY OWNER
Complete set of Encyclopedia Britannica, 45 volumes.
Excellent condition. $200. or best offer. No longer
Needed. Got married. Wife knows everything.

Tiffany put a hand to her mouth to prevent from bursting into loud laughter.

"And have a look at this," Alan said, grabbing the paper from Tiffany's hand, folding it to another page, and putting it down in front of her again.

> ... and a thought from a Great Scottish Thinker, Billy Connolly: "If women are so bloody perfect at multitasking, how come they can't have a headache and sex at the same time?"

"Out of our control," Tiffany said, "that's why – can't do anything when you've got a headache, now can you?" She looked up at the doc.

He shook his head and smiled before saying, "Anyway, why did you want to find me?"

"I've just had breakfast with Babette and Susan..."

"And how is our ballerina today? I haven't seen her in days."

"That's just it, Alan... but let's get out of here; we can't talk in here. I've got an interesting bit of news." She raised her gaze to Alan while they both got to their feet. "By the way, what were you doing in here?"

"Oh I thought I could find a book listing the salvage ships..."

Tiffany literally grabbed his arm and led him outside before he could utter another word.

"What's going on, Tiff?" he then asked.

"I'll explain in your office. Come on, let's go," she urged.

* * * *

Arriving at the medical center, they were surprised to find Gerald waiting for Alan. Evelyn had told him that he would be right back.

"Hi, Gerald," Alan said first, "what are you doing here? Need some more French lessons?"

Gerald guffawed. "No, nothing like that, Doc." He turned to Tiffany. "Hello, Ms. Sylvan, how are you?"

"Just fine, Chief, but if you're here about Mr. Sauvage, I want to hear all about it, because I've got my two cents to add, if you don't mind."

Gerald gaped and then looked at Alan, who shrugged.

"Where did you hear that name, Ms. Sylvan?"

"Why don't we go in my office," Alan suggested, "I have no idea what you two have been up to, but like Tiffany said, I'd like to hear all about it too. Shall we?" He stretched an arm toward the open door.

"Excuse me, Doc," Evelyn called to him, "before you go in, can you tell me if Angie and I should begin distributing the insect repellant we've received? There are boxes and boxes of them."

"Don't worry about that for now, Evelyn. As soon as I've finished with Ms. Sylvan and the Chief, I'll start a distribution list for you, okay?"

"Sure, Doc, no problem," Evelyn said, returning to the stock room.

Alan looked after her for a second before stepping into his office.

Teaching 400 people how to truly protect themselves from virulent mosquitoes in the middle of the Arctic is not going to be a simple task, he mused, rounding his desk and finally returning his attention to Tiffany and Gerald.

"So, what is this all about?" Alan asked, drawing his chair close to the desk.

"You go first, Ms. Sylvan, where did you hear Mr. Sauvage's name?"

"Well, I heard the name at breakfast this morning when I was talking to Ms. Babette and Ms. Ashley…"

"What have they got to do with the guy?" Gerald interrupted, visibly taken aback.

"It's like this, Chief," Tiffany began, and then went on explaining the situation. "You see, Babette has now cast Annette Sauvage in the role of Mrs. McTeege in her play, and Ms. Ashley has fallen head-over-heels for her father," she concluded, looking from Gerald to Alan in turn.

"And I gathered, from what you've just said that Susan Ashley is aware of Mr. Sauvage being involved in salvage operations worldwide?" Alan put in.

"Yes, but when Ms. Babette and I heard that Mr. Sauvage was on board this cruise because he was curious to see the spot where the *Investigator* has sunk, we were thinking that maybe the man has got other motives for visiting Banks Island."

"Okay, Ms. Sylvan, I think you've both hit on something here, because when I asked Interpol to give me anything they had on Annette Sauvage, my friend also forwarded some intel regarding her father."

"And they found something interesting about the man?" Alan queried.

"Not exactly – not about the fellow – but about that boat, the *Itinerant du Nord.* That salvage ship made its way to Hudson's Bay a month ago. However, there's no trace of such a ship anywhere going up the Northern Passage. But, some weeks back the *Northern Rover* made the journey to end up, we presume, three miles' offshore Banks Island."

"So you think the *Northern Rover* belongs to Sauvage and that he's now involved or has taken over the relics' salvage, is that it?" Alan crossed his arms over his chest.

"Yes, that's what I think – there is no other reasonable explanation for the *Northern Rover (or* the *Itinerant du Nord)* being anchored near Banks at this time. Interpol couldn't find any trace of a forty-footer being registered anywhere under the name of *Northern Rover,* but the *Itinerant du Nord* is indeed registered in Liberia (like many boats are these days) and it's usually docked in Boston. The owner being, as I said, none other than our Mr. Sauvage."

"Alright, Chief," Alan said, "I think you should have another talk with Mr. Bornstein and ask him if he knew the owner of the vessel Cecil Legato was obviously using before his demise."

"But shouldn't you guys talk to Mr. Sauvage too?" Tiffany asked, looking at the chief.

"Sure, Ms. Sylvan, but not just yet," Gerald replied. "Before we alert Mr. Sauvage of our discovery, I think we need to re-interview our divers and archeologists and see if they've been bought into the scheme, as you surmised, Doc. After that, we'll see how we proceed."

"Okay, but what do I say to Susan – I mean Ms. Ashley – she's going to be devastated when she hears this..."

"No, Tiffany," Alan interposed, "I suggest you don't say a word to anyone at this juncture. We don't even know if Mr. Sauvage knows where his boat is or what it has been used for – for all we know, Cecil Legato might have rented the *Itinerant du Nord* and changed its name once it arrived in Hudson's Bay, and then sailed to Banks Island to raise the relics."

"That's what I'm thinking, too, Doc," Gerald rejoined. "And talking to Mr. Sauvage wouldn't serve any good purpose right now. We don't want to stir more trouble at this point, do we?"

"I guess not," Tiffany agreed, looking down to her lap. "But what if Ms. Babette starts asking questions? You know how investigative she can be..."

"I know, Tiffany, I think I'll have a word with her before she gets too involved," Alan said, rising to his feet. "I'll have a bit of time this evening and that's when I'll see if I can talk to her."

"Sounds like a plan," Gerald said, getting up and stepping to Alan's office door, "And I think I'll have that chat with Bornstein right now."

* * * *

As soon as Tiffany left the medical center, she made her way downstairs to meet with Babette at the theater – back stage. She didn't want to leave Babette in the dark about what she had found out and felt that her friend needed to know what was going on.

"Hi," Tiffany said, going into Mrs. McTeege's dressing area where Babette was examining some of the costumes.

"Oh hi, Tiffany," Babette replied, turning to her. "Well, what did Alan say?"

"Not much, but we both met with Chief Tolberg who had some interesting info about Mr. Sauvage..."

"Did he say anymore about his salvage operations?"

"Not in so many words, but he's discovered that there is a boat anchored offshore Banks Island now and it probably belongs to Mr. Sauvage – although it has changed name since it left Boston. And the chief suspects Mr. Sauvage doesn't know anything about the illegal salvage operation on Banks Island."

Babette exhaled a heavy sigh. "That's a relief. I hope the man is really an innocent party in this affair, otherwise Susan's gone and done it again, and is not going to take the whole thing very well, I'm afraid."

"That's what I've said to Alan and he said he'll come and talk to you before the day is over – he's afraid you would ask too many questions of Annette if you didn't know."

Babette chuckled. "Yes, I know, I'm the first one to recognize that I'm quite inquisitive when things don't sit right with me, but I wouldn't go as far as risking the success of an entire play – or my life for that matter – by questioning the wrong parties at the wrong time."

Tiffany smiled. "Like the singer said, "know when to fold..." sort of thing."

"Yes, my dear, although I've never learned to play poker or other card games, I always "know when to fold" as you said."

Tiffany turned to the dresses hanging on the rack. "She hasn't got many costumes to wear, I guess?"

"No, she doesn't, but I think I'll need to pin that skirt at the back, because I noticed Annette is quite a bit more slender than our Russian girl was." She took the suit in question off the hanger, sat down and looked at the zipper.

"Do you think she was the killer?" Tiffany asked suddenly.

Babette looked up. "Yes, I think she was. I think the Russians have always had an interest in the Arctic territories, and if there was any way for them to grab that treasure from under the Canadians' noses, they would do everything they could to grab it."

"Are you saying this whole affair is now masterminded by a group like the Russian mafia?"

"Not the Russian mafia necessarily, Tiffany," Babette said, lifting her eyes from the skirt in her hands, "but the Russian government itself."

"Are you kidding me?" Tiffany couldn't believe her ears.

"No, Tiffany, I am not kidding. I think Mr. Bornstein initially hired Cecil Legato and a team of relic hunters to raise the treasure from *The Investigator,* but when Cecil Legato was murdered and Agent Korsakov appeared on the scene, I thought the only explanation was a Russian involvement of some sort."

* * * *

When Gerald reached Isaac Bornstein's cabin, he found the man typing away on his laptop and hardly acknowledging the chief's presence.

"May I ask what you are doing, sir?" Gerald asked, sitting down beside the desk.

"Well, Chief, this story has to be recorded. Somehow, when this is all over, I want the world to know about the McClure Treasure. And if it doesn't exist, I want people to know that piracy still endangers the lives of sailors everywhere on all the oceans."

"So you're writing your memoirs, are you?"

"Not really, Chief, this story is only part of what you call my memoirs. It would take me much longer than a few weeks aboard this ship to write my life's story." Bornstein then finally lifted his gaze to Gerald. "And to what do I owe this visit?"

"Well, several things have happened since we last spoke and I thought we needed to have another chat about the start of this whole affair."

Bornstein crossed his arms over his chest. "But you know how it all started, Chief – it's in my statement, which I'm sure you've read a couple of times since you've put me in protective custody."

"Yes, but there are a couple of items that I frankly forgot to ask, which might be important now."

"What's that then?"

"Well, when you first hired Cecil Legato – I mean when you asked your wife to engage his services – were you aware of his renting a vessel out of Boston to lead the hunters' team to Banks Island?"

"Okay, Chief. Seriously, I have no recollection of a vessel being hired to go to Banks Island. The initial plan was for Legato to arrange for a vessel to sail to the island *after* we had ascertained that there was a treasure aboard the *Investigator*. If our trip down with the sub proved fruitless in that regard, I wasn't going to spend the money to have a vessel sail all the way to Banks Island just to raise the few items left on the wreck."

"So, you're saying that Cecil hiring a vessel and sailing to the coast of Banks Island is news to you, is that correct?"

"Yes. The agreement with Parks Canada was that I would pay for the sub-dive and help the archeologists with completing their catalogue. And as I learned since then, Captain Middleton mentioned that four days would be enough to do that, but if we needed to raise the relics then I should expect it would take longer. And if I recall my conversation with Dr. Lespierre, it was either Captain Middleton or Stephan Ivanov who suggested that *The Contessa* wasn't a salvage boat and that both archeologists should stay behind on the island if we wished to raise the relics left aboard the *Investigator*."

"So, they've kept you informed of what's going on, have they?"

"Yes, they have, Chief. Since I'm paying their salaries on this mission, I wanted to know if there had been any changes in the plans or itinerary."

"And I suppose I'm the first one to inform you that a vessel is currently anchored above the wreck and raising what ever is left aboard the *Investigator*."

Bornstein's face turned bright red. "Are you telling me there are some pirates stealing the relics right now?"

"Yes, that's what I'm saying. And I'm surprised you didn't know about it since Mr. Legato had arrived on Banks Island way before we reached Juneau."

"No, no, Chief. I've admitted to trying to divert the treasure from Canadian hands into mine – if the darn thing exists – but no, I have not engaged Cecil or anybody else to steal these relics…"

"Come on, Mr. Bornstein, what did you think Legato was going to do – go to Banks Island, wait for you to find the treasure with our submarine and then raise it for you without getting his share?"

"He would have gotten his share in cash, not in stealing anything – no."

"Okay, let's get on to something else – that's water under the bridge anyway – we've got that vessel anchored over the *investigator* and it appears to belong to a reputable operator out of Boston by the name of Auguste Sauvage – do you know him?"

"Never heard of him, no."

CHAPTER THIRTY-EIGHT

A Russian government plot?

ON HIS WAY TO have lunch at the officers' mess, Alan noticed the two divers, Edward and Sam, laughing their heads off while watching what was going on the pier below the ship. Since he wanted to talk to them sooner than later, Alan took the opportunity and approached the men.

"Oh hi, Doc," said Edward, a grin on his face. "You've got to hear this one!"

"Oh yeah, what is it?" Alan queried, putting his forearms on the railing and turning to Edward.

"Well, we got a string of jokes from the guys on the rig this morning – they must think we're pretty bored around here – anyway, I've received this one joke that I think is absolutely hilarious."

"Okay, let's hear it then," Alan said, shaking his head, and chuckling a little.

"Okay, Doc, here goes it," Edward began, "Gunter, one of the wipers on another cruise ship, was really turned on by one of the guys in the spa department and wanted to have sex with him, but he belonged to someone else. One day, Gunter got so frustrated that he went up to him and said, "I'll give you $100 if you let me screw you. But the guy said NO. Gunter said, "I'll be fast. I'll throw the money on the floor, you bend down, and I'll be finished by the time you pick it up." He thought for a moment and said that he would have to consult his boyfriend. So, when he saw his boyfriend who worked as a waiter in one of the dining rooms, he told him the story. His boyfriend said, "Ask him for $200, pick up the money very fast; he won't even be able to get his pants down." So he agrees and accepts the proposal. Half an hour goes by, and the waiter is waiting for his boyfriend to come back to the cabin they shared. Finally, after 45 minutes, Gunter comes in all bedraggled and he is asked what happened. He answers, "The bastard used coins!"

Laughing wholeheartedly at Gunter's clever deceit, Alan said, "Let me tell you another one that you might want to send to your friends back in England."

"Is it a doctor's joke?" Sam asked. "I heard they can be pretty hot, is that right?"

"Well, I'll let you guys be the judge," Alan replied.

"Okay, go ahead," Edward said.

"Okay, here's the way I heard it: One night a man and a woman are both at a bar knocking back a few beers. They start talking and come to realize that they're both doctors. After about an hour, the man says to the woman, "Hey, how about if we sleep together tonight? No strings attached. It'll just be one night of fun."

"The woman doctor agrees to it. So they go back to her place and he goes in the bedroom. She goes in the bathroom and starts scrubbing up like she's about to go into the operating theater. She scrubs for a good ten minutes. Finally she goes in the bedroom and they have sex for an hour or so.

"Afterwards, the man says to the woman, "You're a surgeon, aren't you?"

""Yeah, how did you know?"

"The man says, "I could tell by the way you scrubbed up before we started."

""Oh, that makes sense", says the woman. "And you're an anesthesiologist aren't you?"

""Yeah," says the man, a bit surprised. "How did you know?"

"The woman answers, "Because I didn't feel a thing."

When the laughter between the three men had died down, Edward asked Alan, "Did you want to see us for something, other than jokes, Doc?"

"Yes, as a matter of fact I did. But let's not talk over here, if you don't mind…?"

"Okay," said Sam, "why don't we go to the lounge bar for a beer, how's that?"

"Lead the way," Alan replied, walking behind the two men.

As soon as they arrived in the lounge, Alan spotted a table at the back of the room and suggested they sit there to have more privacy.

When they were seated, Edward offered to get drinks for everyone and asked Alan if he wanted a draft or something else.

"Just make it orange juice, no ice for me, thanks," he replied.

"Okay, Doc, no problem," Edward rejoined, squeezing past the tables to get to the counter.

Holding three glasses in both hands, Edward came back to the table a few minutes later and sat down. "Okay, there you go, Doc – 'just what the doctor ordered'," he quipped, grinning and pushing the glass of juice toward Alan.

"Thanks," Alan said, taking a sip.

"Alright, Doc, what did you want to talk to us about," Sam asked, after he had swallowed a long swig of beer.

"Well, let me start by asking you if anyone contacted either of you since we left Juneau (or before that) regarding the salvage of the relics aboard *The Investigator*?" Alan looked at Sam and at Edward in turn.

Edward lowered his gaze to his glass and didn't answer right away. "Why do you ask, Doc?"

"It's because a lot has happened since the beginning of this voyage, as you know, and more is happening at the moment, which had me wondering if there was someone else involved in the salvage operation than the people we know."

"You mean apart from Mr. Bornstein and us?" Sam asked.

"Yes. Chief Tolberg, with Interpol's assistance, has now located a vessel anchored over the wreck three miles offshore Banks Island and it seems the operation in question is funded and managed by someone other than government parties or lawfully hired personnel."

"What about the sub-dive; will it be scrapped then?" Edward asked.

Alan's brow furrowed – it was a strange question, he thought. *Do these guys even care about the dives for the passengers, or are they just here in sufferance?* "I don't believe anybody is planning to scrap any of the plans in that regard, no. But I think the question that you'd want to ask would be; what is a salvage ship doing over the site. What's more, you two didn't even seem surprised that someone else was anchored above the *Investigator*'s wreck."

Sam and Edward exchanged a glance before Sam said, "Listen, Doc, the reason why we are not surprised to hear that a ship is already anchored over the wreck is because it was always part of the future plan. Mr. Bornstein hired us to dive twice, as you know, once to get the archeologists to visit the site as closely as possible, and the second time to have us find out if the relics and the McClure treasure were still aboard the vessel. And if we found a treasure chest or anything like it, we would then be asked to remain on Banks Island – or return to the site at a later date – when a salvage operation would then be started."

"And if someone has anchored a vessel before we got there, maybe that someone has already found out what's aboard the *Investigator*," Edward added.

"What's more, Doc, if that Legato guy was on Banks beforehand, maybe he's the one who's hired the boat. Apart from that, we are not aware of any salvage boat working the area at this time, no, and we haven't been contacted by anyone regarding any salvage operation since we've been hired by Mr. Bornstein," Sam concluded, drinking some more of his beer.

"Okay, guys, I'll accept that," Alan said, taking another sip of juice. "But there's something else I meant to ask you; some time ago you mentioned that you had a friend who was an archer..."

"Oh yeah," Sam said, "that's Harold"—he looked at Edward—"remember, he's the one with the arbalest?"

"Sure, he's that fanatic who's always going shooting something or other when he's on leave from the rig," Edward rejoined. "So, what about it, Doc?"

"Well, since we've ascertained now that Cecil Legato has been killed with an arbalest, I was wondering if either of you guys could show Chief Tolberg and me where on this ship the man could have been killed."

Edward put down his glass and shook his head. "As I've said to the chief, an arbalest is a very accurate weapon and can be fired from anywhere..."

"Yeah," Alan interposed, "but I believe it can be awkward to use at close range – not like a gun or a knife, right?"

"Exactly," Sam answered for Edward. "It's perfect for targeting anything at a distance – up to three hundred yards. But when it comes to firing it at an adversary around the corner, it wouldn't work."

"And that's what I'm getting at," Alan said, "If you could spend some time with the chief or a member of his staff and find out where Legato could have been standing when he was killed, that would be helpful."

"But, Doc, we don't know what sort of arbalest the murderer used..."

"Oh but we do – we actually recovered the weapon a couple of days ago."

"You did?" Sam asked, agape.

Alan's head bobbed up and down. "Yes we did, and it's quite a weapon, as you described, Sam – not your cheap run-of-the-mill crossbow either. To me it looks like a competition or a professional weapon, not that I have much knowledge in that domain, mind you." He smiled.

"Well, if that can help, yes, why don't we do that – what do you say?" Edward asked Sam.

"Sure, okay." Sam returned his gaze to the doc. "When would you like to do that then?"

"Let's make it tomorrow, once we've left Kodiak, the chief and I will have more time to spend on this little experiment. Okay?"

"Sounds fine with us," Sam agreed. "It'll give us something else to do other than exchanging jokes with the guys on the rig."

* * * *

When Alan finally got down to the officers' mess, Tiffany had almost finished eating her lunch. "Where have you been?" she asked reproachfully, but with a smile adorning her lovely lips. "I've been here for a half-an-hour already, and I've got some news for you."

"Sorry about that, Tiff, but I had an opportunity to talk to the divers and I couldn't pass it up. Let me get a salad, and then you can tell me all about your news, okay?"

Tiffany nodded. "Yeah, but make it quick, I've got to get to the Kodiak airport – we've got another virtuoso – a cellist this time – coming in by this afternoon's flight, and I don't want to miss meeting him at the airport."

"Okay, I'll be right back."

Alan was back at their table a few minutes later and while he was eating a scrumptious-looking salad, between mouthfuls, he asked, "Okay, what's the news?"

"Well after we had our chat this morning with Gerald, I went to find Babette backstage…"

"You did, what for? I said I would talk to her this evening."

"It's just because I remembered that we had this concert tonight and that you wouldn't be able to talk to her then and even before that, I knew she would have a rehearsal with the cast of the play. Anyway, I managed to get to her between her many duties. After I explained that Sauvage was probably unaware of what was going on with his salvage boat, we talked about Agent Korsakov again. She told me that she thought the woman was the killer."

"Oh yeah, and did she say why she would think that?"

"Well, that's the strange thing, she told me that the Russians had always been interested in the territories surrounding the Artic Circle and they wouldn't hesitate – given the chance – to grab the treasure from under the Canadians' noses if they could."

"Is she saying it's some sort of Russian government plot?"

"Yes, that's what she said. I still can't believe it, but it makes sense, since the Russians are always trying to steal Arctic land and drilling rights from the Canadians. They say the Russians are behind all the demonstrations with the native Canadian population," Tiffany said pensively.

"Well, that's something I had not considered – but maybe the chief should." He munched on a piece of bread. "As for my bit of news – it's nowhere near as fantastic as yours, but I've talked to the divers, as I said, before coming down, and they seemed disinterested as ever…"

"What do you mean 'disinterested'?" Tiffany asked, finishing her coffee.

"Well, these guys have always shown very little interest in the sub-dives and the visit of Banks Island as a whole, and this time was no different, but they told me that, yes, it was always in the cards to have a vessel coming up to the *Investigator*'s wreck site, if they were to find a treasure during their dives. And they told me – the same as I thought – that Cecil Legato was probably the one who had hired the salvage boat and had come up to Banks to pick the wreck clean before we arrived on site."

Tiffany nodded. "Yeah, that sounds logical, but the big question still is; does Mr. Sauvage know about it. He obviously owns the vessel, but is he involved in any way in the current operation?"

"My thoughts exactly, Tiff, but until we find a thread that could lead us to unraveling this dirty skein of wool, I don't think we'll be going anywhere close to finding a solution, or wanting to speak to him."

CHAPTER THIRTY-NINE

Double dose of Viagra?

GETTING MR. GREGORY STRANDOVSKY, the famous Russian cellist, through customs and onto the ship proved to be an overwhelming task for Tiffany. She didn't know that the man didn't speak English for one thing, that he would be accompanied by his manager and that he had not one but two instruments with him. At her wits' end when it came to translating what Mr. Strandovsky tried to explain to the US customs' officers, Tiffany called Stephan – she knew he spoke Russian fluently.

"Oh hi, Ms. Sylvan, what can I do for you?" Stephan said as soon as he was able to speak out of earshot from the busy bridge deck.

"Glad I caught you, sir," Tiffany replied, "and I'm sorry to disturb you on a busy day, but it's about Mr. Strandovsky..."

"Who...? Is he a passenger?"

"Well, no, not yet... I mean he's our concert cellist and he's just landed from Russia via Juneau, and he doesn't speak a word of English..."

"Doesn't he have an interpreter with him?"

"No, just his manager and he's not much better – would you mind coming to the airport and give us a hand here, again I'm sorry to impose."

"No worries, Ms. Sylvan, but it'll take me about a half-an-hour before I could get to the airport. Do you think Mr. Strandovsky will be okay with that?"

"Maybe you could talk to him on the phone...?"

"Good idea, why don't you put him on?"

"Okay, sir, here he is," Tiffany said as she handed the phone to the cellist.

A few minutes later and now sufficiently reassured that someone other than "these Americans" was going to come and clear customs with him, Strandovsky sat down quietly in the waiting room. The only thing that seemed to disturb him a little at this point was the presence of a uniformed officer at his side. He kept chancing a glance up to the man, who stood impassively waiting with his arms crossed over his chest.

When Stephan finally arrived at the airport, he talked with Strandovsky and his manager briefly, and seemed to explain to both men what the procedure would entail. The only thing that delayed the matter a little more than it already had, were the two cellos.

The officers opened both cases and saw identical instruments inside, which was a puzzler to them. "Why would you want to transport two cellos on this trip, sir?" was the officer's repeated question.

Strandovsky ultimately told the insistent fellow that one cello was to play in public and the other was for rehearsing or 'amusement' as Stephan translated with a smile on his face.

"Alright then," the customs' officer finally said, "let's get you out of here and into a car..."

"I have a car waiting," Stephan cut-in, to Tiffany's surprise.

She wondered where the staff cap had rented a car so quickly – unless he called a hotel.

The car in question was a spacious, black SUV, which accommodated the four passengers with ease. Once the cellos and luggage were loaded, and the cellist and his manager were comfortably ensconced in the back seats, Stephan climbed behind the wheel, and threw a quick glance in Tiffany's direction.

She returned the gaze and asked, "Where did you get the car so fast; I was going to get a car from the airport shuttle company..."

"I thought you'd be asking, Ms. Sylvan, but I've got some friends in Kodiak and they lent me the car for the three days we were here, so picking you up was no trouble at all."

"Wow, that's some nice friends!" Tiffany said. "Do they live in Kodiak?"

Stephan nodded. "They're Russians actually. And, as you know, there are many Russian immigrants living on the islands around here – particularly families who emigrated from northern Russia just after the revolution."

"I guess, as Americans we don't realize how close Alaska is from Russia." She turned her face to Stephan. "Have you invited your friends to tonight's concert?"

"To be honest, Ms Sylvan, I forgot the concert was tonight and I didn't even remember Mr. Strandovsky was playing. But it's never too late to ask – actually it would be a good idea if they came to the ship, since they could take the car back with them after the concert." He smiled. "Thanks for the reminder."

When the car pulled up near the gangway, Gerald, who was standing on the upper deck, wondered why the same car, as the one that had picked up Agent Korsakov, was back alongside *The Contessa*. Obviously there were many black SUV's roaming these parts, but this one had a distinctive light blue strip running from the front fenders to the top of the rear wheel shaft – same as the Russian agent's SUV. Gerald waited until the passengers disembarked and as soon as he recognized Stephan, he ran down to his office.

"Neil, get in here!" he hollered as he pushed the door open.

"What's happened, Chief?" Neil asked, standing in the doorway of Gerald's office. "Something wrong?"

"Would you get on your computer, connect with someone at the DMV around here, and have them check that license plate for me." He handed Neil a piece of paper with the plate number scribbled on it. "It belongs to someone in Kodiak and I want to know who, okay?"

"Who do you think it belongs to?"

Gerald stared at his second-in-command. "Why do you think I've asked you to identify the owner, Neil? If I had any idea who it belonged to,

I wouldn't have asked, now would I?"

"Yeah, sorry, Chief. I guess my brain's not working this afternoon."

"Well, let's get it in gear, because I think we're soon to find out who's been harboring a fugitive in this town." Neil hadn't moved from his spot. "Now, go on, will you?"

* * * *

Returning to the medical center after lunch, Alan found Angie in the storeroom, trying to make space for the umpteen boxes of insect repellant they had received from Health Canada.

"Why don't we find a spot beside the condoms," Alan suggested helpfully when Angie had turned to him – a frustrated look on her face.

"Yeah, I wish they'd keep these things in their cabins so we didn't have to store so many here; these young hunks are always up to no good," Angie remarked, moving the boxes of condoms to make temporary space for the repellent canisters.

Alan always had to deal with crewmembers that had practiced "protected sex". It didn't work very often. Unfortunately, once a female member of the crew was pregnant, she needed to finish her contract rapidly and then be off work until after motherhood. In other words, end of career. The pill was, of course, used religiously. Male and female condoms were a slightly different story. Although they were always thought to be the ideal protection, they tended to perform poorly as a contraceptive in the hands of relatively young "I am indestructible" types among the crewmembers. The company that was always advertising and leaving them samples was Trojan – a mighty name in history and the famous school mascot of the University of Southern California.

Alan always questioned this, and did so right then, "You know, Angie, I would have to ask if that was the most appropriate name for a condom. After all, the Trojans raped and pillaged, and Troy was destroyed – burned to the ground." He added, "One must also remember that if there is a Greek inside, a Trojan could get very hot and uncomfortable, just like in history."

Upon hearing Alan's comments, Angie's fluster seemed to dissipate rapidly into a broad grin, and it was with renewed vigor that she tackled the rest of the lifting and moving of boxes.

Alan was still concerned though. This was a particularly long voyage and he wanted to check that the crew provision boxes that were located in their 'waiting area' were re-filled regularly without fail.

In front of every crew waiting area was a series of boxes. These boxes contained several of the common things crew needed on a regular basis on a ship. These were the meds one would normally be able to get at the local pharmacy or convenience store in any US or Canadian city. Yet, being out in the middle of the great oceans of the world, made going to the corner drugstore a bit difficult. There was a crew store, but the selection was limited. So, to entice crewmembers to pick up and use condoms, etc., there would also be boxes of aspirins, Band-Aids, acetaminophen, meclizine (motion-sickness med), and ibuprofen in their provision boxes.

Getting the contract for supplying the condoms for a thousand or more young, virile, first time away from home males, was a salesman's dream come true. Similarly, the diaphragm company that routinely tried to get the contract to supply the ships medical centers' with diaphragms was called "The Spartan Company".

Picking up several boxes of the Spartan diaphragms, Alan said, "As far as we know, it is not an off shoot of the manufacturers of Trojans. But is Spartan really the most appropriate name for it? Spartan denotes to me: small, thin, thrifty, and probably not very well made. Of course, a diaphragm only gives protection from a frontal assault and has no protection from a rear attack."

"And is that why we're distributing birth-control pills like aspirins?"

"Yes, Angie, it keeps the girls from having to give up their jobs and keeps them out of the back street abortion parlors and the strange ideas various cultures have on local herbal teas and the like for 'natural abortions'."

Alan always insisted that the company paid for these 'little extras'. This was probably one reason the medical department was not the most favorite entity in the corporate structure of cruise ship lines. Along with fine Sherry and Chateau Rothschild wines that the company could charge for, they would also have bills for hundreds of gross of condoms, aspirins, and Band-Aids.

Coming out of the storeroom, Angie asked, "Have you ever prescribed Viagra for any of the passengers, Doc?"

Alan eyed his nurse curiously. "Not that I recall, no – I may have recommended the men that came with such requests to see their own physicians or a GP at the nearest port; but why do you ask?"

"It's just that talking about contraceptives reminded me of a guy who came to the center where I was working before I went to work for the cruise lines. He came in and asked Dr. Gander for a double dose of Viagra," Angie began, while Alan wondered where this story was going. "And Dr. Gander told the guy that he couldn't prescribe a double dose for him. So the man said, "Why not?" And Dr. Gander said, "Because it's not safe." And then the patient said, "But I need it real bad, Doctor. See, my girlfriend's coming to town on Friday; my ex will be here on Saturday and my wife will be home on Sunday – that's why I really, really need it"."

"Is this a joke?" Alan asked smiling.

"Well," Angie hesitated. "Anyway, Dr. Gander finally agreed to give the man a double dose and sent him on his way but not before asking him to come back on Monday to see if the guy suffered from any side effects."

"But, that's…"

"Hold on, Doc, okay?"

"Alright, go on," Alan said, still grinning and thinking that no respectable physician would ever prescribe double doses of Viagra even if the patient had five wives or ex's waiting in the wings for him.

"Well, when Monday came around, the man came in with a sling supporting his right arm. So, when Dr. Gander asked what happened to him, the man said, "No one showed up!"

Guffawing, Alan was slightly taken aback; he had never heard Angie telling a joke of any sort to anyone. "That was a good one, Angie, but did you really worked for a Dr. Gander or did you make that up too?"

"Oh no, Doc, I was his nurse for almost ten years before I decided to travel, but he never prescribed a double dose of Viagra to anybody – not that I know of anyway."

CHAPTER FORTY

An important piece of the puzzle

AS SOON AS TIFFANY had shown Mr. Strandovsky and Mr. Antonov, the manager, to their respective cabins, she made a bee line for the medical center where she found Alan and Angie laughing and piling up boxes of all sorts of paraphernalia in the corridor, presumably ready to be picked up by the various master stewards.

She looked down at the boxes of condoms lined up beside those of insect repellants, and giggled. "Will they use repellants as lubricant now?" she asked Alan.

Laughing some more, Alan said, "I don't think that would make for the best combination, no." He stopped to look at her curiously. "But what are you doing here? I thought I would only see you tonight at the concert..."

"Oh hi, Ms. Sylvan," Angie piped up after depositing a couple more boxes on top of some others. "How are you doing?"

"Just fine, Angie. Thanks. I see you've been busy getting people ready for the *long, long* trip to the Arctic Circle," Tiffany quipped.

"Goodness, not you too, Ms. Sylvan, I dread the next five days, I tell you – thank God we can still joke about it. Because, you know it's usually when we're out in the middle of nowhere that we've got the strangest things happening on our ships." She shook her head. "No, I'm not looking forward to those, I tell you."

"It'll be alright, Angie, I'm sure. Besides, we've got a *select breed* aboard this time; nothing like we've had on the regular cruises. These people appear to really *want* to be here."

"Well, I guess you're right, Doc, but I'll be happy when we get to Banks Island anyway."

"Yes, me too," Tiffany rejoined, smiling up at Angie.

"Okay, ladies, shall we get on with whatever needs to be done?" Alan asked, switching his gaze from Angie to Tiffany. "And I gather you want to speak to me directly?"

"Yes, if you have a few minutes, may I talk to you in your office?"

"Sure, come on in," Alan said, walking ahead of Tiffany toward his opened door.

After they had both taken a seat, Alan asked, "So how did it go at the airport?"

"Well, it went fine, but only after I got Stephan to come and translate and help me with going through customs."

"But I thought your cellist was a guest..."

"He was – I mean he is – but he came with his manager and neither spoke a word of English, so I asked Stephan to join us and translate the questions the customs guys were asking."

"And I gather Stephan obliged, or did he?"

"Oh yeah, he did alright, but that's not what bothered me…"

"What then?"

"It's the SUV, Alan. Didn't Gerald say that Agent Korsakov took off in a black SUV when she left the ship in a hurry?"

"Sure – both Gerald and I saw it drive off, why? Do you think it's the same car that Stephan used?"

"That I don't know, but what caught my attention was the fact that Stephan said that he got the car on loan from some Russian friends he knows on the island and that these Russians were immigrants or some such thing." She paused. "And I suggested that he invite them for the concert tonight…"

"And is he going to do that?"

"I think so, yes. He thought it was a good idea actually." Tiffany stopped talking again and looked at Alan. "Didn't you say that Stephan was an important piece in this puzzle?"

Alan pondered the question for a moment before he answered, "Have you talked to Gerald about this?"

"No, not yet, Alan. I just wanted to know if you guys still considered Stephan as a suspect of some kind."

"Well, I don't really know what to tell you. As far as what Gerald told me: Stephan has no criminal record anywhere and he's probably "squeaky-clean", to use his words. But, from what you've just described, maybe he knows where Agent Korsakov is hiding out."

"That's what I thought. Do you think I should have a talk with him?" Tiffany asked, looking down at her wristwatch. "Not that I have much time before Mr. Strandovsky's rehearsal…"

"No, Tiff, I'll have a chat with him when I go down to his deck to leave some of the repellants in the stewards' waiting area. But if you're right, we might have found our killer – if Agent Korsakov is indeed the culprit."

* * * *

Coming out of his office, Alan noticed a member of the crew sitting in the passengers' waiting room. Crew and staff had their own waiting rooms at the medical center and crew were not supposed to sit with the passengers. Arms crossed under her ample breasts, the young Polish crewmember was indeed a gorgeous looking woman. Beside her sat two older passengers – a couple in their sixties whom Alan knew by sight only. When Tiffany had left, he looked at Angie meaningfully and as Alan was about to ask his nurse to take the crewmember to the examining room while he would take the passengers to his office, they overheard the three of them exchange a few words.

The wife asked the girl, "where did you get such beautiful breasts, dear?"

"I bought them," the young woman replied tersely.

To which the wife said, "I've been thinking of buying a pair of those myself actually."

The husband turned to his spouse and remarked, "That would be like hanging a new chandelier in a haunted house or light bulbs in a funeral parlor."

For his trouble, he received a friendly slap across the face from his wife, who then replied, "I figured that if I put some new lights in the house, you might stay around longer," shrugging.

It was all Alan and Angie could do to keep a straight face when they finally went to take passengers and the crewmember away from the waiting room.

Once Alan had talked to the two passengers and attended to their mild complaints, he reminded the young crewmember that regulations dictated that she was not to wait in the passengers' waiting room.

Alan's arms loaded with three or four boxes of the necessary items he wanted to leave on the third deck, he came out of the elevator to find himself face to face with Gerald.

"We should stop meeting like this," Gerald said, "I was just on my way to see you."

"Okay, I wanted to have a chat with you too," Alan replied. "Do you mind – I'll drop these boxes in the stewards' waiting area, and I'll come to your office?"

"Well, let me help you with these then," Gerald offered, taking a couple of boxes off the pile in Alan's arms.

"Thanks," he said, walking alongside Gerald now. "What did you want to see me about?"

"It's about our staff cap..."

"I guess you've got a bug in your ear, or we'll have to start believing in ESP because that's exactly what I wanted to talk to you about."

"You did?" Gerald sounded surprised.

"Yep," Alan answered, "But let's get this load of boxes delivered and talk once we're back in the quiet of your office, okay?"

Once both men were seated in Gerald's office, Alan asked, "Okay, what's going on with our staff captain?"

"Well, I was on deck coming from the bridge after I talked to Captain Middleton about Bornstein, when I saw that black SUV pulling up alongside our ship and Mr. Ivanov coming out of it. So, I asked Neil to run the plate through the DMV and the car belongs to a Mr. Simirov who lives in Kodiak..."

"And you thought that's probably where our Russian Agent is hiding out, is that it?"

"Well yes. But unfortunately, I don't have any proof that she's suspected of murdering Cecil Legato and even if she's indeed a Russian agent, I've got nothing to tie her to the crime or anything that I could give the local authority to justify issuing an arrest warrant."

"Okay, I don't know if it will help, but since we've recovered the arbalest, which coincidentally found its way to Mr. Ivanov's cabin, I could run a latent print test on it. (I think I still have the luminal that I used a couple of years ago.) And even if our Russian agent has wiped her prints off the weapon, there might still be some traces of blood or fiber that could be linked to her handling it."

"Although, I admire your optimism, Doc, I don't think an agent of her caliber would have left anything behind that would enable an entire CSI lab to find anything on that arbalest."

"But that's assuming that she is indeed the agent she said she was, isn't it? Have we got any proof or reliable confirmation from Interpol of that being the case?"

"Well, no, not that I recall. I remember asking Devon at Interpol about Sam Wilcox, but Korsakov came and went like the wind. It's only when we saw her taking off in that SUV that we became suspicious of everything she said or did while on this ship."

"Alright, Chief, now let me tell you about my conversation with the two divers..."

"Oh, you had time to talk to the blighters, that's good. And what did they have to say for themselves?"

"Nothing more than what we knew about them already, but I've asked them to do a little test once we're back at sea..."

"What sort of test?"

"Well, since we've got plenty of daylight well after dinner and we've got very few passengers – if any – roaming the decks in the late evening hours, I thought, you and I could lead them on a tour of the ship to show us where Cecil could have been killed with that weapon."

"You mean you want them to start shooting arrows..."

Alan had to laugh. "No, Chief, not actually shooting anything, but handling the weapon for one thing – see how dexterous they are with it – and then pointing at a fair distance while hidden and aiming at a possible spot where Cecil could have been standing when he was shot."

"Okay, I'll go along with that test of yours, but remember Legato was shot in the neck..."

"Oh, believe me I remember, and that's another reason for the test, Legato had to be standing still for a second, giving enough time for the shooter's arrow to reach its target with such accuracy."

"Yes, I see what you mean." Gerald paused for a moment, before he asked, "Apart from me talking about Mr. Ivanov, is the test what you wanted to see me about?"

"Actually no, but since I've got your attention before we leave Kodiak, I thought I'd ask."

"So, what was it?"

"It's still about our staff captain. As you probably saw when you noticed the SUV near the gangway earlier this afternoon, Tiffany was with Mr. Ivanov when they arrived..."

"Yes, I saw that, along with individuals, I presumed to be entertainers."

"Well, since we had talked about Mr. Ivanov's possible involvement in this affair when we had dessert together in Kodiak, Tiffany found out that our staff cap has friends on the island and that these friends had lent him the black SUV while we were docked here."

"You mean, Mr. Ivanov admitted knowing the Simirov family?"

"I don't think he mentioned them by name, but he openly admitted knowing the owner of the SUV."

"Alright then, if that's the case, I'll have a talk with our staff captain, as soon as we're done here," Gerald concluded, getting to his feet.

"Hold on, Chief, I think we should wait until tonight – until the Simirov's are most probably aboard the ship…"

"What are you saying? They're coming here?" Gerald erupted, visibly surprised.

"Yeah, Tiffany suggested that our staff cap invite them to attend the concert as his guest."

"Clever girl!"

"That she is, Chief, that she is."

CHAPTER FORTY-ONE

Who's manning the ship?

THERE WERE SO MANY THREADS going in different directions and some leading nowhere but to more confusion, that Alan decided to make a list of who was involved in this affair and how.

Divers: Possible shooters. Sam Ashton knows his way around an arbalest. Possible gain from not finding treasure – they would share in the find if treasure chest is brought back to England after it's raised from the *Investigator*.

Archeologists: they could possibly gain from the finding and removal of the McClure treasure before we reach Banks Island.

Mr. Bornstein: Initiated the salvage of the relics and engaged the services of Legato.

Mr. Sauvage: The salvage boat belongs to him – possibly hired by Legato.

Ms. Korsakov: Might be the shooter (killer) and probably has Russian government connections. The Russians are possibly interested in swiping the treasure from under the Canadians' noses.

Mr. Ivanov: Knows the Simirov family who lent him the SUV.

Simirov: Immigrant family living in Kodiak, possibly harboring Korsakov.

Looking at the list, Alan thought that, apart from Stephan, those were the names of those who could gain from the early salvage of the McClure treasure.

After printing the list, he deleted the document from his computer files and folded the sheet of paper, which he placed in his shirt pocket. *Don't forget to take this when changing for the concert,* Alan thought. And thinking of the concert, he looked at the wall clock – "Two hours before the bell rings," he said to himself, shaking his head. He knew he still had to complete several reports for the corporate office before he could get down to the officers' mess and grab something to eat on his way back to his cabin. This evening wasn't one he wanted to miss – he wanted to meet the Simirov's and talk to them in Stephan's presence.

Alan had known Stephan for some years, and as squeaky clean as he appeared to be, there might be something in his past that would force him today to be part of a conspiracy – such as the salvage of the McClure treasure was. However, Alan could not bring himself to believe that Stephan was involved further than knowing the Simirov's as perhaps longtime friends.

The question that kept coming back to nag him was: Who was now overseeing the salvage operation offshore Banks Island? It had been a given that Cecil had been in charge from day one, but after his death, who was giving orders to continue diving to recover the relics? None of the players on his list were available or near the ship to give any such orders. Bornstein was still under protective custody, the divers and archeologists didn't seem in any hurry to get off the ship to rejoin the salvage operation – on the contrary, they were apparently waiting for the chips to fall where they may. As for Ms. Korsakov, or Scheherazade as Tiffany called her, she was no where in sight and, according to Gerald's sources in town, she had not made a move in any direction since he and Alan had seen her taking off at the end of the pier. "So, who was in charge at this very minute?" Alan asked himself again.

Then a thought occurred to him. What if Sauvage was the overseer now? Since the man was obviously well versed in these sorts of operations all over the globe, maybe he had men aboard the *Northern Rover* who were in contact with him every day. And that may have been another reason for changing the name of the vessel before it reached Banks Island – to divert attention from suspicious visitors or onlookers, such as the passengers on *The Contessa* when they would arrive on site. *He probably hoped to be long gone by the time we arrived,* Alan mused.

Still out of answers and nowhere near finding any at this point, Alan decided it was time, an hour later, to call it a day and make his way to the officers' mess. He was hoping to find Tiffany there, but that was probably not in the cards, since on concert nights, she and her staff would often order a tray of sandwiches to take back stage before the show.

Heading down the elevator, he met Captain Middleton, who was on his way to find Stephan apparently. "Dr. Mayhew," the man said with a genial smile, "have you seen our staff captain in your recent travels by any chance?"

"No, sir, I only know that he was at the airport this afternoon assisting the cellist and his manager going through customs," Alan replied.

"Ah yes, apparently Ms. Sylvan had her hands full with our Russian visitors." He paused as the doors opened on the lower deck. "And you know, Doctor, that's an issue I must address at the end of this voyage..."

"What's that, sir?" Alan asked as both men came out of the elevator.

"The fact that we don't have an interpreter aboard this ship. Mind you we've got many men and women of various nationalities working on our cruise liners, but no dedicated interpreters."

"Yes, I see your point," Alan said politely, "but wouldn't that require hiring a polyglot, given the fact that we meet so many people of different nationalities during our voyages?"

"Precisely. However, if we had someone who could translate the major languages spoken around the globe, we would be ahead of the game in that regard, wouldn't you think?"

"Yes, but these people don't come cheap," Alan remarked helpfully, knowing that the head office would probably put down the suggestion as too expensive and one that could not be billed to the passengers in any way.

"Maybe you're right, Doctor," Middleton concluded. "In any case, I'll just have a look around the mess to see if Mr. Ivanov is there and then I'll get ready for the concert. Will we see you there?"

"Yes, sir. I should be able to make it, yes. But sir, may I ask if you called Mr. Ivanov on his cell?"

"Yes, yes, of course I did, but since he hasn't answered for some reason and I didn't want my first officer to go on a hunt before taking the helm, so to speak, I decided to stretch the old legs a bit and have a look for him myself."

* * * *

The foyer to the theater was abuzz with excitement. Alan thought the whole scene resembled the populated lobby of a Broadway theater before a premiere. He made himself a passage between the passengers and crew attending Mr. Strandovsky's performance until his gaze rested on Stephan. *Ah good – he's still alive and he is here,* Alan mused.

"Oh hello, Doctor," Stephan said when Alan was in earshot, "let me introduce you to Mr. and Mrs. Sirimov, friends of mine from Kodiak."

Alan extended a hand for Mr. Sirimov to shake. "Dr. Mayhew, sir. Quite pleased to meet you and you, Mrs. Sirimov."

"Same here," Sirimov replied with a slight Slavic accent, while shaking the doc's hand in a firm grip. "Very pleased to be here actually. Never thought my wife and I would see the insides of a cruise ship in our lifetime."

"Since you've been so generous in lending me the car for the three days, that's the least I could do, Dimitri," Stephan put in. "And I'm sure you and Tatiana will enjoy Mr. Strandovsky's performance."

"Oh yes we will," Tatiana said, opening her mouth for the first time. "Thank you again, Stephan, for inviting us. I've only heard him play in Moscow – a long, long time ago – and I loved him."

"Are you always working aboard cruise ships?" Dimitri asked Alan.

"Yes, this has been my chosen career practically since I left medical school. Why do you ask?"

"Oh, simply because I imagined the doctors working aboard these big ships would be much younger..."

Alan chuckled amicably. "That's a general assumption, yes. But an inexperienced practitioner would have trouble treating some of the passengers, so age doesn't calculate into the formula that applies to the hiring of ships' doctors."

Tatiana, a portly and affable woman in her late forties with dark eyes and a beautiful tress of blonde hair descending over her shoulder, was about to say something when everyone heard the bell, announcing that the concert was about to commence.

When Stephan turned to lead his guests into the theater, Alan grabbed him by the arm. "Captain Middleton was looking for you, did he find you?"

"Sure did. I was just fetching the Sirimov's to bring them aboard, but when I got back, I called him back."

"Alright then, but you had me worried for a minute there…"

"Why's that?" Stephan asked, peering into Alan's eyes.

"After the performance you and I need to talk, okay?"

"Sure thing, Doc. No problem."

As the people filed past him into the theater, Alan waited at the back of the foyer for a minute before following the throng ahead of him. He hadn't seen Babette – or Susan – whom he had hoped would be here with Sauvage and his daughter.

"If you're waiting for me, Alan, I'm right here," he heard Babette say from behind his shoulder.

Alan swung around and looked at the two people standing beside his favorite playwright. He was immediately surprised not to see Susan hanging on the man's arm.

"Let me introduce you…," Babette offered, noticing Alan's eyes resting on the tall and definitely 'handsome' fellow. "This is Mr. Auguste Sauvage, and his daughter, Annette." Babette looked at the man. "This is Dr. Alan Mayhew, Auguste; he's been aboard one ship or another for as long as I can remember."

"A pleasure, Mr. Sauvage, and Miss Annette," Alan said, bowing slightly. "I'm sure we'll have an opportunity to talk after the performance," he added.

"Of course, would love to have a chat, by all means," Sauvage replied.

"But, tell me, Ms. Babette, isn't Susan with you tonight?"

"Oh dear no, Alan. Poor thing, she's suffering from a terrible migraine and said that she'll join us for cocktails after the performance."

"Do you think I should check on her?" Alan asked.

"No, I don't think that would be a good idea; she took some tablets and is resting for a couple of hours. But, of course, if you think you should…"

"No-no, as you said, it's best to leave her to rest for now."

"Shall we go in then?" Annette then said, looking a little distracted.

"Of course, Miss Sauvage, after you," Alan said, standing back. *Curious young lady,* he thought. *She didn't even respond to the introduction. I wonder what's going on in that beautiful head of hers.*

CHAPTER FORTY-TWO

The "Middle Wife"

THE NEXT MORNING when *The Contessa* began treading the ocean waters that would eventually lead her to Prudhoe Bay, Gerald was sitting at his desk, looking down at the report of his interview with the Sirimov's, which he had conducted the previous night after the concert. They were Russian immigrants who had landed in Alaska shortly after the fall of the Berlin Wall in 1989 and who had obtained US citizenship ten years later. The man was now retired from his occupation as a roughneck on oilrigs. He displayed none of the traits of someone hiding something or being involved with the former KGB at anytime during his life in the then USSR. When asked if he knew a Ms. Korsakov, either by name or by sight, Sirimov burst out in loud laughter.

"Oh no, sir. Never laid eyes or spoke to anybody by that name, no." He chuckled some more. "You see, for us Russians," he added, "Korsakov means that you love playing games and induce women in sharing your bed for a night of pleasure"—he turned a smiling face to his wife— "and I can tell you right now, Tatiana here wouldn't take kindly to that sort of thing – if I had ever been tempted."

"That's all fine, sir, but you see, I've got a problem," Gerald said, "the Ms. Korsakov we know has been seen leaving the ship in a car – in your car actually – a couple of days ago and I was wondering if you know anything about this or if you have loaned your car to anyone else besides your friend, Mr. Stephan Ivanov?"

Simirov crossed his arms over his ample chest after passing his fingers through his graying hair. "I sure haven't given my car to anyone apart from Stephan while he was in town, no. But that's not to say someone else couldn't have used it."

"Yes…," Tatiana put in, nodding emphatically, "we always leave a set of keys in a small box inside the fender, in case we can't get to the house or we lose the keys during the winter."

"Maybe someone from the village knew about this…"

"That's right, Chief Tolberg, and when we gave the car to Stephan we told him to leave it in the parking lot near the ferry pier so that if we needed it, we could get to it without too much trouble."

"So, what you're saying is that anyone familiar with the keys' hiding place could have used your car, is that it?"

"Yes, Mr. Tolberg," Tatiana said, "and we don't know anybody called Korsakov in town – and we know a lot of people since we've lived here for the best part of twenty years now."

Since Gerald thought it was now a police matter and if an investigation was to be conducted, and since it would not be in his mandate to pursue the matter further, he concluded the interview quickly and let Stephan drive the couple home an hour later.

Alan was still concerned about Stephan's possible involvement with the Korsakov woman. While Gerald was interviewing the Sirimov couple, Alan had asked the staff captain to have a bit of a conversation with him at the end of the concert.

"So, what did you want to talk about, Doc?" Stephan asked, sitting down beside Alan in the foyer of the theater.

Alan fetched the list out of his pocket. "Since our last chat about what could be happening out there – offshore Banks Island – and who could be responsible for the murder of Cecil Legato, I've drawn up a list of the people involved"—he handed the sheet of paper to Stephan—"and as you can see your name is at the bottom of it."

Stephan raised his gaze to Alan. "From what I read here, you're suspecting the Sirimov's of harboring a fugitive and because I was driving their car, you suspect me to be an accomplice to criminal activities. Is that the gist of it?"

"In a word, yes." Stephan shook his head and handed the list back to Alan, who added, "but I personally don't believe you to be involved in this affair anymore than knowing the Sirimov's and borrowing their vehicle for the past three days."

"I'm glad that you doubt your own suspicion, Alan, because yes, I've known the Sirimov's for many years – they were friends of my parents – and we kept in touch. And as far as harboring a criminal, I think they would rather slam the door on the Korsakov woman than even speak to her. You see, these people, as many Russian refugees of their era, are scared stiff of knowing anyone from the old country. They didn't trust anybody while they lived in Russia and they surely don't trust anybody now. And that was another reason for choosing to stay in Kodiak rather than moving closer to my family in Boston. They preferred their new life to be solitary – away from the troubles of the big cities."

"And I couldn't blame anyone for the choice," Alan remarked. "But the local authorities – if they ever get involved – could suspect the opposite being true."

"What do you mean?" Stephan asked.

"I mean the fact that they chose to remain 'solitary' in a secluded place, could go against them. They might have retained some ties with the Russian underground, or being suspected of having done so."

"Yes, that's a possibility, of course," Stephan agreed, "but don't you think before they could be granted citizenship, they would have passed through several thorough inspections of their past relationships with people or family in Russia?"

"Probably, especially in the 90's, our immigration policies regarding Russian refugees were quite rigorous, I should imagine."

"From what I heard from my parents, it was sometimes a nightmare." Stephan bent his head to the side, pensive. "Anyway, I hope Chief Tolberg is not giving them too hard a time about this – they've had enough of these interviews to last them a life time."

"Oh I don't think Gerald will be that bad; actually I'd say he thinks the way I do that Ms. Korsakov is probably long gone by now. She might have taken the ferry to another island by the time we began investigating where she could have gone."

"And you know, now that you mention it, it's quite possible that she did…"

"Why would you think that?" Alan asked.

"Because, there's a spare set of keys under the front fender, and anyone could have taken the SUV from the ferry parking lot, where the Simirov's asked me to park it, and used it to take the woman to the ferry."

"But who's the person who picked her up? That's what I'd like to know. It would have to be someone who knew the Simirov's or the car they drive…"

"Not necessarily, Alan. The Simirov's have lived here a long time, and during the winter, practically everyone hides a set of keys under the front or back fenders in case they need to borrow a neighbor's car in a storm or something."

"So, you're saying people leave their cars accessible to anybody who might want to use them…?" Alan was taken aback. This sort of behavior was somewhat foreign to him coming from a big city like Boston.

"Yes, I know that sounds fantastic for us, but around here, everybody knows everybody, so in case of emergency, a car will always be available. It's kind of an emergency measure."

"Well then, I think our Chief better leave the whole matter alone. Now that the body of Cecil Legato has been flown back to Boston, who ever wants or is assigned to deal with this affair, will be faced with interviewing the whole of Kodiak for a start" Alan stated.

That last remark giving rise to a mild chuckle between the two men, they got up and while Alan returned to his cabin for the night, Stephan went to Gerald's office to pick up the Sirimov's and drive them home.

* * * *

When Alan entered the medical center that morning, he found a young woman, visibly a few months pregnant, sitting in the waiting room. He asked her to come into his office. Obviously, Alan was not going to examine anyone before he knew what the matter was, but asking a few questions was okay.

"Please take a seat, Mrs. Dalberg," Alan invited, while he sat at his desk. He knew the lady from having seen her a week or so previously for a minor laceration. "What can I do for you this morning?"

"Well, Doctor, I am feeling so tired lately, I'm wondering if there's something really wrong with me. I'm taking all sorts of vitamins and supplements, as you know, but I still feel like sleeping all day."

"Okay, let me just say that it's quite normal during any pregnancy, but there's an added factor in this part of the world that you might want to take into consideration…"

"What's that?" Mrs. Dalberg asked anxiously.

"It's the longer periods of daylight that we have up here. They play tricks on your circadian rhythm (inner clock)."

"But I feel like sleeping – not staying awake," she argued.

"Yes, and that's because you probably don't get enough sleep during what should be your night." Mrs. Dalberg nodded. "Let me ask you this: do you sleep well every night, or do you toss and turn for a time?"

"Well, to tell you the truth, I usually slept best on my tummy, and now I can't, so I have a hard time falling asleep for one thing, and then I try reading or watching TV, but apart from yawning my head off, I can't seem to fall asleep for the longest time."

"Okay then, let me give you a few suggestions: when you're ready to go to sleep, try shutting off all the lights, making sure the drapes are closed and that there's no noise around you. Go to bed after your husband is asleep, so things are quiet. No TV. No reading, just lie down in a comfortable position and mentally THINK the number one (1) to yourself repetitively. Your thoughts will become calm and even though new thoughts come into your mind, just sweep them out mentally and you'll fall asleep. Alternatively, an old technique is to take deep breaths. If you breathe out one nostril and in through the other regularly, your heart rate will go down and you will also fall asleep."

"Okay, Doctor, I'll try it, because this is starting to drive me nuts," Mrs. Dalberg said. "And I'm not enjoying anything when I feel tired like that." She paused, smiled and then added, "It reminds me of the story of Erica and the birth of her brother."

"Is that the daughter of one of your friends?"

"Well no, Erica was a child in my class a few years back..."

"Oh, you're a teacher; I'm sorry I didn't realize that," Alan said.

"Well, yes, but at the moment I'm on maternity leave and my husband thought we would do well to take this cruise – just the two of us – before the birth."

"Always a good idea – but tell me about Erica then," Alan urged, now curious to hear the story.

"Before I start, you must keep in mind this is from a second grader a few years back." Alan nodded. "When I was a kid," Mrs. Dalberg began, "I loved show-and-tell. So I always have a few sessions with my students. It helps them get over shyness and usually, show-and-tell is pretty tame. Kids bring in pet turtles, model airplanes, pictures of fish they catch, stuff like that. And I never, ever place any boundaries or limitations on them. If they want to lug it to school and talk about it, they're more than welcome.

"Well, one day, this little girl, Erica, a very bright, very outgoing kid, takes her turn and waddles up to the front of the class with a pillow stuffed under her sweater. Then Erica holds up a snapshot of an infant. 'This is Luke, my baby brother, and I'm going to tell you about his birthday. First, Mom and Dad made him as a symbol of their love, and then Dad put a seed in my mom's stomach, and Luke grew in there. He ate for nine months through an umbrella cord.'

"She's standing there with her hands on the pillow, and I'm trying not to laugh and wishing I had my camcorder with me.

"The kids are watching her in amazement," Mrs. Dalberg went on. "'Then, about two Saturdays ago, my mom starts going, 'Oh, oh, oh, oh!' Erica puts a hand behind her back and groans. 'She walked around the house for, like an hour, 'Oh, oh, oh!' Now this kid is doing a hysterical duck walk and groaning.

"'That's when my dad called the middle-wife. She delivers babies, but she doesn't have a sign on the car like the Domino's man. They got my Mom to lie down in bed like this.' Then Erica lies down with her back against the wall.

"'And then, pop! My mom had this bag of water she kept in there in case he got thirsty, and it just blew up and spilled all over the bed, like psshhheew!' This kid has her legs spread with her little hands miming water flowing away. It was too much!

"'Then the middle wife starts saying 'push, push,' and 'breathe, breathe. They started counting, but never even got past ten. Then, all of a sudden, out comes my brother. He was covered in yucky stuff that they all said it was from Mom's play-center, so there must be a lot of toys inside there. When he got out, the middle wife spanked him for crawling up in there in the first place.'

"Then Erica stood up, took a big theatrical bow and returned to her seat. I'm sure I applauded the loudest. Ever since then, when it's show-and-tell day, I bring my camcorder, just in case another 'Middle Wife' comes along."

By this time, Alan was laughing so hard that he and Mrs. Dalberg attracted Evelyn's attention. She didn't want to intrude, but smiled in their direction and hoped Alan would re-tell this obviously amusing story once Mrs. Dalberg had gone.

"Okay, Doctor," Mrs. Dalberg blurted, panting, "I knew that having children was something like adopting a new pet or something, but that story was worth a movie." She tittered some more.

"Oh yes," Alan agreed. "But some memories will keep you awake, I'm afraid. And I understand it may be difficult to chase certain ones out of your mind, but I can only suggest that you try the little techniques I described earlier when you go to bed tonight."

"Yes, I'll try, Doctor, because as I told you, this is driving me round the bend."

CHAPTER FORTY-THREE

The scene of the crime

WHEN ALAN FOUND SAM and Edward at the bar, the place was swarming with passengers having a drink and short order lunches indoors. The weather was not the best for outdoor activities – clouds had gathered over the ocean and every one could feel the cold wind sweeping past *The Contessa* every time they ventured on the outside decks. The two men were in the throes of roaring laughter.

"Oh, hi, Doc," Sam said between chuckles when he saw Alan approach their table. "Have a seat and take a look at the latest joke that one of the rig hands sent us this morning."

Alan smiled and sat down. "Hi, guys, how are you doing?" he said, before he took the printout off Sam's hand.

"Just fine, Doc," Edward replied, "and we're ready for the arbalest test – whenever you are."

Alan nodded. "Good. Now let me read this."

The largest condom factory in the States burned down.

President Obama was awakened at 4:00 am by the telephone.

"Sorry to bother you at this hour, sir, but there is an emergency! I've just received word that the Durex factory in Washington has burned to the ground. It is estimated that the entire USA supply of condoms will be used up by the end of the week."

Obama: "Oh damn! The economy will never be able to cope with all those unwanted babies. We'll be ruined. We'll have to ship some in from Mexico ....."

Telephone voice says, "Bad idea... The Mexicans will have a field day with this one. We'll be a laughing stock. What about the UK?"

Obama: "Okay, I'll call Cameron and tell him we need five million condoms, ten inches long and three inches thick. That way, they'll continue to respect us as Americans."

Three days later, a delighted President Obama ran out to open the first of the 10,000 boxes that had just arrived. He found it full of condoms, 10 inches long and 3 inches thick, exactly as requested, all colored with Union Jacks with small writing on each one:

> **MADE IN ENGLAND – SIZE SMALL**

"Ha-ha, ha-ha," Alan laughed, "yes, I'm sure my American compatriots would have a field day with this one," he added, still grinning.

"Alright, Doc," Sam said, "As you heard from Edward here, we're ready for you. Where's the arbalest, by the way?"

"Oh, Chief Tolberg is bringing it with him; he's actually waiting for us on the upper deck with Agent Wilcox."

"Agent Wilcox? Which agency is he from?" Edward asked.

"He's CIA and he's the one who found the weapon in his cabin shortly after we reached Kodiak."

"Okay then," Sam said, getting to his feet and following Edward and Alan out of the bar.

"Have you had a chance to look around the ship for possible spots from which the arrow could have been shot?" Alan asked on their way to the elevators.

"Well yes," Sam answered. "And there aren't many that could eventually be counted as possibles. But there is one on the third deck, where you have quite a few single cabins located in a row with perfect line of sight for shooting an arrow. But," Sam went on, "there's always the problem of the victim standing for even a fraction of a second and facing his assailant."

As soon as they reached the upper deck, the three men saw Gerald waiting for them in the foyer near the elevators.

"Wow, that's some weapon," Sam exclaimed, seeing the arbalest in Agent Wilcox's hands.

"I'd say," Edward rejoined, as the three of them joined Gerald and Wilcox.

The latter was quick to introduce himself as Hans Grover to Alan's surprise.

"A little bird told me that you're CIA," Sam ventured, smiling amicably at the agent.

"Yes, but between friends, as they say, I'm just Hans Grover."

"Well, is that it then?" Edward asked Gerald. "Are you sure this is the weapon used in the murder?"

"As far as one can be sure of such things, yes," Gerald answered. "And frankly, I can't believe that no one noticed the shooter lugging this thing around before the incident."

"Let me show you how, Chief," Sam offered, taking the arbalest from Gerald, and dexterously folding its arms back into the side slots. Then passing the strap over his head, he lodged the weapon at his back with ease. "See, it's hardly noticeable now."

"I guess I should have taken up a different weapon when I was training years ago," Gerald remarked. He turned a questioning gaze to the CIA agent. "And you didn't know it could be folded?"

"Actually, I had noticed the grooves when I first examined it," Hans replied, "but I didn't want to handle it any more than I had to before the test."

"Okay then," Alan cut in, "shall we move on?" a bit impatient for the group and their weapon to move away from the foyer. This was the deck where most of the condos were located and where the most influential of passengers resided. He didn't want anyone to see men handle the arbalest in this exposed location for any length of time.

"Sure thing," Sam said, "I was just mentioning something to the doc on our way up here…"

"What was that?" Gerald interrupted, falling in step with the divers and Alan, with Hans in tow.

"We've been through the ship's decks and there are only two places where this arbalest could have been used," Sam went on.

"Yes," Edward said, "and if you'd like, we'll show you."

"By all means, that's what we're here for," Gerald said. "Is it on this deck?"

"Well, one of the spots is on this deck, yes," Sam replied. "But it's not the best, given the space needed for the shooter to extend the arms of the weapon; anyway, let's go and see if it could have been used."

The spot in question, however, didn't offer any resolution. The space in which the archer would have had to have taken aim, was a little too restricted for the arms of the arbalest to be extended properly.

While the men were standing in front of the elevators, on their way down to the third deck, Alan heard his name called from behind him. Everyone turned around to see Babette and Annette Sauvage come toward them.

"My, my, is this a gentlemen's conference?" Babette said, smiling up at Alan.

"No, Ms. Babette, we were just on our way down to test a bit of a theory," Gerald replied demurely. "But let me introduce everyone…"

"No need," Babette said, "I think Annette and I know every one of you boys." She looked at Annette.

"Yes, my father and I met Mr. Ashton and Mr. Barrington earlier in the cruise – you're the divers that are going to guide the sub to the *Investigator*, aren't you?"

"We sure are, Miss Sauvage – nice of you to remember."

"Not at all, Mr. Ashton, such dives have always intrigued me since I've heard so many stories about treasure hunting ever since I was a child."

"Are you going to dive with the sub then?" Edward asked, smiling at the lovely woman looking up and down at him appreciatively.

"Oh I don't think so; I think I'll only take a tour of the museum – that's all."

"Well now that we know everybody here…," Babette cut in, but stopped and turned to Hans. "Except perhaps for you that is…"

"I'm sorry, ma'am, I am Hans Grover, pleased to meet you."

"Enchantée, Mr. Grover, I'm sure, and this is Miss Annette Sauvage, one of our cast members," Babette added.

"Nice meeting you, Mr. Grover," Annette said, smiling at the man, "But may I ask what you're doing with an arbalest, Mr. Ashton…?" peering down at the folded weapon in Sam's grip.

"Oh you know this type of weapon then?" Gerald was quick to ask.

"Oh absolutely. I compete in Boston all the time," Annette answered, keeping her eyes riveted on the arbalest. "May I see it – it's quite a handsome weapon you've got there, Mr. Ashton. Do you compete too?"

Alan was surprised to see how comfortable Annette was around the men and how adroitly she lifted the weapon, unfolded it and looked through its scope.

"No, not me, Miss Sauvage, but a friend of mine back in England has an arbalest similar to this one. And he let me handle it a couple of times."

"Well, I should advise you that the more you handle a weapon like this one, the more you realize how much more accurate than a gun it is."

"Is that so?" Gerald queried, frowning.

Alan was also curious about Miss Sauvage's ability and wondered how else she could be involved in this affair. Because it was very clear to him, at this juncture, that Annette could have shot Cecil Legato – she was another suspect on his list. He also realized that she could have been involved in the salvage operation as well.

Shy to have anyone witnessing Annette's little demonstration, Gerald took the weapon off her hands and gave it back to Sam to fold it and fling it over his shoulder before the next elevator came up to a stop in front of them.

"And where were you going?" Alan asked Babette when they stepped into the lift.

"Oh Annette and I are going to put some rehearsing time under our belts," she replied.

As the elevator doors opened on the third deck, the men filed out of it, and Alan said, "See you later then," to Babette and Annette.

"Okay then, fellows, let's get to that second spot of yours," Gerald enjoined, leading the way to the exterior corridor giving access to some of the cabins on the starboard side of the vessel.

"Alright, here it is," Sam said, taking the arbalest off his back, opening it and pointing it toward the cabin where they had found Cecil Legato. "You see, if Legato was standing there, opening that cabin's door and perhaps looking at his murderer; the archer would have had the time to shoot the arrow and for it to reach its target without any problem."

"Good show, Mr. Ashton," Gerald exclaimed, "because that's the most plausible clue we've heard thus far in this bizarre case."

"Oh, why is that?" Edward asked.

"Because the cabin in front of which the victim was obviously standing when he was shot, is actually the one where we found him!"

"You mean he was staying there all the time…?"

"No," Hans put in, "it was only the cabin where the Chief found him. And it makes all the sense in the world for the shooter to lug his victim inside the cabin and shut the door unnoticed."

"Precisely," Gerald agreed. "What's more, our victim had opened the cabin door before he was shot, and our shooter didn't need to transport him very far from where he dropped."

"But then we need to check for traces of blood on the outside," Alan suggested. "Because, that arrow went right through the man's neck and blood would have spewed everywhere before he fell."

"You're right, Doc," Gerald said. "Why don't we go and have a look then?"

"But it's been days since the murder, wouldn't all traces of blood been wiped up or cleaned away by now?"

"Not necessarily, Mr. Barrington," Alan said, "Blood is one of the hardest things to erase from any surface. Apart from bleach there are not many chemicals that will clean blood off anything; hopefully, no super-clean of the deck has been done since the fateful day."

The men walked to the cabin's door and, hoping they would find the place where Legato had been killed – Alan had taken a blue-light torch with him. He pulled it out of his pocket and began panning the light very close to the surfaces that may have been sprayed with blood. It only took him a couple of minutes to show the others where the blue-light reflected off some of the traces of blood left behind.

"And there you are, gentlemen," Alan said, straightening up from examining the skirting board at the bottom of the wall near the cabin, "I think we found the scene of the crime."

"Yes, but we still don't have a suspect, or do we?" Hans asked.

"I think we're closer than ever to finding our culprit," Gerald said, looking at Alan pointedly.

"Is he still on board, do you think?" Edward asked.

"Yes, I believe so," Alan replied for Gerald.

"How you're going to prove this whole thing though?"

"That's my job, Mr. Ashton," Gerald said, "and as soon as we leave here, and I'm back at my desk, I'll start gathering evidence for Interpol – after that we'll see."

"What about the salvage operation; will it be stopped before we get to Banks?"

"That, Agent Wilcox, will be a matter for you and I to discuss at length as soon as we have our murderer under lock and key."

"You think the murderer and the treasure hunter is one and the same person then?"

"That's my contention, Mr. Barrington, but for now, I won't say anymore than that."

CHAPTER FORTY-FOUR

On with the show

THERE WAS A SENSE of gloom and foreboding amid some of the passengers on that day. The weather hadn't been the most pleasant in the past couple of days, and now that wisps of fog and mist seemed to pass *The Contessa* like ghostly figures blowing in the wind, a walk on the promenade deck gave one the eerie feeling of being suspended in time or place.

Alan loved the wisps of fog, making things look so ethereal. Looking at the ever so beautiful scenery going past the ship, Alan was rehashing the meeting he and Gerald had after the arbalest test and was replaying their conversation about Annette Sauvage in his mind.

"Yes, I have to agree with you, Doc," Gerald said, "She is definitely the best suspect yet. But how could we prove it – I mean how can we get her to confess to the crime. We don't have any evidence to suggest that she was near the crime scene at the time of the murder. All we have is the fact that she knows how to handle an arbalest – and that is not nearly enough."

"I know, Gerald. It might be easier to prove that she's been involved with the salvage operation near Banks since the beginning, but proving that she was the murderer might be more difficult, wouldn't you think?"

"Maybe, Doc – and that's a big maybe."

"Let me ask you this then: Didn't you have Interpol intercept conversations between Bornstein's wife and Cecil or between some other parties at some point?"

It was as if a light-bulb had suddenly been switched on over Gerald's head, for a broad grin appeared on his face when he replied, "You're darn right, Alan! Let me get Devon on the line early in the morning, explain the situation and get him to line up his surveillance satellite to monitor Annette's communications from now on."

And that's that, Alan thought as he turned his head to see Babette walking toward him. She was clad in her blue winter suit once again and looked positively charming.

"Alan, what on Earth are you doing out here?"

Alan pointed toward the gigantic iceberg floating amid the fog and mist some distance away from *The Contessa's* port side. "Isn't that an unforgettable sight?" he asked in reply.

"I wish it was about thirty degrees warmer though," Babette said, lacing her arms over the railing beside Alan.

"And what brought you out here then?"

"Annette," was Babette's one word answer.

"What about Miss Sauvage?"

"I may be an old doddering playwright, Alan, but I am no idiot when it comes to weighing someone's emotional attitude. And as far as Annette is concerned, I can tell you that she's a fantastic actress, and because of this, since her little demonstration the other day with the arbalest, I have come to believe that she could kill any one without batting an eyelid."

Alan grinned and turned his head to his friend. "Gerald and I happen to think that she did in fact shoot the arrow that killed Cecil Legato. But proving it is all together another matter entirely. We found blood splatter belonging to Cecil outside of the cabin where he was found, but that doesn't mean Miss Sauvage was anywhere near the place at the time of the murder."

"I see," Babette rejoined pensively. "You'll need for her to confess to the crime then, is that it?"

"In a word, yes, Babette. That's the only way we'll get anywhere with this crime solving exercise."

"Well, how can I help?"

"No need, Babette – but thank you. Gerald and Interpol are currently monitoring her communications, and we hope she's in touch with whoever is overseeing the salvage operation offshore Banks Island. And if we're right, she'll be caught that way. Confessing to the murder will come after we've proved that she's been the mastermind behind an illegal salvage operation."

"But won't the Canadians have something to say about this?"

"Oh believe me, they will. And since they're only too happy to work with Interpol in this case, they'll be very happy to bring charges against the woman – if she is in fact the person we're looking for."

"Sounds good, Alan. And for the time being, I can be as much an actress as she is – I'll forget what you've just said, and wait to see where the chips fall."

* * * *

Two days later, *The Contessa* was nearing Prudhoe Bay and would be dropping anchor the next morning. Interpol hadn't reported hearing a peep out of Miss Sauvage. All of her communications, emails mostly, were messages to her friends in Boston – nothing about the *Northern Rover* or the illegal salvage operation. Gerald and Alan were beginning to wonder if their suspicions had been correct or even warranted, but decided to wait another couple of days to determine whether they were right.

Renowned to be one of the largest oilfields in the world, Prudhoe Bay's population is largely composed of transients working on the rigs and oil plants punctuating the near shore landscape. In the summer the land is barren and mostly covered with lagoons and swamps, which makes visiting the place extremely dangerous. *The Contessa* was not staying long enough in the area to have any of the passengers disembark while they were anchored. This stopover was only designed to pass the ship through an inspection before it would venture into the Arctic waters where there wouldn't be any way for *The Contessa* to stop until she reached Banks Island.

So, on the night before their arrival in Prudhoe Bay, everyone aboard was looking forward to the third act of Babette's play, "Make Mine a Rumba". Every officer was dressed in their whites and the passengers seemed to have taken particular care with their attire also.

Alan caught up with Tiffany in the foyer of the theater. She had been so busy with the passengers' entertainment during the past four days that Alan had hardly had time to set eyes on her before she was off somewhere else.

"And how are you, stranger?" Alan asked as he approached her.

"Ready to collapse, to tell you the truth. You know I love to see the sights when we travel this far outside of our regular routes, but with the cold and these endless days – literally – with no nighttime to speak of, the passengers have been like a restless bunch of demanding kids, running me off my feet."

"Well, let's relax for tonight, and enjoy the midnight sunset and be together after the play, shall we?"

"That's the best offer I've had in days, Alan, thank you."

He wanted to take her in his arms and kiss her, but instead he said, "But for now, let's mingle and put on our best face for all the *children*, okay?"

"Sure," Tiffany replied, giggling a little. "Oh, by the way, have you seen Susan and her Mr. Sauvage lately?"

"No, I haven't seen our ballerina ever since she introduced us to her Mr. Sauvage. Do you know how she is doing?"

"Not really, I saw her at Mr. Strandovsky's second recital – she was with Sauvage and his daughter that evening – but after that not at all."

"Well, I'm sure she'll show up tonight..."

"And Annette said that her dad will be here. He's very keen to see her perform apparently."

"Okay then. And I'll try to see if I can find the von Weglan's – that's another couple that seemed to have disappeared from sight."

"Alright, I'll see you later," Tiffany said, abandoning Alan to his search.

By the time the bell rang, urging the passengers to take their seats, Alan had found Mr. Sauvage and Susan, and had discovered that, these days, he had been grooming his daughter to take over the salvage business.

MAKE MINE A RUMBA

ACT III
SCENE ONE

(Rumba music –Cuando Pienso En Ti – is playing loudly. The stage is empty.)

LEE: (Enters from bedroom. He is in his bathrobe. He goes to mirror, looks at himself – sticks out his tongue.) (Burps loudly) Damn it. Looks the same (Feels voice box). I sound the same (Flexes his muscles) feel the same, or do I? (Stands back, pulls his eyes down and his eyebrows up) How would I look if

I were a woman? Who wants to be a woman? (Exits back into bedroom.)

MR. MCTEEGE: (Enters, looks about - sees the wine bottle.) To hell with this guy! Why doesn't he get some whiskey, drinks blackberry wine – (Puts it down – looks in kitchen and yells) Lee – Lee! (Goes over to table, picks up cigarette, goes to light it, puts it back, picks up a cigar – shrugs shoulders – sticks it into his mouth. Music suddenly goes on.) Hey Lee - I know you're there, I can hear the damn music - (Opens bedroom door) – what do you do in bed all the time?

LEE: (Enters dressed in Elizabeth's clothes) Do I look like I'm in bed?

MR. MCTEEGE: Going to a masquerade?

LEE: You wouldn't catch me dead dressed up like this.

MR. MCTEEGE: Then what's the disguise for?

LEE: An experiment, to see if I really want to be a woman.

MR. MCTEEGE: Don't you know?

LEE: Obviously you haven't heard.

MR. MCTEEGE: I've been away, just got in the door.

LEE: (Whispers in his ear)

MR. MCTEEGE: No - you don't say.

LEE: Of course, they're not sure yet, they're still running some tests. In the meantime I'm doing a little testing of my own.

MR. MCTEEGE: (Watches Lee strut like a woman). You know what I think – you need a good stiff one.

LEE: That never solved anything.

MR. MCTEEGE: How do you know what you'd do if you tied one on. Now you're a thinking reasoning being, right?

LEE: Right.

MR. MCTEEGE: For the sake of science, purely for the sake of science, of course.

LEE: Of course - (Sarcastically)

MR. MCTEEGE: I could watch your reactions when you let your hair down. How can you tell what your subconscious is thinking?

LEE: And you wouldn't be drinking – some kind of a sacrifice?

MR. MCTEEGE: You know me - I can wallow in the stuff and it doesn't affect me. Did I tell you of the time I was in Chicago? Never mind you'd better send for the stuff, call the pharmacy; they have everything, but medicine.

LEE: (On phone) This is Lee Clarkson on Pine St.; would you send over a quart of Baby Duck Rose. And also send three 5ths of Bacardi Rum for a start. I'd appreciate it if you'd send it right over; this is sort of an emergency. (Hangs up.) He'll send it by taxi - should be here in less than 5 minutes. Damn it, when I think of the times I waited for them to send out a prescription.

MR. MCTEEGE: Baby Duck Rose has a mighty fragrant bouquet. I'll get the glasses. (Exits to his property and as he goes out he lets the dog in. The dog looks at Lee, first growls then jumps up and licks him all over.)

LEE: (To dog) It's me, the breadwinner, don't you know which side your bread is buttered - I wish I did.

MR. MCTEEGE: (Re-enters) Allow me (Puts the dog outside, gives Lee the glasses) It can never be said that John Francis McTeege didn't do his bit. (Doorbell rings - goes to door) I'll get it.

(Lee is sitting with his back to door - Enters Mrs. Flater)

MRS. FLATER: That girl Flater is here again... "The first with the finest" (She stops and Looks at Lee.) Honey, your slip's showing.

LEE: I don't want any today; my glands are in dry dock.

MRS. FLATER: I can see that, honey. Say, a little birdie told me that this house is up for sale. You haven't got a sign yet.

(Doorbell rings. Mr. McTeege gets bottles from taxi driver.)

LEE: You can tell your damn birdie he's a Goddamn liar.

MR. MCTEEGE: Will you have one?

MRS. FLATER: You know me, I never say no (Laughs) (Lee is fussing with his clothes). What's going on here, (pause) you know me, I won't talk.

MR. MCTEEGE: It has something to do with hormones.

MRS. FLATER: Come on, honey, I'm a big girl now, you can tell me. Are they really getting a divorce?

LEE: Why doesn't someone ask me? How are you doing with those drinks? I could use one about now.

MR. MCTEEGE: So could I - (Hands one to Lee - Lee hands it to Flater and says...)

LEE: One for the road - (They each get a large one.)

MRS. FLATER: (Nudges Lee) You never can tell anymore who wears the pants in the family. (Laughs vulgarly - helps herself to another. (Lee at this remark takes another one)

MR. MCTEEGE: To you (this is directed at Mrs. Flater) the finest is the first.

LEE: (Goes toward the bedroom) I'm going to be sick.

MRS. FLATER: What's the matter with him?

MR. MCTEEGE: He's kind of mixed up, inside.

LEE: (Re-enters) what I need is another drink.

MRS. FLATER: I can see that I can't do any business here. (Mr. McTeege is tight too, he slaps her buttocks) (Mrs. Flater pats Mr. McTeege's cheek) You've been a naughty boy today. I'd better run along and procure (pauses) houses (Laughs and exits).

LEE: This stuff sort of gets me.

MR. MCTEEGE: When that happens, you just let your hair down.

LEE: I don't have any to let down.

MR. MCTEEGE: You know something; you're right, then let yourself go and rumba (Wiggles his hips).

LEE: (Stops with glass in mid-air) What do you know about that? My wife likes to rumba. She'd rumba every night if - (has another drink) Great little wife, (Loud voice) Good mother too – too damn good - I'll give her to you.

MR. MCTEEGE: (Tight) No thanks.

LEE: That's all right, I don't blame you (starts to cry) I'm all mixed up here inside, and my hormones are on strike. Aren't you hot in those? (Points to Mr. McTeege's trousers.)

MR. MCTEEGE: Getting hotter all the time.

LEE: I have just the right thing to fix that. Come with me (Mr. McTeege starts to follow, goes back for bottle, they exchange drinks back and forth from bottle. They are facing each other and they go into a little dance as they exchange the bottle and exit into bedroom.)

ELIZABETH: (Enters – her arms filled with bundles) Look at this house. It looks as if a cyclone struck it.

MRS. MCTEEGE: Liz, have you forgotten that the Church Circle meets here?

ELIZABETH: This is the first I've heard of it.

MRS. MCTEEGE: I guess I forgot to tell you. I told them to come over to your house. You know with my new rugs and the furniture just upholstered. Well, with your old things I didn't think you'd mind.

ELIZABETH: I don't, Lucrica, but in the future please tell me ahead of time when they are coming.

MRS. MCTEEGE: They are due any time.

ELIZABETH: Oh no, the executive board of the P.T.A. should be here any minute. It's a special meeting and everyone's coming... (Off stage, exits with bundles) What if they see Lee? What will I do?

MRS. MCTEEGE: You'll manage, you always do. Thanks for having Jack this week, poor kid; this is a second home to him.

ELIZABETH: (Elizabeth is bustling about bringing in teacart. Door opens from bedroom. Lee staggers in, with more women's clothes and jewelry on). (Stunned) Just look at you!

LEE: Aren't I pretty - I smell good too - want to sniff? (Dances over to her.)

ELIZABETH: (Stands petrified.)

LEE: (Opens door to bedroom, bows low) Shall we rumba?

ELIZABETH: Get in there, Lee Clarkson, (Pushes him in) and stay there before you disgrace us all. (Closes door - to Mrs. McTeege) Did you see that?

MRS. MCTEEGE: How could I help it? (His eyebrows were up so high they looked like bangs.) What I didn't see, I smelled. Really, Liz, how do you put up with it? I wouldn't stand for it.

BOBBY: (Enters - Rumba music plays - Mr. McTeege now dances on to center stage. He does a female impersonation, then he dances with Lee.) Move over darlings and make room for a pro! (He goes into a dance.)

CURTAIN

CHAPTER FORTY-FIVE

Make Mine a Rumba – Finale

AMID THE FLURRY OF ACTIVITIES during the intermission, Alan found Susan talking wildly to Annette's father, both of them standing by the cocktail table.

"Oh hello, Alan darling; wasn't this scene absolutely hilarious? I love Babette's plays. She's such a talented playwright."

"I couldn't agree more, Susan," Alan rejoined, "and your daughter, Mr. Sauvage, was perfect in the role of Mrs. McTeege I thought."

"Well, thank you, Doctor. Nice of you to say so, I'm sure," Sauvage replied courteously, taking another glass of wine and exchanging it for Susan's empty one.

"Oh I think Annette would be perfect in any role," Susan added, a little inebriated already. "She can take on any personality at the snap of a finger; have you noticed that, darling?" she asked Sauvage.

"Well that's true enough I suppose." He smiled at Alan. "You see, Doctor, when Annette is in the office, you'd think she is this old fearless tycoon that would chew you out for any mistakes you've made. Yet, when she's out somewhere with me and friends, she is the sweetest little girl I have always known."

"She's like a chameleon then?" Alan asked, throwing an amicable smile to Sauvage.

"And you should see her, Alan; the energy this girl has is incredible. I could hardly keep pace with her when we were in Kodiak."

"I'm glad to hear that you had time to take a tour of Kodiak while we were there," Alan remarked.

"Oh yes, we spent quite a bit of time going on a guided hike through a mountain trail – in search of grizzlies, would you believe – and I tell you, by the time we returned to town, I was ready to collapse, but not Annette. Oh no, she would have gone dancing that night, if there had been dancing to be had."

"I am glad to…"

"Doctor Mayhew," Alan heard Gerald's voice call him from over his shoulder. "I'm sorry for the interruption, Doc,"—he bowed to Sauvage and Susan— "but could I see you for a moment?"

"Of course, Chief," Alan replied, turning to look at the couple, "please excuse me – I'll see you both after the performance."

"By all means, Doctor," Sauvage said, "we'll be here or at the cocktail lounge, won't we, darling?" he asked Susan.

"Yes, yes – but go, go – duty calls," Susan added, waving at Alan.

Once both Alan and Gerald had retreated to a corridor leading to the elevators and out of earshot, Alan asked, "What's the matter? I didn't feel my phone vibrate – is anything wrong?"

"Well, actually I'd say everything is finally going right for a change."

"What do you mean? Any news from Interpol?"

Gerald nodded and grinned. "Yes, Alan. You were right. Miss Sauvage has finally made contact with the *Northern Rover*."

"That's good news indeed," Alan said excitedly. "But did she say anything inculpating her in the illegal salvage? Because she could have asked a multitude of questions other than the ones that are of any interest…"

"Let me stop you right there, Alan. She in fact asked how many relics were left to raise out of the boat – is that inculpating enough for you?"

"Wow, that's hardly believable, she must have thrown caution to the wind all of a sudden."

"I don't know what's got into her, but I should think she's getting nervous since she revealed her aptitude to handle an arbalest the way she did."

"And I suppose she thinks there's no one monitoring her communications – or capable of doing so – otherwise, I think she would never have taken the risk."

ACT III
SCENE II

(As the curtain rises the stage is empty – there is dead silence – phone rings off stage. Lee enters from bedroom; he is dressed in pajamas and robe.)

LEE: Damn it can't that thing ever shut up. The phone's ringing.

ELIZABETH: (Off stage) Well, answer it!

LEE: It's probably for you (Holds head) (Jumps at sound).

ELIZABETH: I can't come now.

LEE: (Goes to phone - mumbles "women!") Maybe it's not so bad as that. Hello? (Waits) nobody is home. (Goes to hang up - he hears a voice saying) "I'm from Alcoholics Anonymous…" (Puts phone back to ear as if listening) You say my neighbors and friends gave you my name - some friends - you wouldn't like to tell me what son of a.... No, I'm not drunk - wait a minute (Puts phone down goes over to the kitchen door, opens it slightly, peers in - goes over to patio, looks over fence. (Back to phone) I just wanted to get an address and telephone number for you of somebody who could really use your services. Sure, he wants and needs your help, he's my neighbor, you probably got my number by mistake, when you really wanted him (Looks about) and the name is John Francis McTeege.... You are quite welcome. No really I don't want your help, unless you know what to do for a hangover. Never mind, I was just kidding. (Hangs up) Some joke (Holds head - doorbell rings) Never mind, I'll get it - It's probably the truant officer wanting to know why I haven't been a good little boy - (Off stage) or girl? (Voices – off stage.)

ELIZABETH: (Enters - straightens furniture - then drops wearily on couch.) Who was it?

LEE: (Enters) The police.

ELIZABETH: Not for you. (Elizabeth breaks down and cries.)

LEE: In a way. That isn't what I meant. He wanted to warn me that there's a homosexual in the neighborhood.

ELIZABETH: He knows.

LEE: He knows what? About homosexuals, maybe? Well, if he does, he knows a damn lot more than I do. Why must you jump to conclusions? You're getting like the rest of them around here (Waves arms) yakety-yakety-yak all day. You're not even listening to me, you never listen to my side of it - you're not even fair.

ELIZABETH: I do listen to you; only I've heard the same old tune over and over again.

LEE: So now I bore you?

ELIZABETH: I didn't say that.

LEE: But you meant it, never mind, don't answer. My head is playing the anvil chorus. I'm going to bed (At bedroom door) and I don't want to rumba (Exits to bedroom.)

ELIZABETH: (Goes toward kitchen) I'll get you an ice bag.

(Enters Mrs. McTeege - picks up the two cocktail glasses that were hers - looks around as if to see if there is anything else that belongs to her. Pours herself a drink and quietly starts to exit back toward her own place)

ELIZABETH: Hi, Lucrica.

MRS. MCTEEGE: Hi - I've got to go now, I just came for these glasses - I'm in a big hurry (Starts to go into her own place).

ELIZABETH: (Going after her) Wait a minute. I want to ask you something.

MRS. MCTEEGE : Some other time, maybe (exits).

LEE: (Enters) Where's the icebag ? I thought you were getting it for me.

ELIZABETH: (Still has the ice bag in her hand, returns and goes to phone.) I know she's in (Dials – waits - no answer - Lee takes ice bag from Elizabeth.) Now see what you've done.

LEE: What have I done? You were going to get me an ice bag. You didn't come, so I got up holding my poor head and I walked several painful steps. I take the ice bag intended for me and you say – "see what you've done?" (Louder). What have I done?

ELIZABETH: Shush, you'll wake the children.

LEE: (Loud stage whisper, mouthing his words.) What have I done?

ELIZABETH: (Hangs up phone) Lucrica came in here.

LEE: (Looks at wine decanter). I can see that.

ELIZABETH: Took her glasses and left.

LEE: Maybe she needed them.

ELIZABETH: She wouldn't talk and was very cold.

LEE: Wine affects people in different ways.

ELIZABETH: Then she ran to her house - I followed and rang the bell and she didn't answer.

LEE: Maybe the bell is out of order.

ELIZABETH: I knocked on the door (Lee cringes and holds his head) and I know they are all in that apartment.

LEE: Why don't you phone her?

ELIZABETH: I did and she didn't answer.

LEE: It's very simple - she doesn't want to talk to you. May I go to bed now? (Starts for bedroom. Elizabeth keeps following Lee.)

ELIZABETH: That's just the point, every woman in this town saw you.

LEE: (Moans) and John Francis, too (Exits).

ELIZABETH: You and your rumbas (Exits).

MR. MCTEEGE: (On his side of the fence) Why must it be done now?

MRS. MCTEEGE: You saw her, didn't you. Came right over here. Some nerve.

MR. MCTEEGE: My head is killing me - why don't you let Jack do it.

MRS. MCTEEGE: You know very well they'd start talking to him.

MR. MCTEEGE: They might talk to me too.

MRS. MCTEEGE: Hurry up and get that locked up before one of them comes nosing around (exits into the house).

MR. MCTEEGE: (Pounds and every time he jumps).

LEE: (Enters) What the hell is all the noise about? Will you kids shut up and go to sleep?

CHILD: (Off stage) Mummie!

ELIZABETH: (Starts going to children) Be quiet, Lee, they need their sleep.

LEE: (Over to Mr. McTeege.) What the devil are you doing?

MR. MCTEEGE: Hold the flashlight for me? About there, that's fine, no a little bit more and to the left. Couldn't do it without you, buddy boy, Thanks (takes the flash light back).
LEE: Why the lock?

MR. MCTEEGE: To keep unwanted people out.

LEE: (Turns his back) Don't worry. One question, though.

MR MCTEEGE: (Looks up).

LEE: Who'll hold the flashlight for you? (Mr. McTeege exits - Lee goes back into the living room. Elizabeth enters). Some nerve (pointing towards McTeege's) He had me hold the flashlight.

ELIZABETH: Why?

LEE: I guess, so he could see what he was doing.

ELIZABETH: I mean what was he doing?

LEE: Putting up a lock to keep unwanted people out.

ELIZABETH: They didn't have to do that. (Phone rings.) I'll get it. Hello - oh hi, Dieter - Did I miss an R.E. meeting or something? Good. You what? No, I don't intend to resign from any of my church activities. That's very kind of you to be concerned, that I have too many irons in the fire but I can manage, oh (Pause) yes I'll write it and send it to you tomorrow (Hangs up). The good people of our church want me to write a letter of resignation. In other words – get off all committees.

LEE: Whose idea was that?

ELIZABETH: He said, they agreed unanimously but it was probably, Lloyd Dieter, Bertha Florie and Barbara, all of them (runs off stage to bedroom).

LEE: (Starts to follow - phone rings - Lee answers phone) Hello. I'm sorry she can't come to the phone. Could I take a message? Mrs. Snyder - You have replaced Mrs. Clarkson on the P.T.A. board. May I ask why? I see. Thank you, I'll see that she gets the message. Who am I? Mr. Clarkson. (Hangs up) (Phone rings again) – Hello. Oh, Jane, I'm sure glad you called, you're a nurse and I think maybe you could do the little woman some good. She's pretty low right now. Wait a minute. I'll get her. You want me to give her a message. Sure, repeat that again. My daughter is not to report to her Brownie Troop. Why the hell not? Going to another troop? It's nearer home. (Hangs up phone.) Those damn bitches (Yells); who the hell wants to be a woman? (Doorbell rings - Lee goes to the door – Dr. Asspan enters).

DR. ASSPAN: What do you people do? Sit on the phone, all day-all the time? I've tried to get you for the last hour. As long as I'm going to buy the house next door I won't charge you, this time, for a house call. May I sit down?

LEE: (Motions him to sit.)

DR. ASSPAN: I've been thinking about you and your problem and doing quite a bit of research on it. Now there is a new drug that counteracts the hormone dosage I gave you.

LEE: (Starts rolling up his sleeve)

DR. ASSPAN: Not so fast. I think you should think about it, sleep on it and discuss it with your wife.

LEE: What the hell do you think I've been doing since you told me?

DR. ASSPAN: First of all, you must be prepared to layout a considerable sum of money.

LEE: How much?

DR. ASSPAN: The drug is expensive. I have no control over it - my services are nominal – $10.00 a minute.

LEE: $10.00 a minute – $600.00 an hour!

DR. ASSPAN: (Clears throat, stands) the other aspect is we don't know exactly what the result might be sexually.

LEE: Would I be a man?

DR. ASSPAN: I hope so.

LEE: Could I be a woman?

DR. ASSPAN: I hope not.

LEE: Which would it be, Doctor, man or woman?

DR. ASSPAN: Not both, one or the other.

LEE: That's a relief.

DR. ASSPAN: As your glands go through a changing process, there might be some pain involved, I guess I've painted a rather glum picture. Sorry, Lee (pats him on the back). May I use your phone? (Lee passes the phone - Dr. Asspan dials). Hello, Dr. Asspan here, any calls for me? Maybe I can get to bed for a change. I wonder if you'll call my wife, tell her to wait up for me. I'll be home in a half hour. Oh and by the way, let Dr. Uri take my calls. He spends too much time in bed. (Hangs up.)

LEE: When do I have to let you know?

DR. ASSPAN: Take all the time you need. You can make an appointment with my nurse tomorrow (exits).

ELIZABETH: (Comes on stage just to see the doctor leaving.) Anything wrong, Lee?

(Mrs. McTeege opens her gate and comes in.)

LEE: About the same. (He picks up his instrument – a cello – and starts to play at the back of the stage.)

MRS. MCTEEGE: Am I interrupting?

ELIZABETH: I am glad you came over. I want to talk to you.

MRS. MCTEEGE: Before you start, I haven't much time and I want to say something. You know me; I'm a real sucker for people. I heard what they did to you at the P.T.A. - and all that. I'm sorry for you, kid. I didn't do it for the same reason.

ELIZABETH: Do what?

MRS. MCTEEGE: You want me to say it? (Elizabeth nods "yes.") I am dropping you for a couple of reasons. You can't do anything for John Francis. You know, as a salesman he's got to make the right contacts meet the right people - that's just good business. Who do your kids know?

ELIZABETH: What about the boys? They're such good friends.

MRS. MCTEEGE: They're young, but they have to learn not to associate with the wrong crowd, you know. You and your kids served a purpose, you got Jack out of my hair, but I gave you a gift for that.

ELIZABETH: Is this what you're going to tell Jack?

MRS. MCTEEGE: Sure, he'll understand they have nothing in common. (Elizabeth looks hurt and shocked) You'll get over it, Liz, so will your kids. The trouble with you is, you belong to a decaying generation. You're, you're old fashioned, with your fine manners – honor, integrity and all that. I ask you; will it buy you anything? Look at me; I grew up in the slums. My father and mother couldn't read or write. I went out and worked, while you were in school, and I saw John Francis, big, handsome, masculine, and I went for him but not until I found out his maiden aunt was loaded. It hasn't been easy playing up to his family all these years. I've paid for it. Now we're moving on (pointing up) up there, where the money is. Nothing personal, you know. We've just got nothing in common (exits).

LEE: (Who has been playing his instrument, puts it down) Good riddance. Forget her. What would you do if I suddenly became a woman?

ELIZABETH: (Slowly turns to him) Do you want to be a woman?

LEE: Of course not.

ELIZABETH: Then why do you ask?

LEE: Asspan was here, he recommended a new drug. God is the only one who knows if I'd come out a man or a woman.

ELIZABETH: And if you don't take the medicine?

LEE: Then I stay in a state of suspended animation.

ELIZABETH: What does Boyd say to all this?

LEE: I haven't asked him yet.

ELIZABETH: Why don't you call him?

LEE: You're right (he goes to the phone) Sorry, Boyd, to disturb you at home. But I'm in a hell of a fix, Asspan was here, he gives me till tomorrow... (Voice trails off).

BOBBY: (Enters) Hi, darling (Throws a kiss to Lee and to Elizabeth) how do you like my new hairdo? I put a wave in front this time. I think it gives me height, don't you? You ought to try it sometime.

ELIZABETH (Exits disgusted, takes up her mending; comes back and sits on stage like a chaperone. Lee hangs up the phone.)

BOBBY: Darling, I've found the most adorable man. No, you're not going to stop me this time. You have to make a decision tonight.

LEE: This is the night of decisions.

BOBBY: It sure is, I'll lose him - I tell you and is he cute. Blond hair and great, big, blue eyes and the cutest you know what. Wait until I show you his act. (Bobby goes into an act of a female strip tease dancer) You should see the original like it.

LEE: I don't know.

BOBBY: And there's this dark mysterious one, with the most beautiful voice – "He's my man and he's done me wrong". One note and he suggests things....

ELIZABETH: I suggest something too; that you go home, Bobby, now.

BOBBY: Do YOU want me to go? I'm warning you, Lee Clarkson, if I go now, I'll never, never come back.

LEE: How much can you get them for?

ELIZABETH: Lee, have you gone out of your mind. How can you do this to me?

LEE: I'm doing it FOR you. Who else do you think I'm doing it for? I want to make money for you.

ELIZABETH: I never asked you to do this.

LEE: I know, it's a surprise.

ELIZABETH: Some surprise.

LEE: Wait until the money pours in from the nightclub.

ELIZABETH: Nightclub?

LEE: Sure, we'll do it there.

ELIZABETH: (Screams) NO!

LEE: Well, we can't do it here, they wouldn't license us.

ELIZABETH: I should hope not.

BOBBY: My beautiful boys will be more gorgeous and appealing than any female.

ELIZABETH: Appealing to whom?

BOBBY: The customers, darling. Just think your husband is putting up the money for me to start my own nightclub.

LEE: We'll be partners. Bobby's a good female impersonator and he can get others, it'll be a terrific nightclub. The public will go crazy for it. Think of it, with that kind of money our boys can go to any college they want. (Doorbell rings) I'll get it. (Bobby ad-libs about his clothes etc., off stage) I want to hear you say it again: Thank you officer.

(Bobby stops dead - and looks up, terrified.)

LEE: Don't worry, Bobby, it's not for you – it's for our very good neighbor John Francis (Fairy) McTeege. That great masculine hunk of man is gay, a fairy, a pansy - my apologies to you, Bobby, a homosexual.

ELIZABETH: I know you're mad at them but you really shouldn't say things like that.

LEE: I'm not saying it. That policeman out there, he's the one that said it. For months now, they've had a stakeout watching his place. For awhile they were suspicious of me. Thank God, not for long. He's been contributing to the delinquency of minors.

BOBBY: I'd never do a thing like that.

LEE: Now, they are going to arrest him and do you know, he can't get away because of that lock on his garden gate. I think I'll just make doubly sure. (Gets nails and starts hammering a nail into his gate.) (Doorbell rings)

DR. ASSPAN: (Races in) Is your husband in? I'm in a big hurry.

LEE: I haven't made up my mind yet.

DR. ASSPAN: I wish I had. If only I were at home in bed with my wife. Oh yes, I came to tell you. I made a mistake; you weren't the one I gave the wrong shot to. Well, so long - I can't afford to be found over there (points towards McTeege) Wouldn't do my reputation any good. Any time I can be of service - Good night (Exits).

BOBBY: So long, partner dear. Wait for me darling. I need a lift (Exits)

ELIZABETH: Then you're all right. I'm glad.

LEE: I could ask you to rumba, but I'm afraid it won't do you any good now. Remember my glands have been shot for quite sometime. (Hugs her – rumba music - they start to rumba towards bedroom.)

CURTAIN

THE END

If there was ever a time when Alan was thrilled to be attending one of Babette's plays, this was it. When he stood and applauded, he could have cried. He knew how hard it must have been for Babette to hold it together, while having a suspected criminal among her cast, being a counselor, a friend, and a teacher to so many, and yet, managing to present one of her best plays to an admiring audience. He couldn't have been prouder to be her friend.

CHAPTER FORTY-SIX

A hooded figure

THE *CONTESSA* RAISED ANCHOR in Prudhoe Bay and was now on its way to Tuktoyaktuk - the last coastal stop before heading to Banks Island. Alan spent a long day in the medical center, reviewing once again, all the measures he and his team were going to take with them onto Banks Island. On the island they were hopefully going to prevent any of the passengers from contracting the island's endemic diseases. Firstly, Dengue Fever was present. He especially did not want them to get the virulent strain of tuberculosis mycobacterium that was still omni-present on the island. He decided to call it a day and was on his way to his cabin. En route, he nearly collided with an older fellow who accosted him unexpectedly in the foyer outside of the main restaurant.

"Oh, Doctor," the fellow said, attracting Alan's attention after the two of them collected themselves after the near collision. "I'm sorry to bother you..."

"No bother, sir. How can I help you?" Alan replied, stopping to talk to the man.

"Oh, I don't need any help 'that way', Doctor, but I've heard that you've been in all sorts of places in the world, and I was wondering if you've ever come across a shaman during any of your cruises?"

During previous journeys, particularly in India, Vietnam, Guatemala, China, and Irian Jaya, Alan had encountered various types of healers, shamans, medicine men and others who claimed to have enlisted the powers of a greater being to achieve what their stated goal was. Some of those goals were as lofty as: enlightenment, all seeing power, fortunes, excellent health, and the like. When meeting these individuals, Alan always asked for the latter, even when he was unsure of the authenticity of the 'seer'.

"A shaman? Yes, actually I have, sir, but why do you ask?"

"It's because since we're going to Banks Island, I was curious to know if there are any shamans on that island."

"At this point, I wouldn't know, but if there is one such man or woman on the island, maybe we'll have an opportunity to meet them."

"Oh that would be so nice, so very nice indeed." The man stopped talking and fixed his gaze on Alan's face. "But, I'm sorry, I should introduce myself – Dr. Wasserfall is the name – Ph.D. in ethno biological anthropology, not an MD."

"Doctor Mayhew," Alan rejoined, shaking hands with the well-dressed man who obviously took particular attention to personal details. He must have been in his fifties, although his grey hair and beard made him look quite a bit older.

"...and this cruise is my third journey in and around the Arctic over the last 15 years," Wasserfall went on with a particular brightness in his voice.

"Really? You must have some interesting stories to tell about these trips..."

"Indeed, I have, Dr. Mayhew, indeed I have."

"And have you met any shaman during your travels?"

"Yes, yes – in fact I met 'the man' while visiting Ellesmere Island last summer, and I really enjoyed... no, 'enjoy' is not the right word for it," Dr. Wasserfall said, with a shake of his head. "It was more like an enlightening out-of-body experience, a trip through my mind."

"Hmm, that's sounds fascinating. And, you know, Doctor, I've heard of this shaman while I was talking to some of the locals on Kodiak Island, but unfortunately since we're not planning to visit Ellesmere, I would be very interested in hearing your story of that meeting."

"Well, by all means, Doctor, by all means. Why don't we go to the restaurant's lounge, and I could tell you the story over a cup of coffee...?"

"Thank you, I accept," Alan replied – the fatigue of the day having suddenly abandoned him.

* * * *

After leaving the lounge and Dr. Wasserfall with his many fascinating stories, Alan returned to his cabin – his mind encumbered with all of the questions to which he still hadn't found an answer. Was there any chance of finding a treasure aboard the *Investigator*? Would they be able to reach the wreck without facing any more incidents? Where was Agent Korsakov – and who was she?

Gerald was preparing whatever evidence Interpol had gathered to submit to the RCMP before their arrival in Tuktoyaktuk, which would enable the Canadian authorities to issue a warrant for her arrest. The warrant would charge her with conspiracy to commit fraud against the Crown; given that Parks Canada were now the owner of the *HMS Investigator* and all of its content. As for the murder, Interpol and CIA would have to debate the matter of extradition back to the States once a warrant was issued in Washington.

* * * *

So, it was with a mind full of conjectures that Alan lay down that night and fell asleep, and began dreaming of the shaman he would have loved to meet if he ever went to Ellesmere.

When Alan disembarked in this village, he was met by the man with whom he was to spend the next five hours. Short and wiry, he was a man of about 60, with skin resembling that of a lizard and piercing but kind eyes. Alan rowed with him out to a small island in a rowboat, listening to the lapping of the waves against the sides of the little craft. The island was not much more than a big rock with not a tree there, but even upon arrival, it had a very peaceful feeling to it.

The wind was blowing quite strong and coming off the north, and was quite chilly. Alan was only wearing normal trousers, a shirt and light jacket and even after a few minutes, noted the cold, which did not appear to bother the shaman at all. He and Alan sat on two smooth rocks that had obviously been used before and were somewhat protected from the full force of the wind in the way they were positioned.

It appeared that one of the shaman's assistants had been out to the island just before and had lit a ceremonial fire. It certainly helped with the cold, but not much. Soon after their arrival, the shaman started beating a drum made out of some animal skin stretched over a whalebone frame. He started beating this drum faster and faster, as the wind became stronger and his heart rate obviously increased also. It looked as if he was trying to beat his own heartbeat.... Ice crystals began to form on Alan's eyebrows – it was so cold. The shaman was kneeling but Alan had to keep changing position because of the numbing cold and the painful cramps in his knees. The bottom part of the drum was open, much like those in the Afro-Brazilian tradition. This was to let the spirit into the drum and the shaman. At a certain point, the medium, or priest, metastasized his soul; left his body, allowing another more experienced being to occupy him. There was no particular moment when this happened. Alan tried to empty his mind and disregard the cold wind that was not letting him go.

Alan then opened his eyes and noticed that the shaman was holding some feathers in his hand. This was typical of many cultures as birds are supposed to carry the spirit to the shaman. The wind increased in intensity and Alan was feeling colder still when the shaman took a drink of a foul-smelling liquid. He offered Alan a gulp of the greenish liquid. Out of respect, Alan took a mouthful of the slightly alcoholic, sugary liquid, returned the bottle to the shaman and listened to the drumming once again.

The shaman paused to trace a shape on the ground with symbols Alan had never seen before and which resembled some long since banished form of writing. Then strange noises emerged from the shaman's throat like a greatly amplified cry of a bird. The drumming was getting louder and faster all the time and now the cold didn't seem to bother Alan as much. Suddenly, the wind stopped and the facial features of the shaman changed – he looked younger. The flames of the fire got brighter, and the shaman made more coherent noises now. A vision of what appeared to be birds flying up from the shaman's head and shoulders brought clarity to Alan's thoughts. Then the wind came back up, and Alan quietly, in his dream, boarded the rowboat back to join the others.

Although, the shaman did not give Alan Agent Korsakov's real name or what was to happen on Banks Island, when he finally woke up, it allowed him to organize his thoughts better. Interestingly, the shaman looked old again after the dream session was over. Had his body been taken over?

Alan lay quietly for a while, after waking up with a start, following that significant dream. He felt alert. He also felt that finding evidence against Annette Sauvage had to be done now – in the morning would be too late. He got up and slipped into trousers, shirt and warm jacket before

taking a step outside. He knew Annette Sauvage would be on her guard.
He also felt that she probably wanted to eliminate the remaining witness to
her original crime – letting Cecil hire her father's boat, *l'itinerant du nord*,
from his fleet and participating in the conspiracy. The witness in question
was Isaac Bornstein. Alan knew the man had been returned to his suite on
the sixth deck. He was in protective custody, but he had obtained
immunity from the Canadian Government in order to protect his
investments in the forthcoming sub-dives and future salvage operation of
the relics aboard the *Investigator*. If Bornstein was to remain alive until
Annette's trial, he would spill the beans and inculpate the young woman
with his testimony.

Alan also knew that Annette Sauvage would go to any length to kill
Bornstein. She was a first-rate marksman with a crossbow, and perhaps an
equally excellent shooter with other weapons. Although he was not
prepared for a confrontation with a killer, Alan knew the ship better than
many and he was well aware of the cunning an assassin, the likes of
Annette, could use to enter Bornstein's cabin. So he made his way to the
stewards' quarters on the sixth deck where he knew he would find someone
in attendance, even at this late hour.

* * * *

"Oh God, what have I done now?" Sony, the young steward said
when Alan entered the cabin.

Alan chuckled and went to sit down beside Sony and below the
surveillance screens aligned above their heads. "Nothing that I know of
yet," he replied.

"So, what can I do for you, Doc?"

"Just tell me if you or anyone else here has been called to either the
Sauvage's or the Bornstein's cabins recently?"

Sony turned to the roster and reports, hanging above his desk. "Not
during my shift, but let's see…." He grabbed one of the reports off the
clipboard, and flipped over the first page. "No, nothing, everything has
been quiet, Doc, sorry."

"Okay then, and have you been recording the movements of these
people during the last few hours?"

"Well yes, see, since Chief Tolberg had those surveillance cameras
installed in the corridors of the sixth deck, we've been assigned to record
everywhere these people go – when they come in, when they go out, and all
that – but he told us that we should keep an eye on Bornstein and on the
Sauvage father, and the daughter in particular."

"Good, and have you noticed anything unusual since you began your
shift?"

Sony swiveled his chair to face Alan. "What's this all about, Doc? Has
anything happened that will make a dull job much more interesting?"

"Nothing that I know of, Sony, but Annette Sauvage is the one that
we need to watch very carefully. Has Chief Tolberg told you anything
about her?"

"No, he hasn't said a word. Neil came in a couple of times after we left

Prudhoe Bay, but everything has been very quiet, why?"

"Well, I just wondered, because we've got another three days at sea before we get to Tuktoyaktuk, and I suspect Annette Sauvage to go on the prowl some nights before we arrive."

"On the prowl for what?" Sony raised his gaze to the doc, as the latter was about to get up from his seat. "Come on, Doc. We're only stewards, but if the lady is looking for trouble, we certainly don't want to get in her way. It would cost me my job!!"

"That's why I'd like you to check these tapes again – those you've recorded after the theater play – to see if the woman has exited her suite during the middle of the night or if she carried anything with her..."

"Like what?" Sony asked.

"Like a long bag or case of some sort, or maybe something over her shoulder..."

"Well now that you mention it; there was something that caught my attention earlier tonight. But let me rewind some of the tapes of that hallway."

Alan sat down again. He knew that Sony had a keen eye for detail and that was probably the reason for which Gerald had assigned the young man to this tedious and boring task.

"Ah, there we go," Sony said, stopping the tape at about nine o'clock that night. "You see, she's got some sort of bag slung over her shoulder, would that be what you're looking for?"

"Exactly, Sony, that's precisely what I was looking for." Alan smiled.

"What's in that bag, do you know?"

"I think I do, yes. But now, I want you to call Chief Tolberg and get him up here to see the tape, as soon as possible, okay?"

"Will do, Doc. But where will you be if he needs to talk to you?" Sony asked to Alan's back – he was already out the door.

"Tell him to use my emergency number if he wants me...."

After seeing Annette returning to her suite at 9:00 pm on the stewards' tape, Alan was worried. Isaac Bornstein, he knew, was taking all of his meals in his cabin and Mr. Sauvage was having dinner in the main restaurant at that time of the evening.

He made his way down the corridor to Bornstein's suite, stopped in front of the door and looked up at the camera that hung near the corner of the ceiling a few yards away from where he stood. He shook his head, turned around and retraced his steps to the stewards' quarters. *I should have asked Sony to check that tape as well,* he thought.

As he neared the stewards' cabin, he saw Gerald coming down the corridor.

"Hi, Alan, what's up? Sony called me to say you guys had seen the Sauvage girl entering her suite at around nine with a bag over her shoulder – what do you think it was?"

"Well, you'll tell me, once Sony shows you the clip," Alan replied, opening the stewards' prep area door. "But I forgot to ask him to rewind the tape showing the entrance of Bornstein's cabin before 9:00pm..."

"Why's that?" Gerald asked.

"Hi, Chief," Sony piped up, and then seeing Alan with Gerald, added,

"Oh, you forgot something, Doc?"

"Yes, as a matter of fact I did, Sony," Alan said, going to stand with Gerald at Sony's back. "Could you rewind the tape showing the corridor to Mr. Bornstein's suite to about 8:30 tonight?"

"Sure thing, Doc," Sony replied, already pressing a few digits on his keyboard. "There you go...."

The successive pictures showed an empty corridor until one of the dining room attendants came up on the screen. The man bent down and picked up the empty tray from beside Bornstein's cabin door. He covered it and walked down the hallway out of the camera's scope of vision.

Alan, Gerald and Sony waited a few minutes before they saw someone dressed in a winter suit, hood and gloves, and carrying a long bag on his back, knocking on the door and entering Bornstein's cabin. This was presumably after being admitted inside – by Bornstein himself.

"That's it," Alan said, pointing at the screen in question. "Can you freeze that frame?" he asked Sony.

"Okay, no problem," the young man replied, rewinding the tape and stopping on the clip showing the person standing by Bornstein's door.

"And now can you fast forward the tape to the time that person comes out of Mr. Bornstein's suite?" Alan asked Sony.

The latter nodded and a few seconds later they saw the hooded person exiting Bornstein's cabin and closing the door carefully.

"Okay, I see what you mean," Gerald said to Alan. He pointed to the other clip showing Annette entering her suite at nine o'clock. "These two people are the same. And I would bet my bottom dollar that Miss Sauvage is the one paying a visit to Bornstein on that earlier clip." He tapped on Sony's shoulder. "Good show, son. I knew these cameras would get us some answers one day."

"Shall we go then?" Alan asked.

Gerald shook his head vigorously and looked up at Alan. "Oh no, you don't, Doc. I'll get Neil out of bed and get him up here – but you, you stay right here. If there's something amiss in Bornstein's cabin, I will call you – if your emergency medical or coroners services are required."

"But..."

"No, Doc, I don't want Annette Sauvage to come after you next. If she knows you're the one who's pointed the knowing finger, she'll soon attempt to get you out of the picture rather than surrender. We need you here as a doctor!"

"Okay," Alan replied reluctantly. "I'll stay and watch the show from here then."

Gerald took his cell phone out of his pocket and pressed a digit to get him through to Neil. "Alright, you sleepy head," he said, "get your butt over on the sixth floor and meet me in front of Bornstein's cabin.... Yeah, that's what I said." He paused and looked at Alan who was smiling. "Yeah, that's a good idea. Okay, I'll see you there in a tick." Closing his phone, Gerald added, "Okay, Doc, I'll wave at the camera outside the door of Bornstein's cabin if I need you, okay?"

Alan nodded and sat down beside a bewildered Sony once again.

CHAPTER FORTY-SEVEN

Another arbalest?

AS SOON AS GERALD saw Neil appear at the end of the corridor leading to Isaac Bornstein's suite, he waved to him and placed a finger against his lips, indicating for him to be quiet.

"What's happening, Chief?" Neil whispered as soon as he was near enough to Gerald.

"I don't know if anything has happened yet, son, but from what I saw on the tapes of these surveillance cameras"—he pointed to the nearest one—"Annette Sauvage paid Bornstein a visit earlier this evening. And I want to find out if the man is okay."

"Why wouldn't he be?" Neil asked, looking from the camera to Gerald.

"Think, man. Why would Miss Sauvage want to have a chat with Bornstein? We suspect her to have murdered Cecil to gain control over the salvage operation, but the only person who could link her to that murder or the conspiracy is the man in here." Gerald pointed to the door in front of which they were standing.

"But, Chief, she hired Cecil – not Bornstein – didn't she?"

"Sorry mate, you've got it backwards, Neil."

"How?"

"Well, if you remember what happened; Bornstein hired Cecil, through his wife, to organize the salvage operation *after* we would have visited Banks Island. But, Cecil being the thief that he was, took upon himself to contact Annette Sauvage and hire a boat from the Sauvage fleet, sail it well in advance of our arrival, and once he was on site, must have decided to come up to Juneau to meet with Bornstein's wife to make a deal with her. Recognizing Cecil immediately as he stepped aboard *The Contessa*, Annette had a chat with the man, and soon afterward, decided that if there was a treasure to be had, it would be hers for the taking…"

"And killed the man to take over the entire operation, which was already manned by one of the Sauvage's crews," Neil concluded for Gerald.

"Yes. And the only person, who could, in all likelihood, be aware of the plot and take-over, is Bornstein."

"So, we're here to check on Bornstein…"

"Yes, we are. Sony noticed, on the monitor, that Miss Sauvage was carrying what looked like a possible sheathed arbalest across her back, when she went to Bornstein's cabin."

"Have you seen her come out of the suite?"

"Yes, I did. The tape showed her come out of this cabin and return to her suite a few minutes later."

"Did she have the arbalest with her when she left?"

"It looked like she did, why?" Gerald asked Neil with raised eyebrows.

"Because, Chief, after I looked into the use of these crossbows, it said that you could rig the weapon easily to shoot any unwelcome intruder..."

Gerald swore under his breath. "Do you mean we could find ourselves pierced with an arrow the moment we open that door?"

"Yes, something like that – that's what it said on the Internet," Neil replied. "But if you saw her coming out of here with it, we should be okay..."

"I don't know, Neil. Actually what I saw on the monitor was the sheath, or bag, strapped to her back when she went in and when she came out. We don't even know what that bag contained."

"Okay, Chief. In any case we've got to open that door before anyone else opens it in the morning, agreed?"

Gerald nodded. "Yeah, but how do you want to handle it then?"

"Let me have the pass-card," Neil asked, extending a hand to Gerald.

"Okay," Gerald said, handing him the electronic keycard. "But how are you going to push that door open without standing in front of it?"

"Like this," Neil said, placing the card in the slot, and as soon as he heard the release mechanism and saw the small green light above the lock, he slammed his foot on the door panel and moved aside.

* * * *

In the stewards' monitoring room, Sony and Alan were observing the two men while they had been chatting in front of Bornstein's cabin, and wondered why they were taking their time – until they saw Neil kick the door wide open.

"You know," Sony said, "they're going to wake Mr. Bornstein if they kick the door like that, and give the poor guy a heart attack."

"If there's anyone to wake up," Alan remarked, looking up at the screen.

"What do you mean, Doc? We saw him open the door of his cabin for Miss Sauvage, didn't we? So he should be in there, shouldn't he?"

"Yes, Sony, he should be..."

Alan didn't have time to explain; he was out of his seat like a shot when he saw Gerald wave frantically in front of the corridor's camera.

A couple of minutes later, Alan was standing in front of Bornstein's cabin with Neil and Gerald. "So, what's the news?" he asked.

"Well, if you like déjà-vu situations, this is it."

"Bornstein is dead?"

"As a doorknob, yes," Neil replied, shaking his head and looking down at his feet.

"How did he die?" Alan asked. "May I go in?"

"Sure, go see for yourself, Doc," Gerald said, "he's in the bedroom with a hole in the neck – just like Cecil."

They followed Alan to the bedroom where he stopped in the doorway.

"I see what you meant by deja-vu," he said, taking a couple of steps toward the bed.

Isaac was sitting up; his head hanging to the side, with a hole in his neck – just like Cecil. Except in this case, the victim had been killed in bed, given the blood splatters that surrounded his head and were starting to congeal on his chest.

"Why would he come in here with her though?" Neil asked.

"Well, when someone points a weapon at you, son, I should think you'd do exactly what they say, wouldn't you?"

"And you wouldn't be able to disarm an archer as easily as you would a gunman, I think," Alan suggested, taking a few more careful steps until he reached Bornstein's bedside. "Besides, the man had a weak heart and he may have died of another heart attack before the arrow pierced his throat. I'll have to perform a preliminary autopsy to confirm that possibility." He turned from the bed and walked out of the room.

"But how does Miss Sauvage expect to get away with this, when we've got another three days before we touch land?" Neil asked as the three of them were making their way out of the suite.

"Because she doesn't know we're onto her, Neil," Gerald replied, locking the door of the suite.

"What do you want to do now, Chief?"

Gerald smiled. "Now, we're going to wake our CIA agent and get him to take Miss Sauvage into custody. We don't have the authority to arrest her – not yet – but our friend can at least take charge until we get to Tuktoyaktuk and sort this out."

"If I may make a suggestion, Chief," Alan interposed, "before Miss Sauvage has time to dispose of her weapon, I think it would be a good idea to pay her a visit."

Gerald and Neil looked at Alan, nodding. "Yes, I think that's a very good idea." Gerald turned his gaze to Neil. "Why don't you go and get Sam Wilcox out of bed while the doc and I pay a visit to our murderer?"

"Okay," Neil replied, "I'll bring him to her cabin."

Since the Sauvage's suite was just down the corridor from where Alan and Gerald stood, they found themselves in front of her door in the next minute or so. They were about to open it with the keycard, when the door opened slowly and a hooded person began to slip out of the cabin quietly.

Alan and Gerald, upon hearing the click of the door opening, slammed their bodies against the sides of the doorway and waited for the young woman to come out.

However, and to their surprise, the person who came out of the suite was not Annette but her father. He had the bag, which presumably contained an arbalest, in his hand.

When Gerald stepped in front of the man, he smiled. "I'm sorry, Mr. Sauvage, but may I see what you've got in that bag of yours?"

"Why...? What is this?" a bewildered and astonished Sauvage demanded.

"I think you better let Chief Tolberg look inside that bag, Mr. Sauvage," Alan suggested, coming to stand beside Gerald.

"Doctor! What are you doing here?" Sauvage asked, looking from one man to the other.

"What we're doing here is not as important as what you were intending to do with that bag," Gerald said, pointing to the long sheath still in Sauvage's hand.

"That's my business and none of yours!" he blurted. "I'll have both your jobs..."

"Please, Mr. Sauvage, this is not the Boston shipyard," Gerald retorted, grabbing the bag from Sauvage's hands. "This is a condo cruise ship where our Captain is master and chief, and under his authority, we've got the right to search for any weapon in any of the passengers' possession."

Alan had some doubt as to the total truthfulness of Gerald's statement, but it had been effective in recovering the bag from Sauvage's clutch.

Gerald unzipped the leather case, opened it and looked inside. "Alright, Mr. Sauvage, could you tell us what you were doing with an arbalest in the corridor of this ship at two o'clock in the morning?"

"It's not mine – it's my daughter's," he replied, blurting the words ruefully.

"So, you know what she's been up to, do you?" Alan asked.

"Not exactly, but I've suspected something was wrong for sometime now..."

"Okay, Mr. Sauvage, let me stop you right there. Before you say another word, I'd like you to come with me to the office where we can clear this up..."

"What about Annette? What's going to happen to her – she's just a kid..."

"We've got someone coming for her," Gerald said when he saw Sam Wilcox and Neil come down the hallway. "This is Agent Wilcox of the CIA"—he nodded to Sam—"and he will go in now and take your daughter into custody until we reach Tuktoyaktuk."

"Hi," Sam said to an apparently resigned father. "I'll be looking after your daughter, sir. And don't worry, until we've got an arrest warrant, she'll only be treated as a "person of interest", that's all."

"What about her weapon?" Sauvage asked, looking up at Gerald.

"It's going to be kept under lock-and-key away from her, sir, not to worry. Are you ready to come downstairs with me then?"

"I only wanted to protect her, you understand...?"

"Yes, sir, I do," Gerald said, leading the poor man down the corridor toward the elevators.

"Alright, Doc, do you want to stay around while we take Miss Sauvage into custody?"

"That is like asking me what I would do if there were no hypothetical questions. Yes, I will stick around until the bitter end," Alan replied.

"Okay then." Sam turned to Neil. "Why don't you knock and see if she'll come to the door voluntarily, so the hotel manager doesn't chide us for too many broken door frames?"

CHAPTER FORTY-EIGHT

Like vampires?

IF THE AURORA BOREALIS WERE to take flight from somewhere in particular, some would say Tuktoyaktuk would be the place. Located at the mouth of the MacKenzie Delta, with a meager population of only a thousand residents, the city seemed to rest on the very last piece of land before the Canadian Northern Territories disappeared beneath the waters of the Arctic Ocean. As breathtaking as the view from *The Contessa* was when the ship first approached the coastline, some of the passengers and crew were nowhere to be seen and would not set foot on land, until the RCMP climbed aboard and took Annette Sauvage into custody. There was nothing more to say – nothing more to explain. Mr. Sauvage had suspected his daughter to be more ambitious than he had ever expected, and with that ambition came the dreadful temptation of committing murder against anyone who would obfuscate her plans. With the determination and the anger of a pit-bull, she shot Cecil Legato and Isaac Bornstein in cold blood. However, all the drive and ambition in the world couldn't account for the fact that she ignored the possibility of someone watching her every move and even surveying her correspondence. Perhaps her inflated ego and desire to pluck her own treasure out of the *HMS Investigator* had been too alluring for her to resist. But it was with no resistance and plenty of resignation that Annette Sauvage left the ship the morning of *The Contessa*'s arrival in Tuk.

"Well, I guess we can close the book on that case," Gerald remarked to Neil after the RCMP had left the ship.

"I should say so," Neil replied, sitting down across from the chief. "But now we've yet to find out if these murders and all this trouble was worthwhile, don't we?"

"Yes, and to tell you the truth, I can hardly wait to find out what they've raised from that wreck so far."

"Me too, Chief. Do you think they've recovered the treasure yet?"

"Personally, I don't think so, Neil. If they had, the *Northern Rover* would have left the site long ago."

"So, I guess it's up to Sam Ashton and Edward Barrington to find out, isn't it?"

"Yeah, and you know what the best thing to come out of this ordeal is?"

"No, what?"

"Well, you've read Mr. Sauvage's statement, so you tell me," Gerald said, looking at Neil with a frown.

"He's putting his ship at the disposal of Parks Canada to complete the recovery of the relics – is that it?”

"Yes. And he'll be going aboard the *Northern Rover* to continue overseeing the operation himself."

"Do you think he'll be charged with collusion?"

Gerald shook his head. "I think neither the Canadians nor the Americans will want to spend the money for a trial. They're going to be faced with two sets of legal entanglements – one murder being committed on US "soil", so to speak, and the other, on a ship navigating Canadian waters."

"That's good, because I like the guy. He reminds me of my dad," Neil remarked, looking down at his folded hands, as if he was suddenly traveling down the memory lane of his mind.

"Yeah… and that reminds me; I wonder if Elizabeth Bornstein will have to leave the ship to be taken by social services, as soon as we return to the States."

"I don't think the von Weglans will let that happen," Neil said. "I heard from Dr. Mayhew that they've already contacted the Boston authorities. They will start proceedings to adopt her as soon as we get home."

"Okay then, let's go down to the mess and have some lunch – there's nothing more we can do here," Gerald suggested, getting to his feet.

* * * *

Neil had been right – the von Weglans were already preparing the paperwork with a view to adopting Elizabeth Bornstein. And that morning, while Evelyn and the three technicians had gone to Tuktoyaktuk for a short visit, and Angie had gone down for an early lunch, Herbert, Karen and Elizabeth were in the medical center, talking to Alan about their upcoming visit to Banks Island.

Standing in front of a microscope, Alan was showing Elizabeth one of the mosquitoes he had captured on Kodiak Island and explaining how this little insect could be so dangerous – lethal in fact – for humans.

"It looks ugly," Elizabeth said, after peering through the lens. "And it can kill you?" She raised questioning eyes to him.

"Absolutely. You see, the female mosquito has to feed her developing eggs nutrients that she extracts from human blood…"

"Like vampires?"

"Yeah, like vampires. But instead of just sucking the blood, when she sucks it, she injects an anesthetic into the skin so you don't immediately detect that she is biting you. With this numbing agent is some poison. This gets into her bite. It's that poison that can kill you."

"Wow," Elizabeth exclaimed, returning to look at the mosquito under the microscope. "And where did she get the poison?"

"Well, a long time ago, her great-great-grandmother must have bitten someone who had the disease already. When she was born she already had the poison in her system," Alan explained in the most simplistic terms he could think of.

"It's like my mom," Elizabeth said, returning her gaze up to Alan, "she was always carrying on and being mean like my grandma. She must have some poison in her too."

Alan didn't know what to say. He turned to Karen and Herbert who had been watching their little exchange in silence.

"But your mom didn't bite you, did she?" Karen asked, looking at the little girl intently.

"No, she didn't but she sure had a lot of poison in her – with all that drinking she did every day."

Wanting to change the direction in which this conversation was going, Karen said, "I know, dear. But now we're going to see how Doctor Mayhew is going to protect us against these nasty mosquitoes when we're on Banks Island."

"Will we have to spray that stuff all over us?" Elizabeth asked, grabbing one of the canisters from the counter beside the microscope. "And will that stuff kill the mosquitoes?" She looked up at Alan.

"No, it will just keep them away from where you spray yourself."

"Why don't you have something to kill them, Dr. Mayhew? 'Cause if they can't bite me, they'll go to somebody else, won't they?"

"You're absolutely right, Elizabeth, but you see, we prefer not to use sprays that kill mosquitoes, otherwise we would get sick if we sprayed our bodies with something that is poisonous to the mosquitoes."

"Like that stuff they talked about in school... like... like insecticeed?"

"It's called 'insecticide', but yes you're right. If we used a bad sort of insecticide on our skin, we would die – like the mosquitoes."

Elizabeth turned to Herbert. "Do you have mosquitoes like those nasty ones"—she pointed a finger toward the microscope—"in Australia?"

Herbert guffawed. "No, we don't have those nasty ones at home, no. But we've got plenty of flies. But they don't suck blood, just bite."

"That's good, 'cause I don't want to go to a new home where you've got those nasty mosquitoes." She switched her gaze to Karen. "Do you have to spray yourself with that stuff"—she shook the canister still in her hand—"for the flies too?"

"Oh no, dear, we don't use anything like that. We just do not use any perfume or scented soaps, so that flies won't be interested in us," Karen replied, smiling.

This time it was Alan who wanted to change the topic of conversation. "Now, do you want to see the suit you're going to be wearing when we go to Banks Island?" he asked Elizabeth.

"Yeah!" she screamed happily in reply. "Are they like the astronauts' suits?"

"Not quite, but they're all white too," Alan replied, going to the cabinet where they had stored the protective suits. He opened the doors and pulled out one of the children's pack. "Here you go, Elizabeth," he added, handing her the plastic pouch. "Why don't you open it and try it on, if you like."

Putting the canister back on the counter, Elizabeth unzipped the bag, pulled out the suit and looked at it. "It looks like my pajamas! Is everybody going to wear these when we go to the island?"

"Oh yes, we all are," Karen answered for Alan.

"That's going to be funny – everybody will be in pajamas…" Elizabeth giggled at the thought. "Are we going to wear gloves too?"

"Sure, if you want to," Alan answered, grinning.

"Oh good. That's sounds great." Elizabeth looked down at herself once she had slipped into the suit. "Will you take pictures?" she asked Karen.

"Oh yes, I will, dear. But not now – we'll wait till the time when everyone is in their suits – that will be funnier, don't you think?"

* * * *

An hour later, when the von Weglans had gone back to their cabin to have lunch, Alan was still smiling. He was pleased that he had managed to persuade Karen and Herbert to come on the cruise. Having a new daughter to look after – even an adopted one – would help Karen keep on the positive side of the road of recovery. He would make sure both she and Herbert got all the assistance needed in being able to adopt Elizabeth. That little girl couldn't have found better, and experienced parents than those two.

* * * *

Meanwhile, Babette had managed to rope Susan into having lunch with her. Since Annette's arrest, Susan had spent a lot of time with Auguste Sauvage, who was obviously devastated with the turn of events in the past few days.

"I really shouldn't be here," Susan complained as she took a seat at Babette's table. "Auguste needs me…"

"On the contrary, I think he needs to be alone for a bit right now, Susan. Smothering him won't do him any good either. And you also need to think about yourself, my dear," Babette suggested.

"But I'm nothing without him," Susan said with dramatic emphasis. "He's become my life – do you realize that?"

"Hush, child! There's time enough to talk about what he is or is not." Babette paused, pensive for a moment. "You know that reminds me of something I read recently… Let me see if I can recall the whole thing."

"What's that?" Susan asked, puzzled.

"Well, it describes the attitude you should adopt for your sake, dear." She focused her gaze on Susan. "It goes like this: Be the kind of woman that when your feet hit the floor each morning the devil says, Oh Crap, she's up." Susan laughed. "Sister, life is too short to wake up with regrets," Babette went on, "So love the people who treat you right. Forgive the ones who don't, just because you can. Believe everything happens for a reason. If you get a second chance, grab it with both hands. If it changes your life, let it. Take a few minutes to think before you act when you're mad. Forgive quickly. God never said life would be easy. He just promised it would be worth it. A real sister walks with you when some of the rest of the world walks on you. I think it'll be good for you to think about that advice rather than some of those other feelings."

Still grinning, Susan said, "You know, Babette, I think there are too many men who have walked all over me – and now, I also think I should walk with Auguste."

"Alright then, but for now, let's talk about what you will do once we arrive back in Boston. Have you thought about it?"

Susan looked at her friend curiously. "What on Earth do you mean? I'm going to be there for Auguste – that's what I'm going to do."

"Oh yes? And how are you going to cope with his daughter's imprisonment and undoubted trial? And how are you going to react when he gets all the nasty publicity that's sure to follow after he returns to Boston?"

"I don't know, Babette. Truly, I don't know. But we've got several weeks aboard the ship before we get back, and maybe Auguste and I can figure something out."

"Alright, let's just make sure you don't get hurt, Susan. He's not the only man on the planet, you know..."

"I know, I know, but he's probably the only one who's taken a real interest in me and for what I've become after the cancer – so, I'm not about to lose him because he's got some Paparazzi publicity problems."

"I hear you, Susan, and I admire your courage – always have – but let's take it easy, okay?"

Finally, Susan managed to smile. "Okay, but now can we have lunch? I'm starving."

CHAPTER FORTY-NINE

Mosquitoes with flashlights!

THERE WAS SOMETHING ETHEREAL about the view when *The Contessa* reached the waters near Banks Island. It seemed as if the shore was blanketed in a blue fog that also enveloped the ship as she treaded carefully toward the shore. The rusty colored sun appeared to rise over the teal cloak as if gradually piercing through a knob of land from its hiding place. The passengers' cameras were capturing the scene rapidly, almost incessantly, while Alan and Tiffany were watching *The Contessa's* slow progress from the promenade deck.

"I had never imagined such scenery could be real," Tiffany said, throwing a quick glance to Alan. "I saw pictures of this sort of thing on the Internet and in some movies, but I always thought it was some special effect or something – I really can't believe this is real, Alan."

He chuckled. "Did you know that these types of scenes happen only up here in the northern latitudes, Tiff, and they are often as unreal as this?"

"But why is she going so slowly?" Tiffany asked, looking down at the waves lapping the side of the ship. "Are there other ships in the area?"

"Oh yes – and that's also why she's sounding her fog horn. She's probably approaching the *Northern Rover's* location and Parks Canada's ship."

"So Parks Canada finally decided to join the party then?" Tiffany asked.

"Yeah; once they heard rumbles from the Prime Minister's office that someone had been trying to steal Canadian treasures, Parks Canada suddenly found enough funds to dispatch one of their vessels to the site."

"That's sounds like our public servants in the US – always acting at the last minute, when they're at the edge of a cliff just about to take the plunge."

Alan had to laugh at the rejoinder. "You're right at that," he said musingly.

"And didn't you say that Mr. Sauvage was going aboard his vessel at some point?"

"Yes. He'll be going aboard the *Northern Rover* once our divers have assessed the relics left in the *HMS Investigator*."

"What do you think is still in that wreck?" Tiffany looked up at Alan inquiringly.

"I have an inkling that they're going to find quite a lot of interesting things aboard that ship. There's been too much interest in that wreck for it not to be revealing something important. As for hiding a treasure, I can't tell you. Yet, I wouldn't be surprised that it does."

"You know, I think you're right – about the treasure I mean – there has been so much talk about the vessel, even in the papers, that I wouldn't be surprised if they found something of great value."

A tap on Alan's shoulder interrupted their conversation. He turned around abruptly to face Drs. Sullivan and Lespierre.

"Sorry, Doctor, to interrupt your sight-seeing," the latter said, "but we've been wondering when we are getting our protective suits."

"Didn't you receive the memo that was distributed last night to all the passengers going ashore?" Alan questioned.

"We must have missed it, because neither of us has seen any notice, no," Sullivan replied, looking at his companion.

"I'm sorry about that, Dr. Sullivan, but everyone going to the island is going to be given a suit this morning. It will be dropped in your cabins." Alan looked at both men in turn. "Was there anything else?"

"Well yes, Dr. Mayhew," Lespierre went on, "we have been informed that Mr. Sauvage will be going aboard the *Northern Rover* after the dive, would we be able to do the same?"

"I don't think I am the one to answer that question. Better check with Captain Middleton first and then talk to Mr. Sauvage, since he's the owner of the salvage vessel."

Lespierre and Sullivan nodded in unison. "Okay, that's what we'll do then," Sullivan said, the both of them turning on their heels. "Thanks, Doc."

* * * *

It took the better part of the next two hours before *The Contessa* lowered its anchor near the shore. Advised of the arrival of the ship and some of its passengers' going to visit the museum, the Parks Canada representative and the chief of the local Inuit Band were waiting for the first tender to reach the access beach and pier.

Both dressed in yellow protective suits and gloves, the chief and the rep wore a broad smile on their faces when Captain Middleton, Stephan Ivanov and Alan stepped off the tender.

"I'm Mark Littleton," the rep said, shaking Middleton's extended hand. "And this is Chief Musk Ox." He nodded to the chief.

"A real pleasure to meet you both," the captain said, turning to Stephan and Alan at his side. "This is Mr. Ivanov, our staff captain, and Dr. Alan Mayhew."

"It is a great honor for me and our people to meet you," Chief Musk Ox told them, bowing his head slightly. "We have very high expectations of your people, Captain, but we are humbled by your presence on our little island."

With a genial smile, Middleton replied, "It is thanks to *The Contessa*"—he turned his gaze to the ship behind him—"that we were able to arrive safely at our destination, and we thank God's guidance that we are here."

"What about Drs. Lespierre and Sullivan," Mark piped-up, "Aren't they coming to shore as well?"

"Oh don't you worry, Mr. Littleton," Stephan said, "They'll be here soon, with the second tender. The three of us are only the advance party, if you like. But soon the place will be swarming with many invaders, you can be sure."

"Very good," Chief Musk Ox said, "because my people and I have been expecting your visit for many days now."

* * * *

There wasn't much to see on the island, except perhaps for breathtaking landscapes that seemed to be engulfed in an eerie silence. The birds nesting near shore appeared to be the only disturbance affecting the place when the dozens of passengers disembarked onto the island. They were surprised to see that the ground was covered with millions of little flowers and rugged grass growing timidly amid the rocky and sandy ground. All passengers dressed in their white *pajamas*, as Elizabeth had described them, resembled a group of aliens that had just landed on a strange planet. Again, cameras didn't stop capturing the unearthly landscape and newcomers. That was, until Stephan guided everyone toward the place they had come to visit.

Standing a few hundred yards from the community center and other basic habitations was the temporary museum. It had been erected directly over the site where the first debris of the *HMS Investigator* had been discovered.

Entering the museum in Alan's company, Babette looked around her before her attention was drawn to a long series of chiseled wood planks and other pieces hanging above the display cases.

Yet, what surprised Alan and Babette, when they first walked in the room, was the cold. There was no heat, which prompted Babette to ask with a smile, "Why don't they heat the place? Haven't they paid their bills or something?"

Mark, who had been escorting the visitors inside and had heard Babette's remark, came to stand by the two of them. "I'm afraid keeping these wood boards in a heated room would soon deteriorate them to the point of total decay."

"And they were found on the ground some hundred years after the boat sank?" Alan asked.

"Yes, they were spread all over the beach and rocks nearby – brought in by the tide at the time."

In the display cases, there were only a few artifacts, such as an elegant-looking teacup, a couple vases, an inkwell and some copper and tin plates. Other cases contained some knives and other tools or weapons of some sort. One of these gained Alan's attention. "Would that be an old flintlock pistol?" he asked Mark, pointing to the antique handgun.

"Very good, Doctor," Mark replied. "Yes, in fact this is an original flintlock pistol. We believe it was one of Captain McClure's pistols, and it would be worth its weight in gold – literally – if it were ever sold or auctioned off to a collector."

"How do you know it belonged to Captain McClure?" Babette asked, doubtful.

"Because, even at that time, such a pistol would have been too expensive for any of the crew to purchase."

"But tell me, Mr. Littleton, what do you really expect to find in the wreck?" Alan inquired, fixing his gaze on the man.

"That's anyone's guess, Doctor. Drs. Sullivan and Lespierre have drawn a list based on the manifest that we found in the London archives, but these manifests were seldom complete or even accurate. So, we frankly don't know."

"Would you expect a treasure to be found aboard?" Babette asked.

Mark smiled. "I have heard of the possibility, yes, but there is no evidence that such is the case. We'll just have to wait and see, won't we?"

"I guess you're right," Babette said. "But truth be told, I can hardly wait." A broad smile appeared on her lips.

As they came out of the museum, they found the von Weglans and Elizabeth in an excited discussion and Elizabeth pointing to something in the far distance.

Tiffany, who had been accompanying the little family, turned to call Alan. "Doctor Mayhew...? Would you mind answering Elizabeth's question?"

Alan and Babette took the few steps separating them from the von Weglans. But before he spoke, Alan looked in the direction of Elizabeth's pointing finger. "Wow!" he exclaimed, truly astonished. "This is a herd of musk ox, Elizabeth." He took her hand. "We've got to be very quiet now, okay?"

"What are musk ox?" Elizabeth asked, lifting her querying gaze to Alan.

Without answering, Alan turned to Herbert. "Would you have a pair of binoculars by any chance?"

"Yes, yes, of course," Herbert replied, already pulling the binoculars out of his satchel. "Do you really think these are musk ox?"

Alan took the binoculars from Herbert's extended hand, and replied, "Yes, I think so. But what's surprising is that they came grazing so close to the community." He hankered down to Elizabeth and put the binoculars in front of her eyes. "Look through and tell me what you see."

"Oh my goodness!" Elizabeth said, all excited again. "They're so big, and with long hair.... They're like cows with a fur coat."

"Yes, that's a good description for them," Alan agreed. He stood up to face the little group. "Have a look," he said to Herbert and Karen, handing the binoculars back to him. "This is an exceptional sight. Perhaps, if you had a good telephoto lens for your camera, you could get some great pictures."

"I have one, yes," Herbert replied, searching through his satchel again.

Meanwhile Babette, Tiffany and Karen had been staring in the distance.

Babette said, "Do you think they're liable to start a stampede, Alan?"

"No, I don't think so. And if they don't feel threatened, there's no reason for them to run away, so we can enjoy them while they are foraging."

"That's good," Tiffany said, exhaling a sigh of relief, "because I can't imagine what we would do if they decided to charge us."

"Don't worry, Ms. Sylvan," Mark said, joining the little group, "they're only interested in eating as much as they can while they can. You see, they need to fatten up before the winter arrives so they will be able to survive the lack of food or water for days on end as the first snow storm hits the island."

"They're much like camels then?" Babette remarked.

"No, not really, but they are quite resilient to the climatic conditions around here. And in the winter they stay in the lowland areas in order to be able to dig through the snow to find grass or seedlings."

"Why are they here, so close to the town, do you think?" Tiffany asked.

"That's because it's their mating season and they prefer to stay in a group to protect the calves that were born in April or May, and it's good eating."

"I think it's time for us to return to the ship," Karen suggested. "I feel a bit tired, standing around. Do you mind, dear?" She threw a pleading glance to Herbert, who was still busy taking photos of the herd.

"Yes, yes, of course, Hon, we need to have a good rest before tomorrow's dive anyway," he said, packing his equipment quickly.

* * * *

That night, the ship's main restaurant was abuzz with people recounting their many stories about their visit of the museum, community hall and the surrounding areas, and of course, the musk ox herd sighting.

Alan was quietly happy that everyone had enjoyed their visit in spite of the insects that had swarmed the passengers every time they were outside. It was not only the mosquitoes that had been a problem but the flying ants had demonstrated particular viciousness when literally dive-bombing to bite anyone's face or other exposed skin.

That evening, still dressed in his pajama suit, he decided to take a stroll on the deck to watch the sunset, which promised to be a sight to behold. Many other passengers had apparently decided to do the same. The night was fresh but not too cold. Alan was leaning against the railing when an older man approached him, a bright smile lighting his face.

"Good evening, Dr. Mayhew. Beautiful night, isn't it?" the man said, joining Alan and putting his elbows on the railing.

"It sure is," Alan replied, returning the smile. "Did you enjoy your visit on the island?"

"Oh yes, Doctor. My grandson and I had a ball. Although the mozzies were a bit of a bother."

"I know, but I think setting foot on that island was worth the bother, don't you think?"

"Oh absolutely. And you know, Billy – that's my grandson – he was just as excited about the insects as he was about what he saw in the museum." He chuckled. "You know, when he entered our cabin tonight, we kept the lights off until we got inside to keep the pesky insects out. But still a few fireflies followed us in. And when Billy saw them, you know what he said?"

"No, what?"

"Well, he said, 'it's no use, Grandpa, now the mosquitoes are coming after us with flashlights!' Isn't that priceless?"

"That's one for the books," Alan replied, laughing and noticing that in fact there were quite a few 'mosquitoes with flashlights' roaming the promenade that night, an ethereal sight to say the least, considering where they were.

CHAPTER FIFTY

No one but three loonies!

THE NEXT MORNING CAME far too quickly for Alan. His mind was chasing all of the possible mishaps the sub and divers could encounter during their excursion down to the wreck. As soon as he arrived at the medical center, he re-examined, for the umpteen time, the oxygen tanks, the first aid kits that the divers had brought to him for inspection, and ultimately the suits the diving passengers were going to use today. These were similar to the *pajamas* they had worn the previous day, but with added straps that would latch onto the seats in the submarine.

Satisfied that all was in order, he decided to go down to the temporary buffet set up on the lower deck. This had been organized for the passengers and crew who would go down to the *Investigator*, and wanted breakfast.

And there he was! Dr. Wasserfall – the man with the many stories.

"Oh, Dr. Mayhew, how nice to see you again," Wasserfall said, approaching Alan in the line-up.

"Good morning, Doctor, how are you?" Alan replied, smiling.

"Are you going down with the submarine? I guess you will, seeing that you're all dressed for the occasion," Wasserfall guffawed.

"You guessed right; and are you going to visit the island today?"

"Oh absolutely, absolutely. After what I heard yesterday about the musk ox herd, I wouldn't want to miss such an opportunity," the little man said, filling his tray with everything in reach, it seemed.

"Good to hear," Alan said, grabbing a coffee, whole grain toast and a yoghurt and putting them on his tray. "Do you want to join me…?"

"Yes, yes… if you don't mind. I've just received an email from a friend of mine that I think would interest you."

Alan was curious. "Oh, is someone in your family sick?"

"Oh no, no, nothing like that, I'm glad to say," Wasserfall said, depositing his tray on a table near the window and sitting down. "But my friend Ted is on a cruise with his family, here, I'll let you read his wife's email directly…."

Alan smiled, sat down and took the printout from Wasserfall's already extended hand. Sipping on his coffee, he read:

Ted walked into the ships buffet restaurant with our youngest son. He gave the young boy three loonies to play with to keep him occupied. Suddenly, the boy started choking, going cyanotic (blue) in the face.

Ted realized the boy had swallowed the loonies and started slapping him on the back. The boy coughed up two of the loonies, but kept choking.

Looking at our son, Ted was panicking, shouting for help.

One of the passengers was a well-dressed, attractive, and serious looking woman, who always wore a blue business suit at all of the seatings in the main dining room and even a light blue suit for breakfast. She was sitting, having a coffee and reading the daily ship log newspaper. This passenger looked up, put her coffee cup down, neatly folded her napkin and placed it on the counter, got up from her seat and made her way, unhurried, across the dining room. At the same time, Philippe, one of the waiters who served our table, called an alarm.

At this point, Alan thought how this must have been a crewmember who actually listened to some of the safety talks. As an officer, the ship's doctor was required to give classes on some of the subjects in the *safety series* and many of the crew members, who were required to attend the classes, were not at all interested. Nice to know that some crew did care.

The passenger with the blue suit reached the boy along with Philippe, who we later found out was not only our waiter, but also one of the fire team members. He went to stabilize our son's head and properly determined if there was an airway. The woman carefully grabbed the boy's pants; took hold of the boy's testicles and started to squeeze and twist, gently at first and then ever so firmly. After a few seconds our son had a seizure, and in the process hit his chest on one of the dining room tables. Amazingly, he coughed up the last loonie, which the woman deftly caught in her free hand.

Releasing the boy's testicles, the 'passenger in the blue suit' handed the loonie to Ted and walked back to her table without saying a word. Philippe had to physically close his own mouth.

As soon as he was sure that our son was stable and breathing freely, he and Ted walked over to the woman and thanked her for lending a helping hand during the incident, saying, "I've never seen anybody do anything like that before, it was fantastic. Are you a doctor?"

"No," the woman replied. "I'm with Revenue Canada."

No one has messed with her during the rest of the cruise!

Chuckling heartily, Alan said, "That's the Canadian Government for you: strict, serious, polite, but totally dispassionate when it comes to collecting taxes."

"Oh, but I think an IRS agent would have been even more brutal than this woman was, don't you think?"

"Yes, I believe you're right. When it comes to paying one's taxes no one can escape."

Munching on a mouthful of scrambled eggs, Wasserfall asked, "How many are going down in the submarine then – I mean apart from the divers?"

"Just seven people," Alan replied, putting peanut butter on his toast.

"Did the captain select them?"

"Yes, why do you ask?"

"Oh no particular reason, but I bet it was a difficult choice," Wasserfall commented.

"Yes, partly due to the fact that we had about thirty people wanting to take part in the dive."

"And where is the submarine now?"

"It's been lowered to the gangway level right now so that passengers and divers can access it easily."

"I wish I had been smart enough to put my name down," the doctor said, shaking his head. "You know I really didn't think we would see much of anything down there – but after hearing all of the stories about the wreck and reading about Captain McClure's adventures, I think now, that I should have put my name in the hat.

* * * *

An hour later, Alan and Babette were waiting with the von Weglans and the two archeologists to climb aboard the submarine. It was much longer and much larger than Alan had imagined – probably the size of a minivan – with two sets of propellers at the tail end and a bulbous-looking cabin at the front. When the airtight capsule door opened, and Edward Barrington extended a hand to help Babette climb aboard, she hesitated. "Is there an escape hatch in this contraption?" she asked, smiling up at Alan.

"Yes, there is, Ms. Babette," Edward replied for Alan, "I'll show you once we're all aboard."

"Okay then, let's go," Babette said, somewhat reassured.

The von Weglans and Elizabeth were next – Elizabeth hanging tightly in Edward's arms – and then Drs. Lespierre and Sullivan climbed aboard.

Before stepping into the sub, Alan turned to Captain Middleton behind him. "Sir, are you sure, you don't want to go down?" Alan was all too aware that Middleton would have liked to join the group.

"No, Doc. I have made my decision – you are the one deserving to replace Mr. Bornstein. So, go on and bring me a full report, okay?" And as an afterthought, he added, "Besides, we can't have you navigating *The Contessa* on her way home if anything happened to me?"

With a nod and a grateful smile, Alan stepped aboard the submarine.

Once everyone was seated and strapped in, Edward said, "Alright, folks, the only thing I would like to ask you is to remain seated at all times and if possible, do not make sudden movements, which might alter the sub's balance. We'll stay down for about fifteen to twenty minutes, circling the wreck twice and then come up. So, enjoy the sights," he concluded, going forward to join Sam Ashton at the controls.

"I can't believe I'm actually doing this," Karen von Weglan said, turning to Herbert. "Only three months ago, I didn't think I would even survive another day of chemotherapy."

"Be glad for the science of medicine, dear," Herbert replied, taking his wife's hand in both of his. "And now we'll have grandchildren to tell the story to, won't we?"

With tears pearling at the rim of her eyes, Karen kissed Elizabeth's forehead. The little girl smiled up at her "new mother" in response.

The sub dived down slowly toward its target and offered its passengers amazing sights. Through the small circular windows they admired the many fish and water creatures navigating their way up and down and all around the sub. It was not long though before they saw the wreckage of the *HMS Investigator*. With the powerful headlights illuminating the ship and enveloping it of a golden glow, the old vessel seemed to be resting on a bed of autumn leaves rather than the ocean bed. Much smaller than he had expected, Alan tried to envision the insides of the hull, cabins and quarters.

They circled the *Investigator* twice as planned, but in the course of their coming closer to the hull, Edward remarked to Sam, "It looks like someone has been cracking that side open, doesn't it?"

Sam slowed down the sub sufficiently to examine the hole and nodded. "You're right, that's a fresh cut. And I think it'll be a good idea for us to gain entry that way, since someone has opened the door for us," he sniggered.

As they came up toward the surface, Edward pointed Sam's attention to something else; "look, that must be the salvage vessel's anchor line."

"Yeah, and she's right above us. I'd say a bit too close for comfort," Sam said, maneuvering the sub upward toward the surface.

As soon as the submarine came bubbling up, Captain Middleton was on hand again, to welcome the passengers out of the sub. To say the man was excited to hear what everyone saw would be an understatement, yet he kept his cool until Alan came out. "So, what did you see? Anything interesting?"

"Yes, Captain – one thing for sure is that someone has been aboard the *Investigator* lately. There's a gaping hole in the hull, which probably provided easy access for the divers from the salvage boat."

"Why do you think they had to crack a hole in that hull?"

"Maybe because the hatches on deck were encrusted shut and no one took the time to unseal them properly."

"I wonder if Sauvage will open it," Middleton said musingly.

A couple of hours later, after the submarine had been raised and stored aboard *The Contessa* once again, Edward and Sam were ready to dive to the *Investigator*. Alan and Stephan had accompanied them to the platform from which they were to dive, to help them strap their oxygen tanks properly while Sam gave Alan the last instructions regarding the handling of their two-way radios. All checks being completed, the two men rolled backwards into the dark waters of the Artic Ocean. As soon as they were a few feet below the surface, Edward was the first to call Alan.

"Everything is okay down here, Doc. We'll call again in ten – as agreed."

"Copy that," Alan replied. He felt funny saying that. It reminded him of some TV show.

However, and before the ten minutes were over, Alan heard Sam say,

"What the hell is that?"

"Sam? Are you okay? What did you see?" Alan called down, anxiously.

"There are some jokers around here," Edward said. "It must be guys from the salvage boat or from town…"

"Nobody is supposed to be down there…" Alan told them, turning to Stephan who was standing beside him.

"Let's get down to the wreck," Sam said – he was probably talking to Edward. "We don't have enough air to mess with these guys."

The radio then went dead for a few interminable minutes. Meanwhile, on the platform, Stephan said, "I'll contact the *Northern Rover* and see what these guys are up to," already walking back inside the corridor leading to the elevators.

Alan remained on the platform, more worried than ever. No one was supposed to be diving from the salvage boat until Sauvage and his crew received the green light to raise what ever relics Sam and Edward would have found aboard the *Investigator*. He was still wondering what could be going on down there, when Sam's voice resounded over the two-way radio.

"We're about to enter the hull through the hole and will be in touch as soon as we reach the bridge or McClure's quarters."

"Copy that," Alan repeated. If both divers were okay and didn't mention who ever interrupted their descent, he was not about to detract their attention from their tasks.

"Doc," Edward shouted suddenly, "I think we found something!"

"Where?" Alan asked.

"We're in a room with table and chairs and there are some unusual partitions behind one of the walls…" Edward paused while Alan heard some gurgling noise. "It looks like someone was hiding something behind the wall." He paused again. "We'll bring down some chisels to move the boards on the second dive."

"Copy that," Alan said again, before he heard Stephan come back to the platform. "What's up then?" he asked the staff captain.

"Just two "pot-heads" – as Sauvage described them – who were dressed like mermaids (over their dive suits) messing with our guys."

"Were they working divers?"

"Apparently yes, but on this occasion they simply wanted to fool around."

"They're back on the *Northern Rover* then?" Alan asked with a scowl.

"Sauvage said they were climbing back on board as we were talking, yes."

Twenty minutes later, Sam and Edward were heaving themselves onto the platform. They then divested themselves of the tanks while Sam said, "I don't like to give anyone instructions around here, Doc, but having two guys fooling around while we're diving on a timer in cold water, is not only dangerous but quite unnecessary. Who were they?" He looked at Stephan.

"Divers from the salvage boat," the latter replied, visibly embarrassed.

"Well, since we've got to go down again – and as many times as it will take, I suggest you keep everyone away who is not officially working, okay?"

Captain Middleton, Drs. Lespierre and Sullivan, Alan and Stephan were assembled in the captain's office waiting for Sam and Edward to come and report on their first dive, when Middleton asked, "Have you made it clear to Mr. Sauvage that we will not tolerate any interference from his crew?"

Stephan's head bobbed up and down. "Absolutely, Captain. The two jokers are in the brig now – curing their hangover apparently."

"Okay then," the captain replied at the same moment as Edward and Sam entered the office.

"Well done, gentlemen!" Middleton exclaimed, as the divers took their seats.

"Thank you, Captain," Sam said. "But we've only had time to take a look in that one room. As you know we were interrupted by those two nuts..."

"Yes, yes, I know, Mr. Ashton, and I can assure you the problem has been resolved."

"That's good, because we wouldn't want to dive again if we can't be assured that we have all the time necessary to accomplish our task," Edward rejoined.

"Quite, gentlemen. But do tell us now what you found," Middleton asked.

Sam described the room into which they found the unusual panel and told the archeologists that they were certain there was something large – like a box – sealed behind the panel.

"That's very interesting," Lespierre remarked. "And will you be able to take that container out of its hiding place then?"

"Yes, we're confident we'll be able to free it when we break through the panel boards," Edward said.

"And when are you planning to dive next?" Alan asked, conscious of the danger accompanying successive dives.

"Probably later this evening, Doctor. We need about five to seven hours between dives to be safe."

"Have you been able to find anything else beside that box?" Dr. Sullivan asked, pausing from his taking notes.

"We didn't get to the captain's quarters yet, but there seemed to be many items under the dust that should be raked and retrieved properly."

"It sounds like Cecil Legato didn't pay much attention to salvage rules," Stephan remarked.

"I'd say you're right, Mr. Ivanov," Sam agreed. "It seems to me that they were searching for the treasure and picked up the first items they found along the way, and nothing else."

CHAPTER FIFTY-ONE

Snow White and the Seven Dwarfs

AS THE AFTERNOON DREW to a close, Tiffany and Alan were sitting at the café on the upper deck. Alan had spent some time with the Health Canada technicians who had managed to capture some mosquito specimens on Banks Island to examine the Dengue fever strain existing in these nasty little vectors. He had been amazed at the resistance this strain demonstrated to any of the usually available common antidotes, albeit, supportive therapy at best.

And it was with some of these results in mind that he had made his way to join Tiffany for some refreshments.

"How was the visit of the island today," he asked, steeping the tea in the pot on the table carefully.

"Apart from these infernal insects – I really don't know how these people can stand these things day after day – everything went fine."

"Was the herd of musk ox still there?"

"Oh yes," Tiffany replied. "And it was much more of an attraction for the passengers than the museum or anything else. Oh, and to top the day off, I had the 'honor' of meeting your Dr. Wasserfall, by the way."

"Ha-ha-ha. And did he tell you any of his famous stories?"

"Oh gosh, the guy is impossible, Alan; I couldn't get rid of him – until he finally went to take pictures of the herd."

"I think the man should write a book of stories; he is a good story teller."

"I'll say. But really, once he latches on to you, there's no way to get rid of him."

Alan poured the tea.

"But do tell me," Tiffany went on, "did Edward and Sam find anything in the wreck? And how did it go with the sub-dive?"

"Well, the sub-dive was a success – no question. Elizabeth couldn't stop talking about everything we saw around the ship." Alan paused, recalling the little girl coming to the center before lunch and thanking him profusely for allowing her and her "new mom and dad" to venture under the sea with the submarine. "She's bound to enjoy her new life, you know."

"I hope she will," Tiffany replied, taking a sip of her tea. "Wow, that's good – is that a special concoction?"

Alan smiled. "I just thought you might enjoy that herbal blend I had bought in Kodiak. I didn't want to open the sachet until you were with me to enjoy it."

"You're right – we haven't been able to spend that much time together lately. But wait until I get you alone once we leave the island – I'll have you caught up with me in no time." Tiffany tittered at the thought. "And I'm happy you've waited to introduce me to this tea – it's great!" She drank some more. "What about the dive – did they find anything?"

Alan shook his head and replaced a nearly empty cup in its saucer. "They found a panel, hiding what appears to be a blank space with a box in what was probably the surgeon's cabin. They're going down again tonight to get the panel off so they can get the mysterious box out of its hiding place."

"What do you think is in that box?"

"Frankly, and since I haven't seen it – except for some blurry pictures that Edward took of the panel – I couldn't tell you."

"It makes you wonder why the Legato team didn't pull it out before we arrived, doesn't it?"

"Yeah, but I think Legato was thinking the treasure or coffer would be in evidence among the rubble in the hull of the ship. I don't think he wanted to spend too much time on searching for hidden boxes or old crates in walls."

A tap on Tiffany's shoulder prevented her from asking the next question. She turned around with a jerk to find Babette standing behind her – all smiles. Alan, for his part, had seen the playwright approach and had kept a straight face. But he now burst out laughing when he noticed Tiffany's astonished face.

"How are you, my dear?" Babette said, sitting down between the two of them.

"Just fine, Babette, thanks, but why the sneaking around?"

"Because I haven't seen you smile in a while and I thought giving you a little jolt was in order."

"You don't know the half of it, Babette; I am actually worried for the kids aboard or more specifically those going ashore. These northern varieties of insects are a real nightmare."

"Yes, they are, but you shouldn't let them ruin your visit or your diligent work." Babette smiled kindly at her friend. "And, talking about kids, as a matter of fact, I've got a little story that I think you two might enjoy."

"Oh yeah, what's that?" Alan asked, already hoping to hear the introduction of Babette's next play. "And where did you hear it? Or is it one of your own?"

"Oh no, it's not my own, no, Alan. It's something I picked up this morning while Edward and Sam were diving. We were all watching them as they dove when suddenly we saw a couple of sirens..."

"What are you saying," Tiffany cut-in, "you mean sirens like girls with fish tails?"

Babette shook her head, laughing. "No, I don't think they were real mermaids, no, I believe they were a couple of local potheads. But I was watching them when one of the passengers – he was looking over the railing as I was – told me that it reminded him of Snow White and the Seven Dwarfs."

"That doesn't sound like a mermaid story," Alan remarked.

"You're right," Babette replied, "but let me tell it...."

"Okay," Tiffany said, "but before you start, shall I get you a cup so that you could taste that magical tea Alan got in Kodiak?"

"Oh no, dear, but thanks all the same."

"Alright then, let's have the story," Alan encouraged.

"Okay, here goes: Snow White and the Seven Dwarfs are roaming in the forest when they come across a lake. The water was enticing and Snow White decides to take a bath. So she tells the Dwarfs to turn around while she is taking a bath in the lake. The Dwarfs protest vehemently because they want to take a bath too. Snow White relents and says, "When I get into the water and you hear the splash, you can turn around." Snow White undresses and as she is about to jump into the water, at that very moment, she is startled by a frog who jumps into the water before she can. The moment the Dwarfs hear the SPLASH, they turn around and see Snow White standing NAKED. This situation was apparently the idea for a TV ad. Can you guess what product is being advertised?" Babette stopped and looked at her companions' puzzled faces. Receiving no answer, she chuckled and said, "That's easy ... 7 Up!"

Alan couldn't stop laughing and Tiffany had to wipe the tears coursing down her cheeks. "That's beautiful, Babette. But do tell us, who was the story teller?"

"Oh, I think his name is Dr. Wasfall or something like that..."

Both Alan and Tiffany's laughter were re-ignited upon hearing the doctor's name – once again he had told a good story.

"Why...? Do you know him?" Babette asked, agape.

"Oh yes, Babette, we do. His name is actually Dr. Wasserfall," Alan replied. "He latches on – as Tiffany says – to people just to tell his stories."

"Has he got many of them?" Babette queried, looking at Alan and Tiffany in turn.

"We've only met him on a couple of occasions and already we've got half a dozen of these little tales to remember," Alan said.

"Well, I think I'll make it my business to find him again," Babette said with a determined look on her face. "I could probably use him in my next play." She stood up. "But for now, I better go and get dressed for dinner – I've got to meet Susan at the restaurant in about an hour..."

"Oh and how is Susan? We haven't seen her in days," Tiffany asked.

"She's fine, my dear, now that she's got Auguste to take care of her, and vice-versa, everything is fine. But I'll know more after tonight." As she was about to leave the table, Babette stopped. "At what time are they diving again, Alan?"

He looked at his watch. "Actually I should go down right now – they're diving in about a half-an-hour." He got up from his seat. "Why don't we go down together?" he suggested, looking down at Tiffany.

"Okay – good idea," she replied, standing up too.

Once again standing on the platform, Alan and Stephan assisted Edward and Sam in getting everything ready for their next dive. They were taking some tools with them and, this time, Sam had strapped a video camera around his head, which would enable him to film the procedure and hopefully a discovery. For his part, Edward had a strong cable attached to his waist, which they would loop around the box once they had it out of its hiding place.

"Alright, everything ready?" Alan asked as he checked the diver's monitors, the two-way submersible radio already in his hand.

"That's a roger, Doc," Sam and Edward replied in unison, fitting their oxygen mouthpieces to their lips.

And with these words, they dove into the black waters.

Alan turned to Stephan. "Let's hope they find something...."

"You said it, Doc. I'm sure they'll find the box alright..."

"It's what's inside it that will be interesting," Alan finished for Stephan.

A few minutes later, they heard Edward say, "Okay, we're down and through the hole. Everything is clear."

"Copy that," Alan said, smiling to Stephan.

It took another ten minutes before Alan heard his radio crackle again.

"Alright, Doc," Sam said. "We've got the box out of the wall, and secured with the cable. Activate the pulley when I give you the signal."

"Copy that," Alan repeated.

Stephan was already stationed by the electric wench, ready to wind the cable. "Here comes the moment of truth," he said, grinning.

"Okay, wench it up," Sam called up.

After pressing the button, all they heard was the noisy sound of the cable coiling back around the spool for several minutes.

As soon as the 'box' surfaced, Alan and Stephan couldn't help but burst into joyous laughter. The tension that accompanied weeks of waiting for this moment had been broken. They high-fived each other as Edward and Sam surfaced.

"Isn't that the perfect picture of a treasure chest?" Edward exclaimed, once he had removed the oxygen tube out of his mouth.

And in fact, it was. The old wooden chest was as everyone would have pictured it to be – completely encrusted and with a heavy lock on the front of it.

"Does anyone have a key?" they heard Gerald say from over their shoulders.

Still excited, the men erupted in renewed laughter.

"I think we better carry it inside to the loading room," Stephan said, already crouching down to grab the chest.

"Hold it," Gerald said, "let my guys do that for you, Mr. Ivanov."

At these words, four hefty-looking security men came onto the platform, heaved the chest and carried it to the nearby loading room.

In the meantime, Drs. Lespierre and Sullivan, who had been observing the whole procedure from the lower deck, and Captain Middleton came rushing in.

"So we've got a treasure chest after all, have we?" Middleton burst out, entering the room and focusing on the large coffer.

"Yes, Captain, we have," Sam Ashton said, all smiles. "You wouldn't happen to have a key, would you?"

Chuckling, the captain crouched down to examine the lock. "I think we could open it easily enough with a crowbar," he said, standing up.

"Hold on a moment," Alan said, remembering what he saw at the museum. "I think I know where the key is."

Everyone in the room turned to the doc, agape.

"Yes, yes, you're right, Doctor. The key is in one of the display cases at the museum," Lespierre rejoined. "Let me call Mr. Littleton. He could be here in ten minutes." He phoned the man.

"Okay, Mr. Tolberg, why don't you take a tender and escort Mr. Littleton back to the ship, will you?"

"Yes, Captain – on my way."

CHAPTER FIFTY-TWO

A Russian Coat of Arms

AS SOON AS MR. LITTLETON came in the loading room, key in hand, he stopped and stared. "That's incredible!" he erupted to all the smiling faces that returned the stare.

"Well, Mr. Littleton," Captain Middleton began, "I think you should do the honors." He pointed to the lock in the impressive chest.

"Yes, yes, of course, Captain," Littleton replied, shaking from head to toe and crouching down in front of the coffer.

The silence that permeated the room at that moment was almost palpable.

As everyone expected, the key fitted in the lock easily and as Littleton turned it, they all heard the click that released the crossbar inside the chest. The Parks Canada rep then looked around him as if asking for someone to authorize him to lift the lid.

"Go ahead, man," Lespierre burst out, "we've been waiting years for this; so please open the darn thing!"

Nervous laughter accompanied the creaking hinges when Littleton finally raised the lid of the coffer.

What they saw took their breath away – it was filled to the rim with gold coins.

"You said it, Mr. Littleton, *that's incredible,*" the captain said, stepping to the open chest. "But where do you suppose these coins came from?" He took one out and passed it to Dr. Sullivan, who hadn't moved from his spot a few feet in front of the chest.

"Hummm... let's see," he mumbled, taking the coin from Middleton's hand. He looked at it closely and then shouted, "*This is a Russian ruble!*"

"Let me see," Lespierre demanded, grabbing the coin from Sullivan's trembling hand. He, too, looked at the gold coin carefully. "You're right, by God, you're absolutely right."

"But what would Russian rubles be doing aboard an English ship?" Stephan piped up.

"I could think of several reasons," Alan interposed, "one of which being that our Captain McClure was at the tsar's stipend and this gold would have been destined to ensure the purchase of what ever land was available around the Arctic Circle at the time."

"Clever of them," Stephan remarked, receiving a nod of acquiescence from the archeologists.

Gerald stepped closer to the chest. "And that's probably why we had a Russian agent aboard our vessel – Ms. Korsakov was anxious to put her hands on this treasure before anyone other than Cecil Legato found it."

"Let's see if it contains anything else," Alan suggested.

"Let me," Dr. Sullivan said, finally moving to the open chest. He knelt down beside Littleton and slipped a hand in between the coins and suddenly lifted it out. "There is some sort of cloth or linen parchment underneath the coins. We should pull it out carefully – it maybe frayed and moisture ridden by this time."

"Okay, let's get some clean containers from your medical center, Doc, if you don't mind, and get the coins out from the top of this parchment…"

"Sure, Captain," Alan replied, "I'll be right back," already out of the loading room.

As soon as Alan was out, Gerald turned to the security guards that had brought the chest in the loading room, and said, "Alright, guys, I want two of you to stay here – inside this room – for as long as it will take us to make arrangements for this chest to be transferred aboard the Parks Canada vessel. We don't want one coin out of this coffer to disappear, understood?"

"Yes, sir," the two men replied in unison, but apparently unable to take their eyes off the treasure.

A few minutes later, Alan reappeared with two large plastic containers and two pairs of surgical gloves, and placed them beside the chest. He let the archeologists slip the gloves over their hands, and take out hands-full of coins to pour them into the boxes until they uncovered the linen parchment. It had been rolled but had been flattened under the weight of the coins laid over it. Before unrolling it, they brought it to a nearby table and examined the outside of it carefully. "We need to dry this off under a heat lamp before we open it," Sullivan said, turning to the assembled men behind him.

"Let's take it to the medical center and dry it in our sterilizer," Alan suggested.

"Very good idea," Lespierre said, already taking the parchment off the table.

"Let's put the coins back in the chest," Stephan said to the divers who had been watching the scene, standing by the door.

"No problem, Mr. Ivanov," Sam said, nodding to Edward.

When the chest was closed and locked again, Captain Middleton said, "Okay, men, let's get back to our duties and please, everyone, let's not breathe a word of the find to any of the passengers, shall we? It's enough that most of them saw the treasure chest being lifted on board, we don't want to spur anymore thieving aboard my ship, okay?"

Receiving a unanimous nod from everyone present, the captain preceded the group down the corridor, leaving the security guards inside the loading room with the treasure.

Alan and his two companions made their way to the elevators and to the medical center in silence.

* * * *

An hour later, Drs. Sullivan and Lespierre were standing in front of the sterilizer waiting for Alan to open it. "It should be dry and sterilized now," he said, smiling up at the two men. With gloved hands, Alan opened the glass door, retrieved the parchment and handed it to Sullivan.

"I'm glad to be here – in a medical center – Doc, because I don't know if my heart will be able to take much more of this suspense." A tentative smile appeared at the corner of his lips.

Handling the parchment as carefully as they could, Sullivan and Lespierre unrolled it over a table while Alan held it open.

"My God, would you look at that!" Sullivan exclaimed when he saw the Russian coat of arms at the top of the parchment.

"What does it say?" Alan queried. "Do you read Russian?"

A shake of both men's heads was the answer.

"Perhaps Mr. Ivanov would be able to translate it for us?" Lespierre suggested. "Although the ink is very faint in places, maybe he could give us the gist of the missive."

Not fifteen minutes later, Stephan was looking down at the parchment with a loupe. "This is a confirmation of what you suggested, Doc. The coins were destined to buy land and chattels from any inhabitants McClure encountered during his journey."

"But one question," Lespierre piped up, looking at Alan. "Why do you think it was found in the medic's quarters and not in the captain's cabin?"

"Ah yes, I've been wondering about that myself, and the only reason I could think of was the fact that no one was allowed to visit the medic's quarters unless the person was sick. It was the best place for it, I would have thought."

"Well then," Sullivan said somewhat decisively, "if a medical center is the best place to hide treasures, why don't you keep this one in a safe place, Doc?"

Alan chuckled. "Alright, I'll do that, but I promise you I won't sleep here to guard it though."

"As long as it's not in plain sight, it should be okay," Lespierre rejoined.

* * * *

When Lespierre and Sullivan left the medical center, Stephan stayed behind, apparently wanting to have a chat with Alan.

"So, what's on your mind, Stephan?" Alan asked, sitting at his desk.

"I've been thinking of that Russian agent – Ms. Korsakov. Where do you think she is now?"

"Difficult to say, really," Alan replied, leaning to the back of his chair, "but I would be surprised if she isn't aboard the *Northern Rover* right now."

"Really? But what would she hope to gain by being there? It's not like Sauvage and his crew will be able to recover much else aboard the *Investigator* now, especially if it was the treasure she was after."

Alan laced his fingers in front of his chest. "Yes, of course, the treasure has slipped from her hands now, but there might be something else aboard she wanted…"

"Like what?" Stephan queried.

"The parchment for instance," Alan replied, pausing to let the suggestion sink in.

"Oh, I see what you mean, she would have hoped to retrieve the parchment so not to incriminate her government for past misdeeds, is that what you're thinking?"

"Something like that, yes. Although I don't think we'll ever find out what this was all about."

"And what about Sauvage; do you think he's aware of what's going on with her? Does he even know her?"

"That I don't know, Stephan. But I am quite sure Ms. Korsakov wouldn't advertise her presence to anyone at this juncture. And there again, it wouldn't be anything we would have to worry about. You see, as soon as the treasure and the parchment are in the hands of Parks Canada and safely aboard their vessel, we will be on our way out of here – and thankfully so," Alan concluded.

"You said it, Doc!"

* * * *

It wasn't long before Evelyn returned to the medical center for her night shift. Tears rolling down her cheeks and giggles escaping her mouth, she burst into Alan's office. "You've got to hear this one, Doc, it's too funny!" She plopped down on the seat facing his desk.

Alan smiled, *this has to be a good one,* he thought. Actually, he had never seen Evelyn, the quiet and reserved woman she was, in such a state of hilarity. "Okay then, let's have it," he said.

"Okay," Evelyn replied, wiping her eyes with a tissue, "...a cabbie picks up a Nun. She gets into the cab, and notices that the very handsome cab driver won't stop staring at her. She asks him why he is staring. He replies, "I have a question to ask you but I don't want to offend you."

"She answers, "My son, you cannot offend me. When you're as old as I am and have been a nun as long as I have, you get a chance to see and hear just about everything. I'm sure that there's nothing you could say or ask that I would find offensive."

""Well, I've always had a fantasy to have a nun kiss me."

"She says, "Well, let's see what we can do about that: #1, you have to be single and #2, you must be Catholic."

"The cab driver is very excited and says, "Yes, I'm single and Catholic!"

""Okay," the nun says. "Pull into the next alley."

"The nun fulfills his fantasy with a kiss that would make a hooker blush. But when they get back on the road, the cab driver starts crying.

""My dear child," said the nun, "Why are you crying?"

""Forgive me, but I've sinned. I lied and I must confess, I'm married and I'm Jewish."

"The nun says, "That's okay. My name is Kevin and I'm going to a Halloween party."

If Alan's mind had been cluttered with any of the bothersome possibilities that accompanied the safe keeping of the parchment, right then, all of his preoccupations vanished, only to be replaced with loud laughter.

CHAPTER FIFTY-THREE

Returning home

AFTER A COUPLE OF DAYS seeing to the transfer of the treasure aboard Parks Canada's vessel and after taking care of their many duties, Tiffany and Alan were finally alone, to enjoy some of the sceneries following their departure from Banks Island. Somehow the calmness that had enveloped *The Contessa* after leaving the strait that was now leading them to the east coast of Canada was unreal. They had had time to find themselves in the throes of making passionate love as if they were rediscovering each other after a long absence. Their love seemed to be sweet, and enduring the hassles of their occupations with ease.

Waking up the next morning in his cabin, Alan decided it was about time to see if his computer had been able to receive emails from his friends. The Internet connections were at best temporary and erratic and at worst totally inexistent. But today, since they were approaching civilization again – so to speak – he was hopeful.

And yes, he had a couple of emails from Sharon. She and her husband had been long time friends and they had recently traveled through northern Canada, and Alan was anxious to read what they had encountered.

Hi to you all,

I am so sorry that you have not received my last few picture-grams. I have certainly been trying to send them, but Greenland and Newfoundland are, for some strange reason, far more difficult to send emails out from than one would have thought. Especially when you consider the isolated places I have been sending to you from during our voyage.

So, although I have tried (and still am), it looks like no more photographs will be forthcoming, at least not from this trip.

For those of you who were using the blog site, it is no longer being added to as the expedition part of the voyage is completed. It was over when we successfully landed at Nuuk in Greenland.

Thereafter we spent 3 very rough days sailing to Newfoundland – well Norby and I didn't think they were rough, but many passengers did.

We are currently sitting at the entrance to a magnificent, but tiny fjord on the coast of Newfoundland near a teeny-weeny little village called Francois. Population 115.

For the previous two days we were at St John's the largest city in Newfoundland, which is affectionately called "jellybean town" by the locals, because of the plethora of extremely colorful buildings. It is a truly beautiful city, with an amazing history, and we loved every moment of our stay there. The city was named by John Cabot when he visited on the Feast Day of St John the Baptist in 1497. However St John's would not become a permanent settlement until the 17th century. It is the capital of the province of Newfoundland and Labrador, and it is considered as the birthplace of the Information Age. It was here in 1901 that Italian inventor Marconi received the first wireless transatlantic signal.

Today has been our first reasonably warm (19 degrees and very sunny) day since we left St Paul way over on the east near the coast of Alaska, and we all sweltered today when we went ashore to explore the delightful little village. It too has lots of jellybean multicolored houses…so quaint! The town is small, but survives because of the fishing. There is still an abundance of crab, crayfish, cod and halibut in the waters here. The town is very isolated, reachable only by helicopter or boat, but the locals love it and most have lived all their lives here.

Tonight we set off again for our last sea days before arriving in Quebec. We shall then take a week to drive via Niagara Falls to New York, hopefully getting a chance to admire the fall colors on the trees on our way.

We have had the most wonderful trip of a lifetime. We have seen amazing sights, had unbelievable experiences, met wonderful people and witnessed the best (and sometimes the worst) that Nature and people have to offer.

But, as much as I don't want to leave this fantastic lifestyle, it is time to head for home and face the real World. We have made many new and firm friends along the way.

My hope is that I can take you all along with me again one day.

Till then . . . *Fair Winds and Safe Harbors to You All*
Sharon

Alan was a little disappointed to read that Sharon had so many difficulties in sending her messages, and scrolled back to a few days prior to the most recent email. He wanted to see if perhaps the server had downloaded something when they were on Banks Island. It took a few minutes but he finally found another message from their friends.

Hi,
It just so happens that we will be in Cambridge Bay in a week or so, all being well. We have finally arrived at Herschel Island just inside the Canadian Border, off the north coast of the Yukon

Territory. It is known as "Qikiqtaruk" which means "island" in Inuvialuit. Archaeological sites show this site as being occupied as early as 700 years ago.

After a customs clearance we shall finally be able to step ashore. This has in fact proved to be a very complicated and expensive procedure, because the customs men, 2 more Inuit guides for the ship, a helicopter and its two pilots, and our Canadian Ships pilot and an ice captain have all had to be flown to this extremely isolated place.

Looking out over our deck all I see is a very low lying, barren tundra type island. There are several historical buildings on a small land spit and it is very cold and windy. There was a time when commercial whaling was carried out here, but it was short lived and then it became a center for the fur trade in the western Canadian Arctic. Herschel Island is now a Territorial Park administered by the government of the Yukon...

For some reasons, these emails brought to mind some of Alan's encounters during the voyage. Babette and her very funny play, Susan in the arms of Auguste Sauvage, the two divers who had stayed behind with Drs. Sullivan and Lespierre on Banks Island, while not forgetting Elizabeth, the little girl who found new parents in the von Weglans – their images seemed to parade before his mind's eye as if collected in an album of memories he would cherish for a long time to come.

* * * *

As Alan came to the end of the contract on *The Contessa*, following a few more weeks of treading the waters of the Arctic Ocean and later returning to the east coast of the United States, the bitter sweet aspects of the end of a cruise for the crew were again evident. First of all, there are hundreds of forms that need to be filled in and reports completed that need to be up to date as of 24 hours of arrival in port, and numerous others that need to be completed as of the day of arrival. As the head of the medical department, the doctor has to ensure that all the reports that are the responsibility of the nurses are also completed before he can submit his. Inventories, maintenance records of the laboratory and x-ray equipment, cleaning records, sterilization records, etc. are all included in the summaries.

A report to the physician taking over also has to be done. This includes crewmembers and passengers remaining on the ship with major ongoing medical issues. Of course, one is not allowed to discriminate for medical reasons in most jobs, including on a ship, so the new doc needs to know about the chronic arthritic deckhand and the diabetic chef, and any passengers remaining aboard.

Alan recalled on one contract his ship had a 93-year-old woman passenger patient who *lived* on the ship. Ethel Goodacre had lived on the ship for 5 years almost continuously. The only times she was off it was during the ports that she enjoyed walking around for a few hours and, of course, for the few weeks every so many years when the ship was in dry dock. When a ship is in dry dock, passengers are never allowed to stay aboard. There is a flurry of repairs, redecorating, making new additions and whatever else the cruise line can cram into a one or two week period. That is generally all the time they schedule to take a ship out of profitable cruising, for repairs. Some crew are even housed at local hotels or guesthouses. At certain times the dust and fumes are toxic to ones' health unless one is wearing appropriate personal protective equipment (respirators and the like). Mrs. Goodacre did have ongoing medical issues, but none serious enough to keep her from cruising. She regularly got her checkups in the medical center and was essentially considered by most crew as the ships' godmother. Her rationale for living on board was her pat statement, "Where else can I live with as much food as I need whenever I want it, entertainment every day, people who clean my bedroom daily and always make my bed, and always someone to talk to. The cost is not any more than assisted living anyway, and as long as my health holds out, I get to see different scenery daily instead of the same old facility. If I don't feel like leaving my room for a few days, I always know that someone will come and look in on me and bring me room service." Since Ethel had not been traveling on a five-star cruise line, the costs were probably not much different, and the lifestyle was definitely better.

Officially, one physician has to be on board at all times. Consequently one had to balance trying to get a flight that was late enough to accommodate getting everything done on day of disembarkation with the arrival of the new physician. Since cruise line companies seldom ask the crew to fly in early to the port of destination so that extra nights in a hotel are avoided, it is often difficult to coordinate the changeover smoothly. Consequently, one's reports need to be as complete as possible, which Alan always tried to do.

On this occasion, the reports were done, Alan was packed and with airline tickets, passport, disembarkation papers and all in hand, he awaited the arrival of the new doc and the announcement that the immigration authorities were ready to start their process of letting the crew off. Of course, that could not happen until the passengers had all disembarked.

While he was waiting to be authorized to get off the ship, Tiffany came knocking. And it was with a broad smile on his lips and a quivering heart that Alan took her in his arms.

"So are you all packed and ready to go home?" he asked as he released his embrace.

"Not really – although this trip was perhaps one of the hardest I've ever experienced, I will miss the Artic, the mosquitoes, the Inuit and their drums, the icebergs and the magnificent ocean. I truly can get over how lucky we were, Alan, to being able to make the journey on *The Contessa.*"

"She is a grand lady, isn't she?"

"You said it. But I will be happy to return to terra-ferma too." She looked up at him with loving eyes. "Do you have any plans for the next month, before your next contract?"

"I had a little idea, but I don't know if you would agree to it…"

"Oh-oh," Tiffany said, giggling already, "What have you got in mind?"

"I just thought that you might like to spend a couple of weeks in Paris – how's that sound?"

Screaming her joy, Tiffany wrapped her arms around Alan's neck and kissed him, but not before saying, "I would be a fool to say no!"

Paul Davis MD

Cruise Ship Crime Mysteries (Number 4)
Murder at Northwest Passage

Paul Davis MD is the author of *Cruise Ship Crime Mysteries: A Medical Murder Mystery; The Curious Cargo of Bones, The German Intrigue* and *Murder in the Northwest Passage.* He was trained in Family Practice and Emergency Medicine in Canada, the United Kingdom and the United States. Dr. Davis uses his insider knowledge, as his novels are based on his ten-year career as a cruise ship doctor. He currently lives in Canada and is the director of a medical specialty group.

Visit his websites at:

http://www.cruiseshipcrimesite.com

http://cruiseshipcrime.wordpress.com

Dr. Paul Davis is available for lectures and readings. For information regarding his availability, please contact Skye Wentworth, Publicist, at 978-462-4453 or email skyewentworth@gmail.com.

www.ingramcontent.com/pod-product-compliance
Lightning Source LLC
Chambersburg PA
CBHW070829250626
47159CB00003B/705